"IT'S GETTIN
TO BEHAV
AND KEEP

Zane's head lowered just as Riley's lifted, and his mouth covered hers. He'd intended it to be no more than a simple good-night kiss, but the instant their lips met, everything changed.

His arms wrapped around her, drawing her close. While his mouth moved over hers, he could feel her in every part of his body. The softness of her breasts against his chest. The press of her thighs to his. The tingle of warmth as her arms slowly lifted until they closed around his neck. And clung.

He heard her little sigh of pleasure as she offered her lips for more.

Somewhere in his mind an alarm bell went off and he realized that he needed to take a step back.

But not just yet. He wanted, needed, one more taste of her. One more kiss before leaving.

Zane took Riley fully into the kiss and could feel himself sinking into her. Into all that sweetness. And losing himself completely...

"A popular writer of heartwarming, emotionally involving romances."
                                              —*Library Journal*

*Please turn the page for
more praise for R.C. Ryan...*

Raves for
Montana Destiny...

"5 Stars! Watching this wild rebel and independent woman attempt to coexist was so much fun...The author, R.C. Ryan, delivers an ongoing, tantalizing mystery suspense with heartwarming romance. Sinfully yummy!"
—HuntressReviews.com

"Ryan's amazing genius at creating characters with heartfelt emotions, wit, and passion is awe-inspiring. I can't wait until MONTANA GLORY comes out...so that I can revisit the McCord family!"
—TheRomanceReadersConnection.com

"The series continues to intrigue, and each page brings you closer to finding the treasure. Another terrific story from R.C. Ryan."
—SingleTitles.com

"Sure to entertain. Enjoy."
—FreshFiction.com

"[A] wonderful series...The characters are extremely well developed . . . I couldn't put this book down. I can't wait until Zane's story comes out."
—NightOwlReviews.com

MONTANA GLORY

R.C. RYAN

FOREVER

NEW YORK   BOSTON

This book is a work of fiction. Names, characters, places, and incidents are the product of the author's imagination or are used fictitiously. Any resemblance to actual events, locales, or persons, living or dead, is coincidental.

Copyright © 2010 by Ruth Ryan Langan
Excerpt from *Montana Legacy* copyright © 2010 Ruth Ryan Langan
Excerpt from *Montana Destiny* copyright © 2010 Ruth Ryan Langan
All rights reserved. Except as permitted under the U.S. Copyright Act of 1976, no part of this publication may be reproduced, distributed, or transmitted in any form or by any means, or stored in a database or retrieval system, without the prior written permission of the publisher.

Book design by Giorgetta Bell McRee

Forever
Hachette Book Group
237 Park Avenue
New York, NY 10017
Visit our website at www.HachetteBookGroup.com.

Forever is an imprint of Grand Central Publishing. The Forever name and logo is a trademark of Hachette Book Group, Inc.

Printed in the United States of America

First Printing: November 2010

10 9 8 7 6 5 4 3 2 1

To our very own Riley. And to Kelly and Courtney, Annie, Nicole, Gabby, Aubrey, Macey, Kelsey, and Haley.

And, as always, to my love, my best friend, Tom.

PROLOGUE

——◆◆◆——

The Lost Nugget Ranch
Montana, 1986

Hey, guys. Wait for me." Six-year-old Zane McCord struggled under the weight of the saddle and watched in consternation as his cousins, eight-year-old Wyatt and nine-year-old Jesse, started out of the barn on horseback.

"We're heading up to Treasure Chest Butte." Jesse pulled down the brim of his hat. "Catch up if you can. We don't have time to wait for babies."

From his position in one of the stalls, wrangler Jimmy Eagle watched as the little boy used an overturned bucket to finally get the saddle in place. Chubby little fingers struggled to tighten the cinch.

It was on the tip of Jimmy's tongue to offer to lend a hand, but he knew he would be rebuffed. Zane McCord may be the youngest of the three cousins who lived here on the Lost Nugget Ranch with their parents and grandparents, but he was already a tough-minded, independent little cuss.

Minutes later Zane used the same overturned bucket to

pull himself onto the back of his horse. By the time he'd cleared the barn, he could just make out two wide-brimmed hats in the distance as his cousins' horses topped a ridge.

Half an hour later, when Jesse and Wyatt finally slowed their mounts to a walk, Zane and his pony caught up to them.

"You should've waited." His face was red, his shirt stained with sweat from the broiling sun.

Jesse grinned at Wyatt. "You should've asked one of the wranglers to help you with that saddle."

"Why should I? You don't ask for help."

"I'm not little."

"Neither am I. And I don't need anybody's help."

His two cousins shared a laugh before starting up at a brisk pace.

If they'd thought to leave Zane behind again, they were soon reminded of his steely determination when he urged his pony into a gallop to take the lead, leaving them to eat his dust.

Hours later the three boys sat on a rock shelf, surveying the lush rangeland spread out before them as far as the eye could see.

Wyatt polished off the last of the sandwiches the ranch cook had provided. "What're you going to be when you grow up, Jesse?"

Their oldest cousin never even hesitated. "A cowboy. Like my dad and Coot."

Their grandfather, called a crazy old coot for spending a lifetime searching this land for a fortune in gold nuggets that had been found and then lost by his ancestors, had embraced the nickname. Even his grandsons called him, with great affection, Coot.

"How about you, Zane?"

"Yeah. A cowboy. But I don't want to work with cattle." The youngest chugged from a canteen of lukewarm water. "See those mustangs?" He pointed to a herd of wild horses grazing across the valley. "I'd love to spend time with them. See if they'd trust me enough to let me ride one."

Wyatt chuckled. "You've been watching too many movies. People don't live with mustangs."

Jesse nodded. "Coot says they eat our crops, trample our rangeland, and steal some of his best fillies every spring."

Zane got to his feet, shading the late afternoon sun from his eyes. "I think they're beautiful."

"Don't tell Coot that. He says the only thing they're good for is the glue factory. Come on." Wyatt pulled himself into the saddle. "We've got a long ride ahead of us if we're going to make it home by dark."

As they headed back to the house, Zane trailed behind, his gaze wandering again and again to the herd. He was fascinated by the way the stallion patrolled the perimeter, keeping his mares safe from predators.

He knew what the ranchers around here thought of mustangs. It didn't matter. There was just something about a herd of wild horses living free on open rangeland that stirred his young heart. Not every creature, he thought fiercely, should be tamed.

1992

"Here, now." Jimmy Eagle had spotted a light on in the barn and ambled in only to find twelve-year-old Zane

McCord busy tying a bedroll behind his horse's saddle. "It's almost midnight, son. You ought to be asleep up in the big house. What're you up to?"

Zane ducked his head, hoping to hide his tears. He was too big to cry. If his cousins found out about it, they'd never let him live it down. "I'm leaving."

"I can see that."

Very deliberately the wrangler forced himself to lean on the rail and assume a relaxed pose. He'd already heard about the latest fight between the boy's folks, Melissa and Wade. For years Wade's wife had been pressing to leave the ranch and its simple lifestyle for a more glamorous life far from Montana. If the rumors were true, this time she'd managed to push Wade over the edge, and he'd agreed to take her wherever she chose to live.

"Where're you headed?" Keeping his gaze averted so the boy had time to wipe away his tears, Jimmy stuck a piece of straw between his teeth.

Zane pulled himself into the saddle. "I don't know. I just know I can't stay here."

As he started out of the barn, Jimmy opened a nearby stall and led his horse into the night air. He had no need of a saddle. A full-blooded Blackfoot, he'd spent his childhood on the reservation riding bareback. It was second nature to him.

When Zane heard the sound of a second set of hoofbeats, he turned. "You going to try to stop me?"

Jimmy shook his head. "Just figured I'd ride along. That is, if you don't mind some company."

"Suit yourself." Zane dug in his heels and his big black gelding broke into a run.

Behind him, Jimmy's spotted pony kept up an easy

pace as they ate up the miles of rangeland under a full moon.

When at last they came to the top of a rise, Zane slowed his mount and slid from the saddle by the banks of the creek. Jimmy did the same. The boy dropped down in the dew-dampened grass, choking back the lump in his throat.

A short distance away the two horses stood, blowing and snorting from the exertion.

Zane looked up at the moon. "Dad said we have to leave the Lost Nugget. He said he's been selfish to keep Mom here all these years. Now it's her turn for some happiness, and we just have to suck it up."

Jimmy held his silence, knowing the boy needed to get it all out.

Zane turned to the man who had always been his best friend. "How can I leave here, Jimmy? How can Dad ask me to? I love it here. I can't stand the thought of not being with Coot. With Jesse and Wyatt. With you."

Jimmy took a blow to his heart.

"Oh, Jimmy." The boy buried his face in his hands and gave in to a fresh round of tears.

Jimmy gathered him in his arms and let him cry until, with a shuddering sigh, Zane pushed away and blew his nose in his bandanna.

A light came into his eyes as a thought struck. "You think maybe I could find a herd of mustangs and just live with them?"

"I suppose you could. If you were older. Right now, you've just got to do what your ma and pa want you to do. Whether you like it or not."

"But what am I supposed to do in California?"

"Is that where you're headed?"

"Hollywood." Zane spit the hated word.

Jimmy chose his words carefully. "The way I see it, wherever you're planted, you'll need to go to school and do a heap of growing up. And when you're old enough to make your own choices, you'll have the smarts to make wise ones."

"What if I never get to see you or Coot or this ranch again?"

Another blow, and Jimmy absorbed the pain. He knew exactly how Zane felt. He couldn't imagine life here on the ranch without this boy who had been his shadow since he was little more than a pup.

"The good thing about life is that we can't see what tomorrow will bring. If we did, son, some of us wouldn't want to live another day. But this much I know: You're tougher and smarter than most. For now, for the next few years, you just have to stay the course and endure whatever life hands you. And if it's meant to be, you'll find your way home."

He dropped an arm around Zane's shoulders as the two walked back to the horses.

They rode the entire distance back to the ranch in silence.

By the time the sun rose, the boy and his parents were in their van, heading down the long, gravel road. Away from all that was familiar and loved, and toward the unknown.

Jimmy Eagle stood in the dust and watched until they were out of sight, and fought back tears of his own.

CHAPTER ONE

H oo, boy." Zane McCord grinned when he walked into the big kitchen of the Lost Nugget ranch house and caught sight of his cousins, Jesse and Wyatt. "You two look a whole lot better'n those cows I've been tending."

Jesse grinned. "Two weeks up in the hills, and you look more like a grizzly than a human."

Zane ran a hand over his rough beard. "The cattle don't care what we look like as long as we deliver food in the snow."

Though spring had arrived in Montana, the mountains were still hip-deep in drifts. A storm had dropped nearly a foot of snow the previous weekend.

Cal Randall, foreman of the Lost Nugget, turned from the stove where he was filling a mug with coffee. "These late snowfalls play hell with the calving."

"Yeah. But the flip side is"—Zane pulled a tiny video camera from his shirt pocket—"I got some fabulous shots of the hills buried in fresh snow. They'll make a great background for the introduction I'm planning for my documentary. I can see the camera panning a vast, snow-covered wilderness, while a voice intones, 'When Coot McCord died, the town of Gold Fever called him crazy for having spent a lifetime searching for the lost treasure of his ancestors. How could anyone in his right mind believe one man could find a sack of gold nuggets in such a primitive setting? But Coot's grandsons pledged at his graveside to carry on his search. This, then, is the record of one family's dream, and the successful conclusion of a treasure hunt that began in 1862, at Grasshopper Creek, in the Montana wilderness.'"

"Sounds great, cuz." Wyatt punched his arm. "Especially that part about the successful conclusion. The sooner the better."

"Yeah. Hey, it's slow going, but we're all committed."

Jesse nodded. "I've found another piece of equipment I'd like to have shipped out here as soon as the snow melts up in the hills."

"Good. I wish we could find a piece of radar that could see through tons of rock."

The three shared a grin as Jesse added, "If such a thing is ever invented, we'll be the first to buy it."

"Hey, Zane." Jesse's wife, Amy, stepped into the kitchen. "Welcome back to civilization."

Jesse and Amy embraced and even when they moved apart, Amy kept her arm around his waist.

"You staying for supper?" she asked Zane.

"Depends. What's Dandy fixing?"

"Slow-cooked pot roast."

Their ranch cook had been with the family for more than

thirty years, and he knew just how to please a hardworking cowboy. From fiery chili to perfectly grilled steaks, nobody in Montana made better meals than Dandy Davis.

"I'm definitely not giving up Dandy's pot roast for Daffy Spence's greasy burgers."

At his reference to Daffy, owner of the Fortune Saloon in the nearest town of Gold Fever, the others began laughing just as Wyatt's bride, Marilee, stepped through the doorway and paused to brush a kiss over her husband's cheek. "Hello, you."

"Hello, yourself." Wyatt affectionately brushed a lock of red hair from her eye.

Zane turned to Cal with a mock shudder. "There's just way too much of this newlywed affection going on here. I hope it isn't contagious."

"I wouldn't worry, if I were you." Cal shared a laugh with the others. "We've seen the way you keep cutting fresh fillies out of the herd and then discarding them."

Zane smiled. "So many women. So little time."

"So I've noticed." Cal grinned. "I think your bachelor days won't be threatened until you're old and gray."

"Like you, Cal?"

The old cowboy chuckled before ducking his head in embarrassment.

It occurred to Zane that the only woman who ever really got Cal's attention was their aunt, Cora McCord. An artist who was a bit of an eccentric, she was more comfortable wearing her brother's cast-off clothing while she worked in her studio. And though her paintings brought fabulous sums of money from art patrons around the world, she remained a simple woman who had turned her back on the European art scene to live in her beloved Montana.

"Where's Aunt Cora?"

"Off on one of her nature campouts. While a spring blizzard rages."

Zane heard the worry in Cal's voice and was quick to soothe. "She'll be fine, Cal. And if she doesn't check in tonight, we'll send the cavalry after her."

"I'll be leading the charge," the foreman said firmly.

Zane gave him a long look. "Is that a clean shirt in the middle of the day?"

Cal nodded. "Thought I'd clean up for the interview."

"Interview?" Zane glanced around. "What've I missed?"

Cal took a sip of coffee before saying, "With Coot gone, I'm buried in paperwork. I complained to our accounting firm in Helena, and they agreed to send me their new hotshot bookkeeper to clean up the mess."

"A hotshot bookkeeper is coming all this way?"

"Schooled in the East." Cal took a sip of coffee. "Guy named Riley Mason."

"A city boy?" The cousins shared a grin. "How long do you think he'll last out here?"

Cal shrugged. "Depends. The last one they sent lasted all of four days before he said he needed to get back to civilization. Can't say I blame him. If he's used to spending his off-hours at coffeehouses or bars, there's just not that much to entice him into feeling at home here. And after a visit to town, and a night at the Fortune Saloon, what's left? So I told them to send someone who's not only sharp, but willing to spend a lot of his downtime doing ordinary things like reading or watching old videos."

Zane nodded in agreement. "How long would you like him to stay?"

Cal thought about it. "I guess that depends on what he finds. I figure he's going to need a couple of weeks, maybe months, to get everything into a computer database so the Helena firm can handle all those mysterious government forms that need to be filled out in triplicate."

"Where will he stay?"

Cal pointed his mug toward the doorway. "He can have his pick of empty rooms. There's that bedroom next to the office that would probably work best."

"If he doesn't mind living in a cave." Marilee gave a throaty chuckle. "Maybe you can keep him chained to his desk, Cal. Then he can clear up the paperwork in half the time."

"Believe me, I'd be happy to, as long as I wouldn't have to deal with legal documents ever again. I don't know how Coot could stand doing all the paperwork involved in running this place."

"Good luck with the interview. I'm more interested in supper." Zane turned away, rubbing a hand over his bristly beard. "Excuse me while I head upstairs for the longest shower and shave in history."

He ambled out of the kitchen and was heading through the great room on his way to the stairs when he heard a knock on the front door.

Since nobody but a stranger would ever use the front entrance, Zane was grinning good-naturedly as he grasped the knob and threw open the door to admit the accountant.

"Hello."

Zane knew he was staring, but it took him a moment to switch gears. He'd expected a dark suit and he wasn't disappointed. And a firm handshake, which he returned woodenly. But the image of the nerdy accountant in his mind was replaced by a gorgeous female, dark hair slicked back into a knot at the back of her head, trim figure encased in a knee-skimming dark skirt and figure-hugging jacket. And that was quite a figure to hug.

Then there was the voice. Soft and breathy, with just a hint of nerves.

"I'm Riley Mason. Are you Cal Randall?"

"No. Cal's in his office." Because she was female, and because it came naturally to him, Zane gave her one of his most charming smiles. "My name's Zane. I'll show you the way."

"That's all right." She took a step back, studying him warily. "Maybe I'll just wait here and you can tell him I've arrived for my interview."

He realized, too late, that he probably smelled like a barnyard and looked like a trail bum, causing her to be completely repelled.

"At least wait inside." He held the door wider, and she was forced to accept his invitation to step inside.

She did so hesitantly.

As she brushed past him, he breathed her in. Her hair smelled like a spring garden. Something light and floral and fresh as a breeze.

For two long weeks he'd smelled nothing but horses and saddle leather and unwashed wranglers.

Pure heaven, he thought as he gave her one last look. "I'll go get Cal."

He sauntered away, leaving her standing in the foyer, staring after him.

Riley didn't relax until the cowboy disappeared along a hallway. She'd known, of course, that the Lost Nugget

was a working ranch. But she'd assumed that she would
be isolated from the wranglers, since she'd been told they
lived in bunkhouses scattered across thousands of acres
of rangeland.

Not that she felt herself above working cowboys.
She'd been working since she was fifteen, and she was
proud of it. But if the men on the ranch looked anything
like that one, she preferred to give them a wide berth.
There had been a fierce, dangerous look to him. Like a
throwback to the cowboys of the Old West who could
calmly shoot a gunslinger, toss back a glass of whiskey,
and ride out of town without a backward glance.

Silly, she knew. She'd always been cursed with a wild
imagination. But being on a ranch in Montana was about
as far from her comfort zone as possible.

"You're not in Philly anymore, little girl," she muttered.

She watched the approach of a handsome, white-
haired man. Now this was how she'd envisioned Cal Randall, foreman of the Lost Nugget. Tall, rangy, weathered,
and extremely courtly as he extended his hand.

"Riley Mason? Cal Randall."

"So nice to meet you, Mr. Randall."

"That's too formal for my taste. Call me Cal." He put
a hand beneath her elbow. "Let's go to my office and
chat."

They passed through an enormous room with a four-
sided fireplace surrounded by comfortable furniture.
The floor-to-ceiling windows offered an incredible view
of the towering spires of the mountains in the distance.
Riley caught her breath at the sheer beauty of it.

Before she could take it all in, Cal led her along a
hallway and paused to open a set of double doors. Inside

was a purely masculine retreat, complete with walls of shelves holding an assortment of leather-bound books and yet another fireplace.

Cal settled himself into a leather chair behind an oversize desk littered with paperwork. He indicated a chair across from him and Riley perched on the edge of the seat.

Seeing her nerves, he strove to put her at ease. "Tell me about yourself, Riley."

"I'm twenty-four. Fresh out of college." She flushed. "I took some time off to work, so that set me back a bit. I've worked since I was fifteen. Mostly as a clerk in a local store, and at a coffeehouse off-campus. I'm trained in accounting. But I have to be honest with you." She stared openly at the mountains of paperwork that spilled from open file drawers and was piled haphazardly on top of every available surface. "I just don't know how much help I can be until I have a chance to look over some of this. It looks—"

Cal interrupted. "I know what you mean." He tapped a pen against the desktop. "It intimidates the hell out of me."

That had the desired effect, causing her to relax a bit as she matched his grin.

"I'm current with state and federal guidelines on fees and assessments, and even though I haven't been in Montana long, I know I can get up to speed on local issues as well."

She dug an envelope out of her pocket and set it on the desk. "Our firm suggested independent assessments of my work. These are the e-mail addresses of my immediate superiors at our Philadelphia firm, and also my college professors who are familiar with me. They agreed to answer any questions you might have about my abilities. They were in contact with the firm in Helena before I was hired."

She took in a breath. "I've been apprised of your business and I'm of course prepared to handle daily sheets and payroll. I think I could get all the necessary paperwork ready for our CPA firm in Helena. And though I can't promise miracles, I'm pretty sure I could get most of this"—she indicated the desk—"cleaned up and in some sort of order. But, as I said, neither of us will really know what I'm capable of until I take a look at the work you need done."

Cal grinned. "That was quite a mouthful."

Riley flushed, knowing he had seen through her prepared remarks. She'd rehearsed them all the way out here.

"I don't value speed nearly as much as I value efficiency. I told the firm that I want someone who will take the time to simplify this paperwork and make my job run smoothly." Cal leaned back in his chair. "And, to make your job a bit easier, I'm prepared to offer you a room here."

She seemed surprised. "The firm didn't say anything about living on the ranch."

"Is that a problem?"

She hesitated. "Before driving out here, I arranged for a room in Gold Fever, with a lady named Delia Cowling, who was recommended by a banker in Helena."

Cal smiled. "I know Delia. Her brother was owner of the Gold Fever bank before his untimely death." He thought a minute. "As you know, the ranch is an hour's drive from town. Living here could save you time, as well as gas and wear and tear on your car."

The way she was chewing on her lower lip told Cal that something was bothering her. "Of course, the decision is up to you, Riley. I certainly don't want you to find yourself in an uncomfortable situation."

She took a deep breath. "I didn't come to town alone. I have a four-year-old daughter."

"Oh." It was Cal's turn to be surprised. "Is your husband okay with the hours you'll be away?"

Her head came up. "My husband?"

"I figure he'll be stuck with some of the child care if you sign on for this."

Riley realized she'd been sitting on the edge of her seat. She sat back in the chair and met Cal's questioning look directly. "I didn't mean to mislead you. I don't have a husband. I've never been married. There's just Summer and me."

"I see." He saw more. Much more. Though the job interview may have unnerved her, questions about her private life were infinitely more painful. This was obviously not the first time she'd been asked about her unmarried status. Though she was direct and honest, she didn't volunteer any more information than necessary. Despite her honest explanation, he could see the way her chin came up, waiting for him to throw the first punch.

"You haven't said if you'd be willing to live here on the ranch."

"I...I'd be more than willing, as long as you understand that I'd be bringing along my daughter."

"That's fine with me." Cal stared at the envelope she'd dropped on his desk. "I don't need to check any further references, Riley. Our firm in Helena had nothing but good things to say about your work. That's good enough for me. So, if you're agreeable, I'd like you to get started as quickly as possible."

His abrupt end to the interview caught her by surprise. She'd expected Cal Randall, once he'd heard about her daughter, to use her references, or possibly her lack of experience, as an excuse to dismiss her. She'd expected him to be like so many others who judged her without even knowing her.

And he had, she realized. But he was judging her by her work ethic, and not by her personal life.

Cal got to his feet and leaned across the desk to extend his hand. "If you'd like to wait in the great room, I'll phone the firm in Helena and affirm your employment."

She was reeling from the speed with which he'd come to a decision.

She stood and offered her hand. "Thanks for giving me this opportunity, Cal." She turned toward the door.

"Can you find your way?" he called to her retreating back.

"Yes. I'm fine with it." Riley closed the door and backtracked until, pausing in the massive great room, she sank into an overstuffed chair, feeling a wave of giddy relief.

Needing to calm her nerves, she closed her eyes and took long, deep breaths until her heartbeat returned to normal.

Zane was whistling as he descended the stairs and headed toward the kitchen. He'd noted the door to Cal's office was closed, and he wondered about the foreman's reaction to the new guy, Riley. That had Zane grinning. It was a natural mistake, and they'd all been guilty. Who'd have believed the new hire would be female? And so darned pretty.

In the great room he came to an abrupt halt. The object of his thoughts was seated in a chair, hands folded in her lap, head back, eyes closed, practicing some sort of deep breathing.

Yoga? he wondered.

He took that moment to study her more closely, enjoying the way a lock of dark hair had fallen from that prim knot to curl against her cheek. Such a pretty, dimpled cheek. Everything about her was pretty. And soft. From the lips, pursed as though in prayer, to the gentle curve of her eyebrows.

Just then her eyes opened and she caught him staring.

"Hi again."

At the sound of his voice her eyes widened in recognition. "You're ... the one I met at the front door."

"Zane."

"Yes, of course. Zane."

"When do you get to tackle Cal's office mess?"

"Whenever he wants me to start."

"I'd say the sooner the better. Cal doesn't have much patience with paperwork."

"That's what he told me." She laughed. "Fortunately, it's what I do best."

Just then Cal stepped into the room. "You two getting acquainted?"

"Yeah. When does Riley start?"

Cal turned to her. "You'll need tomorrow to move your things out here and get settled in. Then you can start the following morning. How does that sound?"

"Perfect." She offered her hand. "I'd better get back to town now. I have to get the rental car back before closing."

Cal accepted her handshake. "Rental car? How did you get here from Helena?"

"Bus."

"Well, then, you'll need some help getting your stuff out here."

"Oh, I don't think…"

Zane interrupted. "I'm free in the morning. I could take one of the ranch trucks into town and lend a hand."

"No. That isn't neces—"

"Perfect." Ignoring her protest, Cal gave Riley a smile. "How does eight o'clock sound?"

"Yes. All right." She turned to Zane. "Thanks for the offer. I'm staying at Delia Cowling's place. Do you know it?"

"Sure thing." Zane's smile grew. "I'll see you at eight."

When she and Cal walked to the front door, Zane stood admiring her backside.

Minutes later, when Cal closed the door and joined him, he was grinning like a conspirator.

"Very slick," Cal muttered as they made their way to the kitchen.

"I was thinking the same thing. Thanks for giving me that perfect opening. It'll give me a chance to get to know our pretty new accountant."

"A word of warning." Cal paused at the kitchen door. "She's going to be an employee now, Zane. You make the wrong moves, she could sue you for harassment."

"Me?" Zane threw back his head and roared before dropping an arm around the foreman's shoulders. "When have you ever known me to make a wrong move on an unwilling female?"

"Willing or unwilling, Riley Mason is off-limits. And if she doesn't sue your hide, I'll do it for her."

"Thanks for that fatherly advice. I'll keep it in mind."
Zane was still chuckling as he joined the others.

Riley drove the rental car down the long, curving driveway leading away from the Lost Nugget Ranch.

She was still reeling from her second encounter with the cowboy. She'd had to keep from staring at the change in him. Gone was the dark beard, the filthy clothes. He'd been freshly showered and shaved, with little drops of water still glistening in his hair. Dark hair, she'd noted, that just brushed the collar of his plaid shirt. Long legs were encased in faded denims. On his feet were scuffed boots.

He had piercing blue eyes in a tanned face that wasn't so much handsome as commanding. With that killer smile aimed at her, it was impossible to look away. But she wasn't interested in a fling with a cowboy.

A man was the last thing on her mind.

But a job...

The magnitude of what had just transpired came over her in waves.

She had the job.

Right this minute, nothing else mattered except that.

She had the job.

This wasn't just the start of a new job. This was the start of a brand-new life.

A new life, in a place so far away from where she'd begun, nobody searching for her would ever be able to find her or Summer.

Not ever again.

CHAPTER TWO

———◆———

Zane was whistling as he descended the stairs and walked to the kitchen.

At the Lost Nugget Ranch, breakfast was an important meal, bringing everyone together before they went their separate ways for the day. And, because ranch chores started at dawn, the men had often put in several hours of hard work before breakfast.

Jesse and Amy were already seated at the table, along with Wyatt and Marilee.

Cora, who had returned to the ranch sometime during the night, was engaged in a familiar argument with Cal.

"I was never in any danger, Cal." Cora's tone was patient.

"So you say. But you admitted that the heavy snow brought down a tree right beside your tent. You could be lying out there right now, pinned and gravely wounded, and we wouldn't have a clue."

"Cal, I always have my cell phone under my pillow."

"A lot of good that would do if you were crushed beneath a tree. The calendar may say it's springtime, but somebody forgot to tell Mother Nature. If it isn't a tree falling, it could be an avalanche. And there you are, all alone in the wilderness, at the mercy of any number of dangers."

Cora gave a long, deep sigh. "You know I'm not going to give up my art excursions. It's where I do my best work. I love it too much to ever stop."

"And I'm not going to stop worrying. I've been doing it too long."

"Now, children," Jesse said with a laugh. "There will be no fighting at the table."

That eased the tension as everyone, even Cal and Cora, joined in the laughter.

Jesse turned to Zane. "You look awfully happy this morning."

Cal sipped orange juice. "Could it be because you're driving into town to pick up Riley Mason?"

"The new accountant that everyone figured was a man?" Jesse's remark brought a round of laughter.

"A man?" Cora looked intrigued.

"Because of the name, I guess." Zane merely smiled as he settled himself at the table. "Actually, Aunt Cora, she's a real looker."

Jesse winked at his wife. "I heard a cowboy say that about Daffy Spence last week. Of course, that was after his tenth beer."

Daffy and her twin sister, Vi, owners and operators of the Fortune Saloon in Gold Fever, were both stick-thin, and wore their purple hair spiked, their eyes ringed with enough jet-black liner to give them the appearance of

flirty raccoons. Their age was a source of constant specu-
lation, though one thing was certain. Whatever their birth
certificates said, they were still young and frisky enough
to bed the occasional bartender or willing customer.

"Good one, cuz." Zane slapped him on the back. "It
wouldn't take getting drunk to find Riley Mason easy to
look at."

Something in his tone had the others studying him
more closely.

"This sounds interesting." Wyatt dropped an arm
around Marilee's shoulders. "You thinking of getting better acquainted with easy-to-look-at Riley Mason?"

"It may have crossed my mind. But just in the interest
of good business relations, of course."

When Dandy began passing around platters of sausage and toast and omelets, Zane turned to Cal, ready
to change the subject. "I happened to get a look at your
office on my way in here. It looks like a tornado blew
through. Good thing you're getting some much-needed
help with the paperwork."

The ranch foreman ran a hand through his white hair.
"I'm buried under a mountain of bank ledgers and legal
documents."

Cora laid a hand over Cal's. "It would certainly ease
your burden if you'd just move into Coot's suite upstairs.
That way you could work on some of the books after
supper, instead of getting talked into playing poker in the
bunkhouse."

Jesse winked at his cousins across the table. "Let's
see. Spend your evenings poring over bank ledgers, or
playing poker with the wranglers. Hey, everybody knows
that boring paperwork wins every time."

Cal chuckled. "Given a choice, I'd rather skip both and be up on the range, especially with spring calving here and the herds mired in snow."

"Most of the wranglers are feeling the same way." Jesse dug into his meal. "They've spent way too many hours cooped up and can't wait to get back to the hills along with the herd. Not even a good poker game can hold a candle to that."

Cal nodded. "It's that old springtime itch. I've got it bad." He turned to the woman beside him. "As for moving into Coot's rooms in this big house, we've been over this before, Cora. I'm just not ready. I may fill some of the hole left by Coot, but as for the rest..."

His words trailed off, but everyone in the room understood his reluctance. His best friend's things were just as Coot had left them. From the wide-brimmed hats and custom-made boots in the closet to the books he'd devoured and the letters he'd saved from family and friends, Coot's presence could be felt everywhere on this vast ranch, but the feelings were strongest in his own suite of rooms, where nothing had been touched since his death nearly a year earlier.

To ease the tension Jesse abruptly turned to the foreman. "So, where are you going to put your new accountant, now that you've learned she's a female? I don't think she'd be comfortable in the bunkhouse."

Cal turned to Cora. "I was thinking about the room next to the office. But that's when I thought we were hiring a guy. Now that I've learned that she has a four-year-old, I'm thinking maybe she'd be more comfortable in Annie's Retreat. What do you think?"

Zane looked thunderstruck. "A kid? Riley Mason has a kid?"

"Named Summer," Cal said easily. "Did I forget to mention her?"

"Yeah. You did." Zane tried to picture the gorgeous accountant in the role of mother. Somehow, the image didn't fit. And wife. Her image blurred a bit more.

Cora's smile bloomed. "A little girl. How sweet. I'm sure she'll love living on the ranch." She turned to Cal. "Annie's Retreat." Her voice turned dreamy. "I remember when my sister-in-law decorated those rooms and turned them into her hideaway. Cal, it hasn't been put to use in years. It's perfect for a family."

Cal shook his head. "There's just the two of them. No husband, she told me."

That sparked Zane's interest. No man in her life. At least not now.

Cal's words broke through his musings. "That's it, then. As long as Cora agrees, it looks like you'll have to carry their things up a flight of stairs."

"No problem." Though Zane was still reeling from the revelations about their pretty new bookkeeper he managed to say, "Being a pack mule is one of my many talents."

That had the others laughing before Jesse said, "Let's just hope our new accountant has enough talent to clean up the mess in Cal's office."

Cal gave a shake of his head. "I'm not worried. She had excellent references, going all the way back to working at a coffee shop near her campus."

That had Cora smiling. "I remember my first job in college."

"At a coffee shop?" Amy asked.

Cora chuckled. "They weren't popular then. I applied for a job as a waitress in an off-campus bar. I got the job and hated every minute of it. I'd rather work alone in the dreariest job imaginable than have to put up with dozens of drunks all demanding attention at the same time, especially as it got closer to quitting time. I found myself forgetting drink orders, making mistakes on the bills, and spilling more drinks than I could keep track of."

That had her great-nephews smiling.

Wyatt shook his head. "It's hard to imagine you working as a waitress in some college-town bar, Aunt Cora. Were you wearing Coot's overalls back then?"

The older woman put a hand to her hip. "I'll have you know I was once considered quite a babe."

While the others were grinning, Cal rushed to her defense. "Still are to me, Cora."

Then, realizing what he'd just said, his face reddened.

His discomfort wasn't lost on the others.

Amy and Marilee exchanged meaningful looks, while Jesse, Wyatt, and Zane jumped at the chance to start teasing him.

"Careful, Cal." Jesse winked at his cousins. "Next thing you know, Aunt Cora will invite you to her studio to pose for a portrait."

Wyatt chuckled. "Just remember to keep your boots on, Cal."

Clearly flustered, Cora pushed away from the table. "I'd better get to my studio and finish what I started out at camp."

Cal got to his feet, grateful for a chance to escape. "I'll bring in the rest of your things."

She gave him a tender smile. "Thanks, Cal, but you have enough on your plate these days. I can manage."

"I know you can, but I want to help." Before she could protest further, he turned and made his way to the mudroom off the kitchen, where the custom wagon he'd made for her years earlier had been left crammed with supplies from her latest overnighter.

When he was gone, Cora glanced at Amy and Marilee before taking in a deep breath. "One day soon I intend to tackle Coot's rooms and see if I can't make some order out of them. With the anniversary of my brother's death looming, I think most of his things should be put in storage. That would go a long way toward making Cal feel more comfortable about moving in. And I know I'd feel better sorting through Coot's belongings. I hope I can count on both of you to lend a hand."

Amy spoke for both of them. "You know we'll help whenever you're ready to face it, Aunt Cora."

"Thank you." She turned away and headed toward her studio in the rear of the house.

Minutes later Cal Randall followed, hauling in her supplies.

When they were alone, Wyatt turned to the others. "I'm glad Cal is getting the help he needs to ease some of the load from his shoulders."

Jesse nodded. "I was just thinking the same thing. He's taken on too much." He got to his feet. "I'm going to head the first group of wranglers up to the high pasture."

Zane glanced out the window, where a thick blanket of clouds had obscured the sun. "If this weather keeps up, we may have to skip spring altogether and go right to summer."

Jesse drained his coffee. "I figure this is winter's last hurrah. By this time next week I'm betting the last of the snow will be melting and the high country will be abloom with acres of green grass."

"I'll take that bet." Zane whipped out a twenty and slapped it on the table. "I'm betting this latest storm will dump enough snow to stick around for two weeks or more."

"Sucker." Jesse dropped his own twenty and leaned over to kiss his wife. "Baby, I'll be treating you to a couple of cold longnecks on Zane's money this time next week."

"In your dreams." With a grin Zane sauntered away, leaving his cousins to stare after him.

In the barn Jimmy Eagle looked up from a stall where he'd been wrapping a mare's leg. Spying Zane's polished boots beneath new denims and shirt, he leaned on the rail. "You ducking ranch chores, son? You sure aren't dressed for mucking stalls."

Zane shot him a grin. "I volunteered to pick up Cal's new accountant in town and help her move her stuff out to the ranch."

"Her stuff? I thought he'd hired a city boy."

Zane's smile grew. "That's what we all thought. Turns out Riley Mason is a female." He peered over the stall. "What's wrong with Vanilla?"

"I didn't like the look of a cut on her leg. Treated it with some of my special ointment."

Zane chuckled. Jimmy's mysterious ointments were regarded as something of a miracle around the ranch. "I've had that treatment myself a time or two."

Jimmy nodded and glanced at the scar on the younger man's jaw. "I thought your mother would horsewhip me when she found out I'd stitched up that cut and treated it without a doctor so you could get back out on the trail with your cousins."

"As I recall, I was more concerned with missing an afternoon up in the foothills than I was about splitting my jaw clean open in that spill from old Skeeter."

"He was a mean pony." Jimmy slapped Zane's shoulder. "You were the only one who could ever ride him."

"Thanks to you." Zane shook his head. "I believe you were the original horse-whisperer. Whatever you said to that pony, it turned things around. After that, he was as docile as an old plow horse."

"I told him he possessed the spirit of my father's father, and that it was his duty to make our family proud."

"That's what you say now. At the time, Jesse told me that you threatened Skeeter with the glue factory if he ever tossed me again."

The old man looked Zane in the eye. "Which one of us do you choose to believe?"

"You've never steered me wrong, Jimmy."

The two men shared an affectionate smile before Zane sauntered away, jingling the keys to a ranch truck.

Zane parked the truck at the curb outside Delia Cowling's neat white house. On the ride to town he'd had plenty of time to wrap his mind around the fact that Riley Mason had a daughter. He'd begun to imagine the fun of teaching the kid to saddle a horse and ride across the hills. Four wasn't too young to start. Hadn't his old friend and mentor Jimmy Eagle put him on a horse's back as soon as he'd been old enough to walk?

He climbed the porch steps and knocked.

When Riley opened the door, he found himself staring.

"Hey." It was all he could manage.

She was wearing skinny jeans and a T-shirt that hugged every curve. Her dark hair fell in soft waves to her shoulders. She wasn't wearing a bit of makeup, and he found himself looking at perfect porcelain skin, laughing dark eyes, and a pale mouth rounded in surprise. If possible, she looked even better than she had, all prim and proper, in that business suit.

"Hi. We're just about all packed. Would you like to...?"

Her words ended abruptly when something careened into Riley's legs, propelling her forward. If Zane hadn't caught her, she'd have been knocked clear off the front porch.

Riley stepped back, gathering as much dignity as she could manage. "Sorry."

"Don't be." His entire body was still tingling from that sudden, shocking impact with hers. He managed a dangerous smile. "It was my pleasure." He looked down at the little girl peering through Riley's legs. "Now, who's this?"

He found himself staring at a miniature Riley. Big, laughing eyes in a tiny, heart-shaped face framed by a wild tangle of dark curls.

She was so small. Once again he had to adjust his thinking. Maybe saddling a horse and riding the range wasn't in the cards after all.

"This is my daughter, Summer." Riley's voice had gone from tense to soft and proud in the space of a heartbeat.

The little girl was wearing leggings under some sort of short skirt, topped off with a denim jacket. In her arms was a floppy-eared stuffed dog.

He knelt down on the porch so that his eyes were level with the little girl's. "Hi, Winter."

She wrinkled her nose. "Not Winter. I'm Summer."

"Now how did I get that wrong? Hello, Summer. How old are you?"

"I'm this much." She held up four fingers.

"Four. Wow. You're almost all grown-up, aren't you?"

She nodded proudly. "Mama says I'm a big girl, not a baby. What's your name?"

"My name is Zane."

"That's a funny name."

"Funnier than Winter?"

"Not Winter. Summer." She glanced up at her mother. "He's funny."

"Yes, he is. Did you remember to pack all your toys?"

Summer nodded. "Now can I have a snack?"

"Yes, you may. I thought you could eat it on the drive to the ranch."

"Okay." The little girl skipped away.

Delia Cowling walked up behind Riley. "Good morning, Zane."

"Delia." He gave the old woman a smile. "I'm sorry you're losing a boarder."

"So am I." She held the door. "Come on in. Their bags are all packed."

He took in the tiny wheeled suitcase standing alongside the larger one. "That's everything?"

Riley ducked her head. "We like to travel light."

"I'm not complaining." He chuckled. "You've made my job easy."

Summer came barreling down the hallway carrying a little bag. "Mama, look what Auntie Delia made me." She opened the bag to reveal a cinnamon biscuit, several raspberry-filled cookies, and a small bottle of water.

Riley glanced at the old woman. "What happened to the carrot sticks I cut up?"

"Summer and I nibbled them while you were finishing your packing, dear." Delia tried for an innocent smile. "But I know how long the drive to the Lost Nugget is. A growing child needs her energy, so I thought I'd just add a few goodies."

Before Riley could voice her disapproval Delia opened her arms and gave the young woman a hug. "I'm so glad I had a chance to meet you and Summer, though our time together was too brief. If you ever need a sitter, I hope you'll call on me."

"Thank you, Delia." Riley stepped back a pace, while continuing to hold the older woman's hands. "It was so kind of you to take us in on such short notice. I won't forget your kindness."

Delia scooped up the little girl. "Good-bye, Summer. I hope you'll come back to visit me often."

"And we'll have tea and raspberry cookies?"

"Of course we will." Delia kissed the little girl's cheek before setting her on her feet.

"And Floppy can have some, too?"

"Floppy will always be invited to tea here, sweetheart."

Zane thought about the woman he'd known in his

childhood as the stern gossip of Gold Fever. In the past year, after the painful loss of her brother, she'd transformed into this kindly stranger he barely recognized.

Who would have believed she'd be melting into a puddle over one little girl and her stuffed dog?

Riley picked up a child's car seat and held the door as he hauled the luggage down the porch and out to the waiting truck. Summer skipped along behind them, gripping her bag of goodies, her stuffed dog, and a toy shaped like a television remote. She paused to turn and wave several times at the old woman who stood in the doorway.

Zane stowed the luggage before opening the back door of the truck. "I'd give you a hand with that, but I've never dealt with a kid's car seat before."

"That's all right. I'm used to doing it."

As she moved past him, he inhaled the fresh, lightly floral fragrance of her perfume, and felt a quick rush of heat that caught him by surprise.

He watched as Riley deftly inserted the seat belt through the slots of the seat before helping Summer up and into the truck.

With a click of the seat belt Riley turned and found him standing close. Too close. She took a quick step back. "Simple and safe."

"So I see. Looks easy enough." Zane held the front door and waited until she was seated before closing the door and hurrying around to the driver's side.

As they started away, both Riley and Summer waved and blew kisses toward Delia Cowling, who did the same.

"Now can I eat my snack?" Summer asked.

Riley turned. "Yes, you may."

In the rearview mirror Zane saw the little girl unwrap her biscuit and hold it toward the stuffed dog before taking a bite. "Mama says I have to share. Isn't that good, Floppy?"

Minutes later he heard questions in an adult voice, followed by answers in childlike tones. A glance in the rearview mirror had him smiling. Summer was pressing buttons on her toy, which asked questions about simple things like the color of the sky or the sound made by a horse. Each time Summer answered correctly, the gadget praised her, and she in turn would relate her brilliance to her stuffed dog.

"See, Floppy. The sky is blue. And a horsey says neigh, neigh."

Zane looked over and shared a smile with Riley. "For a minute there I thought we had a stowaway."

Riley laughed. "I guess, if you're not used to being around little kids, the sound of all those strange voices could throw you."

"I'll say. She's a cutie. Looks a lot like her mother."

"Thanks." She turned to study the passing scenery, as though deliberately turning away from any form of flattery. "Once you get out of town, it's really beautiful countryside."

"Yeah. I've always loved the look of this part of the country. You have it all. Mountains. Rivers. Meadows. Forests."

Riley nodded and continued drinking in the scenery, grateful for the chance to stare at something besides the driver. He was too handsome. Too charming. Too... distracting, with that dangerous smile and those laughing blue eyes.

She had no intention of being tempted by a smooth-talking cowboy, no matter how good-looking he was.

They veered off the highway and began the long stretch of road that gradually became gravel and dirt.

She turned toward her daughter in the backseat. "We'll be at the Lost Nugget pretty soon, Summer."

"Actually, you've been on Lost Nugget property for the past half hour," Zane corrected.

Riley caught her breath. "I had no idea this was all part of the ranch."

"The house is just beyond that rise."

He pointed.

Up ahead the sprawling, three-story house came into view and she caught her breath at the sheer size and beauty of it. "I was so preoccupied on my first drive here, I didn't really appreciate how big it is."

"Biggest ranch in Montana." Zane couldn't hide his love and pride. "The original building was started by my great-grandfather, then the majority of the place finished by my grandfather and father and uncles."

"You're"—she swallowed—"a McCord?"

He glanced over with a look of surprise. "I thought you knew."

"You never said your last name." Her face flamed. All this time, she'd thought him one of the hired hands.

He was one of them. And that meant he wouldn't be riding off to join the others. He would be living here. Sharing the same house… "Have you lived here all your life?"

He shook his head. "There was a long stretch of years when I was away." He glanced over. "Long story. Maybe I'll tell you some day."

As they drew nearer and then drove around to the back of the house, Riley fell silent, awed not only by the size, but by the number of outbuildings. As if the house wasn't impressive enough, with its three stories and wide, cathedral windows looking out on the most amazing vista, there were the barns, each one the size of a football stadium.

Zane brought the truck to a halt at the back door and opened the passenger side so Riley could step out and free little Summer from her car seat. Staring around with big eyes, the little girl kept hold of her floppy dog with one hand, the other tucked firmly in her mother's. For her part, Riley seemed relieved to have a hand to cling to, as well.

As they walked through the mudroom, Zane paused to explain. "Our cook, Dandy, is a stickler for neatness. Anybody who doesn't bother to clean their boots before stepping into his kitchen will get his famous hairy eyeball."

Summer held back. "Mama, what's a hairy eyeball?"

"The look you get from me when you forget to pick up your toys."

"Oh." The little girl smiled at Zane. "Does he take away your snack if you forget?"

"Yes, he does." Zane kept a straight face as he showed them the big sink, where a foot-operated pedal turned on a giant stream of water. "Especially if we don't scrape our boots or forget to wash our hands."

As he stepped on the pedal, Summer gave a delighted squeal. "Look, Mama. No hands."

Riley pretended to be amazed. "How did Zane do that?"

Summer shrugged before asking timidly, "Can you teach me?"

"Sure thing." He lifted his foot, showing her how to step on the pedal.

She was absolutely thrilled when water spilled out.

"Can I do it by myself?"

"You bet." Zane stepped back and Summer gingerly touched her little foot to the pedal, starting the water flowing again.

"Careful," Riley said in an aside to Zane. "She may want to stay here for hours just turning on and off that spray."

"I don't mind." Zane held the door to the kitchen. "But you may want to come back here later. Right now, I think I smell something sweet. Which means that Dandy must be baking some goodies."

That was all it took to persuade Summer to leave the magic sink and follow her mother and Zane into the kitchen.

Dandy was just straightening from the oven, removing a cookie tin before setting it down on a trivet.

When he looked over, Zane was grinning from ear to ear. "What perfect timing. Do I smell chocolate chip?"

"You do."

"Dandy, this is Riley Mason and her daughter, Winter."

"It's Summer," the little girl corrected.

"Oh. Right. Summer. I keep forgetting." He winked. "While you get acquainted, I'll bring in your things."

Dandy tossed aside his oven mitts before extending a hand. "Riley." He smiled down at the little girl beside her. "Summer, I hope you like chocolate chip cookies."

"I do." She eyed the tray. "Are those as good as Mama's?"

"Probably not. Nothing's ever as good as Mama's. But as soon as these are cool enough to eat, you can judge for yourself."

"I can tell you right now, there's no contest." Riley was laughing. "Mine are actually from the store. I don't think Summer has ever tasted home-baked cookies."

"Why, that's almost sinful. We'll have to correct that problem immediately." Dandy was chuckling. "No child should have to grow up eating store-bought cookies."

"Okay. I have your luggage." The door slammed behind Zane as he made his way through the kitchen. "Follow me." He hefted their bags and led the way from the kitchen and through the enormous great room to the stairs leading to the second floor.

As Riley caught her daughter's hand and followed, she struggled to hold back the nerves she'd been fighting all morning.

She desperately wanted this to work. Not just the job, which was critical for their survival, but also the location.

The Lost Nugget Ranch was as different from her life in Philadelphia as night was to day. She wasn't at all certain she could fit in here, but she was determined to try.

Her safety, and that of her daughter, absolutely depended on it.

CHAPTER THREE

───◆◆◆───

"Here we are." Zane opened the door and waited until Riley and her daughter stepped inside the room before following them.

Was it his imagination, or had Riley stiffened before moving past him? Whenever she was forced to get close to him, he could almost feel a chill in the air.

He left them in the parlor while he carried their bags into the adjoining bedrooms. When he returned, they were standing where he'd left them, staring around with matching looks of wonder.

He felt the need to explain. "Sorry. Some of the furniture is old-fashioned, and..."

"No. It's lovely." Riley studied the feminine floral sofa and two pale-peach rocking chairs positioned in front of a white marble fireplace.

On the floor was a rug in muted tones of peach and white and pale apple green.

"We've always called this suite of rooms Annie's Retreat. It's named for my grandmother, who used this as her getaway from her men. With a husband and three sons, and later three grandsons, she needed to escape all the manly talk of ranch chores and broken fences and wayward cattle. She used to come up here and sew or just sit by the fire and read. And when Coot was gone for weeks at a time, she even slept up here."

"I can see why she loved it." Riley clasped her hands together to keep from hugging herself. "It's so much more than I expected."

Zane grinned. "That's a relief. Well..." He started toward the door. "I know you'll want to explore and unpack." He glanced at Summer, who was yawning and rubbing her eyes. "I think maybe someone is going to want to try out her new bed before long."

Riley followed him to the door. "Thanks again, Zane, for picking us up and hauling in our stuff."

He turned abruptly, and she froze.

Sensing her discomfort, he gave her a smile that sent a tingling awareness along her spine. "It was my pleasure."

When he stepped out and pulled the door shut, Riley leaned against it for just a moment, hoping to get her bearings.

What was it about that cowboy? She'd become very adept at avoiding men, especially those who sent out signals that they were attracted to her. Zane hadn't said or done anything that even hinted at attraction. He hadn't so much as flirted with her, but she was aware of him in a way she hadn't been aware of any other man.

Nerves, she told herself. It was just the result of all the chaos in her life. Once she had time to sort things out, she would be back in control of her emotions, and she could resume her ice-maiden attitude around men in general, and Zane in particular.

"Come on, honey." Taking Summer's hand, she led her daughter, still clinging to Floppy, on a tour of their rooms.

Late afternoon sunlight streamed through the big windows and splashed a pool of golden light across the bed where Summer lay, her arm flung across Floppy as she napped.

Riley turned from the closet where she'd been hanging the last of Summer's clothes. One glance at her daughter had her moving to stand beside the bed, watching her sleep. It had been an exhausting day, beginning much too early because of nerves. But she had accomplished so much. And now, seeing her daughter at rest, she felt a wave of such gratitude. After the nightmare of the last few years, this peaceful setting was like a soothing balm to her heart.

She perched on the edge of the mattress, careful not to wake Summer.

This was what she'd wanted for her daughter. What she'd dreamed of. Someplace clean and cheery and safe. A place where Summer could grow and learn and develop into the wonderful person Riley knew she could be.

She picked up Summer's favorite faded blanket and draped it over her, smoothing out each wrinkle and tucking it around her little shoulders before walking from the room. Across the hallway was a second bedroom where she had already put away her few clothes and belongings. Precious few, she realized. But, thankfully, these rooms were already furnished with beds and dressers and chairs.

All of them empty and waiting to be filled with things and people. And dreams.

They may belong to somebody else, but for now, for this precious little time she would spend working at the Lost Nugget Ranch, they were hers to enjoy.

She paused beside the big soft bed, now dressed in fresh linens from the closet. It had been years since she'd slept alone, without her daughter sharing her space. She wasn't certain just how Summer would adjust to these new arrangements. If her daughter appeared troubled by the changes in her life, Riley intended to give up her own comfort to sit beside the little girl's bed and read to her each night until she was comfortable being alone in a new room.

She walked to the pretty parlor, with its soft, feminine furniture arranged around a cozy white fireplace. It was a room fit for a queen. Or at least a princess, she thought with a smile.

Had Annie McCord felt like a queen when she'd used this space? Had she looked out at that amazing countryside and gasped at the beauty of it? Or had she, like so many born to this part of the country, grown so accustomed to it that she'd taken it all for granted?

The name this family had given the suite suited it perfectly. Annie's Retreat. It was a lovely hideaway inside the labyrinth of this enormous, masculine house, where a rancher's wife had sought peace and solitude.

Besides the two bedrooms and this lovely sitting room, Riley had discovered, much to her delight, that it had its own washer and dryer, and a small galley kitchen equipped with a sink and a microwave.

Riley dropped down into one of the lovely peach

chairs drawn up beside the fireplace and let her head fall back. Her eyes closed.

This was better than a retreat. After years of loss and struggle, of damaged self-esteem and desperation, of despair that she would ever climb out of the hole she'd dropped into, this lovely little cocoon was pure heaven.

The temperature hovered just above freezing, turning the snow to a bone-chilling rain. Under a leaden sky the rain caused the thawing riverbanks to swell, sending the overflow cascading over pastures, flooding roads.

Zane dragged himself out of the drainage ditch and wiped his muddy hands on his pants. "Okay," he shouted. "Give it a try."

Jesse, huddled under a poncho while seated on a back-hoe, lowered the claw into the snow-clogged ditch and scooped out a mound of half-frozen earth. When nothing happened, he lowered the claw a second time, scooping out more dirt and ice, depositing it onto the mountain of debris already removed.

There was a sudden whoosh when the water that had been backing up across the road suddenly began spilling into the freshly opened drain.

Zane and his cousin watched the swirl of water until, satisfied that it was flowing freely, they turned away. While Jesse drove the backhoe to the barn, Zane slogged through ankle-deep mud past the bunkhouse, past the row of outbuildings and barns, and on to the main house.

Outside the door he pried off his boots and set them aside to be hosed down later. In the mudroom he paused, barefoot, to roll up the sleeves of his filthy shirt before washing the worst of the mud from his hands and arms.

Except for his feet, he was caked with mud. It had even managed to coat his hair, leaving tufts of it sticking out here and there.

He climbed the stairs to his suite of rooms and was nearly there when the door to Annie's Retreat opened.

Riley and Summer stood, hand in hand, looking so fresh and clean they could have been models for a magazine.

"Well." He paused, unaware of how he must look to them. "All settled in?"

Riley went as still as a statue before taking a step back and drawing her daughter with her. "Yes. Thank you."

In that instant he realized that he probably smelled like a sewer.

Beside her, Summer stared at him wide-eyed. "Does your mama let you play in the mud?"

"Oh." He glanced down at himself before breaking into gales of laughter. "Yeah, I guess that's what I was doing. But around here, play is the same as work."

"You work in mud?" The little girl turned to her mother. "Could I watch Zane work in the mud some time, Mama?"

"Why would you want to do that?" Riley wrinkled her nose, refusing to look at him.

"'Cause I think it would be fun. Did you have fun, Zane?"

He thought about that for a moment. "Yeah, I guess I did. My cousin Jesse probably had more fun. He got to drive the backhoe."

"What's a backhoe?"

"A big tractor with a giant claw that eats dirt."

He could see her trying to picture that in her mind.

"If you really want to watch me work, and see a back-hoe in action, I'll be sure and let you know the next time I have to crawl around in the mud opening up a drainage ditch." He started away. "I guess I'd better get cleaned up if I want to have some of Dandy's chicken and dumplings."

Behind him, he heard Summer asking, "What are dumplings, Mama?"

He couldn't hear Riley's response, though he enjoyed the low timbre of her voice.

He was grinning as he let himself into his rooms. When he caught sight of himself in the mirror and realized just how bad he looked, he stopped dead in his tracks before shaking his head.

No wonder Riley seemed to freeze and take two steps back whenever she saw him. Anybody who didn't know him would think he was a drifter, or maybe a serial killer.

It wasn't going to be easy to impress a pretty woman when he was constantly engaging in ranch chores that left him looking and smelling like something she'd find stuck on the sole of her neat little boot.

It was, he realized, going to take a very long, very hot shower before he dared to show his face at the dinner table. And a much longer time to get past the wall that Riley Mason put up whenever he came near.

An hour later Zane walked into the kitchen to find most of the family gathered there. From the sound of their voices, the introductions had already been made.

Jesse handed him a frosty longneck. "Glad to see how well you cleaned up."

The two cousins shared a grin.

Zane nodded toward Amy and Marilee, chattering like magpies. "I see they're getting acquainted with Riley and Summer."

Jesse's voice softened. "Look at Amy. She's hovering over that little girl like a mother hen."

"I guess that comes from her days as a teacher."

Jesse nodded. "She never talks about it, but I know she misses it."

The two turned as Wyatt said, "And this is my great-aunt..."

At his words, Riley smiled and turned to the older woman who had walked up to stand beside her.

"...Cora McCord."

Riley's hand was halfway toward the woman's outstretched hand when Zane's words registered. "Cora McCord? The artist?"

"That's right, dear."

Riley's mouth opened, then closed, and she swallowed twice before she managed to remember to shake hands. "I never put it all together until just now. Of course. McCord." She knew she was babbling, but she couldn't seem to stop herself. "I knew Cora McCord lived and worked somewhere here in Montana, but I just never dreamed I'd get to actually meet her. I mean, meet you," she quickly corrected.

"You're familiar with my work, dear?" Cora laid a hand over Riley's.

"I've seen dozens of your paintings. Hundreds. I love them. Everything you paint is so vibrant. So amazing. The color. The texture..." She gave a shake of her head as though words couldn't convey all that she was thinking.

It was, Zane thought as he watched the scene unfold,

the most he'd ever heard Riley reveal. Not that she was making a lot of sense, but at least she was opening up. For the moment, she looked pretty emotional.

"Thank you." Cora nodded toward Summer, nibbling a piece of cheese. "I have to say that your work is pretty amazing, too."

It took Riley a moment to realize that Cora was talking about her daughter.

"Thank you." Her smile bloomed and she forced her attention to Summer. "Summer, say hello to Miss McCord."

The little girl followed her mother's example and extended her hand. "Hello, Miss McCord."

"Hello, Summer. Welcome to the Lost Nugget Ranch."

"I've never been on a real ranch before. Mama says there are horses and cows and"—she fumbled for words—"baby cows, too."

"Calves. Yes, indeed there are. More than you'll be able to count."

"I can count to ten. Want to hear me?"

Riley put a hand on her daughter's shoulder. "Maybe later, honey."

"Okay."

When the little girl returned her attention to her appetizer, Cora couldn't help chuckling. "Your daughter is indeed special. And having both of you here is quite a treat for me. After a lifetime of only men and boys, it's comforting to have so many women coming into my life."

Jesse, Wyatt, and Zane exchanged arched looks as the realization dawned. For the first time in her life, Cora had as many women in her home as men.

Seeing Dandy ladling soup into a tureen, Cora turned

toward the table. "I think we'd better take our seats so Dandy can begin serving."

They all moved to take their places. With Cal at one end and Cora at the other, Jesse and Amy sat beside Wyatt and Marilee, leaving Zane to sit beside Riley and her daughter on the other side of the table.

During a leisurely meal of hearty soup, and slow-cooked chicken and dumplings, the conversation centered on the heavy runoff of melting snow from the mountains that was taxing both fields and roads.

"I don't mind getting down and dirty," Zane said with a laugh. "But I really think we're going to need to take on a few more hands to deal with the clogged drainage ditches until the rainy season ends."

Cal nodded. "I'm way ahead of you. Since I can't spare any of the wranglers up in the highlands until after the calving, I put in a call to Stafford Rowe to see if he'd heard about anybody looking for work. He sent me a couple of prospects, and I put Jimmy Eagle in charge of them."

Zane chuckled. "Good move. If anybody can figure out the good workers from the lazy ones, it's Jimmy."

"And if anybody in town would know who's in need of a job, it's our mayor." Jesse winked at his aunt. "Mayor Rowe seems to have taken over Delia Cowling's position as town historian and all-around keeper of everybody's secrets, now that she's been transformed into your new best friend."

While everyone around the table began laughing, Zane turned to explain the joke to Riley.

"The sweet lady who allowed you the use of her home the other night has made quite a transformation in the past months. There was a time when she knew everybody's business, and was more than happy to share it with anyone who would listen."

Cora shook her head. "That's old news now, Zane. She and I have become quite good friends, and every time I see her, I discover more and more of the old Delia I knew as a girl."

Jesse nudged his wife. "So, Aunt Cora, you're saying an old tiger can change its stripes?"

That brought another round of laughter.

Summer's eyes grew round. "Are there tigers on the ranch, too?"

"Not a single one," Jesse assured her. "But we've got plenty of horses. If you ever want to see some, you should ask Zane to show you around. He's our resident horse expert."

"What's a horse ex...sert?"

"He's the guy who can eat, sleep, and live with horses." Jesse shot a quick grin at his cousin before deciding to play a trick on the family's confirmed bachelor. "I bet, if you ask him, he'd give you a tour of our horse barn."

Summer turned to Riley. "Oh, boy. Could I, Mama?"

"We'll see, honey."

Zane winked at the little girl. "That's mom-talk for 'Eat all your vegetables, pick up your toys, and maybe you'll be rewarded with a trip to the barn.'"

"I can do that." She looked very solemn. "I know what horses say. Neigh. Neigh."

"Did you hear that?" Jesse looked around the table. "Summer's just like Zane. She knows how to talk to horses."

"I do?" She looked very pleased.

Jesse nodded. "You'll just have to see for yourself. If

you go with Zane, I'm betting that in no time at all the horses will be talking to you."

The little girl eyed the last two green beans on her plate. Very deliberately she picked up one, then the other, and ate them, before glancing up at her mother. "See, Mama? I ate all my 'begibles."

Seeing the smiles on the faces of those around them, Riley felt a swelling of such pride. "I see, honey. I think, just for that, I'd better give you my word that you can visit the horses in the barn tomorrow."

"Can I really?" The little girl clapped her hands together before turning to Zane. "When will you take me?"

He sliced a killing look at his cousin for setting him up. "Whenever your mama says it's all right."

"Okay." Satisfied, she sat back and allowed the adult conversation to swirl around her.

But from the smile that lit her eyes, Zane realized that what he considered a minor blip on his crazy work schedule was a major event in the life of this four-year-old.

He tried to remember what it had felt like to be four and learning something brand-new each and every day. The thought had him remembering.

He had been absolutely horse-crazy. He'd had pictures of them taped on his walls. The only bedtime stories he would listen to were the ones about horses. And thanks to Jimmy Eagle's patience, he'd been introduced to riding and grooming his own mount as soon as he was old enough to handle such grown-up chores.

He came to a sudden decision. He couldn't let this little girl down. No matter how busy he was, he would make time tomorrow to take Summer to the horse barn. It would be fun to see her reaction to her first real live horse.

"Yeah, Riley. If anybody can introduce your daughter to horses, it's Zane." Wyatt dropped an arm around Marilee's shoulders and the two shared an intimate smile. "I don't know if you're aware that our cousin is about to become famous."

Riley arched a brow.

"He spent the past couple of years trailing a herd of wild mustangs across the wilderness and filming it for a Steven Michaelson documentary that's going to air on TV next month."

Zane chuckled. "My cousin has it wrong. I'm not going to become famous. The horses are. In fact, except for my voice doing the narration, you'll hardly ever see me. I'm just the guy trudging through waist-high snowdrifts and hunkering down in one of the worst thunderstorms I've ever encountered in the wild."

"You lived in the wilderness with mustangs?" Riley turned to study him more closely. "That's pretty awesome."

"If you like living in a furnace all summer and surviving blizzards and wolves all winter," Jesse added with a grin.

Riley gasped. "That sounds dangerous."

"Not to mention downright dismal," Wyatt deadpanned.

"Hey. It isn't as bad as it sounds." Zane was forced, as usual, to defend himself against the constant teasing. "In fact, I loved every minute of it. Living with mustangs was a dream of mine since I was no bigger than Summer."

"And you made it happen." Riley's voice turned wistful. "Not everybody can say that."

He shrugged. "Dreaming is the easy part. Making it

come true takes some work. But you have to figure, if I can do it, anybody can."

Wyatt shared a wicked grin with Jesse. "Life in the wilderness had to be quite a step down. How about this for a subtitle? From Hollywood heartthrob to dancing with mustangs."

"Hollywood?" Riley looked from one cousin to the other. "You're kidding, right? Isn't this your family home?"

"It was until our parents decided to dip their toes into the ocean of that big world out there." Wyatt grinned. "My folks dragged me around the world, while Zane's folks settled in la-la land."

That brought a round of laughter from everyone.

Riley smiled along with the others. But she found herself intrigued by the man seated beside her daughter.

Every time she saw him, he was a different person from the day before. One day a rough cowboy. The next a foul-smelling ditchdigger. But the most intriguing of all was the free spirit who could go from a glitzy life in Hollywood to spending years living in the wilderness with mustangs.

No wonder Zane McCord seemed like such a man of mystery.

CHAPTER FOUR

———◆◆◆———

Dinner was perfect as always, Dandy." Cora glanced at the others. "Shall we take our coffee and dessert in the great room?"

Riley couldn't recall a better meal. This excellent food would have cost a fortune in a fine restaurant in Philadelphia. But the food had become secondary to the warmth of the people gathered around the table. Their easy conversation and raucous laughter were infectious. She'd watched the interaction between the three cousins and couldn't detect so much as a trace of jealousy or mean-spiritedness. It was the same with Amy and Marilee, and Cora and Cal. Despite the generational gap, the teasing, there was a depth of love and affection that was so real, it had her throat closing.

"Thank you, Dandy."

He gave Riley a big smile. "You're welcome. Do you prefer coffee or tea with your dessert?"

She touched a hand to her stomach. "Neither. I don't believe I have room for dessert tonight. But thank you."

She caught Summer's hand as they trailed the McCord family.

In the huge great room a roaring fire blazed on the hearth.

Riley watched as they all seemed to fall into a routine.

Zane and his cousins gathered around a map filled with colorful pins, and began talking in low tones about a path they were charting for their trek into the wilderness as soon as the snow melted.

Cora and Cal stood in front of the fire, discussing plans for the morning, while Amy and Marilee, comfortably seated on a sofa, began studying blueprints and chattering about new house designs. From the conversation, it would seem that Jesse and Amy were planning on building their own home, not far from this grand house.

Riley stood in their midst, feeling like an intruder. An outsider.

To no one in particular she said, "If you don't mind, Summer and I will skip dessert and go up to our rooms."

Conversation ceased and heads came up.

Uncomfortable being the center of attention, she felt the need to come up with an excuse for their imminent departure. "Neither of us will need any coaxing to fall asleep tonight."

Cora walked over to take Riley's hand. "What were we thinking? I'm sure you're both feeling exhausted and more than a little overwhelmed. I hope you're comfortable in Annie's Retreat."

"More than comfortable, Miss McCord. It's a beautiful suite of rooms. I couldn't have asked for anything more."

"I'm so glad." Cora gave her a gentle smile. "Good night, Riley." She bent down so that her eyes were level with the little girl's. "Good night, Summer."

"'Night," the little girl said, keeping her hand tucked firmly in her mother's.

As they climbed the stairs, Riley could hear the rumble of conversation beginning again. Masculine voices talking about trails and caverns and treasure. Feminine voices discussing master bedrooms and guest rooms, closets and storage rooms.

Cal's voice, discussing the pressing issue of calving. Cora encouraging him to ride up to one of the northernmost pastures.

They may as well be speaking a foreign language. She was as out-of-place on this ranch as the McCord men would be in Philadelphia.

The McCord men. They were all so rough and handsome. And intimidating. Especially Zane McCord. He actually seemed to revel in looking like some sort of wild mountain man. He wasn't a bit apologetic about being covered in mud and coming across like a gunslinger in the Old West. Just being close to him stirred all sorts of uneasy feelings in her.

Uneasy? She knew that was a misstatement, to cover the truth she was trying to deny.

She was attracted to him.

That fact bothered her more than she cared to admit. But though she worked hard to ignore him, in the small, dark recesses of her mind, she was forced to concede what her heart couldn't hide. Just looking at him did strange things to her pulse rate.

Not that she would ever act on such feelings. He was

one of the privileged members of this family, while she was merely here for a few weeks to do a specific job. When the job was done, she would be moving on. She couldn't afford to forget that fact.

As she opened the door to her suite, she stopped in mid-stride at the sight of a man across the room.

His head whipped around. His eyes narrowed on her.

Instinctively she drew Summer behind her. "What are you doing here?"

His gaze moved over her, then fastened on the little girl peeking out from behind her. Though he smiled, his eyes remained cold. Cold enough to turn the blood in Riley's veins to ice.

"Just bringing you firewood." He touched a hand to his wide-brimmed hat before adding, "Ma'am."

He brushed past her and walked down the stairs without a backward glance.

As soon as he was gone, Riley closed the door and locked it.

"Who was that, Mama?"

"One of the wranglers." Her voice trembled. As did her hands.

"What's a wrangler?"

"A cowboy who works here. Come on, honey. Let's get you ready for bed." On legs of rubber she moved toward the bedroom, where she helped Summer into her pajamas.

As she helped her daughter, she struggled to calm her frayed nerves.

She would have to stop jumping every time she saw a stranger. She was in Montana, she reminded herself. On a ranch in the middle of nowhere.

It was time to get a grip, she told herself.

• • •

Summer snuggled in her mother's arms beneath an afghan, turning the pages of the book while Riley read a bedtime story.

It was the third story, and Riley knew that her daughter was very close to sleep. Still, she resisted taking her into the bedroom. She needed to feel Summer here, safe in her arms.

Safe.

Now that she'd had time to mull over that frightening scene, she was beginning to second-guess her own reaction. Had he been openly surly and mocking, or had he simply been as startled by her presence as she'd been by his? After all, if one of the wranglers had been ordered to fetch firewood to her apartment, he had every right to be here. Knowing the family was gathered downstairs, he wouldn't have been expecting to have someone walk in on him.

Still, she couldn't completely put aside her sense of unease. Knowing a stranger had access to her suite of rooms made her feel vulnerable and...violated. There was an easy remedy. She would remember to keep her door locked.

The warmth of the fire and the soothing motion of the rocking chair were beginning to work their magic. She could feel the fear slipping away. In its place was a feeling of contentment.

There had been so few precious moments like this in Summer's young life. Riley wanted nothing more than to keep her daughter in her arms for a while longer.

Summer looked up through her lashes. "Then what did little Sarah do?"

"She climbed up into her brother's treehouse and..."

A knock on the door had them both pausing.

Riley's heart took a hard, quick dip, and the fear was back, stark and terrifying.

Holding Summer firmly in her arms, she walked to the locked door. She hated the ripple of fear in her voice as she called, "Who's there?"

"Zane."

At the sound of that deep voice she felt a rush of relief that left her weak.

She unlocked the door and opened it, then stepped back, giving him a wide berth.

Summer put her chubby hands up to her mother's cheeks. "I bet you thought it was that man again."

"Man?" Zane looked from mother to daughter.

"A...wrangler was in here when we came up after dinner. He left a supply of firewood."

Zane nodded. "Cooper Easley. One of the new hires. I hope he didn't do anything to bother you?"

Riley shook her head. "I was just startled. I didn't expect to find a stranger in our rooms."

Zane offered Riley and Summer his most charming smile. "I'll see that it doesn't happen again." He nodded toward the tray. "Dandy thought, since the two of you skipped dessert, that you might enjoy some hot chocolate. Since I was on my way upstairs, I volunteered to bring it."

"Oh, boy." The book slipped from Summer's hands. "Can I have some, Mama?"

"I don't know. It's awfully late. A minute more and we'd have both been asleep."

"Sorry." Zane stood, uncertain whether to stay or leave.

"Please don't apologize." Unnerved, Riley set her

daughter down and picked up the fallen book, setting it atop the pretty afghan she'd found draped on the back of the sofa. "Summer's not the only one who would love some hot chocolate."

He set a silver tray on a side table. "Well then. Enjoy."

Before he could turn away, Riley stopped him. "Didn't you bring any for yourself?"

"I had coffee and fudge cake with two scoops of ice cream. Anything more and you'll see a grown man explode."

Summer's eyes went wide. "Do you have a tummy-ache?"

Before he could respond she said, "My mama knows what to do for that."

The little girl looked so serious that Zane couldn't help teasing just a bit. "She does?"

"Uh-huh. I lie on my side while she rubs my back. It really tickles. And after a while, I forget all about my sore tummy. You want Mama to do that for you?"

Riley's face turned several shades of scarlet while Zane struggled not to laugh out loud.

"That sounds really...soothing." He winked at Riley. "I'm not sure about my tummy, but the rest of my body would be grateful. Thank you, Summer. I'll keep it in mind for the next time I get a tummyache. But for now, I think I'll just go to my room and try to fall asleep."

The little girl picked up the mug of hot chocolate, topped off with a generous dollop of whipped cream. One taste and she turned to her mother with a look of wonder.

"This is the very bestest hot chocolate I've ever had. Try it, Mama."

Riley picked up the cup, aware that Zane was watching. "Oh, my. What in the world does Dandy do to make it taste this good?"

"Magic." Zane watched as she licked the whipped cream from her upper lip. He felt a sudden tightening in his loins. "Everything that man touches turns to pure magic."

She took another long drink before setting the mug aside. "What a thoughtful thing for Dandy to do."

"He has a soft spot for..." Zane caught himself. He'd been about to say "strays." Instead he quickly inserted, "...pretty little girls and their moms."

Summer gave a delighted laugh. "Zane called us pretty."

"You bet." He got down on one knee and touched a finger to her whipped-cream mustache. "You're one lucky little girl to have a mom this pretty. Every day you can look at her and see exactly how you'll look when you grow up."

"I'm going to be just like my mama."

He straightened and looked directly at Riley. "Smart girl."

Riley could feel her face growing hotter by the minute. Why did he have to stand so close? Why did she have to feel so stiff and awkward around him? "That's my aim. To raise a smart girl. Smarter than her mother."

He arched a brow. "Cal says you're one smart accountant."

"Thanks. But there's more to life than crunching numbers. Some of us just work. Others follow their passion. I still can't get over the fact that you followed your dream to live with mustangs."

"Just pure dumb luck." Seeing the smudge of whipped

cream on the corner of her mouth, he tucked his hands in his back pockets to keep from reaching out to it. "I happened to be in the right place at the right time, and the opportunity was dropped into my lap."

"I had a professor who told us that there is no such thing as luck. People who say they're lucky are actually well-prepared, so that when the opportunity presents itself, they're ready to take up the challenge at a moment's notice."

Zane thought about that. "I've never heard it stated that way before, but your professor may be onto something. All I know is, once the offer was made, I grabbed on to it with both hands. It was a dream job, and I never once felt like I was working."

She nodded. "A labor of love. I suppose that's the way your aunt feels about her art."

"Yeah." That had Zane smiling. "Aunt Cora is obsessed with her art. And she's a true artist. She never did it for the money. In fact, she turned away from some pretty tempting offers in Europe to return to her roots and paint this land that she loves."

Seeing Summer yawn, he reached a hand to the door. "I'd better get out of here and let you get some sleep. Good night."

"'Night. Thank you for the hot chocolate," she called.

He paused in the doorway. Turned to her with a smile. "You can thank Dandy in the morning. He did the work. I was just the messenger."

He stared with naked hunger at her lips before pulling himself back. "Sleep tight."

He pulled the door closed and made his way to his own suite.

As he walked he thought about the pretty picture Riley and Summer had made when he'd first opened their door. Bare toes peeking out from beneath their robes. A modern Madonna and child, dark hair loose and falling over their eyes, looking all warm and sleepy and thoroughly content.

There was something about the way Riley protected her child that touched a chord in him. He admired the fact that she was willing to forgo her own pleasure for her daughter's comfort. She was the direct opposite of his own mother, who'd sacrificed her husband and son for her own selfish desires.

As always, he had to exert great effort to put the past out of his mind. He'd learned early in life that it did no good to dwell on old angers.

Now Riley was a subject he could enjoy lingering over. There was something about her. She was as skittish as a mustang. He'd done his best to put her and her daughter at ease. But though Summer enjoyed his humor, her mother was still wary around him.

He'd thought at first that it was due to the way he'd looked at their initial meeting. He would have frightened any sane person. Again today, she'd seen him at his worst. But now, tonight, even when he was freshly showered, bearing gifts, she still went to great pains to hold him at arm's length.

That intrigued him. It wasn't the usual effect he had on women. Of course, he didn't know her. Didn't have a clue about her history. Maybe she'd been hurt in the past. Or maybe she was still carrying a torch for Summer's father.

That thought sent a quick, sharp dart to his heart that caught him by surprise.

Hell, maybe she just didn't like him.

Whatever the facts, he intended to find out all he could about the lovely Riley Mason.

And to learn why she was so cautious around him.

Riley tiptoed into Summer's room and studied her daughter at rest. Just seeing that sweet face smiling in dreams, her arm draped carelessly over Floppy, was enough to send her spirits soaring to the moon.

If she never had another good thing in her life, this would be enough. Knowing Summer was safe and happy meant everything to her.

She stood there, enjoying the moment, before picking up the empty tray of mugs and slipping from the suite.

By the light of the moon she made her way downstairs to the kitchen. Once inside she switched on the light and carried the tray to the sink.

As long as she was here, she decided, she may as well make herself a cup of tea.

While she waited for the kettle to boil, she washed the mugs and tray and set them aside.

She was just pouring boiling water into a cup when the door opened, causing her to slosh hot water over the rim, burning her hand. That, in turn, had her dropping the kettle onto the stove with a clatter while she gave a gasp of pain.

Zane, barefoot and naked to the waist, stood staring at her with a look of surprise before he crossed the room in quick strides. "Hey, you're hurt."

She winced. "Just a little burn. It's nothing."

"Nothing?" He caught her hand in his and studied the red mark. "I'll get some ice for that."

"No, it's…"

Ignoring her, he pressed the ice-maker lever on the door of the refrigerator and wrapped an ice cube in a napkin. "Here. Hold this on the burn for a few minutes."

"Thanks."

Instead of moving away, he remained beside her. So close, she could feel the warmth of his body enveloping her, causing a strange tingle along her spine.

"I figured you'd be asleep by now."

The deep timbre of his voice had her looking up to find his gaze centered on her, and for the first time she became aware of how she must look. Hair tumbled. Feet bare. Wearing nothing but soft, clingy pajama bottoms and a cami that revealed more than it covered.

Just having him so close had her body reacting, her flesh hot and cold, her nipples growing hard.

Oh, why hadn't she stayed up in her room? At least she could have taken the time to put on a robe, if only she'd had her wits about her.

"I couldn't sleep. I was…making tea."

"I'll make it."

"No." The word was out of her mouth before he could turn away.

He turned back to look at her.

"I mean…" She could feel her cheeks burning. "I'll just go up to bed."

"Don't let me send you away. While you're living and working here, Riley, this is your home, too."

"Thanks, but…" She backed away.

His voice lowered. "I notice how you…shrink from me…"

"I don't…"

His eyes narrowed slightly. "Look. I don't want to make you uncomfortable. If you'll tell me what I'm doing wrong, I'll take steps to correct..."

"Zane." She touched a hand to his mouth to halt his words. "It isn't anything you do. It's..."

The minute her fingers came in contact with his flesh she felt the rush of heat and realized her mistake. But it was too late. Now that she was touching him, she couldn't even remember what she'd been about to say.

The words died in her throat.

Before she could lower her hand he caught it and continued holding it while his narrowed gaze burned over her.

"So, it is me."

"It's not what you think. I don't...dislike you. On the contrary, I really..." She sucked in a breath and tried again. "You aren't blind, so you have to know that you're easy on the eyes."

He studied the high color on her cheeks and knew what it had cost her to make that simple admission. His smile was back, quick and charming. "Well now, that's a relief. I was afraid I'd grown some warts that I wasn't aware of. So, if you don't find my looks repugnant, it must be my boring personality."

She decided to play along. "Well, there is that."

He chuckled. "Okay. Now I get it. I need to work on my conversational skills and polish my dull wit."

She joined in the laughter. "Nobody could ever accuse you of being dull or bland."

"Thanks." He smiled down into her eyes. "You know, Riley, you ought to laugh more often. You have a really wonderful laugh."

"Thank you. While you're working on your dull personality, I'll work on my laughter."

He tugged on a lock of her hair. "With all that hard work and polish, in no time the two of us ought to be just about perfectly suited."

His fingers continued to play with her hair, sending a tingle along her spine.

She looked up and could tell, by the simmering look in his eyes, that he was aware of his effect on her.

He brought his hands to her upper arms.

Though she wanted to run, she stood rooted to the spot, unable to move, or even breathe.

Without a word, keeping his eyes steady on hers, he lowered his face. His mouth moved over hers like the merest whisper of a snowflake, tasting, testing.

She knew she ought to resist. That hesitant kiss meant that he was giving her the chance to decide. If she had half a brain, she'd turn tail and run up to the safety of her room. Now. This instant, before it went any further.

But the kiss was so unexpectedly sweet. And the warmth of his body, along with those strong hands touching her as gently as if she were some fragile piece of glass, was her undoing.

The ice she'd been holding dropped unnoticed to the floor. With a little sigh she moved in and wrapped her arms around his waist, offering more.

And he took like a man starved for the taste of her. Suddenly the kiss wasn't gentle, and the hands that drew her firmly against him were now moving over her with a fever, a possessiveness that had the breath backing up in her throat.

She could feel her bones begin to melt. Her legs nearly

buckled as the kiss spun on and on, clouding her mind, heating her blood.

"Zane." She pulled back, sucking air into her starving lungs.

Though he lifted his head, he continued holding her close while he stared down into her eyes. "I've been wanting to do that since the first time I saw you standing on the doorstep." His smile was quick and dangerous. "In fact, if you don't mind, I'd like to do it again."

"No." She put a hand to his chest to hold him back, and felt a tingling in her fingertips at the contact with his bare flesh.

She knew, if she didn't get out of here right this minute, this was about to lead to something they'd both regret.

"I have to go." She turned away and prayed her trembling legs wouldn't betray her.

She was grateful to make it to the door.

"Riley."

At the sound of her name she turned.

His eyes flashed with a glint of humor. "I hope you don't expect an apology, because I'm sure as hell not sorry about this."

She opened the door and fled.

Even after she'd made it to the safety of her room, she could feel the warmth in her fingertips where she'd touched him. And could still taste him on her lips.

Zane stood perfectly still, listening to the creak of the floorboards as Riley climbed the stairs.

What in the hell had just happened here?

Apparently Riley Mason wasn't nearly as disinterested as she'd let on. That was the good news.

The bad news was Cal would have his hide if he thought he was playing with the affections of an employee. Especially one whose excellent work Cal valued so highly.

At least that's the excuse he would admit to. There was a deeper problem, one that he'd constantly denied whenever he found himself too attracted. Once a woman knew how a man felt, she had the power. The power to demand, to push, to inflict pain. His mother had used her power to destroy Zane's father. By the time he'd died, far from the comfort of his family, he'd been a whipped dog. A shell of the rugged, hard-driving cowboy Zane had worshipped.

After settling in Southern California, Zane had endured the taunts of Beverly Hills–hip classmates who'd ridiculed his cowboy boots in middle school, and his battered, no-name denims in high school. He'd learned to use his fists, and had watched helplessly as his mother had heaped humiliation on her ex-husband and son while hooking up with a dizzying array of married directors, producers, and even a few aging washed-up actors, searching for her elusive happiness. Zane had survived, but the wounds had left scars. He touched a finger to the scar on his chin. Not physical scars, but deeper, invisible scars on his soul.

Still, he thought as he turned out the light and started toward his room, there was something different about Riley Mason. Maybe it was the fact that she was such a devoted mother to Summer. He'd never met anyone quite like her before.

Despite her attempt at keeping a wall between them, he couldn't put aside the fact that she'd been a willing participant in that kiss.

He smiled in the darkness. And what a kiss. There'd been any number of women through the years. But now that he'd kissed this pretty little accountant, he couldn't recall the name or face of one of them.

He knew one thing. There had never been one that had ever rocked his world like this, with but a single kiss.

A dangerous fact, he thought. But there it was.

CHAPTER FIVE

Y ou're up early." As Zane walked into the kitchen, Dandy turned from the counter where he was filling glasses with freshly squeezed orange juice. "You heading up to the north pasture with Jimmy?"

"Not today." Zane drank a glass of juice before pouring a steaming cup of coffee and settling himself at the big table.

"Ready for some breakfast?"

"No thanks, Dandy. I'll wait for the others."

He didn't have to wait long before Jesse and Amy entered the kitchen together, followed by Wyatt and Marilee. All four of them looked rested and radiant. That only made Zane more aware than ever of the restless night he'd just put in.

He'd like to blame it on the lousy weather that was causing them to work overtime to keep their countryside from becoming a sea of mud. But in truth, most of his sleeplessness had been caused by Riley Mason.

First of all, there was that kiss. Not an easy thing to dismiss.

And then there were the questions.

Why would a bright student from Philadelphia come all the way to Montana for a job? He could understand it if her area of expertise were animal husbandry. Soil erosion. Mineral deposits. But accounting? Wouldn't she have made a much better salary right in her own backyard? Or New York City? What was the appeal of a far-flung ranch in Montana to a woman like Riley Mason?

"Good morning." Cora's cheerful voice broke his train of thought.

Zane was the first to greet his aunt as she stepped through the doorway.

This morning, he noted, she seemed in a thoughtful mood.

"Oh." Cora sighed. "It's just so grand seeing all three of you together. Those years you spent away from the Lost Nugget were difficult enough for me, but I know your grandfather missed all of you with a passion. Even though his wish for a family reunion was denied him, I can't help but think he's here with us. And seeing you all grown up and looking so much like him, he must be smiling."

Jesse brushed a kiss over her cheek. "I feel him here, too, Aunt Cora."

They all looked up when Cal walked in from the direction of his office and called out a greeting.

"How's it going, Cal?" Jesse handed a glass of juice to Amy before taking the seat beside her.

"Good. Great, in fact." Cal smiled at Cora before accepting a mug of coffee from Dandy. He ran a hand through his mane of hair, its whiteness in sharp contrast to his ruddy, handsome face. "I thought I'd stop by my office and try to put it in some kind of order, but Riley beat me to it."

Cora looked surprised. "She's already at work?"

"Yeah." He grinned. "She set up a little table for Summer to draw while she tackles that mountain of paperwork. She said she wanted me to know I was getting my money's worth." He looked around at the others. "You could have knocked me over with a feather. I told her this was a ranch, not an office. She doesn't have to clock in at eight and clock out at five. In fact, I told her she could set any hours she wants, as long as the work gets done."

"Will she be joining us for breakfast?" Amy asked.

"She'll be right along. I told her that was another thing about living on a ranch. Our day starts early, and with lots of hearty food."

The words were no more out of his mouth than the door opened and Riley and Summer walked in.

"Good morning." Riley greeted all of them with a polite smile.

She turned to the cook. "Thank you for last night's hot chocolate, Dandy. That was thoughtful of you. Summer and I really enjoyed it."

"I'm glad." Dandy pointed to a row of glasses on the counter, and beyond those, mugs. "Orange juice there. Coffee over there. I have milk for Summer."

"Thank you." Riley helped her daughter to a seat at the table with a glass of juice before fetching a cup of coffee.

While she stood at the counter, Zane studied the way she looked, all prim and proper, her dark hair tied in some kind of knot at the back of her head, her slim black pants and crisp white shirt looking out of place beside their denims and boots.

Zane turned to Cal. "When Riley and Summer went up to their rooms last night, they walked in on Cooper Easley, one of the new hires, setting logs on the hearth."

"Sorry." Cal shot her a quick smile. "I didn't realize he was up there. Jimmy said he was giving the new guys a variety of jobs before settling on something regular. I hope you didn't mind too much."

"It's fine. I was just caught by surprise."

"The regulars all know that the house is off-limits unless they have specific chores inside."

"After that, how did you sleep, dear?" Cora smiled when Riley returned to the table. "I hope those old beds are comfortable."

"Everything about Annie's Retreat is comfortable, Miss McCord."

Cora turned to Summer. "How about you, dear? How did you sleep?"

The little girl shrugged. "I don't 'member. Mama read me so many stories, I fell asleep on her lap, and when I woke up this morning, I was in my very own room."

While the others grinned, Cora nodded. "I'm so glad it feels like your very own room, Summer. That's what I was hoping to hear."

While Dandy served a breakfast of steak and eggs and fried potatoes with sourdough toast, Riley sat back, sipping her coffee and occasionally chancing a quick look at Zane.

Had she imagined the passion beneath that simple kiss?

There was no way of telling. This morning he was all fun and laughter as he talked with his family.

She listened to the buzz of conversation.

Cal glanced around the table. "Got a call from the mayor. Some big-shot investor just landed and he's promising the town the moon if we'll let him have a chunk of our land. He's asking for a tour."

"Not again. Doesn't Mayor Rowe ever give up?"

Jesse chuckled. "Coot used to say that Stafford Rowe didn't even know how to spell no. When he sees dollar signs for his town, the man's like a dog with a bone."

Zane turned to Cal. "I hope you intend to tell this investor we aren't interested."

"I will. But I doubt that'll stop our mayor."

Jesse reacted with frustration. "I don't care how much Stafford nags, let him know we have no intention of selling off any of our land."

"Want to go with me and tell him yourself?" Cal sipped his coffee. "Apparently this investor has gone to Stan Novak, putting a bee in his ear about millions of dollars ready to be poured into the town if Stan will commit to building a shopping center."

"A shopping center in Gold Fever?" Zane's words had all of them laughing. "Doesn't this guy realize he needs shoppers? Where's he going to get them in a one-horse town like ours?"

"Exactly." Cal joined in the laughter. "Anyway, I'll phone Stafford and say no, one more time."

To Riley this all sounded so strange. And yet, even though she felt as if she'd been dropped into an alien landscape, there was something so very sweet and normal about this land, this ranch, and this big, noisy family. And especially one very handsome, rugged, sexy cowboy.

While Dandy served their breakfast, Cora went to great pains to engage Riley in conversation.

Though the young woman seemed reticent, she was soon swept up by Cora's charm and couldn't help remarking, "I suppose you have to bar the door to keep your family from spending all their time in your studio."

Riley's words had Cora laughing. "Heavens no. My family wisely avoids visiting my studio. If the lovely fragrance of paint and turpentine isn't enough to scare them off, the chaos of canvases stacked everywhere drives most of them crazy. Of course, as I've pointed out to all of them, being an artist and being slightly crazy go hand in hand."

The two women shared a laugh at her joke.

Cora added, "But if you'd care to visit my studio sometime, I'd love to show you around."

Riley was quick to shake her head. "I wouldn't want to be a distraction."

"My dear." Cora put a hand over Riley's. "When I'm working, I'm not even aware of what is going on around me. The place could be burning down and I wouldn't notice the heat. But when I'm not at work, I'd be happy for your company."

"Thank you, Miss McCord. I'd really be honored to visit your studio some time when it's not inconvenient for you."

"It's a deal."

While the two women talked Zane glanced at the little girl seated beside him. She was staring at her plate with a mixture of curiosity and surprise.

He leaned close to whisper, "What do you usually have for breakfast?"

"Cereal and fruit. Or peanut butter on toast."

"Would you like Dandy to fix you some?"

She shook her head. "Mama said we shouldn't make a fuss."

"I see. That's probably a good idea, because Dandy likes to think he's fixing a manly breakfast for all of us, even the women." He realized his audience was too young to appreciate his humor. "Tell you what. You taste this, and if you'd rather have cereal and fruit, you let me know."

Without a word she gamely tasted first the eggs, and then the potatoes.

He winked. "You like those scrambled eggs?"

She nodded and smiled before taking another taste and pronouncing loudly, "Oh, yes. I love strangled eggs."

Everyone had a chuckle at her choice of words. Though the little girl didn't understand why they were laughing, she joined in.

Zane looked at her plate. "Want me to cut up that meat?"

"Yes, please."

Without a word he leaned close and cut the meat into tiny bite-size pieces.

Her cheeks dimpled with another smile. "Thank you."

She was so proper, and so sincere, Zane could feel his heart actually melt. "You're welcome."

He watched as she took a tentative bite of the steak before spearing a second bite and then a third.

He leaned close to whisper, "How about it? Want to trade that in for cereal and fruit?"

She shook her head and took another bite. "The only meat I know is chicken nuggets. But this is good, too."

"That's good, because on a cattle ranch, we like our beef."

He was smiling as he finished his own breakfast. What had started out as a real effort on little Summer's part had turned into a surprising pleasure. Apparently she approved of Dandy's choice of food.

He sat back, sipping strong, hot coffee, listening to Riley explain about the table she'd added to Cal's office.

"...just a small table I found in the bedroom. I thought it would be the perfect place for Summer to draw while I'm busy."

"That's very wise. I'm sure you enjoy having her close."

"I do. I'd been mentally preparing myself to leave her with a sitter I could trust while I made the long drive out here each day, but this is so much more satisfying."

Jesse looked over. "I hope you'll trust Zane to take Summer to the barn after breakfast. It seems to me we forced him to promise her a chance to see the horses."

"Oh, boy." The little girl's eyes rounded. "You didn't forget."

Zane arched a brow. "Did you think I would forget a promise?"

"I was afraid you would. Mama said it isn't nice to remind people about broken promises." She turned to her mother. "See, Mama. He didn't forget. Can I go see them now?"

"Not until after breakfast," Riley said. "That is, if Zane really wants to do this."

"I'm fine with it," he said, though in his heart he wasn't

at all sure about how he would handle a four-year-old girl. She seemed so much more…fragile than he'd been at that age.

Summer took a big bite of potatoes and managed to polish off the last of her egg before draining her glass of milk. "I'm finished, Mama."

Riley carefully wiped her daughter's mouth with her napkin. "That's good, honey. But you're not excused yet. We'll wait for everyone to finish."

Summer dropped her hands in her lap. But though she didn't issue a word of protest, she was wriggling like a puppy, her little feet keeping time to some music in her head.

When the others had finally finished, she glanced hopefully at her mother.

Riley looked past her daughter to where Zane sat watching. "I don't want her to rush you. Are you finished?"

"I am." He drained his cup.

Riley gave her daughter a gentle smile. "You may be excused, honey."

Summer turned to Zane with her eyes wide as saucers. "Are we going to see the horses now?"

"You bet." He shoved away from the table and, as an afterthought, offered his hand.

Catching it, she paused to wave good-bye to her mother and the others, who were heading off in different directions to deal with their morning chores.

Riley paused. "I think I'd better go along."

"There's no need…"

Before Zane could finish Riley was reaching for her daughter's hand. "Summer isn't used to being away from me."

"We aren't going far. Just to the barns. We shouldn't

be more than an hour." Zane smiled down at the little girl before turning away.

"An hour? That long?"

"There are a lot of horses," Zane reminded her.

Riley stepped back. "All right. You'll bring her right back to Cal's office?"

He nodded.

Riley watched them walk away.

As she made her way to the office, she was wearing a little frown, and biting her lip.

Riley struggled to keep her mind on her work. It wasn't easy when she was feeling so torn. On the one hand, she knew that Summer was safe so far from the big city. On the other hand, she'd become so accustomed to keeping her daughter close, it was difficult to let her out of her sight for even a moment. And especially with a big, rough cowboy who had probably never been alone with a little girl in his life. What if she tripped and fell? What if the horses frightened her? What if that wrangler with the angry eyes was out in the barn? What if...?

She pushed aside the troubling thoughts to concentrate on the work at hand. An hour, Zane had said. She glanced at the clock and forced herself to get busy.

Before breakfast she'd sorted the documents into several piles. The first needed to be dealt with immediately. The second ought to be completed by the end of the week. The third, and largest, could be set aside until she'd dispensed with the others.

She chanced another look at the clock before chiding herself. She wouldn't permit herself to worry until the hour was up. By then, if Zane hadn't returned Summer to the office, she would go in search of them. For now, she would begin on the first pile of documents.

Zane led Summer into the cavernous barn.

She wrinkled her nose. "It smells funny."

"You think so?" He chuckled. "I guess it does. I'm so used to this smell, I don't even notice."

When a dark-haired wrangler ambled over, Zane said, "Summer, I'd like you to meet Jimmy Eagle. Jimmy, this is Summer Mason."

"Hello, Summer."

The little girl gave him a shy smile and put her tiny hand in his big, calloused palm.

Jimmy said, "When Zane was just your age, I taught him how to ride."

"You did?" She looked from Zane to Jimmy. "Is he your daddy?"

"No, but there were times when I wished he was." Zane laughed. "Jimmy taught me more about ranching than anybody else. When my own dad was busy with ranch chores, Jimmy always found time for me."

"Because you pestered me to death," the older man said with affection.

"I pestered you because I knew you wouldn't brush me off." Zane's voice had gone gruff with emotion.

The older man clapped a big hand on Zane's shoulder before tipping his wide-brimmed hat to the little girl. "It was nice meeting you, Summer."

As he ambled away, a horse in a nearby stall lifted its head and whinnied.

"Ooh." Summer turned with a look of surprise and pleasure.

Seeing her reaction, Zane chuckled. "Vanilla is saying hello."

"Vanilla? Is that his name?"

"Her name. Vanilla is a mare. That means she's a lady horse. She's going to be a mama."

"She is? Where's her baby?"

"Still inside her. But soon enough you'll get to see it. If you'd like, I'll introduce you to her older son when we get to his stall."

"Why doesn't he stay with his mama?"

"Because he's old enough to be on his own now. Want to meet Vanilla?"

"Okay."

Zane lifted Summer to a wooden rail of the stall and held out her hand. At once the mare lowered her head, allowing the little girl to rub her palm along her muzzle.

Riley giggled. "She feels as soft as Floppy."

"Yeah." Setting her down, Zane followed suit, rubbing a big hand along the mare's forelock.

Riley looked over at him. "She likes me."

"I can tell. I think you like her, too."

"I do. Could you teach me to ride her?"

"I'll make you a deal. Whenever your mama says you're big enough, I'll teach you how to ride."

"You will?" Her eyes were glowing. "Just like Jimmy Eagle taught you?"

"Just like Jimmy taught me. For now"—Zane reached into a bucket—"you're going to have to get to work."

"I am?" Big brown eyes went wide with wonder.

"Uh-huh. I'm going to need some help here. Vanilla expects a treat, so, now that you're here..." He handed Summer a carrot. "Vanilla loves carrots."

He took the little girl's hand and showed her how to offer up the food. The mare dipped her head and latched onto the treat, much to Summer's delight.

As the mare happily chewed, Summer was jumping up and down with excitement. "Can I give her another?"

"You wouldn't want her to get a tummyache, would you?"

"No."

She was so serious, Zane found himself laughing aloud. "Besides, there are a lot more horses here in the barn, and now that they've seen you give a carrot to Vanilla, they're going to expect the same treatment, or they'll be jealous."

"Can I feed all of them?"

He shrugged. "I don't see why not." He filled his pockets with carrots and sugar lumps and led her from stall to stall, where she happily handed out treats to each of the horses.

At the end of a long row of stalls Zane paused to run his hand along the muzzle of a pale two-year-old. "This is Dusty, Vanilla's son."

"He's bigger than his mama."

Zane chuckled. "Yeah. That happens a lot. Who knows? Maybe some day you'll be bigger than your mama."

The little girl giggled at the impossible thought.

When they finally left the barn and stepped into bright sunlight, Summer tucked her little hand in Zane's as they crossed the yard to the house.

Again he felt that quick little tug at his heart and wondered about it.

He'd never been around kids. None of his friends had

children, and the few ranchers with wives and families lived on far-flung areas of the spread where Zane rarely came in contact with them.

Yet this little girl, with her sweet, sunny nature and a face like an angel, had a strange effect on him.

He'd been reluctant to be alone with her. Yet the time spent with her in the barn had flown by in the blink of an eye. And though it had been his intention to merely entertain her for an hour or so, he had been the one who'd been entertained.

He'd certainly never given any thought to having kids of his own. After the mess his mother had made of their once-happy family, he figured it just wasn't in the cards for him. And now, here he was, having more fun with a four-year-old than he'd had in a very long time.

When they drew near the ranch house, Summer, her dark hair windblown, her cheeks pink from the spring breeze, danced ahead of Zane toward the house, where she dutifully scraped her little shoes before stepping on the foot pedal and washing her hands at the big basin.

Beside her, Zane was grinning. "You take to ranch rules like a pro. I'd say you'll be joining the wranglers up on the range in no time."

When they stepped into the kitchen, Dandy turned from the stove. "How was your visit with Vanilla?"

"She likes me," the little girl said matter-of-factly.

"I'm not surprised. Did you bring her a treat?"

"Uh-huh. A carrot."

"That's her favorite. She'll be your new best friend forever, as long as you bring her a carrot."

Dandy and Summer looked over as Zane's cell phone rang.

"Wait 'til I tell Mama." Summer danced from the room, with Zane trailing behind to answer his cell phone.

"Hey, cuz." Zane paused at the sound of Wyatt's voice. "You going to join us up on the south ridge, or are you going to play nursemaid all day?"

Instead of taking offense at Jesse's jibe, Zane merely grinned. "I'll be there in half an hour."

He tucked away his cell phone and paused in the doorway of Riley's office.

She stopped her pacing to grab up her daughter in a fierce hug, breathing her in. "I was getting worried. Silly, I know." She tightened her grasp, unwilling, unable to let go.

The little girl was wriggling with excitement, eager to be free. "Mama, Mama, you should have seen all the horses. I met Vanilla, she's so pretty and loves carrots, and she's going to have a baby soon. And her son, Dusty, who's bigger than her. And..."

While Summer danced about the room, extolling the virtues of each horse in the barn, Riley just stood quietly, drinking her in. There was a look of fierce intensity on her face.

Finally she looked over at Zane. Though she'd been achingly aware of him, she'd remained completely focused on her daughter.

He leaned against the doorframe. "Your daughter's a natural with horses."

"Really?" She felt a flush of pleasure. "So Vanilla really likes her?"

"Vanilla and every other horse in the barn. She showed no fear at all. She just fed them carrots or sugar lumps and talked to them the same way she talks to Floppy."

Riley glanced at her daughter. "Do they answer?"

"Uh-huh. They went neigh neigh, just like I told Floppy they would."

"And if you visit them often enough," Zane added, "you'll get to know what every little ear-twitch and neigh means."

"I will?"

"You bet." Zane winked at Riley and the two shared a laugh.

Zane could see Riley beginning to relax. The little furrow between her brows that had been evident when he'd first stepped into the office was beginning to smooth away.

"Well." He turned. "I've got some chores to see to. I tried to avoid them, but my cousins just phoned to remind me, so I'd better get going."

"Zane."

At the sound of his name he turned back.

"I'm sorry for being so nervous. Thank you." Riley glanced at Summer, who was already getting out her crayons and books. She lowered her voice. "You've made my daughter very happy this morning."

He grinned. "My pleasure. She made me happy, too. Almost as happy as that kiss we shared last night."

Riley's face flamed.

Zane pretended not to notice. "Bye, Summer."

The little girl looked up with a wide smile. "Bye, Zane. Thank you. I loved my visit with Vanilla and all the horses."

"So did I. We'll have to do it often."

He caught Riley's hand and examined her palm. "How's the burn?"

"The burn?" She was so mesmerized by the touch of his hand, she'd completely forgotten.

"Last night's boiling water."

"Oh." She pulled her hand back. "It's fine. Hardly a mark."

"Good. See you later." He walked away, deep in thought.

It hadn't been his imagination. Riley wasn't immune to his touch. That knowledge should be enough to carry him through the day.

But there was something more. Riley had been absolutely terrified for her daughter. The way she'd pounced on Summer when she'd walked in, she acted like her daughter had been gone for days instead of an hour.

What was going on here? Why in the world had she been so fearful?

Maybe she was afraid of horses. Or maybe, coming from the East, she was feeling out of her element on a ranch and afraid that her daughter could be harmed.

Still, it had been a pretty radical reaction to such a minor separation.

Summer Mason enchanted him. And her mother was a puzzling challenge.

He was intrigued. Hooked, in fact. And more determined than ever to learn more about Riley, about her past, her likes, her dislikes, her childhood, what she wanted in the future. He wanted to know everything about the mysterious Riley Mason.

He'd never been able to resist a challenge or the chance to solve a mystery, and this woman was all of that. A puzzling challenge, and a beautiful, beguiling mystery.

CHAPTER SIX

At a knock on the office door Riley looked up to see Dandy standing in the doorway, holding a tray.

"I figured you'd be too busy to think about lunch." Dandy set the tray on her desk and uncovered it to reveal two bowls of hearty beef-and-vegetable soup and gooey grilled-cheese sandwiches made with thick slices of home-baked bread fresh from the oven, along with an individual pot of tea and a glass of milk.

"I hope you drink tea."

"I do. It's my usual drink with lunch."

"Good." He lifted the dome of a pretty platter to reveal a plate of warm-from-the-oven cookies.

"Look, Mama. Chocolate chip. My favorites."

"Mine, too," Riley said.

"I just took them out of the oven." Dandy looked over at Summer. "If you'd like, you could help me bake cookies one day soon."

"Oh, honey, what fun." Riley turned to Dandy. "I have to admit, my daughter has never had the chance to bake cookies."

"Then it will be a treat for both of us," the cook said. "I've never had the chance to bake with a helper."

When he left, the little girl pulled her chair close to her mother's desk. The two shared a wonderful lunch.

Summer looked over at her mother. "This is nice, Mama. I like being with you while you work."

"I like it, too. In fact, I love having you here." It was, Riley thought, the most relaxed she'd been in a very long time. And it was all because of the fact that she wasn't spending time worrying about whether or not her little girl was being well cared for when she was out of her sight.

Riley sat back. "Have you been having fun, honey?"

"Um-hmm." Her daughter ate the last of her sandwich. "Zane said I can go with him when he feeds the horses. And when I'm big enough, he'll teach me to ride them."

If only that could happen, Riley thought. But within a matter of weeks this job would be completed. Once she'd worked her way through the overflow, Cal could easily take over the simple office chores required to run the ranch.

Still, what was the harm in allowing her daughter to dream?

"Wouldn't you be afraid to sit way up high on a horse's back?"

The little girl thought about it. "Not if Zane held me. He's big and strong. And funny, Mama. He makes me laugh."

Her words had Riley going very still. There was

definitely something about Zane McCord. He had an easy, gentle way about him, especially with her daughter. That was one of the reasons why she was being very careful around him. He was too attractive. Too perfect. She was certain, as she got to know him, that she'd find the cracks in that facade.

When she'd watched him cut Summer's steak this morning, she'd felt a sudden ache around her heart, knowing that her daughter was being denied what most children took for granted.

Would she always carry this guilt? When Summer started school, and her classmates talked about doing things with their daddies, would her daughter feel jealous that she was different? Did all single mothers worry, as she did, that they were cheating their children because there wasn't a man in their lives to protect them, a man willing to die, if necessary, to keep them safe? Would it be enough for Summer to know that her mother had made every sacrifice, paid every price, to make her life as full, as rich, as balanced as possible? Or would she be found lacking because she had chosen to raise her child alone?

She had no idea what their future would hold. Perhaps some day there would be a man she loved enough, trusted enough, to share her life. But only, she thought fiercely, if he also loved her daughter so much that he couldn't imagine a life without the two of them.

She and Summer were a package deal. No man could have her heart without first winning the heart of her daughter.

Zane McCord was being surprisingly tender with Summer. But then, she barely knew him. What he found amusing about a four-year-old girl in the short term could prove to be irritating when he was exposed to her over time.

In the meantime, all Riley could do was wait, watch, and observe. Zane was, after all, a handsome and probably spoiled playboy accustomed to doing as he pleased, whenever he pleased. Going out of his way to cater to the needs of a child could wear thin in no time.

She smiled, thinking about the way Summer had warmed to him almost from their first encounter. Hadn't it been the same for her? There was just something so sweet and surprisingly funny about Zane.

With thoughts like that, she would need to guard her foolish heart.

They both looked up when a knock sounded.

Amy paused in the doorway. "Hi. I hope I'm not disturbing anything."

"Not at all. Come on in." Riley gave her a welcoming smile. "Do you need a file?"

"No." Amy looked around with interest. "This is the cleanest I've ever seen Cal's office. Last time I was here it looked like a mountain of junk."

The two women shared a laugh.

Riley looked pleased. "I have to admit, it was pretty intimidating when I first came in here. But I'm slowly chiseling away at the mountain." She returned her attention to Amy. "What can I do for you?"

"I was hoping you'd lend me your daughter."

Riley blinked. "I don't understand."

"Let me explain. I was a teacher in Helena until I came back here to care for my father during his illness. Then Jesse and I married, and I realized I'd have to give up teaching, because I'm just too far from town to make that daily drive back and forth. But I miss it. And I've been thinking. While Summer is here, it might be fun to see if I still know how to be a teacher."

"I don't know…"

Amy went on quickly. "We have an old classroom that was once used by Jesse, Wyatt, and Zane when they were boys. And I have lots of old textbooks and teacher's aids."

Riley turned to her daughter. "How about it, honey? Would you like the chance to go to school?"

"Oh, boy! A real school." Summer was out of her chair in an instant. "Can we go now?"

Riley knew defeat when she saw it. How could she possibly say no, now that she'd seen her daughter's face?

She sighed. "I guess so. If it's what you really want."

"I do, Mama. I do."

Amy took the little girl's hand and shot Riley a wide smile. "Now that's what I call an eager pupil. Don't worry. We'll be back whenever Summer starts to tire of me."

Riley watched them walk away. Then she cleared away the remains of their lunch and returned her attention to her work.

Riley sat back, rubbing at the knotted cord at the back of her neck. A glance at the clock had her gasping. Summer and Amy had been gone for most of the afternoon. She'd become so absorbed in her work, she'd forgotten all about them.

She pushed away from her desk and stepped into the hall, listening to any sound that might alert her to their location. She should have asked Amy where the classroom was before letting her get away.

A ripple of childish laughter had her climbing the stairs.

She followed along the upper hallway until, noticing a shadow, she rounded a corner to see a man straining to look through a doorway. The sight of him had her stopping dead in her tracks.

His head came up sharply, and she saw his eyes narrow on her. She realized at once that it was the same wrangler who had delivered the firewood to her suite. She felt a shiver along her spine at the coldness in those eyes.

Swallowing back her fear, she lifted her chin and prayed her voice wouldn't betray her nerves. "Can I help you find something?"

"No need. Just finished my chore and I'm heading out to the barn." He scuffled past her.

She turned and watched as he descended the stairs. When she heard the front door close, she continued along the hallway until the sound of voices drew her into one of the rooms. It was the very room he'd been staring at.

Summer was seated in a child-size chair at a tiny table, painstakingly printing in a lined tablet. Seated beside her was Amy, head bent, voicing her encouragement.

"Oh, Summer. That's excellent."

"Thank you." The little girl looked up, her face wreathed in smiles when she caught sight of her mother in the doorway. "Mama. Look. My very own schoolroom and my very own teacher, Miss Amy."

"I see." Riley let out the breath she'd been holding and waited until her heartbeat returned to normal.

She glanced around. "So this is where Zane and his cousins attended classes?"

Amy studied the room, seeing it through Riley's eyes. "They were homeschooled for years, because they lived too far away to drive into town each day."

Riley fell silent, trying to imagine three wild and restless little boys, studying in this cozy room before being turned loose to ride out into that magnificent countryside.

Mistaking her silence for condemnation, Amy said quickly, "I'm sorry, Riley. I shouldn't have kept Summer here so long, but the truth is, I was having too much fun to let her go."

"Amy." Riley laid a hand over hers. "Please don't apologize. I can tell by the look on Summer's face that she's having a wonderful time."

"So am I. I've really missed teaching."

"Then…" Riley bit her lip. "If you really want to keep her here, I have no objections." She turned to her daughter. "Would you like to stay awhile longer in your new classroom?"

"Oh, yes, please." The little girl's excitement sparkled in her eyes. "I'm writing all the letters I know. Miss Amy says I can take the page up to my room with me if I'd like, and you can help me match the letters to words."

"That sounds like fun, honey." Riley turned to Amy. "When you see her losing interest, or you feel you've had enough, would you mind bringing her back to my office?"

"It's a deal." Amy couldn't help gushing. "She's so smart, Riley. The more time I spend with her, the more I realize what a sweet, darling girl you have."

"Thanks." Riley's heart soared at such praise for her daughter. "I think she's pretty special, too."

She started out of the room.

When she turned for a last glimpse, both teacher and pupil were bent over the tablet on the table, lost in the lesson at hand. As she made her way back to the office, her mind was filled with many conflicting emotions.

She'd felt such a rush of pride when Amy had praised Summer. There was a real sense of satisfaction in knowing that others saw what she knew to be true. She supposed every parent hoped the world recognized all the wonderful traits in their child. But it was especially sweet praise indeed to a single parent, doing the work alone.

Alone. And yet, she was learning, she and Summer weren't alone. Summer now had another friend. A friend and teacher. Was that twinge she felt in her heart a trace of jealousy?

She paused. Time for some honesty. Maybe she was just a bit jealous that her child was having so much fun, not only with Amy, but also with Zane and his family. For so long now there had just been the two of them against the world. Now, suddenly, Summer's life was opening up to all kinds of possibilities. School. Friends. Activities that she couldn't share with her own mother, like visiting the horses.

But by opening up her world, she was also leaving herself open to danger. Riley thought again of the wrangler, whose presence had caused such a prickly sensation along her spine.

For now she would watch. She would be vigilant. Her daughter was far too precious to leave anything to chance.

• • •

Riley stood by the window of her suite, staring at the lovely scene spread out below. Though there were still tiny pockets of snow here and there along the hillsides, the first spring ferns had burst from the soil and were beginning to unfurl. The shadows of late afternoon were lengthening. In the distance, the sun was already beginning to drop behind the peaks of Treasure Chest Mountain. Today she'd learned the name of that mountain, when her daughter had returned from her classroom.

Her classroom.

That thought had Riley smiling. Who would have believed that she would find such luxury in this isolated place? She'd come here seeking safety and solace, and was beginning to feel as though she'd landed in the middle of a dream.

If she was dreaming, she hoped she would never wake up.

"Mama?"

At the sound of Summer's voice she looked over. Her daughter, hair still damp from her bath, was holding up one tiny white sneaker.

"There's a knot in the laces."

"Here." Riley held out her hand and took the shoe, working the laces until she'd untied the knot.

Kneeling, she slid Summer's foot into the shoe and neatly tied it before giving the little girl an approving look. She was wearing neon-yellow tights under a little denim skirt and a fluffy top embroidered with daisies.

Riley stood and caught her daughter's hand, as much for her own comfort as for Summer's. "Let's go downstairs to supper."

"Dandy said he was making Zane's favorite food."

"What would that be?"

"Meat..." The little girl shrugged. "Meatbread."

It took Riley a second to figure that out. "Oh. Meat loaf?"

"Uh-huh." Summer smiled. "Will it be as good as strangled eggs?"

Riley was still laughing as she and her daughter descended the stairs and stepped into the kitchen to find the others already standing around, sipping cold drinks and nibbling cheese-filled appetizers.

"Hi, there." Amy was the first to greet them. "Here's my favorite pupil."

That had the others turning to call out their greetings.

Riley returned their greetings and felt her cheeks grow hot when she realized that Zane was staring.

He separated himself from his cousins to cross the room. Kneeling in front of Summer, he said, "I hear you started school today."

"Uh-huh." She dimpled. "With Miss Amy."

"You're a lucky little girl."

Her eyes flashed. "I'm not little. I'm a big girl now. Mama says only big girls go to school."

He clapped a hand to his mouth while the others chuckled. "Sorry. Your mama's right. What was I thinking? If you're in school, you're definitely a big girl now."

Dandy held out a tray of appetizers. Summer watched as her mother chose one and took a bite.

"What's in it, Mama?"

"Cheese. You'll like it. Want to try?"

After one taste Summer smiled.

She turned to Zane. "Is this your meatbread?"

"Meat loaf," Riley corrected.

That had Zane grinning. "No, these are just the beginning. But wait until you do taste Dandy's meat loaf. It's the best in the West."

As the family took their places around the big table, Dandy began to serve. They passed around rolls fresh from the oven, and a mixed green salad with beets and a sprinkle of feta cheese. Once again Summer wrinkled her nose, but gamely tasted it. When Zane offered her a dollop of garlic mashed potatoes, the little girl nodded.

"And this," he proclaimed, "is Dandy's famous meat loaf." He cut a thick slice for himself and a smaller one for Summer.

Once she'd tasted it, she looked over with a smile. "It's good."

"Of course it's good. You think I'd lie?"

"Mama says it's wrong to lie."

She was so serious he had to bite back the laughter that threatened. "Your mama's right." Zane looked past her to wink at Riley. "Always listen to your mama. She'll never steer you wrong."

"What's steer?"

"You ask a lot of questions, don't you?"

"I do?" Her tone was so innocent, everyone around the table burst into laughter.

"Another question?"

While Zane fumbled with answers for all Summer's questions, Riley found herself laughing along with the others.

Oh, she thought as she sat back and studied all these happy faces, it was good to be here, spending time with people so full of life. People who obviously enjoyed one another's company.

This ranch, this family, was very quickly becoming a soothing respite from the turbulent past.

But were they real? The question assaulted her out of the blue, causing her to stare around in silence.

Her own home life had been so different, she may as well have been living on the moon. She studied Cora, seated beside Cal, laughing and chatting with her great-nephews as though she were visiting her best friends. And Amy and Marilee. Though they claimed to have come from very different backgrounds, they seemed so compatible. And all of them, from the handsome, earthy cousins to the cook who served their meals with such obvious relish, seemed so delighted to be here, sharing all of this together.

Whether this was real or just a glorious facade masking something altogether different, she was willing, for now, to bask in their reflected sunlight and be warmed by it.

Cal accepted another cup of coffee from Dandy and turned to Cora, who was seated at the kitchen table. "Each day that passes shows me just how amazing Riley is. Not only is my office being restored to some kind of order, but the firm in Helena can't stop raving about the fact that we're finally filing all our tax forms on time, without having to nudge me three or four times before I follow through."

"You moved awfully quickly on this." Cora regarded him over the rim of her cup. "Actually, I was surprised that you hired her without checking all of her references."

"The firm trusts her completely. She's their go-to person." His tone lowered. Warmed. "Besides, I just liked her the moment I met her. I had a good feeling about Riley."

Cora's smile bloomed. "You've always been able to read people, Cal. If she meets with your approval, you know she meets with mine. You and I are in complete agreement on this."

Zane listened in silence and found himself wishing that both he and Riley had more time. He made it a point to take Summer with him for a morning visit to the horse barn several times a week. But though he always returned her to the office, hoping to chat with her mother, they rarely had time for more than a quick word before the office phone would ring and Riley would dash away to lose herself once more in her work. To make matters worse, the calving, along with a series of early spring snowstorms, had the wranglers on high alert. He'd spent as much time bunking up in the hills as he did here at the big house. It didn't look as though things would slow down anytime soon, since he and his cousins were getting ready to resume their hunt for the family treasure, now that the spring thaw was setting in down here in the lowlands.

Fate, he decided, was determined to keep him from ever getting to know the fascinating Riley Mason. In no time her work here would be over, and she and her daughter would be gone.

His loss. And he didn't see any way of changing things in his favor.

As the days passed, Riley and Summer settled into a routine. After breakfast with the McCord family, Summer would accompany Zane to the barn to visit her new best friends, the horses, leaving Riley to get to work on the ledgers.

Riley wondered if Zane had any idea how much her daughter enjoyed these outings. She'd often seen the little girl twitching with excitement until Zane arrived. After their trip to the barn, Summer spent endless hours talking about Vanilla and the other horses, which had become her pets.

What was more, her daughter repeated every word Zane had said to her. It would seem that he had captivated Summer as easily as he'd captivated her. And though it worried Riley, she couldn't see any solution to the problem. Both she and her daughter were falling under the spell of Zane's easygoing charm.

After lunch Amy would stop by the office to fetch Summer for a few hours of classroom study before returning her to her mother's side in time for a brief nap.

After dinner Riley usually took her daughter up to their rooms, in order to give the McCord family their privacy. Though they always invited her and Summer to join them in their evening ritual of gathering around the fireplace for a family conference, Riley still felt like an intruder. They deserved some time alone, without always having to include her and her daughter. At least that was what she told herself. In truth, she had to work very hard to put as much distance as possible between herself and Zane McCord. The man was just too much of a distraction to her. She couldn't allow herself to become attracted to a free spirit like Zane. If even half the tales being told at the dinner table were true, he'd led a romantic, larger-than-life existence during those years he'd been gone from the ranch.

She couldn't even imagine attending school as a teen in Hollywood with fellow students who were now appearing regularly in movies and on TV. Had he romanced any of those gorgeous girls? Did he miss them now, and wish he could return to that lifestyle? That thought had her frowning, though she didn't know why.

Then there was that important documentary about wild horses filmed across thousands of acres of wilderness. A documentary that would soon be televised all over the country.

At all the thoughts swirling through her mind, she blinked. Time for some honesty. This wasn't about Summer. She was on very shaky ground here. She was actually feeling jealous about fictitious women in Zane's colorful past, even though she and Zane were practically strangers.

Despite the fact that he was being very kind to her daughter, he and Riley had nothing in common. They rarely had time to talk. They'd shared exactly one kiss. And though it may have stopped her heart, it hadn't exactly stopped his world. He hadn't even attempted to get close to her again. And wasn't it best to leave it that way?

She'd vowed to make a fresh start. She couldn't afford to invest any part of herself in a man, only to have her world shattered.

Though she hadn't quite figured out how, she was determined to keep herself and her daughter from getting too attached to Zane and his family. There was a danger in caring too much, whether for a family, a home, or a way of life. Summer may be too young to understand, but Riley knew only too well that nothing lasted forever.

• • •

It was one of the prettiest spring mornings Riley had yet seen here in Montana. The sun had burned off the morning mist and now, under a clear, cloudless sky, the temperature had begun to climb. Cal had predicted shirt-sleeve weather by the end of the week, and his prediction was coming true.

In her office Riley was able, through sheer discipline and determination, to put her thoughts about Zane McCord aside while she worked on the thorny issue of payroll.

Cal had admitted to doing it all from a handwritten ledger that had belonged to Coot. Now it would be up to Riley to bring it into the twenty-first century, via computer program. Though the initial process would be horribly time-consuming, she knew that once it was in place, it would save countless hours each month.

She opened the leather-bound ledger and flipped through the first few yellowed pages. She sat back and grinned. Cal Randall was the epitome of a dying breed—the strong, silent cowboy. Tall, bronzed, and handsome in a weathered way that could cause the hearts of women of all ages to flutter. But his handwriting was little more than a scrawl. It would take many hours to decipher the names he'd entered, and even longer to determine the number of hours each had worked. Thankfully he or someone at the accounting firm had provided a typed cross-reference list, so that she could check the proper spelling of each name.

As the clock on the desk silently ticked, she lost herself in the job at hand, pausing only to field several calls from the accounting firm in Helena. Each required that she sift through the file cabinets until she'd located the proper tax form, canceled check, or document requested and fax it for their records.

"Even though your record-keeping is sloppy," she muttered after the third such call, "at least you manage to keep every little scrap of paper with even a tiny bit of information I might need, Cal. Otherwise, I'd be asking myself if this job was worth the hassle."

She returned to her desk and took up where she'd left off, painstakingly recording each name from the ledger and entering it into the computer database.

"Mama." Summer stood in the office doorway, wearing an oversize apron, a sure sign that she'd been helping Dandy in the kitchen. "Everybody's waiting for you so we can eat dinner."

"Oh, my." Riley looked up from her desk. A glance at the clock showed her that it was well past time for her to end her workday. "I'll be right along, honey." She closed the old ledger.

In her haste to stow it in the drawer, she brushed the ledger with her arm, knocking it off the desk. It fell to the floor with a thud, sending up a cloud of dust that had her shaking her head. The ledger was so old it had accumulated the dust of many years.

When she bent to retrieve it, several yellowed documents drifted to the floor.

When Riley picked them up, she could see that they didn't really belong in this ledger. Instead of names of employees and number of hours worked, they appeared to be handwritten notes, as well as some crude drawings.

Puzzled, she shoved them into the back pages of the

ledger before stowing it in the deep lower drawer of her desk. She would study them more carefully when she had more time.

"Mama. Come on."

"I'm coming, honey."

Turning off the light in her office, she followed her daughter along the hallway to the kitchen.

Once inside she greeted the McCord family and picked up a glass of lemonade.

While talk about ranching swirled around her, she gave a sigh of quiet satisfaction.

When she'd first come here, she had been prepared to rent a room in the town of Gold Fever, pay Delia Cowling to babysit Summer, and do her best to hold both her job and her personal life together while commuting an hour or more each way. Now, just thinking about that commute had her inwardly shuddering. She would have spent all her time wondering and worrying about Summer's safety. Here, in this isolated place, she could finally draw a breath.

Knowing that she could enjoy a hot meal prepared by the most incredible cook, take her daughter upstairs to a gorgeous suite of rooms, and let the day slip away before falling into bed, was the sweetest of luxuries.

And right now, listening to Zane's deep voice as he told some silly story about something that happened out on the range earlier today had a dreamy smile playing on her lips.

She was content to just sit here and let the others carry the conversation. She dropped an arm around her daughter's shoulders and the two shared a smile.

Life, she thought, didn't get much better than this.

CHAPTER SEVEN

———◆———

Riley's office chores increased when a call from the firm in Helena requested detailed information on the number of part-time employees. This required scouring the files for addresses, only to learn that many of the wranglers were itinerant workers who moved from ranch to ranch during the various seasons. She had to dig even deeper to locate Social Security numbers and medical information required by the state. All of this hampered her ability to complete the database for the looming payroll.

She was grateful to Zane and Amy and Dandy for stepping in to keep Summer busy.

"Mama. We baked something special."

Riley looked up to see Summer, wearing the now familiar oversize apron, standing in the doorway of the office with Dandy behind her.

"You did? What did you bake?"

"I can't tell you. It's a secret." Summer turned to the cook. "Isn't that right, Dandy?"

"That's right. No telling until dinnertime. But you're going to be awfully proud of your little girl when you see what she made."

Riley smiled. "I'm already proud of her. But now I can't wait to see the surprise." She paused. "Why aren't you in the classroom with Miss Amy?"

"This was part of today's lesson," the little girl said with a knowing grin. "Miss Amy said I can learn my numbers by . . ." She turned to the cook.

"By measuring. One cup of flour. One-half cup sugar. Like that," Dandy explained.

"Uh-huh." Summer beamed with pride. "So I was helping Dandy bake, and learning my numbers, too."

"Brilliant." Riley could see the logic of it, and she found herself once again thrilled that Amy had taken her daughter under her wing. "Are you going to stay here with me now? Or is there more mysterious work to be done in the kitchen?"

Summer turned to Dandy, who winked. The two shared a smile before Summer said, "I have to go now, Mama. I'll come back when we're finished."

Summer skipped away, holding the cook's hand.

Riley sat back and wondered at the lightness around her heart. With every day she spent here, more and more of the tensions seemed to lift from her shoulders.

But that sense of peace lasted less than a minute, when she saw the name of one of the wranglers who had failed to provide any of the required information.

Cooper Easley.

. . .

Riley stashed the last of the paperwork and looked around the office with a sense of satisfaction. She'd managed to accomplish much more than she'd hoped to when the day had begun.

When she stepped out of the office, she heard Summer's voice calling to her from the kitchen.

"Mama. I'm in here."

Riley turned and made her way to the kitchen, where most of the family had already gathered. Jesse, Wyatt, and Zane were standing near the counter, enjoying frosty longnecks with Cal, their heads bent in quiet conversation. Cora, Amy, and Marilee were seated at the big wooden table, sipping from stem glasses filled with pale white wine.

Though she smiled and greeted all of them, Riley was aware of only one pair of midnight blue eyes watching her. Just seeing Zane had her pulse speeding up.

For some strange reason, she had a sense that he'd been talking about her. But that was crazy. What would he possibly have to say to his family about her, since she had been so careful to avoid him after that one shattering kiss?

He shot her one of those heart-stopping smiles before returning his attention to the others, and Riley could almost taste him on her lips.

Amy held up a wineglass. "Will you join us?"

"Yes. Thanks. Are we celebrating something?"

Amy merely shrugged before pouring some wine and handing the glass to Riley, who took a seat beside Cora. While they visited, Riley watched Summer and Dandy laughing and whispering together. The little girl used a small stool to reach the counter, waiting patiently while

Dandy filled the salad bowls. When they were ready, it was Summer who carried them to the table and began setting a bowl at each place.

One by one the men began to drift to the table, while Dandy placed a steaming platter of sizzling steaks and grilled vegetables in the center. Riley took her place beside Summer, with Zane on her left. With a great deal of laughter the others began to pass the food.

Zane held a platter toward Riley. "I'll hold this while you fill your plate and Summer's."

"Thanks." While she did as he'd suggested, she could feel his gaze on her. It was the strangest sensation, and one that had her cheeks flaming.

Sometimes, when he stared at her with such intensity, she had the feeling that he could see clear to her soul.

"Now I'll hold it for you." She took the platter from his hands. When their fingers brushed, she absorbed a quick rush of heat and hoped to heaven her face wasn't as red as it felt.

"Thanks." He filled his plate and she passed the platter on.

While they ate, Riley sat quietly, allowing the conversation to flow around her.

"…have to be heading up to the north ridge tomorrow. Fuller said there were dozens of new calves today, and more expected to drop by morning." Cal glanced at the ridge of clouds on the horizon. "At least the weather has finally decided to cooperate."

Zane winked at Amy, seated beside her husband. "Hey, Jesse. Want to bet another twenty bucks on the weather?"

Jesse laughed. "I'd have thought getting stung once would be enough, cuz. Besides, I think spring is finally here to stay."

"Amen to that." Cal gave a glance around the table. "All that snow in the mountains brought out the predators, hungry for helpless new calves."

Jesse looked over at the foreman. "Maybe we'd better post a few more wranglers with each herd."

"It's already done." Determined to change the subject, Cal turned to Riley. "How'd the payroll go today?"

"Fine. I'm nearly finished getting everybody into the database. As soon as I get the last ones done, I'll leave a printout on your desk. Once you've looked it over and approved it, I'll start feeding in their hours and I can print out the paychecks."

"So soon?" His face creased into a smile. "I expected you to need a couple more weeks with all the disruptions caused by the firm's questions. Then there was the problem of deciphering all my chicken-scratching."

Summer's head came up. "You scratch like a chicken?"

"Just my handwriting, honey." He winked at her. "I'm betting yours is much better'n mine."

"Miss Amy said I know all my letters."

"You see? And soon you'll be helping your mama in the office."

That had the little girl smiling with pride.

When the meal was finished, Dandy asked if they'd like to take their coffee and dessert in the great room.

Cora nodded. "I'd like that."

With a conspiratorial wink, Dandy said, "Summer can stay in here and give me a hand with the desserts."

The little girl put a hand over her mouth to hide her giggles.

As the others made their way from the kitchen, Cora saw Riley glance at her watch. With a mysterious smile she tucked her hand through Riley's arm. "Worried about the time?"

"Just thinking that Summer will be getting ready for bed soon."

"I'm betting she'll be too keyed up to sleep for some time." Cora settled herself on the sofa pulled up in front of a roaring fire, and she drew Riley down beside her. "You have a sweet, bright child, Riley. And she seems to be having such a grand time here. She's completely captured Dandy's heart."

"I've noticed." Riley sighed. "I was concerned about what I'd have to do to fill her hours on a ranch. But now her days are so full, I can hardly find any time alone with her."

"Do you mind?"

"Not at all. Well, that's not exactly true. I found it hard at first to share her with all of you. For so long it's just been the two of us."

Cora nodded. "I understand."

"But now it's such a joy to see her making friends and blossoming under all this attention."

Cora's mysterious smile remained as Dandy arrived with a cart containing assorted coffee cups, cream and sugar, and a covered tray.

Summer removed the cover to reveal a plate of sugar cookies, each carefully decorated with colored frosting and bright sprinkles.

Riley studied the cookie in her daughter's hand. "Does that have your name on it?"

Summer nodded. "Dandy and I baked it together, and he let me print my name. See?" She traced a chubby finger over the letters in bright red frosting. "S-u-m-m-e-r. That spells Summer."

"See how quick she is?" Amy glanced around at the others. "For a four-year-old, she's really smart." She smiled at the little girl. "We've been working on our letters, haven't we, Summer?"

The little girl nodded, flushed with pride at her accomplishment. "And Dandy says next week I'm going to help him bake tarts. Know what tarts are, Mama?"

"I do. Did he tell you what they are?"

Summer nodded. "Little tiny pies. I told him you love cherry pie. So we're going to bake you a bunch of them."

"Wow." Zane looked suitably impressed. "I hope you'll make enough for me, too. I know I'll want seconds."

"I'll want thirds," Jesse said.

"Me, too." Marilee glanced at Summer. "Honey, do you know how special you are? I've never once been allowed to learn Dandy's secret recipe for his sugar cookies, and here you are, not only watching him, but helping him."

Riley saw the way each little bit of praise had her daughter's smile growing. She could have hugged each and every one of the McCord family for making Summer feel so special. For a child with only her mother as family, this was a great feast, a magnificent banquet, and one that would be remembered for a very long time.

"I made a cookie for each of you with your very own name," Summer announced proudly before delivering a special treat to each of them. "Dandy helped me spell them."

Riley sat back, enjoying the moment.

As she sipped her coffee, Cora began to speak and the others, as though by mutual consent, fell silent.

"Riley, I hope you don't mind, but while you were busy today, we had a little family conference."

Riley's smile began to falter. She'd known, of course, that once everything was in the database and the payroll checks were issued, everything would be operating on an even keel. Now her efficiency had rendered her position here unnecessary.

She braced herself.

Cora turned to the ranch foreman. "I think this should be your announcement, Cal, since you're the one who suggested it."

Cal cleared his throat, clearly uncomfortable at making speeches. "Riley, you've probably noticed that since you arrived, I've spent as little time as possible in the office."

She nodded, but before she could say a word he went on.

"With the calving season, and the need to get the rest of the herds up to the hills, I'm being stretched too thin. There are only so many hours in the day, and I've had to pick and choose how to spend them. My first priority has to be the operation of this ranch. But that presents a big problem, because the smooth operation of any business depends on bills being paid on time, and local, state, and federal documents being filed in a timely manner. Until you came along, I was trying to do it all, and I only succeeded in doing none of it well. Now, with the luxury of having you handling the office work, I'm free to do what I do best."

He smiled. "Though I haven't spent as much time in the office as I used to, I've been keeping a close eye on your work. Our firm in Helena confirms that you're not only smart, you're efficient. Since your arrival, things have been running so smoothly, their complaints about late payments and lost documents have ended. What's more, I'm comfortable going up to the hills with the wranglers, knowing the paperwork is in your capable hands. So…" He cleared his throat again, and Riley couldn't help holding her breath.

Cal glanced at Cora for confirmation before adding, "We realize that this is a big adjustment for you and Summer. So we thought we'd give you some time to get the feel of the place and see if it's something you'd like to do for the foreseeable future."

It took Riley a moment for his words to sink in. "Are you offering me a…permanent position here?"

"That's right. But we'd like you to take your time to consider the implications. Coming from a big city, you may find this isolation too big a hill to climb. And then there's Summer to consider. There aren't any other kids for her to play with way out here."

Riley mulled his words, until a new thought struck. "What about my contract with the firm in Helena?"

Cal nodded. "That's another problem you'll have to consider carefully. If you decide to make this permanent, you'll have to leave the employ of the firm and become an employee of the Lost Nugget Ranch. We would match their salary and benefits, of course, but if you decided to leave us and go back to the city at a later date to seek employment, you wouldn't have the cushion of a big firm as reference. I doubt employment at a ranch in Montana would go very far in getting you a job with one of the top firms."

Riley could feel the others watching her.

She took a deep breath. "Thank you, Cal. This is so generous of you. I'm flattered that you would want me to stay. As you said, there are a lot of things to consider besides just a paycheck. Since you want me to give it some serious thought, I'll do just that."

"Good for you." Cora laid a hand over Riley's. "I told Cal that's what you would say. I've noticed that you're by nature a careful person. You'll want to consider this from all angles before making a decision."

Riley glanced toward Summer, who had curled up on a rug in front of the fire. "My first consideration has to be Summer. And as you said, Cal, I was worried about the fact that she wouldn't have access to day care and other children. But she has been thriving on all the attention she's getting here."

She gave a deep sigh. "I'm so honored that you would ask me to stay. But right now, I'd better say good night and carry one very tired little girl to her bed."

"I'll do that." Zane crossed the room and scooped Summer into his arms.

She was so sound asleep she barely stirred, except to wrap her chubby little arms around his neck and bury her face against his shoulder.

Riley could do nothing more than stare in stunned surprise at the sight of Zane holding her daughter. A tall, muscled cowboy should look awkward holding a sleeping child. Somehow, he made it look like the most natural thing in the world. As for Summer, she looked completely at home in his strong, capable arms, as though she'd always been there.

When at last she managed to compose herself, Riley

bid good night to the others before following Zane up the stairs.

As she walked, the sight of her daughter's face nestled against Zane's shoulder caused the sweetest of aches around her heart. It was a picture she'd carried in her heart for a very long time now. A picture of a man who would be both tender and strong. A man who wouldn't find Summer a burden, but rather a joy. But this tall, rough cowboy certainly didn't fit the image she'd had in her dreams.

Zane paused to allow Riley to unlock the door to her suite. Once inside she snapped on lights as she led the way to Summer's bedroom. In the little girl's room she turned down the bed linens and watched as Zane lowered her daughter to the bed.

"Tell me where to find her pajamas."

"There's no need." Riley shook her head. "I'll just slip off her skirt and shoes. She'll be fine in her top and tights."

While she was busy doing that, Zane glanced at the framed artwork hanging above the bed. It was a three-dimensional drawing of Floppy, but as he studied it more closely, he realized it also very cleverly spelled out Summer's name.

"Who made this?"

Seeing the direction of his gaze, she shrugged. "I made it."

He continued studying the clever piece while Riley tucked the blankets around her daughter's shoulders.

She sank down on the edge of the mattress and lifted a hand to smooth a lock of hair from Summer's face.

Seeing the look of tenderness in Riley's eyes as she studied her daughter, Zane couldn't help smiling. "The angels have to be jealous."

His words touched her more deeply than she cared to admit.

Pressing a kiss to Summer's cheek, she stood and followed him from the room, switching off the light before closing the door.

In the sitting room she turned. "Thank you for carrying her up the stairs. I didn't mean to take you away from your family."

"I don't mind. I can see them anytime. It isn't often I get the chance to hold an angel in my arms."

Riley gave a throaty chuckle. "She does look like an angel when she's sleeping. But I'll remind you of your words some time when her temper flares."

"If there's a temper in her, I have yet to see it."

"So far, she's been on her best behavior."

He smiled. "I'd know a thing or two about that. I've been on my best behavior around you, too." He touched a finger to her cheek. Just a touch, but it sent the most amazing rush of heat through her veins.

His gaze burned over her. "But it's getting harder and harder to behave like a gentleman and keep my hands off you."

She fought to ignore the little thrill that shot through her.

"Maybe"—she ran a tongue over lips that had gone dry—"we'd better say good night."

He kept his fingertip at her cheek, and though the touch was whisper-soft, she could feel it all the way to her toes. "Is that what you really want?"

His abrupt question had her struggling for composure. Caught by surprise, she answered without thinking. "I've learned that what I want and what I need aren't always the same."

His eyes remained steady on hers. "Good night, Riley."

"Good night."

Instead of turning away he allowed his hand to follow the curve of her cheek to her jaw.

His head lowered just as hers lifted, and his mouth covered hers. He'd intended it to be no more than a simple good-night kiss, but the instant their lips met, everything changed.

In his life he'd been kicked by an angry bull. Tossed from the back of a skittish stallion. Clubbed by a falling tree limb. Nearly drowned in a raging river. And none of those experiences compared with the jolt he was absorbing to his system. A rush of adrenaline had him vibrating with need.

His arms wrapped around her, drawing her close as he took the kiss deeper. While his mouth moved over hers, he could feel her in every part of his body. The softness of her breasts against his chest. The press of her thighs to his. The tingle of warmth as her arms slowly lifted until they closed around his neck. And clung.

He heard her little sigh of pleasure as she offered her lips for more.

Somewhere in his mind an alarm bell went off and he realized that he needed to take a step back.

But not just yet. He wanted, needed, one more taste of her. One more kiss before leaving.

He took her fully into the kiss and could feel himself

sinking into her. Into all that sweetness. And losing himself completely in her, his head spinning, his world tilting, his heart doing a crazy dance in his chest.

His hands were in her hair, though he didn't know how they got there, and he had her backed against the wall.

All he could think of was taking her here, now. The hard, driving need had him by the throat until he could barely breathe. He couldn't remember the last time he'd been so aroused by nothing more than a kiss.

He lifted his head, staring deeply into her eyes as he drew air into his starving lungs.

"You're right. Want and need have a way of getting really tangled up." He took another long breath. "Good night, Riley."

He turned away and felt her watching him as he descended the stairs. When he reached the landing, he paused and listened to the sound of her door closing.

He wasn't ready to join the family just now. He wanted to be alone, to sort through the thoughts and emotions twisting around inside.

Shifting gears, he headed toward his own suite of rooms. Once inside he moved to the window and stared at the darkened outline of Treasure Chest Mountain in the distance.

That kiss had been a revelation. The first time, he'd thought he'd merely imagined all that heat. Now he knew better. That cool, distant wall of reserve that Riley had built was a cover. The ice maiden was a flesh-and-blood woman hiding a deep well of passion.

He'd thought, after their first kiss, that he'd be prepared for all the flash and fury, but he'd been wrong. So wrong. Even anticipating it, he'd been completely taken over by a need stronger than anything he'd ever known.

He began to move restlessly around the room. He'd hoped to spend a few hours editing some of his latest film. Now the thought of keeping his mind on his work seemed an impossible task.

He paused in mid-stride, seeing her in his mind as she'd looked when he left her. Hair disheveled, lips pursed in a little pout of wonder.

He had no doubt that she'd been as aroused by that kiss as he had.

That thought made him feel a little less edgy.

He paced to the window once more, arms crossed over his chest, hip against the sill, and this time he smiled. He was going to have to tread carefully here. If they struck sparks each time they kissed, they could easily start a raging wildfire.

Starting a fire wasn't the problem. Putting it out, if and when it became necessary, was another issue altogether. Along the way, somebody was apt to get badly burned.

CHAPTER EIGHT

Riley squared her shoulders before stepping into the kitchen with Summer. After a sleepless night, she steeled herself for the jolt she knew she would feel when she had to face Zane this morning.

Her heart plummeted when she looked around and realized he wasn't with the others.

"'Morning, Riley. Summer." Dandy returned his attention to the pancakes on the griddle. "Help yourselves to juice."

"Thank you." Riley carried two glasses to the table and greeted the others before taking a seat beside her daughter.

"Where's Zane?" the little girl asked.

Riley was grateful for her daughter's question.

"Out in one of the barns." Jesse held a chair for Amy. "Knowing Zane, he'll be along soon. I've never known him to miss breakfast."

Dandy began passing around a platter of sausage and pancakes just as Zane walked into the mudroom, trailed by Jimmy Eagle.

The two men hung their hats, scraped their boots, and carefully washed at the big sink before stepping into the kitchen.

Though the talk and laughter continued around her, Riley was aware only of the tall, rangy figure making his way toward the table.

"Jimmy," he said, "this is Riley Mason."

Riley's palm was engulfed in the old wrangler's work-roughened hand. "Riley, this is Jimmy Eagle, who's been here almost as long as Cal."

"Hello, Jimmy. It's nice to meet you. Summer has already told me that you love the horses as much as Zane."

"Yes, ma'am. I guess I do."

When Zane took the seat beside Riley, she felt the brush of his thigh on hers and dropped her fork with a clatter.

His deep voice, so close to her, had her forgetting all about retrieving the fork. "'Morning."

She struggled for something light and meaningless to fill the silence. "You were up early."

"Yeah. Figured as long as I couldn't sleep, I may as well get some of my chores started." He met her steady gaze. "How about you? Get much sleep last night?"

She was grateful that the others were too busy talking to hear her conversation with Zane. "Not much."

His smile grew. "Sorry to hear that."

She couldn't help smiling. "You don't look sorry."

He chuckled. "I can see that I'm going to have to start

working on my poker face so you can't see what I'm really thinking."

Summer looked past her mother. "Will you have time to take me to see Vanilla today, Zane?"

"You bet. When I saw her earlier, she asked where you were."

"She did?" Summer's eyes went wide.

Seated on the other side of her, Jimmy Eagle pressed a sugar lump into the little girl's hand. "You might want to give her this when you see her."

"Thank you." Summer treated the small cube as if it were gold as she tucked it into her pocket. "Vanilla loves treats."

"I think she likes you more than the treats."

Summer beamed.

"You're in for an even bigger treat," Zane said casually. "A couple of the mares foaled overnight, and they've got brand-new little foals to show off."

"What are foals?" Summer asked.

"Baby horses."

"Babies. Oh, boy." Summer clapped her hands in delight. "Can I go see them right now?"

Zane chuckled. "I think you'd better finish your breakfast first. There'll be plenty of time to make a fuss over the new foals. By the way, one of those babies belongs to Vanilla."

"She has her baby now?" Summer's eyes grew round. "How did it get here?"

"I walked into her stall and there it was." He turned to Riley. "If there's anything more you want her to know, I'll leave it up to you."

Riley laughed. "Thanks. I think. I guess I'll just have to see how many questions she has about this."

Jesse broke into their conversation as he turned to his cousins. "I'm heading to the south ridge today. You two coming?"

Wyatt nodded. "Count me in."

Zane merely smiled. "Sorry, cuz. Didn't you hear? I have a date." At Jesse's arched brow he added, "I promised a certain young lady that we'd visit the horse barns today and meet the new babies."

After thanking Dandy for the fine meal, the others were soon going off in different directions to see to their morning chores. Riley watched as Summer turned eagerly to Zane.

"Are we going to visit Vanilla now and see her new baby?" As always, she was twitching with anticipation.

He couldn't help chuckling at her reaction. "I think we'd better hurry. Vanilla's been waiting a long time for her treat." He turned to Riley. "I'll bring Summer to the office when we're through."

While Riley watched, the little girl tucked her hand in Zane's as they made their way from the room.

Summer had become comfortable enough with the routine in the barn that she needed no coaxing to reach into the bucket and retrieve a handful of carrots before heading toward the first stall.

"'Morning, Vanilla." She climbed up onto the bottom wooden rail and waited until the mare was close enough to pet. She ran a tiny hand over the velvet muzzle. "Did you miss me?"

As if on cue the mare bobbed her head, tossing her mane and forelock.

"I missed you, too. Look what I brought you."

Zane stood back, recording the scene on his video camera. With the eye of a professional he studied the little girl through his viewfinder. At such a tender age she didn't have a clue that she was a photographer's dream. Sweet, natural without a trace of artifice, and glowing with delight.

"Oh, look, Zane." Summer spied the tiny foal standing behind its mother. "She looks just like Vanilla. What's her name?"

"We haven't given her a name yet. Can you think of one?"

She thought for only a moment before saying, "She has a star right there." She pointed to the foal's muzzle. "Can we call her Star?"

"I think that's a perfect name." He moved close to capture a shot of both Summer and Star together.

"Want to see the other babies?"

"Yes, please."

As she moved from stall to stall, he continued recording her, sometimes pausing to chuckle at her conversations with the horses, and their sweet antics as they accepted the treats she offered.

By the time they returned to Vanilla's stall, Summer was bubbling with happiness. She stood on the wooden rail and watched as the newborn stayed close to its mother, resisting all her attempts to coax it with treats to come closer.

"The new baby is too young to eat carrots or sugar lumps yet," Zane explained. "Right now her mama is the only one who can feed her. But I'm sure you can tempt her mother with a carrot or two."

While the foal watched from across the stall, Vanilla eagerly accepted Summer's offerings.

She looked over at Zane. "Can I pet the baby?"

"As long as her mama doesn't object. New mothers can be a bit protective of their babies."

Summer climbed up yet another rail of the stall and leaned far over to touch the velvet muzzle of the downy foal. The look on the child's face was one of pure joy.

"I touched her. I did."

"And she didn't seem to mind a bit. In fact, Summer, I think she likes you. Almost as much as Vanilla does."

The little girl walked away on a cloud.

When she'd assured herself that she'd fed every one of the animals, she and Zane stepped from the barn into bright sunlight.

Zane dropped the camera into his shirt pocket. "Know what I think?"

"What?" Summer paused to look up at him.

"I think the day is too pretty to go inside yet." He glanced toward one of the utility carts parked in the yard. "How about a ride?"

"Oh, boy. Can we?" Summer danced ahead of him and climbed into the passenger side of the vehicle, which was little more than a glorified golf cart with a big metal box in back for tools.

Zane slipped on his sunglasses before climbing in beside her and turning the key. "Let's take a look at some of the horses out here in the corral."

As they drove slowly around the enclosure, Summer had dozens of questions.

"Why are some brown and some black and some white?"

"Because they had different parents. Just like people, who come in all different colors."

"But how come those are spotted?"

He winked. "Maybe they fell into a bucket of paint."

Though she wasn't sure whether or not he was joking, she laughed along with him.

"How come they're out here and the others are in the barn?"

"The ones in the barn are either too young or too old to go up into the hills. And then there are the new mothers and their babies. They need to be pampered for a while."

"What's pampered?"

"Spoiled. Given extra food and treats and comfort while they grow strong enough to go into the hills with the others."

"Why would they go to the hills?"

"Sometimes the wranglers prefer riding horses to driving trucks or all-terrain vehicles."

"What are all-terr..." She stumbled over the word.

"All-terrain vehicles. That just means they go up over hills and rocks and through streams."

"Like horses."

He smiled at her logic. "Yep. And a lot of the old-timers here still prefer all-terrain horses to all-terrain vehicles."

"I like horses best," she said matter-of-factly. "But"— she patted the seat of their cart—"this is fun, too."

He watched the breeze take her hair and thought how much she resembled her mother.

She turned to him. "When I get big, I'm going to ride horses instead of a car."

"A girl after my own heart."

"Mama says you like horses."

"I love horses. I've loved them all my life."

She sat back, not completely certain just why she felt so warm and content, but knowing that it had something to do with this man and his easy nature. "Me, too." She looked over at him with a smile. "I love horses, too. Just like you. All my life. Even when I was little."

His laughter was rich and warm as honey as it washed over her, making her laugh along with him.

Riley paused in her work to glance once more at the clock. Where were Zane and Summer? How long could they spend admiring new foals? They'd already been gone far longer than she'd expected.

She struggled to return her attention to the payroll, but it was impossible to concentrate.

Half an hour more, she thought, and then she would simply have to go searching for them.

Riley stepped into the kitchen and was dismayed to find it empty, except for Dandy.

He looked up. "Hi, Riley. Something I can get you?"

"No thanks. I was wondering if you've seen Summer and Zane."

"Haven't seen them since they left for the horse barn." He returned his attention to a pot of chili simmering on the stove.

Riley hurried through the mudroom and out the back door toward the distant barns. It shamed her to admit to herself that she wasn't even certain which of the buildings housed the horses. She'd become so complacent that she allowed her daughter the freedom to roam this vast space without even knowing specifically where she was.

She stepped into the first barn and peered around. It took a moment to adjust to the gloom. Then, seeing the horses' heads over the doors of their stalls, she felt a rush of relief.

Cupping her hands to her mouth, she shouted her daughter's name and waited, expecting to hear a response. Instead, except for the occasional blowing and stomping from the stalls, there was only silence.

"Summer." She shouted the name now, and began running from stall to stall, peering into each one.

By the time she'd reached the last stall, her breath was coming hard and fast, and her mind was conjuring images that had her close to tears. Hadn't she heard of horses going on a rampage and stomping their owners to death? What if Summer had been bitten, and Zane had already rushed her to the hospital? Would he have time to contact her, or would he just go on instinct and drive her daughter into town?

What if a stranger had found Summer and snatched her away, without anyone's knowledge? Her helpless little girl could be miles from here by now, and in desperate danger.

It was then that she saw the wrangler. The one she'd seen in the house on several occasions. Cooper Easley. The very name sent chills along her spine.

He was bent over in the last stall.

"Summer?" Her daughter's name was little more than a choked sob as Riley charged into the stall.

The wrangler looked up, his eyes locking on hers.

Except for this man, the stall was empty. "I'm..."

Riley could hardly breathe. "I'm looking for my daughter. Have you seen her?"

He straightened. A harness dangled from his hand.

Staring at his raised hand, she backed up a step. "Have you seen my daughter?"

His lips thinned. "On a ranch this size, she could be anywhere."

On a ranch this size, she thought as she turned and raced out of the barn. Summer could be anywhere and there were thousands of acres. She was heading toward the next outbuilding in the distance when she caught the sound of childish laughter rippling on the breeze.

She turned toward the sound and froze as Zane and Summer, seated in a little cart, rounded the building and rolled to a stop in front of her.

"Hi, Mama. Look. Zane let me steer and I..." Summer's words faded at the look in her mother's eyes.

Riley swooped closer, hands on her hips, her tone close to hysteria. "Do you have any idea how long you've been gone?"

Zane glanced at his watch. "Sorry. We were having so much fun I forgot all about the time."

"You forgot? You have my child in your care, and you forgot?" Her eyes narrowed on him and he could feel the pent-up fury as she reached out a hand to her daughter.

Before she could grab Summer's hand Zane turned off the engine, stepped out and rounded the front of the cart, stopping directly in front of her.

"What's going on here, Riley?"

"What's going on? I'll tell you what's going on." She had to fight back the tears that threatened. Now that she'd found her daughter safe and sound, a reaction was setting in. She could feel her entire body trembling. She wanted to sink to her knees and weep with relief, but she didn't dare show such emotion in front of an audience.

Instead, she lifted her chin and faced him. "When you didn't return Summer in a reasonable time, I got worried and came searching for her."

Sensing the nerves beneath her facade, Zane deliberately kept his voice low, reasonable. "I'm sorry that I forgot about the time. And you have every right to worry. This is a big ranch, with a lot of places for a kid to get lost. But I promised to bring her back to you."

"Promises aren't always kept."

"Mine are." He touched a hand to her shoulder and felt her shivering response. Instead of lifting his hand away he deliberately kept it there. "Something else is going on here, Riley. What's wrong?"

She lifted pleading eyes to his. "I don't want to talk about it. I just want to take Summer in the house now."

He continued watching her chest rise and fall with each labored breath. He could see that she was very close to losing control.

"I'll drive you up to the house." He indicated the cart. "Climb in."

Without a word she settled herself beside her daughter.

Zane rounded the cart and sat down before turning the key. When they pulled up to the back door Zane stopped the cart and watched as Riley climbed out and helped her daughter down beside her.

Before they could climb the steps he called, "After I return the cart to the barn, I'll stop by your office. We need to talk."

Riley paused, but she didn't turn around before taking Summer's hand and leading her up the steps. She was already regretting that ugly scene. Not just because of the things she'd said, but because of the naked fear she'd revealed.

Naked. That's how she felt right now.

She had no idea what she would say when Zane returned and demanded answers. But this much she knew. Zane McCord wasn't the kind of man who would swallow a half-truth. No matter how much she told him about her past, he would demand to know everything. And that she was not prepared to give. Not to him. Not to anyone.

Zane parked the cart beside the barn and walked back to the house, deep in thought. The fear he'd sensed in Riley may have been extreme, but it was also very real. It mirrored the fear he'd sensed when she had first arrived here and had been reluctant to let Summer out of her sight. In the past couple of weeks he'd begun to believe he'd only imagined her earlier reaction. Now there was no doubt in his mind. She was obsessively overprotective.

He intended to find out why.

In the mudroom he took his time scraping his boots, hanging his hat, washing his hands, all the while replaying that little scene in his mind.

As he made his way along the hall toward the office, he heard Amy's cheerful voice.

He paused in the doorway of Riley's office.

"...sent away for some neon-colored construction paper. I thought Summer and I could make something special today," Amy was saying to Riley.

"Oh, boy." Summer's smile rivaled the sun. "Can I draw anything I want?"

"Whatever makes you happy." Amy took her hand. "And when we're finished, Dandy said we can tape it on the door of the refrigerator so the whole family can see it at dinnertime."

They turned and caught sight of Zane in the doorway.

Summer danced over to him to whisper loudly, "I'm going to draw something we both love."

He winked at her. "I wonder what that could be."

"Shh." She put a finger to her lips. "Don't tell."

"Okay." He gave her a wink and a big smile. "It'll be our secret."

"Come on, Miss Amy. Let's go up to the classroom."

"Bye," Amy called as she followed the little girl, who was skipping ahead of her.

Zane shook his head as he watched them go. "I don't think I was ever that excited to go to school."

Riley sighed. "Bless Amy. Whatever magic she's using, I've never seen Summer so eager to please."

Zane regarded her. She was seated behind her desk, her hands nervously working a pen, clicking it on, then off. On, then off.

When she realized what she was doing, she set the pen aside and folded her hands in her lap.

Her chin came up in that way she had when she was facing something unpleasant. "I'm sorry for that scene."

"You were worried about Summer."

She nodded.

"Why?"

She swallowed. "I told you. I looked at the clock and realized you were late bringing her back."

"We were a few minutes late and you were falling apart."

"I wasn't…"

He held up a hand. "Riley, I know what I saw. My question is a simple one: Why? What had you so worried that you were close to tears?"

When she remained silent, he walked closer and perched on the edge of her desk.

She reached for the pen and he took it from her before closing his hand over hers. "The truth, Riley."

She took a deep breath. "Before I came here to Montana, the authorities in Philadelphia tried to remove Summer from my care."

"Why?"

"There was an…incident involving the woman I'd hired to watch her during the day when I returned to school."

He continued holding her hand. "Tell me about it."

"Charlotte was the friend of a friend. I'd used day care, but it was expensive. I had already dropped out of college and was working two jobs to make ends meet. I decided that I needed to get my degree so I could make a better life for myself and Summer, and when this friend told me that Charlotte would work for half the price, and care for Summer in my apartment, I jumped at the chance."

When she fell silent, Zane prodded. "You mentioned an incident."

Riley looked away. "Just weeks after I hired Charlotte, Child Protective Services arrived to say that they had proof she was neglecting the child in her care, and they were moving the child to foster care."

"How did you stop them?"

"One of my professors at the university had a brother who taught law and did pro bono work. He offered to help me. Shortly after he got involved, the case was dropped because he threatened to sue for entrapment. He suggested that I'd been set up."

Zane's eyes narrowed. "Set up? Who would do that? And why?"

She withdrew her hand and clasped it in her lap. "It's complicated."

When she didn't offer more, he said, "Summer's father?"

Riley shook her head. "Nick is dead."

She looked up to see Zane's eyebrow lifted.

She sighed, wondering how far to take this. "Summer's father was serving in Special Forces. He was shipped to a location in the Middle East. He...never made it back."

"I'm sorry." He regarded her. "Did Summer get to know her father?"

She shook her head. "He was gone so quickly, he never even got to hold her."

"He wasn't there for her birth?"

She gave a quick shake of her head.

"But you had someone with you?"

"No one."

He tried to imagine what it had been like for Riley, giving birth alone, without anyone there to offer a word of encouragement, a smile, a hug. "How about family? Yours? His? Weren't they reluctant to see you move so far away?"

She ducked her head, avoiding his eyes. "I have no family except an aunt and an uncle. Nick grew up in foster care and never knew his family."

"And this aunt and uncle of yours. Aren't they hungry to know their great-niece?"

Her voice wavered slightly. "Not all families are like yours, Zane." She stood. "And now, I really have to get back to work. I spent way too much time this morning worrying about Summer."

He caught her by the chin and lifted her face to keep her from avoiding his eyes. "Why do I get the feeling there's a lot you're not telling me?"

"Please, Zane. Let it be."

"Okay. For now." He lowered his hand to his side and took a step back. "See you at dinner."

As he walked from the office, he could almost hear her sigh of relief.

Part of him, the sensible part, had wanted to stay and pry the truth from her. But his heart had won out over his head. Because of his growing feelings for her, he'd decided not to pursue it.

At least not for now, he repeated in his mind. But the day would come when he would probe deeper. Maybe, if she returned those feelings, she would be persuaded to confide in him. Because he knew in his heart that she hadn't told him the whole truth.

Riley Mason was proving to be a complex woman. She reminded him of the waters of Grasshopper Creek. Anyone who saw it on a calm, sunny day could be fooled into believing it was nothing more than a clear, shallow body of water. But those who knew it intimately realized that there were deep currents beneath that surface. Currents that had revealed some of the finest gold in the land, while taking the lives of countless unsuspecting miners.

CHAPTER NINE

———◆———

W ell, Riley." Cal paused in the doorway of the office.
From the growth of stubble on his cheeks and chin, it was
plain that he'd just returned from the high country after
more than a week with the herd. "Since there weren't any
grumblings from the wranglers, I'm guessing your first
payroll went off without a hitch."

She laughed. "There may have been one or two, but
they were minor glitches that were straightened out at the
bank without having to jump through too many hoops."

"That's good." He stared pointedly at the desktop,
clean of all paperwork, and at the file cabinets, all neatly
closed, without a trace of the chaos that had been there
when he'd left. "Looks like you took care of business."

"I tried." She got up and walked around the desk. "I'll
get out of your way."

"Hold on." He lifted a palm. "I hired you to do the
one job I don't feel qualified to handle on this ranch.

I've been a cowboy all my life. I can wrangle a wayward heifer, nurse a sick cow, and birth a calf without breaking a sweat. I can sleep under the stars, trudge through mud up to my knees, and happily huddle under nothing more than a saddle blanket in a blizzard. But believe me when I say I'll be the happiest man in the world if I never have to handle another paycheck, tax form, or official document in my lifetime."

Riley stood facing him, shaking her head from side to side until she broke into a wide smile. "Is this your way of saying that you'd like my answer about whether or not I intend to stay on permanently?"

"Not at all. What I'm saying is I'd like you to sit back down. I don't want to interrupt your work. For as long as you're working here, Riley, this is your office."

He fixed her with a look. "I'd like you to remove one of the wranglers from the payroll—Cooper Easley. It seems Jimmy warned Cooper several times about the house being off-limits to the wranglers unless they had specific duties here. The fact that Cooper chose to ignore those orders sealed his fate. He's gone from the Lost Nugget."

"Cal..."

He held up a hand. "Jimmy told me that he hadn't been satisfied with Cooper's work since taking him on, but we were so desperate for extra hands, he decided to keep him on the payroll. Today was the last straw."

"Today?"

"Jimmy caught him hauling a ladder back to the barn."

"A ladder." She thought about her suite of rooms on the second floor. She'd never thought to check the windows. Were they locked? Could they be opened from the outside?

"We don't know what he was up to. It's not as though we keep valuables around. But I'm thinking he may have been targeting Cora's studio, and the paintings she keeps there. I told Jimmy to pass the word that at the first sign of Cooper back on the premises, we call the law."

Riley felt like cheering. Her suspicions had been correct. That wrangler had been up to no good. And now he was gone.

As Cal turned away, he called over his shoulder, "I'm going to shave this beard and settle into a tub of hot water. Then I'm going to sleep for about twenty hours in a real bed."

When she was alone, Riley raced up the stairs to her suite. She looked around but could see nothing out of the ordinary. When she checked the window, it was slightly open, allowing the curtains to billow. She hadn't opened that window.

Cooper Easley had been in here. Of that, she was certain.

She peered into Summer's room, noting her neatly made bed, with Floppy still lying on the pretty pink pillow.

After several deep breaths, Riley took a turn around the apartment, testing each window and carefully locking any that weren't secured. She then let herself out of her suite, taking care to lock the door behind her.

She returned to the office deep in thought and sank slowly into her chair, staring around as though seeing it all for the first time.

Though she hadn't officially given Cal her answer, he'd given his. He wanted her to stay.

She wiped the back of her hand over her eyes to stem the tears as the thought slowly formed. This was real. Not some dream. The job was hers for as long as she chose to stay. And now, with the threat to her safety gone, at long last she could put aside the daily struggle just to survive, and begin to plan for Summer's future.

"I don't know about you." Zane and his cousins circled the map they'd set up in the great room, dotted with little flags to show where they had already searched for the lost treasure before the winter snows had stopped them in their tracks. "But I'm itching to try out some of that exotic equipment we've had shipped out to the wilderness."

Jesse nodded. "I'm with you, cuz. We were making progress until the first snowfall. Then we got buried."

"Which isn't all bad." Wyatt had an arm around Marilee's shoulders. "It gave us some extra alone time."

"Newlyweds." Zane gave a mock shudder. "Do you guys ever think about anything else?"

"You mean there's more to life?" Wyatt nuzzled Marilee's cheek.

Zane glanced over their heads to where Cal and Cora were seated by the fire, enjoying coffee and dessert. "Cal, I need another bachelor over here. I'm outnumbered."

Cal merely grinned.

They all looked up when Riley walked down the stairs and stepped into the great room.

"Oh." She paused. "I didn't realize you were still here. I'll just go to the kitchen."

"Don't be silly. We'd love for you to stay and join us. Our guys are plotting the next moves in their treasure hunt..." Amy looked up. "That's probably all a puzzle to you. I'm sure you don't have a clue about our family history." Amy caught her hand and drew her into the circle. "Stay. We'll talk. Did you have dessert?"

Riley shook her head. "After a second helping of Dandy's pot roast, I was too full. I guess Summer was, too, because that's the first time I've ever seen her refuse one of Dandy's brownies."

At the mention of Summer, Amy's face softened into a smile. "Is our girl asleep?"

"Yes. I barely got through the first bedtime story when I realized she was already out."

Amy touched a hand to Riley's. "It was probably all that fresh air today. Zane took her to the barn to feed the horses and see the brand-new foals, and then drove her out to one of the ranges to see the calves."

Riley nodded and turned to Zane. "Summer was so thrilled. She kept calling them baby horses and baby cows. I heard everything. How soft they are. How one newborn could barely stand. How protective their mothers are. And how you lifted her up and carried her on your shoulders through the field so she wouldn't step in any cow patties."

That brought a round of laughter from everyone.

Zane chuckled. "Most of those cow patties are bigger than her little feet. I didn't want her to get scolded for losing a boot out there."

Riley couldn't hide her happiness. "I want to thank all of you for making us feel so welcome. Summer can't stop talking about how much she loves having her very own teacher, Miss Amy, and going to sleep in her very own bed at night."

Jesse circled an arm around his wife's waist. "I don't

know who's having more fun with this. Summer or Amy. I didn't realize just how much she missed teaching until Summer moved in. I have to tell you, Riley, I haven't seen Amy this happy since our wedding day."

"I can understand that, cuz." Wyatt punched his arm. "Now that she's settled in for the long haul, she's probably wondering what in the hell she was thinking, taking you on for a lifetime."

Riley joined in the laughter before squeezing Amy's hand. "Thanks for asking me to stay and join your evening's discussion, but I think I'll just take a cup of tea upstairs, in case Summer wakes and needs me."

She headed toward the kitchen. In the doorway she paused.

Though her gaze swept everyone in the room, it lingered on Zane. "Good night."

It was nearing the end of another very busy day of paperwork.

Riley opened the dog-eared pages of the ledger and began painstakingly checking each entry against the ones on the computer screen. She hoped this would be the last time she would need to make corrections to the errors that had shown up on the first payroll. Though the bank had been patient, there had been a few misspelled names, and a number of incorrect digits on official documents.

Now, with the information already entered, it would be a simple matter to make a few changes to the database.

As she flipped pages, she came across the yellowed papers that had fallen out of the ledger days earlier. With all the work she'd been doing, she'd completely forgotten about these.

She studied the words of a long, rambling note, trying to make sense of it. Some of the words were smudged. Others were missing altogether, no doubt erased by time or weather. No matter. Whatever this was, it needed to be turned over to Cal.

She set the papers aside on her desk. This time, she wouldn't tuck them away and forget about them.

When Summer stood in the doorway wearing her oversize apron to announce it was time for dinner, Riley stowed the ledger in a desk drawer and picked up the yellowed papers.

"Hurry, Mama. Me and Dandy made a special dinner."

"Dandy and I," Riley corrected. "What did you make?"

"Fried chicken and lasa…" She paused and tried again. "Lasa…"

"Lasagna?"

"Yes. How'd you know, Mama?"

"I may have heard it a time or two," she said with a smile.

When she and her daughter stepped into the kitchen, the others were already there. The men were drinking longnecks. Cora was sipping tea. Marilee and Amy were gathered around a set of blueprints for the new house planned by Jesse and Amy.

Seeing Cal talking to Zane, she walked over and held out the papers.

"I don't know what these are, but I thought you might want to look them over."

Cal's eyes widened as he studied the pages.

His head came up sharply. "Where'd you find these?"

From the fierce look in his eyes Riley realized that he considered them important. Her heart started pounding.

"They fell out of the ledger when it dropped on the floor. I guess they must have been stuck to one of the back pages, and that sudden drop loosened them. It happened days ago, but I completely forgot about it until now when I came across them again."

"Cora. Take a look at this." At the urgency in Cal's voice, the rest of the family fell silent and gathered around.

"Oh, my heavens." Cora read the pages before putting a hand to her throat.

Without a word she passed the pages to Jesse, who in turn passed them to Wyatt and then to Zane. Each of them studied the pages with great deliberation, as though memorizing their contents.

None of them spoke, but Riley had the sense that they were all deeply touched by what they were seeing.

"I'm sorry. Have I brought you bad news?"

Zane's eyes crinkled with laughter. "Bad news? Is that what you think?"

He knelt down and faced the little girl so that his eyes were level with hers. "What your mama found is just about the best news ever."

"It is?"

Riley arched a brow, grateful for her daughter's question and eager to hear Zane's explanation.

"It is indeed." He got to his feet. "Aunt Cora, maybe you ought to explain."

Cora nodded. "In 1862, at Grasshopper Creek, our ancestors found a treasure of gold nuggets, some as large as a man's fist. That ancestor, Jasper McCord, was murdered, and his sack of gold nuggets stolen. His son, Nathanial, at the time only fourteen years old, vowed to find the prospector who committed that terrible deed and retrieve the gold. Nathanial McCord spent the rest of his life searching for the lost treasure. And since then, our family's goal has been to follow his lead and find our rightful fortune, which we believe is still somewhere on our land."

Cora was clinging to Cal's arm and he gently led her toward a chair at the kitchen table, where she sat down heavily, still staggered by the latest discovery. "This"— she held up one of the yellowed papers—"is a page from Nathanial's diary. I know because we've found many of them through the years. The size of the paper and the very distinctive handwriting make it easy to identify. And this," she continued, holding up the other paper, "was written by my brother, Coot." Her tone softened at the very mention of his name. "Many of these have been found scattered across the countryside. But this one is different." Her voice trembled as she said, "All the others were merely crude maps that made sense only to Coot. This one identifies the location. And the fact that he drew a star in a particular area may mean something important."

Around the room, her nephews could be seen nodding in agreement.

Riley felt a wave of giddy relief. "For a minute there I was worried. You seemed really shaken by what you saw. I'm so glad I was able to bring you good news, Miss McCord."

"This is more than good news, dear. It's fresh hope." Cora's smile bloomed. "This is a very important piece of the puzzle. How appropriate that it should be revealed to us now, at the beginning of spring, just as my great-nephews have resumed their search."

When Dandy indicated that he was ready to serve their dinner, they took their places around the table.

Before they could begin to pass the food, Summer looked around with those big, innocent eyes. "When Mama and I were alone, we always said a blessing before we ate."

Riley looked horrified. "Summer—"

Before she could say more, Cora stopped her. "That's lovely, Summer. When my brother and I were little, we always said a blessing, too. Then, somehow, through the years, we forgot." She smiled at the little girl. "Why don't you lead the blessing tonight?"

Feeling very important, Summer held out her hands to her mother and Zane, and the others followed her lead around the table.

"Bless this food," Summer said in her most solemn tone. "And bless all of us here."

It was Cal who said softly, "Amen."

The others chimed in.

With a sudden burst of conversation they began passing the fried chicken, the lasagna, the freshly steamed carrots and early peas, and the rolls still warm from the oven.

As they ate, they began to speak passionately about this new piece of evidence. The room vibrated with an air of expectancy, as though something monumental had just occurred that had altered the course of this family's future.

Riley felt a warm glow at the knowledge that she

had been the messenger of such happy news. News that, apparently, would aid all of them in their search for the lost treasure.

Beside her, little Summer merely smiled and listened to the chorus of voices flowing around her. Voices that made her feel like an important member of this big family.

While Dandy served coffee in the great room, little Summer carefully passed around a tray of chocolate chip cookies that she'd helped him bake earlier that afternoon. With each compliment from various members of the family, her smile grew.

Riley was content to sip her coffee and nibble a cookie in silence. From the noise level, it was clear that the McCord family was caught up in the excitement of her discovery.

The three cousins were gathered around their map, pinpointing various places they felt the document referred to. While they argued among themselves, Riley sat back as the realization dawned. For the first time she felt as though she belonged here. Always before she'd felt like an intruder. But now, with the discovery of their ancestor's papers, and a history lesson from Miss Cora, she understood what they were talking about. Almost as though she were one of them.

One of them.

She set aside her coffee to mull this sudden thought. There had been times before in her life that she'd believed herself to be part of a family, only to learn that it had all been a false impression. She'd belonged only as long as she played by certain rules. Once she broke the rules, she'd found herself on the outside looking in. It had been a painful lesson, but one that she wouldn't soon forget.

"...like the others, this trail leads directly to Treasure Chest." Zane ran his finger along the map, and his cousins nodded in agreement. "This has to be what Coot was saying."

"Okay." Jesse crossed his arms over his chest to stand and study the map. "But that's a huge area to cover."

"Not nearly as big as all this." Wyatt indicated the vast wilderness that stretched from the high meadows to Treasure Chest Mountain. "At least now we've narrowed the search considerably."

"And with the latest technology available, it doesn't seem nearly as impossible a task as it did this time last year." Zane smiled at Riley across the room. "With Coot directing us, thanks to the discovery by our brilliant accountant, how can we fail?"

Cora looked up. "My brother never permitted the word *failure* to be spoken in his presence. Neither will I. We're in this to win."

Zane crossed the room and kissed his great-aunt's cheek. "Well said, Aunt Cora. And I say the sooner we get started, the better."

She patted his arm. "I'm feeling really positive about this, Zane."

"Me, too." He looked over at Summer, who was lying on her stomach on the hearth, coloring a picture for her mother. "I think, while a certain someone is otherwise occupied, this might be a good time to fill Riley in on some of our family history."

Riley chuckled. "You mean there's more than a lost treasure?"

"Lots more. But it's all tied to that historical fact." Zane turned to his aunt. "Want me to bring Nathanial's diary?"

"Would you mind?"

He gave a nod before strolling away. Minutes later he returned with a wooden box, which he placed on the table beside his great-aunt. After lifting the lid, she held the yellowed papers in her hands with the same great care she would give to holding a treasure.

"Let me read to you from our ancestor's diary, which he started keeping during one of the coldest winters in Montana's history. Though he and his father nearly starved to death, and were forced to burn their wooden handmade furniture to keep from freezing, they endured. And Nathanial, hunting game as he crossed Grasshopper Creek, claims in his diary to have found the most amazing gold nuggets ever recorded. Dozens of them, and some as big as a man's fist."

Cora began reading aloud from the faded yellow pages, and Riley, along with the McCord family, was spellbound by the tale that emerged. A tale of hunger, despair, desperation, and then jubilation. But then, as the diary ended, Nathanial recorded his horror at waking from an exhausted sleep in a room above the saloon to find his father beside him, the mattress soaked with blood, Jasper's throat slit, and the sack of nuggets missing.

In the utter silence that followed that passage, Riley felt tears fill her eyes.

"How could he bear it?"

Cora closed the tattered book. "How could he not?

He had tasted hardship and then triumph. And in a single night it was stripped away, and all that was left was his faith in himself and his determined will."

Cora peered at Riley. "Isn't that all any of us really have in this life? Faith and strength of will can see us through the toughest of times."

Riley went very still as the older woman's words washed over her. How strange that an ancient story recorded by someone she'd never met could touch her heart and give her renewed hope that she could make wise choices in her own life that would affect her destiny.

She felt someone staring at her and turned to see Cal, seated across the room, fixing her with a steady look. Caught unaware, she managed a tremulous smile.

When he realized that he'd been caught staring, the foreman returned her smile before giving a slight nod of his head.

Riley didn't know why, but his courtly gesture always seemed to touch her heart. There was something very tender beneath the face this tough cowboy showed the world.

She busied herself in draining her cup and setting it aside, all the while indulging in a strange glow of contentment. Maybe it was the knowledge that it had been her discovery of the faded documents that had given this family a renewed sense of purpose. But she thought it was more than that. Her discovery, and the McCord family's excitement, had given her a sense of belonging. From the moment she'd entered this household, they had gone out of their way to make her feel welcome. But now, finally, she had allowed herself to open up to that welcome, and to believe that she deserved to be here.

For Riley, this was an amazing epiphany. Could it be

that she was finally coming out of the fog that had kept her mired in her own misery?

Her hands stilled. Or was this newly discovered feeling of belonging just a myth? One that could cause her to let down her guard and open the door to even more misery and danger?

Zane knelt beside the still little figure on the hearth. "I think your angel has gone to dreamland."

Riley pulled herself back from her thoughts and hurried across the room. "I'll take her up to bed now."

"I'll do that." Before she could bend toward Summer, Zane had the little girl in his arms. "You lead the way."

Riley called good night to the others before heading toward the stairs, with Zane behind her. At her suite she held the door and watched as Zane carried Summer to her bed.

While Riley undressed her daughter and pulled the covers over her, Zane studied the framed photos of Summer that adorned the walls of the hallway leading to the sitting room. "Did you take these?"

Riley nodded. "It's a passion. I didn't want to forget a single thing about Summer's early years. Each new discovery, from her first snowfall to her first Halloween pumpkin, was so precious. And I realized that she would never have those firsts again."

Zane patted the tiny video camera in his shirt pocket. "I'd know a little about that. I should warn you. I've been recording Summer interacting with the horses in the barn."

"Oh, Zane." Without thinking, Riley caught his arm. "I'd love to see them."

He looked down at her hand and wondered what she would think if she knew what her touch was doing to him. "I'll edit them and put them in some kind of order before I show you."

"I'd like that."

"And I like this." He closed his hand over hers.

"Don't, Zane."

He shot her a wicked grin. "Don't hold your hand?"

"Don't try to hand me some slick line. Don't whisper sweet things that are meaningless. Those may work with other women, but I have a built-in immunity."

"I see. Once burned…"

"Exactly. I'd be a fool to fall for a tired line."

"You don't strike me as a fool."

"Thank you." She started to turn away.

His hand tightened on hers, holding her still. "But I still like this." He glanced at their linked hands. "And that's no line."

"Zane…"

He touched a finger to her lips. "I get that you have to be careful. Having Summer is an awesome responsibility." He could feel her beginning to relax. "I didn't come up here to ravish the fair maiden."

That had her actually smiling.

"See there? Life doesn't have to be all high drama. Sometimes it's enough to just share a laugh, a smile…" He brushed his mouth over hers. "A kiss."

She drew back enough to look into his eyes. "You're very smooth, Zane McCord."

"Thank you. I try."

"But I still say it's all just a slick line, and you're just trying to see how long it takes to get me in the sack."

"Mind reader." At her quick hiss of breath he held up a hand. "Okay. Kidding. Listen, Riley, if I'd wanted quick, mindless sex, I'd be in the Fortune Saloon over in Gold Fever. There are half a dozen women who'd be more than happy to oblige any cowboy with a few bucks in his pocket."

She couldn't help laughing. "Now that sounds so very romantic. What's stopping you, cowboy?"

"A very serious-minded accountant who has me tied up in knots."

At his tone her smile faded. "I told you…"

"Sorry. I can't hear you." He dragged her close and covered her mouth with his in a kiss. There was nothing soft, or gentle, or tentative about this kiss. It was as hot, as hungry, as the look in his eyes. And as demanding.

She could do nothing more than hang on. When his hands moved along her back, heating her blood, she responded with a hunger, a fierceness of her own. She knew she shouldn't be indulging herself like this, but it was too late for recriminations. There would be plenty of them later, when she got back her brain. Right now, she couldn't hold a single coherent thought. All she could do was hold on to him while he continued kissing her with a depth of passion that had her blood heating, her bones melting, her entire world spinning out of control.

He changed the angle of the kiss and took it deeper. She responded by running her hands down his chest. Oh, the ripple of all that corded muscle made her fingertips tingle. She couldn't hold back the little purr of pleasure in her throat.

As the kiss spun on and on, she wrapped her arms around his waist and clung, afraid that at any moment her knees would buckle and she would drop like a dish-rag to the floor. But she was even more afraid that the kiss would end, and she would be left feeling cold and empty. And so she clung, and kissed him with a sense of sheer joy.

Here was a man who knew how to kiss a woman, making her feel absolutely cherished. His lips moved on hers with a thoroughness that had her sighing with the pure pleasure of it. He kissed her as though she were the finest of wines, the sweetest of confections. She could feel him drinking her in. Feasting on her. And she could do nothing more than offer him all he wanted. And more.

Just as her mouth softened to him, opened to him, he abruptly jerked away, as though yanked by an invisible chain.

She blinked to clear her vision.

He stepped back, keeping his hands at her shoulders, holding her body away from his.

She was grateful for his hands. Without them she wasn't sure she could remain upright without staggering. That kiss had completely rocked her world. She was already feeling lost without his mouth on hers. Without those strong arms around her.

"Sorry." The word was as gruff as the look on his face. "I'd better go."

"Yes, well..." Her throat was so constricted, she could barely get a word out.

She reached around him and opened the door. If he was going to pretend that nothing had just happened, she'd play along. In fact, it was probably better this way. They would both pretend this was nothing more than a moment of weakness that would never happen again.

"Good night, Zane."

His look burned over her, causing a rush of heat that had her holding tightly to the door.

"'Night, Riley."

Without another word he turned away and started down the stairs.

She watched until he reached the landing. Then, closing the door, she pressed her forehead to the cool wood and wondered at the way her poor heart was racing.

She'd been completely engaged in that kiss. Had felt a need so overpowering, she would have willingly invited him into her bed, and into her life. It shamed her to admit that, even now, knowing he was the one who'd found the strength to stop before they'd crossed the line, she wanted him. And she felt a terrible aching loss now that she was alone.

With her arms hugging herself she turned and stared at the empty room.

Wasn't this what she'd wanted? What she'd fought so hard for? A place of her own, where she and Summer were safe from the world, and completely alone? Why, then, did it suddenly feel all wrong?

"Damn you, Zane McCord. Damn you for turning my life upside down."

She stalked to her bedroom and began removing her clothes, angrily tossing them into a ball on a chair. When she was dressed in a sleep tee and drawstring pants, she walked to the window and stared out at the sky, where millions of stars winked in the darkness.

All those fine promises she'd made to herself. All the hard lessons she'd been forced to learn. And they fell by the wayside the minute Zane so much as touched her.

What was she going to do about this? With a sigh she plucked an accounting textbook from her nightstand and carried it to the other room, curling up in front of the fireplace. She couldn't think of a better way to shut down all these raging hormones than with a couple of chapters of financial planning, tax audits, and the rules for preparing profit-and-loss statements.

CHAPTER TEN

———◆———

The next morning Cal walked into the kitchen to find Jesse, Wyatt, and Zane hunched over the map, charting a path. He glanced at the backpacks and duffels in the corner of the room. "What's this? You three ready to take up the search?"

"Yeah," Jesse answered for all of them.

"This was kind of sudden, wasn't it?" Cal snagged a mug of coffee.

"Zane's idea." Jesse looked over. "But Wyatt and I agree it's time to get started, now that the snow's melted." Jesse gave a quick grin. "I'm dying to try out all our latest high-tech gadgets."

Cal glanced up. "Starting early, aren't you?"

"Yeah. No use wasting time." Wyatt helped himself to coffee. "And with the snow melted and calving over, we figure you can spare us for a week or so."

Zane studied the map, avoiding their eyes. After that

scene in Riley's suite, he knew he needed to put some distance between them. It was the only way he could be sure of keeping his hands off her. Living under the same roof was proving too much of a temptation. The thought of a week away seemed the perfect cooling-off time he needed.

He'd been trying to tell himself that he was doing all this to appease Cal. After all, he'd given his word that he would keep his distance. But this was more. Much more. He needed to work out for himself just how he was feeling about Riley. There was no denying the attraction. And though he tried to tell himself it was pure lust, last night had left him more than a little shaken by the feelings she'd stirred up in him. Feelings he hadn't believed himself capable of. He was beginning to entertain thoughts of love and family and happily-ever-after. Silly, he knew. Hadn't he seen what such things had done to his father? To him? And hadn't he vowed to never let himself get hurt that way? Yet here he was, thinking about things he had no right to.

"A week? No more?" Cal glanced from one to the other.

"Maybe two. But no more than that." Zane spoke this time for all three. "There's no sense just working piecemeal. We lose too much momentum. I thought maybe this time we'd take along enough provisions. You know, sort of like Aunt Cora's marathon painting sessions."

Cal shook his head, muttering almost to himself, "Just proves that insanity runs in the family."

That had them all laughing just as Cora walked in. "I'll have you know I heard that."

Cal could tell, by the warmth of her tone, that she

hadn't taken offense at his joke. Her sense of humor was just one of the many things he loved about her.

Seeing the gear, she smiled. "So. You three are finally getting back into the hunt."

Zane brushed a kiss over her cheek. "If it's springtime in Montana, it must be time to resume Coot's search for the family fortune."

She nodded, and it was obvious that she was in perfect agreement with her nephews.

When Riley walked into the kitchen trailed by her daughter, Zane felt the quick sexual tug, and he marveled that he'd been able to walk away from her last night. A minute more and he'd have stepped over the line for good.

Though he'd fully intended to treat her with indifference, it simply wasn't possible. While everyone around them was talking at once, he stood silently studying the way she looked, hair damp and curling around her face, a simple cotton shirt hugging her breasts, her long legs encased in narrow jeans that displayed that lean, taut body.

He could still feel the press of that body on his.

He wanted her. Right this minute, with the entire family standing around, and the lure of the treasure hunt fresh in his mind, he wanted to take her away somewhere and make mad passionate love while the rest of the world passed them by.

Wasn't that why he'd insisted on leaving today? As early as possible?

"Isn't that right, Zane?"

At Jesse's words he mentally shook off his thoughts and forced himself to join the conversation.

"Yeah. That's right." He dropped to one knee in front of Summer. "I hope, while I'm gone, you'll give Jimmy Eagle a hand in the barn."

"Will I help him muck the stalls?"

Zane chuckled. "I think you'd better leave that for the men. But you'd be a big help if you'd go out and assist Jimmy in giving the horses their treats."

"Okay. That will make Vanilla happy, too. How long will you be gone?"

He stood and saw Riley watching him a little too closely. He managed a casual shrug. "A week or two."

Seeing the look of stunned surprise in her eyes, he turned away. "We'd better eat and get on the road."

Dandy looked up from the coolers he'd packed with perishables. Meat. Cheese. Rolls and bread. "You guys want milk, or would you rather just have a case of longnecks?"

"Milk," Jesse said.

"Longnecks," Wyatt called at the same time.

They all burst into laughter.

"That answers that," Dandy muttered as he turned away, determined to cram everything he could into the coolers.

As they were sitting down to breakfast, Amy and Marilee walked into the room together, heads bent, voices low. As though making plans of their own.

"Jesse." Amy held out a hooded rain poncho. "You'd better take this along. If you don't, it's bound to pour rain for days."

He shot his wife a lopsided grin. "Are you saying that if I take it, we can count on sunny weather?"

"Absolutely. It's like washing your car. You know, the minute you get it dry and shiny, it's going to rain on your parade. If you have the right gear, you won't need it. But if you leave it behind, you're bound to wish you had it." She paused to kiss his cheek before tucking the slicker into his duffel.

"And Wyatt, I figured you'd want these." Marilee held out his mirrored sunglasses. "I found them on the hall table."

"Whew. Thanks, baby." He slipped them into his shirt pocket before filling his plate with three eggs and several strips of sizzling bacon. "Another reason to be glad I have a wife looking out for me."

His words weren't lost on the others, who couldn't wait to tease him.

"What'd you do before Marilee?" Cal asked.

"I stumbled around blindly, for the most part," he admitted with a grin.

That had the others laughing good-naturedly.

While they ate, they talked of nothing but the treasure hunt.

"Where are you planning on making camp?" Cal held the platter of eggs for Cora.

"Somewhere in the foothills of Treasure Chest." Jesse patted the cell phone in his pocket. "As soon as we set up camp, we'll call and let you know exactly where we are."

Zane held out the little pot of strawberry preserves to Summer and leaned close to whisper, "Want to try some of this?"

"Okay."

While Zane slathered strawberry preserves on her toast, she looked up at him with big eyes. "Will you sleep in a tent?"

"Yeah."

"Will you be cold?"

He smiled. "I have a sleeping bag. It'll keep me warm."

"Is it scary?"

"No more scary than being up in the hills with the wranglers."

"Will you see wolves or bears?"

"Maybe. But we have our rifles."

Her eyes grew bigger. "You wouldn't shoot them, would you?"

Dangerous ground, he realized. "Probably not. But if we fire a shot into the air, it should be enough to scare them off."

"Oh." She thought about that and nodded. "Do you miss being in the wilderness? Mama said you lived with wild horses."

"Mustangs." He looked over her head to where Riley was sitting quietly.

Their gazes met. Held. And he wondered just what he was seeing in her eyes. Was that sadness because he was leaving? Or was that just wishful thinking on his part?

All too soon the meal was over and Jesse and Wyatt were kissing their wives before taking up their gear.

Zane gathered Summer close and hugged her. "Bye, Summer. See you soon."

She surprised him by wrapping her chubby arms around his neck and kissing him on the cheek. He felt his heart melting.

When he stood, he found himself wanting, more than anything, to embrace Riley, too. Instead he merely touched a hand to her arm. Even that simple touch had his blood heating.

"Stay safe." His voice was gruff.

"You, too."

He turned away quickly and brushed a kiss to his aunt's cheek before shaking Cal's hand.

Without a backward glance he picked up his gear and headed outside to the waiting truck.

As the family gathered around on the back porch, the three cousins finished stuffing their equipment into the back of the truck before climbing inside. With Zane at the wheel, they took off.

Amy and Marilee blew kisses to their husbands.

Zane turned for a last glimpse of Riley. She was standing alongside Summer, holding the little girl's hand and watching as they drove away.

In the rearview mirror he saw the others begin to drift inside until Riley and her daughter were the only ones left.

It was the last view he had of her before he turned the truck sharply and they headed up into the hills.

"Okay." Jesse turned to Wyatt. "What's the plan?"

"Step one. Establish a campsite on ground high enough that we don't wake in the night flooded by rain or melting snow from the mountain."

At Wyatt's words, Jesse nodded. "Okay. Since you've been all over the world, I figure you know something about having a plan. But since Zane actually lived in the wilderness, I'm going to figure he has something in mind besides setting up a tent on high ground."

Zane chuckled. "Actually, I agree with Wyatt. High ground works. Also a supply of fresh water. So, we find a stream. And since we're inching toward Treasure Chest, I figure we'll drive to the foothills and something will present itself."

"And all that equipment in the back of the truck?" Jesse jerked a thumb.

"At camp we'll unload it and get started. I'll make a video record of everything, so there's no second-guessing later."

Wyatt pulled on his sunglasses. "I've got a really good feeling about this."

"Me, too." Jesse watched the countryside flow by outside the truck window. "I'm glad Amy packed that poncho. That's my good-luck charm against nasty weather."

The three shared a laugh as the truck climbed higher into the hills.

By noon the three cousins had set up camp in a grassy area in the foothills of Treasure Chest that afforded them a view of towering buttes on one side of them and a pine forest on the other.

As soon as the tent was secured and their supplies unloaded, they set out under a clear, cloudless sky, eager to test the expensive equipment that had been shipped over the winter. Now, finally, they would be free to indulge their love of high-tech gear while they fought to control the flutter of nervous anticipation that always surfaced when they were on the trail of the lost treasure.

"Coot would love this," Jesse breathed as he turned on the metal detector.

"Coot's loving all of it," Wyatt said emphatically.

"Amen to that." Zane stood a little away, video camera whirring, recording everything for posterity.

"Can't beat this weather." Zane returned to the campsite, barefoot and naked to the waist, a pair of faded denims riding low on his hips. His hair still glistened from his quick wash in the stream. He pulled on a sweatshirt before lounging with his back against a rock, his long legs stretched out to the heat of their campfire.

"Yeah. We really lucked out." Jesse sipped a beer. "I was afraid we'd run into flooding from the snowmelt, but so far it's been great."

After a day of hard work under a clear, cloudless sky, they were enjoying Dandy's spicy-hot chili and ice-cold longnecks while seated around a blazing fire.

Wyatt stared into the flames. "This is the time of day I miss Marilee the most."

Zane snorted. "That's what you said at noon. And again around three, when we uncovered that old box that turned out to be nothing more than tobacco."

"I really thought, for one minute, it was going to be the gold, and I wanted my wife to be with me when we opened it."

Zane and Jesse shared a grin.

"Tell the truth, cuz," Zane taunted. "You weren't ready to leave your bride for even one day."

"True enough." Wyatt sipped, then leaned his head back and fixed Zane with a look. "You, on the other hand, seemed awfully eager to get out of Dodge."

Jesse turned and joined in. "Yeah. I noticed that. One minute you're carrying a sleeping Summer up the stairs. You're gone way too long to be just tucking her in. The next you're downstairs, looking a little too flushed, and making plans to start the treasure hunt right away. I think, if you had your way, we'd have left last night instead of waiting until morning."

Zane took a long pull on his beer and held his silence.

"Come on, cuz," Wyatt prompted. "What's up between you and our pretty little bean counter? Did you two have a fight last night up in her room?"

"Don't be stupid."

"Ah." Wyatt drew out that single word on a slow breath. "I get it. Not a fight."

Seeing the way Zane's lips thinned, both men knew Wyatt had hit a nerve. It was all they needed to dig deeper.

Jesse winked at Wyatt before turning to Zane. "Hey. You getting in over your head, cuz?"

"Better be careful," Wyatt added. "If Cal finds out you're toying with the help, he'll have your hide."

"I'm not toying."

Zane's tone was entirely too angry.

That had Jesse and Wyatt exchanging knowing looks before Jesse said, "When a guy protests that loudly, you just know he's covering something up." His look sharpened. "You sleeping with Riley?"

"Hey." In an instant Zane was across the space that separated them, his hand at his cousin's throat, pulling him to his feet.

Jesse's beer dropped from his hand and fell, foaming, into the grass. His fingers dug into Zane's shoulder.

Like two bulls, they faced each other, eyes blazing.

"Cut it out." Though it took an effort, Wyatt managed to pull them apart before standing between them.

He fixed Zane with a look. "Are you?"

Zane's hand fisted at his side, but he managed to keep from throwing a punch.

He turned away and returned to his place by the fire. After an interminable length of time he said glumly, "No."

Jesse cupped a hand to his ear, grinning wickedly. "Huh? Speak up. I didn't hear you."

"You heard me." Zane tossed a log on the fire and watched it hiss and sputter before bursting into flame.

"I think that's a no." Wyatt walked around the fire to slap a hand on Zane's shoulder. "So that's what's troubling you, cuz. You're not sleeping with the lady." He waited a beat before adding, "But you'd like to."

"Yeah." Zane slumped against the fallen log that served as a backrest.

Wyatt pulled two cold longnecks from the cooler and handed one to Zane and one to Jesse before sitting back down across from them. "Now that wasn't so hard to say, was it?"

Zane blew out a breath.

"So this is a trial separation, to see whether or not you miss the lady?"

Zane shook his head. "This is my attempt to cool things down, so Cal doesn't have to nail my hide to the wall."

His quiet admission broke the ice and had his two cousins growing serious.

Jesse studied Zane more closely. "Riley doesn't strike me as someone who'd welcome a casual fling."

Zane's tone was harsher than he intended. "There's nothing casual about the way I feel."

"How do you feel?"

Zane took a long drink before leaning his head back to stare at the night sky. "I'm not sure. I mean, it's never been like this with anyone else. She's on my mind way too much. I feel tense, and edgy, and sometimes I just feel like I want to walk away and forget I ever met her." He glanced over. "That sounds crazy, doesn't it?"

"Yeah." Wyatt exchanged a look with Jesse. "Crazy in love."

At Zane's look of surprise he added, "My romance with Marilee wasn't all rose petals. There were a lot of thorns. But the truth is, I could no more walk away from her than I could stop breathing."

"Yeah." Zane fell silent and sipped his beer.

Jesse leaned back to study him. "The lady comes with baggage. How're you with that?"

Zane's head came up. "Summer?" His smile was quick. "What an amazing kid. I've never spent much time with kids before, and especially a little girl. But she's got it all going on. She's bright, and funny, and pretty much fearless. I wouldn't be surprised if I have her in the saddle and riding in a couple of months."

Jesse grinned. "I hope you realize that you just made noises like a proud papa."

Zane thought about that before giving a shake of his head. "I hadn't thought about it, but I guess I was bragging about her. I feel kind of...possessive about her." He shrugged and his smile widened. "The kid grows on you."

"Yeah." Jesse shot him a look. "Just like her mom is growing on you." He gave him a thumbs-up. "Don't worry, cuz. It happens to the best of us."

"Not to me." Zane's frown deepened.

"What's that supposed to mean?" Jesse asked.

"I don't believe in love and marriage." He held up a hand. "I know it's working for the two of you, but I'm not wired that way. I saw what it did to my dad. By the time he died, my mother had ripped his heart to shreds. She didn't give a care about his feelings or mine. I'm not about to set myself up for that kind of heartbreak."

Jesse and Wyatt exchanged a knowing look. As boys they'd heard the battles behind closed doors, and they had watched as their uncle finally caved in to the demands of a selfish wife, wrenching Zane away from the only home he'd ever known.

Jesse took a pull on his beer. "Give it some time, cuz. You'll work it out."

Wyatt shrugged. "Some people never do. But I'm putting my money on you to work your way through all the old baggage and put it behind you for the sake of love."

"Love?" Zane arched a brow. "Gee, thanks. I think."

Sensing his reluctance to continue the conversation, they managed to turn to their plans for the following day, the route they would take, and the equipment they would need.

Hours later, when Jesse and Wyatt were snoring, Zane sat alone by the hot coals and stared at the night sky, wondering why, even from so great a distance, he could see Riley's face as clearly as though she were right here beside him. And could almost smell her perfume.

Love? It didn't feel like love. In fact, he couldn't recall a time when he'd felt this conflicted or this miserable.

CHAPTER ELEVEN

———◆———

Are you sure you're up to this, Aunt Cora?" Amy led the way up the stairs to Coot's suite of rooms.

"Yes, dear. I'm so glad you and Marilee thought of it. With your men gone, it's the perfect time to tackle this." Cora paused in the doorway and looked around, as though expecting to see her brother seated in the chair in front of the fireplace, a cigar in his hand.

Tentatively she moved around the room, touching a finger to the wooden desk, running her hand over the heavy brown throw at the foot of the big bed.

"Everything is just as Coot left it."

"If you'd rather not change anything…," Amy began, but Cora stopped her with a hand in the air.

"I've put this off for far too long." She squared her shoulders, mentally girding herself for the battle of emotions she knew she would have to deal with.

"Where do you want these, Miss Cora?" Riley stood

in the doorway, arms laden with nested plastic storage tubs.

Behind her, little Summer carried a carton of plastic trash bags.

"Right over there will be fine." Cora gestured to a vacant spot in a corner of the room. "I believe we should tackle the closet first. Marilee, I'm grateful for the name of that charity in town that offers clothing to the needy. You'll see that they get Coot's things?"

"Yes'm." Marilee indicated the bed. "Why don't you let us set everything there, and you can go through the pockets and such before deciding what you want to donate, and what you'd like to keep."

"That sounds fine." Cora stood beside the bed and watched as the young women began taking shirts, pants, and jackets from the closet, removing them from their hangers and spreading them out on the bed.

Cora went through each item, checking for anything Coot might have left in the pockets, and checking for rips and tears before sorting them into a pile for the plastic bags, which would go to charity, and a pile for the plastic tubs, if there were things Cora wanted to store.

"So many things." After an hour of concentrated work, Cora sank down on the edge of the bed. "Coot was such a simple man, with simple tastes. Yet look at the number of hats and boots and clothes."

"Don't forget," Amy said gently. "This was the accumulation of a lifetime, Aunt Cora."

"Yes, I know. Still…" She sighed and reached for yet another shirt. Feeling the softness of the fabric, she hugged it to herself and marveled at the fact that, after all this time, she fancied that she could still smell Coot in the folds. "I believe I'll keep this one for myself."

The women exchanged smiles. Cora's love for her brother's clothes was legendary.

Little Summer sat on the floor at Cora's feet, arranging the boots into neat pairs, after having set half a dozen wide-brimmed hats on the other side of the bed.

Seeing her, Cora couldn't help but smile. "I used to do that for my father when I was your age, honey. Every Sunday evening my daddy would bring in his boots and the polish and rag, and he and I would sit together in front of the fire and polish all his boots for the coming week. Oh, my, some of them would be so dirty. Mud-spattered, rain-soaked, scratched and torn from brambles or barbed wire. But when we lined them up by the fireplace, after an hour of cleaning and polishing, they would shine like new."

She touched a hand to her heart. "I haven't thought about that in years. I always loved working alongside my father. It was just a little ritual, but because we did it together, it was always special to me."

She saw the little girl watching her and realized that the others had stopped work to listen.

Across the room, Riley felt the sudden knife of pain to her heart, as the fact was brought home to her once again that Summer would never have precious memories with her daddy. She'd thought of it so many times since Summer's birth, but Cora's memory made it all the more poignant. All the simple little things that other young girls shared with their fathers were being denied her daughter.

To hide her emotions, she turned to stare out the window.

Seeing her, Cora understood what effect her words had had on the young woman. On impulse she got to her feet and crossed the room to stand beside Riley, laying a hand on her shoulder.

"I wish you could have known my brother. He loved looking at this land, and knowing that, for as far as the eye could see, it was all his."

Riley cleared her throat, swallowing back the lump. "It's hard to conceive of owning this much land. It's so much bigger and grander than I could ever imagine."

"It is, isn't it? When I was young and impulsive, I traveled across Europe, studying art and living in so many glamorous cities. Rome. Paris. London. Madrid. I thought of myself as sophisticated." She laughed softly. "So very continental, with a new hair color and style to suit my moods, and a new beau in every town." She sobered. "And then, after a particularly difficult time in my life, with my dreams battered along with my heart, I phoned my brother in tears. Like a child I babbled on about the handsome, very powerful French art critic who had won my heart. For months we'd been inseparable, planning a future together. I'd been deliriously happy, dreaming of a life with a man who would understand my passion, and nurture my talent. Imagine my heartache when I realized that it was all a game to him. After being charmed into his bed, I learned that he had a wife and child, and I was merely one of a very long list of rather-famous women he'd taken great pleasure in seducing and then abandoning. I felt so betrayed. So utterly foolish and useless. How could I not have recognized him for the shallow, unfeeling creature he was? But I'd been blinded by his exquisite chateau, his worldly friends, his sophisticated lifestyle." She gave a shake of her head. "I expected Coot to curse the man, and to remind me that I was still, after all, an artist of some repute. Instead he said simply, 'It's time to come home to Montana, Cora.'"

Riley's eyes went wide. "Did you?"

Cora nodded. "I came home feeling shattered. I wanted nothing to do with my art. For months I never picked up a brush or looked at a blank canvas. All I did was ride by horseback into the countryside. Day after day I rode about, sweating in the sunlight, shivering in the night air. And one day I looked around at the sun-washed landscape, at the towering buttes and endless fields of wildflowers, at the exquisite beauty that was all around me, and it struck me that I absolutely had to make it come alive on canvas."

Riley was as caught up in the narrative as Cora. "It happened just like that?"

"Just like that. One minute I was wallowing in misery and self-pity. The next I was filled with the most burning ambition I'd ever known. Not even the awe-inspiring art capitals of the world had made me burn with such zeal. It was as if some miraculous hand had touched my soul. And when Coot found me, days later, working feverishly in my room filling canvas after canvas with the images in my mind, he said simply, 'I knew this land would restore you.'" Cora sighed. "And so it has."

"Oh, Miss Cora." Riley felt her eyes fill. "I'm so happy for you. And happy for all of us who love your work."

Cora sandwiched the young woman's hands between hers, clasping them firmly. "It's my wish for you, too, dear. At one time or another we've all had our dreams trampled. Give this land a chance to work its magic."

When she walked away to resume her work, Riley remained at the window, her throat clogged with unshed tears. She was so grateful to this dear lady for sharing her story. Maybe everyone had secrets they were afraid to share with even their closest friends. Yet, in sharing, Cora McCord had revealed her great strength. She had risen above a painful episode in her past to carve a rewarding life for herself.

Riley's thoughts drifted to Zane, somewhere in that vast wilderness, searching for the impossible.

Maybe, she thought, they were all searching for the impossible. But at least, she realized, glancing at Cora across the room, one very lucky person had already found it.

"Time for lunch, ladies." Dandy carried a tray laden with sandwiches and tea, and a little pitcher of milk for Summer. Under a domed glass was a platter of fruit slices and a variety of cheese wedges and biscuits.

He set up their meal on a round table he'd positioned in front of the fireplace. From various parts of the suite he found enough chairs for all of them.

By the time he left, the four women and little girl were happily seated by the fire, enjoying a break from their chore.

Marilee glanced at the filled bags and containers across the room. "We've made quite a dent in that closet, Aunt Cora."

"Indeed. I wouldn't have believed Coot had so many clothes if I hadn't seen it myself. I believe by tomorrow we'll be ready to start on his desk."

The others looked at the hand-carved wooden desk,

with its deep drawers and dozens of compartments, and knew it would take days to wade through everything in there. But at least, except for a few misty moments, Cora had managed to keep her composure in the midst of such an emotional journey.

They all hoped, once the personal items in Coot's closet were sorted, the worst of the job would be behind them and they could sail through the rest of his rooms in good time.

Amy poured tea and passed it around. "Did this suite belong to your parents when they were alive, Aunt Cora?"

"Oh, no, dear." Cora sipped her tea. "They had their rooms downstairs, where Cal's office is now. Coot added this upper wing later. He wanted a desk where he could gather his private papers, just as he wanted a small parlor off this room where he could sit and gather his thoughts. He always said, after his daily chores were complete, he liked being high enough to see out over the land."

"I can see why." Marilee pointed to the big high windows and the vista spread out beyond. "What a view he had."

"Like a king in his castle," Amy said with a laugh.

"Not at all." Cora looked around. "Coot never thought of himself as the one in charge of all this. He always said this land was his master. He was its servant."

"Your brother was ahead of his time," Riley remarked.

When the others looked at her, she flushed. "Today, everyone talks about being good stewards of our natural resources. I'm sure that wasn't something talked about when Coot started out ranching. But it sounds as though that's exactly what he was."

Cora nodded. "I never thought about it that way, but you're right, dear. Coot felt a real responsibility to leave this land as he'd found it for his grandsons and for theirs."

"Not just the land, but the fortune as well." Amy propped her elbows on the table and rested her chin on her hands. "I wonder how they're doing on their search."

Cora drained her tea and smiled. "I'm betting they're having as grand a time in the wilderness as we're having right here. And all because we're sharing it with people we love. Now," she said, getting to her feet, "it's time we got back to work."

"I believe that's the last of the clothes." Cora dropped another scrap of paper on Coot's desktop, already littered with the papers she had found in the pockets of his shirts and pants. Most were scraps of his primitive drawings. One had even been found in the toe of his boot. But none of them made any sense, and though they were important to Cora for their sentimental value, they wouldn't add any vital information to the search for the gold.

"What about Coot's hats?" Amy asked.

Cora turned toward the bed, and all of them paused to stare at the sight of little Summer, sound asleep, surrounded by a jumble of wide-brimmed Western hats.

"Some people just know how to relax," Cora remarked. "After the day we've put in, I wouldn't mind joining her."

The rest of them chuckled.

When Riley walked over, intent on carrying her daughter to their rooms, Cora stopped her. "Let her be, dear. If she can sleep through all the laughter of this past hour, she can sleep through anything."

"You're right." Riley covered her daughter with a throw and returned her attention to cleaning the closet.

Within the hour the floor and the shelves had been thoroughly emptied and cleaned, leaving the closet smelling of soap and furniture polish.

The four women stood back, enjoying the satisfaction of a job well done. A dozen garbage bags held clothes that would be donated to charity. A single plastic tub held the few articles of clothing that Cora had been unable to part with. A cowhide parka that Coot had worn for years. A couple of soft shirts that Cora would claim as her own. A pair of bib overalls suitable to wear for painting. And Coot's favorite, hand-tooled leather boots, made for him by Jimmy Eagle's wife twenty years earlier.

Just as they made ready to haul the containers down the stairs, Summer awoke from her nap.

Sitting up, she rubbed her eyes and slid from the bed. "I want to help."

"You've been a grand help, dear." Cora handed the little girl the carton of unused garbage bags. "You may return these to Dandy," she said. "And be sure to thank him."

"I will." Feeling useful, Summer danced ahead of them down the staircase.

Behind her, the others made numerous trips up and down the stairs, until everything had been disposed of.

The days that followed found the four women back in Coot's rooms, tackling cupboards, closets, dressers, and his desk, which contained another monster stash of his worldly goods. The wooden desk was at least eight feet wide and deep enough to contain dozens of cubicles and drawers, all filled to the brim with papers, ledgers, note-books, and mementos of a life well-lived.

Because every item was personal, it fell to Cora alone to make the decision to keep or toss. The others simply carted garbage bags and plastic tubs from the corner of the room to the desk, and from there to the mudroom downstairs or to Cora's suite of rooms across the hall.

At least every minute or so Cora would exclaim over another discovery.

"Oh, my. I can't believe he saved this silly caricature of me drawn by a street artist when I was in Rome."

They would all gather around her to look, to laugh, to appreciate.

"Oh. Papa's old belt buckle."

The ornately engraved silver winked in the sunlight.

On a sigh, "Our mother's locket."

The women stood around her chair to admire the tiny photos of a prim woman in a long gown and a tall, weath-ered man with a bushy beard.

A whispered "Oh, Coot," as Cora uncovered a letter she'd written to him from Paris, carefully folded and in its original envelope, brought them back to watch and listen as she read aloud to them.

When she found something tucked into the farthest corner of a drawer, she felt the tears well up and spill over down her cheeks.

"What is it, Aunt Cora?"

At Amy's question, the others gathered around to offer their consolation.

"Just an old cigar box." Cora was holding a long, nar-row wooden box, dull with age, the engraving on the lid barely legible.

Taking a magnifying glass from the top of the desk, she held it over the engraved words and read aloud, " 'To my only true friend.' "

She read further and added, "The initials C.R."

"Cal Randall," Amy said.

Cora opened the lid and stared at the faded photograph inside of two handsome young cowboys in leather chaps, boots, and vests, each holding a wide-brimmed hat while leaning against the rails of a corral. Their eyes stared unblinking at the camera, their lips split in unmistakably cocky grins.

"Oh, just look at them." Cora couldn't contain her tears.

Amy smiled. "I remember Coot looking just like this when I was little."

Marilee nodded. "I only met him a couple of years ago when I settled into Gold Fever. By then his hair was gray, but those eyes were always sparkling with mischief."

"That's my brother." Cora managed to smile through her tears.

Riley studied the photograph carefully, glad for a chance to see the man she'd never met. It was easy to see his grandsons in his face.

But it wasn't Coot's image that held her attention. One glance at Cal and she couldn't hold back a sigh. "Now that's one handsome cowboy." She glanced over at Cora. "Cal hasn't changed a bit. He's still the best-looking man around."

"Considering the competition on this ranch, especially from the McCord men," Marilee said with a laugh, "that's a really high compliment."

"But it's true." Riley glanced at Amy for confirmation. "He's just a serious hunk."

"Absolutely." Amy gave a wolf whistle for emphasis, causing the others to break out into gales of laughter.

Riley stopped laughing long enough to ask, "Don't you agree, Miss Cora?"

When she handed the picture back to Cora, the older woman stared at it for long, silent minutes After touching a handkerchief to her eyes she pressed the photograph to her chest for long minutes, her breathing shallow, her lips quivering until, realizing that the others were watching, she became suddenly busy tucking it into the box and setting the wooden box atop the desk. "Since Cal gave this to Coot all those years ago, it only seems right that I should give it back to him. I have the feeling he'll treasure it just as he treasured Coot's friendship all these years."

Though these days had been filled with emotion, none of the women had ever seen Cora's passion this raw, or so close to the surface.

Around the room the conversation was muted as they returned to the job at hand.

CHAPTER TWELVE

"Oh, Aunt Cora. Just look at this." Amy stared around Coot's old suite of rooms. "It's hard to believe this is the same place."

Cora nodded as the others picked up the last of the cleaning supplies and stood back to admire their work.

After nearly two weeks, the wooden floors, once scratched and dingy from neglect, had now been polished to a high shine. The draperies at the windows had been removed, allowing sunlight to stream in and fill the rooms with light. The fireplaces had been scrubbed of soot, leaving the stone, mined from Treasure Chest Mountain, glinting with imbedded flecks of silvery and bronze mineral deposits that hadn't been visible for years.

They had stripped the bed, replacing the heavy comforter and throw with ivory-striped sheets and pillowcases and a russet duvet that picked up the coppery glints in the fireplace surround.

"It's funny." Cora ran a hand over the now empty desk. "Even though this suite of rooms has been stripped of Coot's belongings, I can still feel his presence here."

"That's as it should be, Aunt Cora." Marilee paused to lay a hand on the older woman's shoulder. "To you, it will always be your brother's ranch, his home, his rooms. But it's all yours, too, and I think it's good that you're able to move on."

Cora touched a hand to the young woman's cheek. "It is good, isn't it?"

Around the room the others nodded in agreement.

"I wasn't sure I'd be up to this. But now I'm so glad I had all of you to share the work. Thank you for suggesting that we do this together."

With a deep sigh Cora turned away. "I just hope that Cal will be able to move in now and make this his."

"Why is that so important to you, Miss Cora?" Riley asked.

"Cal has loved this ranch for so many years, caring for it as though it were his own. But he has always held back doing things his way, in deference to Coot, even continuing to sleep in the bunkhouse rather than move into the main house. Now, I truly believe that it's time for him to put his own brand on this place. My great-nephews respect Cal. He's as much a father to them as their own fathers were. I think they want Cal to step up and take charge, but they don't quite know how to say so."

"You're an observant woman, Miss Cora." Riley dropped an arm around her little girl, who was holding a dustcloth. "That probably comes from being an artist."

"I suppose so." Cora gave a shake of her head. "But

only insofar as others are concerned. When it comes to my own life, I've never had a clue."

"That's true of most of us," Marilee said with a laugh. She turned to the others. "Now, I say we've earned an afternoon off. Our work here is done. I don't know about the rest of you, but I'm going to take a very long bath before dinner."

"Oh, that sounds heavenly." Amy started out behind her.

"Come on, Summer." Riley caught her daughter's hand. "You can grab a nap while I soak in the tub."

When they left, Cora remained behind, walking from the bedroom to the sitting room, pausing to stare around, as though absorbing her brother into every pore of her being. For she knew that when she walked out and closed the door, she was also closing the door on an era.

It was a bittersweet moment for her as she steeped herself in memories of a time that would never come again.

The big ranch house rang with masculine voices and laughter as the three cousins returned from their trek to the wilderness.

Doors upstairs were flung open and the women hurried downstairs to greet their men.

Because Summer was napping, Riley opened the door to her suite and stood gripping her hands together, drinking in the sight of the bearded man walking toward her.

"You're back." Her voice sounded a bit too breathy.

Zane stopped dead in his tracks to stare. The woman facing him was even better than the image he'd carried in his mind. Dark hair soft and curling around her shoulders. A summery shirt and stonewashed denims accentuating her feminine curves. And a face wreathed in smiles.

She was so pretty, she nearly took his breath away.

When he was able to compose himself, he burst into laughter. "Why do you always see me at my worst?" He glanced down at himself, then over at her. "Here you are, looking like you've spent the day at a spa, and I look like some kind of wild mountain man." He sniffed. "And smell like one, too."

"I think you look…" *Wonderful* came to mind. She caught herself in time and added lamely, "…just fine."

"As long as you don't get too close to me." He was about to move on when Summer slipped out of bed and came racing to the door.

"Oh, boy. You're home." Without waiting for his response she threw herself against his leg and clung. "You were gone too long."

Zane was so startled by the rush of emotions that engulfed him, he had to take a minute to find his brain. He bent down and scooped her up into his arms.

Breathing her in, he muttered, "Yeah. Way too long. But I'm home now."

"Are you going away again?"

"Probably. But I'll always come back."

"Promise?"

"I promise."

"Good. Mama and I missed you."

"I missed both of you, too." He glanced over her head and thought he detected tears in Riley's eyes. When he looked again, she'd blinked, and he wasn't certain just what he'd seen.

He set Summer on her feet. When he straightened, he winked at her. "I'm going to shave and shower now. But when I come down for dinner, I'd like to hear just how much you and your mama missed me."

"We missed you a whole lot." She spread her arms wide. "At least this much. Didn't we, Mama?" Without waiting for a response she added, "Maybe more."

"That much?" He threw back his head and roared with laughter. "I've never been missed that much before." He tipped his hat. "I'll see you ladies downstairs."

As he walked away, he thought how wonderful it was to be home. And to have somebody who'd missed him.

Dinner was so festive, it felt like a holiday. The table groaned under the platters of whole roasted chickens and mounds of whipped potatoes, gravy, tiny peas from the garden, and biscuits so light they melted in the mouth.

Dandy had made a salad of garden lettuce, orange slices, walnuts, and a sour-cream dressing that tasted like heaven.

Cal, fresh from a week in the high country with the wranglers, remarked that his timing couldn't have been better. Not only did he get to hear about the fortune hunt firsthand, but he got to enjoy a feast instead of a cold meal in the saddle while riding herd on the cattle.

The men, freshly showered and shaved, were eager to relate their adventures in the wilderness.

"Did you see any bears?" Summer asked.

"We did. And coyotes. And lots of deer and elk. And we heard a mountain lion one night, though we never spotted it."

Her eyes got big. "A lion?"

"Well, not exactly. But a really big cat," Zane said with a straight face.

"What about the gold?" Amy looked into Jesse's eyes.

The two were sitting so close together, Zane noted, that they were practically sharing a single chair.

He felt a quick rush of jealousy and glanced at Wyatt, who was smiling down into Marilee's eyes with a smug look. The two had been late coming to dinner, and everyone knew why.

"We didn't find the fortune." Jesse looked around the table. "But we're convinced we're on the right track."

"Why?" Cal looked up quickly.

Wyatt helped himself to more potatoes. "We found places where Coot had been digging. What's more, we found a grouping of rocks that were placed in a precise pattern to form an arrow pointing toward Treasure Chest."

"Couldn't they have been put there by anybody, for any reason?" Marilee asked.

"They could have. But when we came across it, the three of us all felt strongly that the rocks had been left there by Coot."

"Now what?" Cora asked.

"We plan on heading back up there as soon as we get caught up with ranch chores."

Cal sat back, grinning. "Glad you're taking the chores into account. Still…" He chose his words carefully. "I think you're right about those stones being put there by Coot. He and I have been doing that for thirty years or more to mark something important. The weather here in Montana can change awfully fast, but it would take a heap of weather to rearrange a pile of stones."

Zane, Wyatt, and Jesse exchanged wide grins.

"Thanks, Cal." Zane spoke for all of them. "We figured if anybody would know, it was you."

At Dandy's suggestion that they take their coffee and dessert in the great room, their conversation continued as they settled themselves in front of the fire.

"We found lots of old stuff buried in the sand. Rusted prospector's picks and shovels. Old boots. Tobacco tins." Jesse stretched out his long legs toward the warmth of the blazing logs, keeping an arm firmly around his wife. "Tomorrow we'll show you some of it. We stashed most of it in the back of the truck."

Cal smiled. "We've got so much of that stuff set aside on shelves in the barn, we could open a miners' museum."

"Not a bad idea." Wyatt drew Marilee close. "With the McCord nuggets as the centerpiece, we'd probably get lots of attention."

"With the McCord gold we could build a monument of marble and hire our own curator." Zane chuckled. "In Paris."

That had everyone laughing.

Cora, who had remained silent throughout most of the meal, accepted a cup of coffee from Dandy and sipped before turning to Cal. "I'm glad we have you... all our men back home," she corrected. "The house was so empty without you." She waited a beat before adding, "Speaking of empty, the girls and I tackled Coot's rooms while you were gone. The family charity in town now has dozens of pairs of pants and shirts and parkas, not to mention hats and boots for the needy."

Cal lifted his cup in a salute. "That's mighty fine, Cora. It can't have been easy for you."

"Actually, it wasn't all that hard to do, once I got started. The hardest part was making up my mind to do it. After that, with the help of all my girls here, we just sailed through it. And now, it's like a completely new suite of rooms. Just waiting for someone to take it over."

They fell silent as Dandy wheeled in a serving cart laden with a huge chocolate cake. While Dandy cut the cake, Amy disengaged herself from Jesse's arms long enough to add a dollop of ice cream to each of the slices before passing them around.

Wyatt took a first bite and closed his eyes. "Now this is worth coming home to." He offered a bite to Marilee. "Not that you weren't enough, babe. But this is just"—he winked—"icing on the cake."

That had everyone grinning.

When at last they'd eaten their fill and were sipping second cups of coffee, Cal looked over at Cora. "I'm thinking, since you went to all the work of cleaning out Coot's rooms, that you're hoping I'll move in."

"That was my plan." Cora's eyes were shining.

"I'll give it some thought." He held up a hand. "But not right now."

"You can move in tomorrow, Cal."

He shook his head. "No time to pack up my gear. I'm probably heading back up to the hills first thing tomorrow. I just came home to sign some papers." He glanced at Riley. "I got a call from the firm that they need them faxed as soon as possible."

She nodded. "They really wanted the government forms signed days ago. I told them this is a working ranch, and you'd get to them when you could."

He grinned. "Good for you. It's nice to have you watching my back, Riley."

She returned his smile. "Just doing my job."

"Well then." He stood. "Why don't I sign them now, so I can get on the trail first thing tomorrow?"

Jesse chuckled as Cal and Riley headed toward her office. To Cal's back he called, "Knowing the hours you put in with the herds, you probably won't have time to move into Coot's rooms until next winter."

"At least I know it's all ready for me," Cal called over his shoulder.

Cora watched him leave and sat back while the others caught up on all they'd accomplished in the past week. Even if Cal wasn't ready to move into the big house just yet, she was content in the knowledge that her men were all home, at least for the night.

As expected, everyone seemed eager to turn in early.

Jesse and Amy were the first to say good night, followed by Wyatt and Marilee.

Zane nodded toward Summer, asleep, as usual, on the rug in front of the fire. "She made a noble effort to stay awake."

Riley smiled. "She was so happy to see... all of you."

He crossed to the hearth and lifted the little girl easily in his arms. She stirred enough to wrap her arms around his neck and snuggle her face against his chest.

When he turned, Cora and Cal both got to their feet.

"Well, I'll…" Cora started to turn away, but Cal's hand on her shoulder stopped her.

She turned back. "What is it, Cal?"

"I just want to thank you for going to all that trouble with Coot's rooms."

"It's long overdue."

"I guess. But I know it had to be hard for you."

"It was an opportunity to say good-bye. I had a chance to see a lot of the things that Coot considered important in his life." She thought about the cigar box and the photograph. "I left a few things there for you. Things I thought you'd like to keep."

"I'll be sure to look them over when I get more time." He bent close and brushed a quick kiss on her cheek. "Good night, Cora."

"'Night, Cal." With a hand on her cheek she watched him walk from the room. Then, with a quick good night to Riley and Zane, she hurried up the stairs.

Zane climbed the stairs slowly, with Summer still asleep in his arms. Riley followed.

When they reached her suite, she held the door while Zane deposited Summer on her bed.

Minutes later Riley walked from her daughter's bedroom. "She didn't even move."

"I guess that's what they mean by 'sleeping like a baby.'"

"Yeah." She remained several paces away, her hands twisting and untwisting at her waist.

"Was she telling the truth earlier?"

Riley arched a brow.

"She said you both missed me."

Riley swallowed. "Summer talked about you constantly. And asked every morning when you were coming back."

"And her mama?"

Riley looked down. "I...missed you, too."

"Thank heaven." He took a step toward her and saw her head come up sharply. "I had a great time with Jesse and Wyatt. It was a good experience for the three of us. And in truth, I can't wait to continue the hunt for the treasure. I have a good feeling about it. But I missed you and Summer. More than I expected to."

"Zane..." She was shaking her head.

"I know." He put a hand on her arm. Just a touch, but he felt the rush of heat and was shaken by it. "But I'm not going to deny the truth. I thought about you. A lot."

"I...thought about you, too. More than I wanted to." Her smile trembled.

"What'll we do about this?"

"Nothing." She said it firmly, as though she'd had plenty of time to rehearse.

"Okay."

She stared into his eyes and saw the glint of humor there.

He shrugged. "I'm trying to be agreeable." His mouth curved into a hint of a smile. "Is it working?"

"It is."

"Good. Now, about that good-night kiss."

"What good-night kiss?"

"This one." His hand snaked out, dragging her into his arms.

Without a word he dipped his head and covered her mouth with his.

She didn't resist. Instead, as if controlled by some unseen force, her arms slid around his neck and she was as fully engaged in the kiss as he was.

"Oh, now this was what I wanted. Just this." He brushed kisses over her upturned face, kissing her eyes, her nose, the corner of her mouth. "I was starting to feel very jealous, watching the way Amy and Marilee were falling all over my cousins. It's nice to know I have my very own welcome committee."

Just as suddenly Riley pushed free of his arms.

"Is it something I said?" Though he was trying for a light touch, the frustration was evident in his tone.

"I can't do this, Zane. I won't play house. You have to leave."

He could see the nerves, could hear the near panic in her voice.

He stood a moment longer, watching the way she struggled to hold herself together. He didn't know what he would do if she fell apart. If she started to cry . . .

"Good night, Riley."

He turned and walked from the room. Before he could say a word the door closed, and he heard the sound of the latch being turned.

Seething with frustration, he climbed the stairs to his own suite. Once inside he kicked off his boots and tore off his shirt, tossing them into the corner with a muttered oath.

He strode to the window and stared out at the peaks of the mountain in the distance, illuminated by moonlight. Did she simply have no feelings for him? Or was she, like him, feeling way too much, and fighting every bit as hard as he was to keep it all under control?

In the small hours of the night, when he finally fell asleep, he had no answers.

All that time in the wilderness, and it hadn't helped to cool a thing. Just hours home and he was right back where he'd started.

So damned hot for her he couldn't think straight.

CHAPTER THIRTEEN

———◆———

Cal trudged in from his morning chores in the barn, depositing his wide-brimmed hat and jacket on a hook by the door and then scraping his boots and washing his hands at the big sink.

In the kitchen he greeted the others before wrapping his hands around a steaming mug of coffee. "Got a call from Fuller up on the north range. Just as I figured, I'll be heading up in about an hour." He glanced toward Jesse. "You free to head into town?"

Jesse shook his head. "Wyatt and I promised to join the wranglers in the south meadow."

"How about you, Zane?" Cal turned to where Zane and Jimmy Eagle were helping themselves to tall glasses of orange juice.

"Sure. I've got time." Zane's attention shifted to the doorway when Riley and Summer walked in.

"Good morning." Riley was careful to direct her

greeting at everyone, even though she was aware of only one person in the room.

She could feel Zane's gaze riveted on her.

Amy looked up from the table. "'Morning. Summer, did you tell your mama what we're doing today?"

The little girl's eyes went wide. "Miss Amy, it's a surprise. We aren't 'posed to tell anybody."

"Oh." Amy covered her mouth with her hand, as much to hide the grin as to convey her dismay. "What was I thinking?"

Riley paused. "What's this about?"

"Nothing, Mama." Summer's eyes danced with unconcealed joy. "Miss Amy and I are making something, but you can't know what it is."

"Oh." Riley snagged a cup of coffee, then thought better of it and added a glass of juice for her daughter before taking her place at the table.

Zane pulled out the chair beside her. "I just thought of something. You haven't taken a day off since you started."

Riley shrugged. "I don't need a day off."

"Everybody needs a break from work now and then." He glanced at Cal. "As long as Summer is going to be busy with Amy, why don't I take Riley to town with me? That way she can shop for anything personal she and Summer might need, and then we'll have lunch at the Fortune Saloon."

Riley was already shaking her head. "We don't need anything."

Cal ignored her protest. "I think that's a fine idea." When she opened her mouth to say more, he held up a hand. "Even the toughest wranglers get burned out if they don't take some time away from the cattle. You've been going full speed ahead since you arrived. I say go when you have the chance. You may not get it again for a long time. Besides, this weather is just too pretty to spend the day indoors."

"That's true." Riley thought about that for a moment. "I guess there are a few things Summer and I could use."

"There you are." Zane shot her a smug smile. "We'll leave in about an hour." He turned to Summer. "You sure you don't want to go with us?"

The little girl stared at Amy across the table. "I'd rather stay with Miss Amy, and we can make our surprise."

Riley shot her daughter a look. "Miss Amy doesn't have the whole day to—"

Amy interrupted. "I'm flattered that you'd like to stay with me. I think it's perfect." She glanced at Riley. "Jesse and Wyatt are heading up to the south meadow. I have the day to myself, and I can't think of anything I'd enjoy more than working with Summer on our surprise. So the two of you can take your time. We'll be too busy to miss you."

While Dandy served a breakfast of eggs and pancakes, Riley forced herself to relax. "If you really don't mind."

"I insist," Amy said firmly.

"All right." Riley dug into her meal, and decided to simply enjoy the freedom. It had been a very long time since she'd had a day to herself.

"Bye, honey." Riley leaned out the window of the ranch truck. "You be good for Miss Amy."

"I will, Mama." As Zane put the truck in gear, Summer skipped up the back porch steps beside her teacher.

The two waved before disappearing inside.

As they drove along the dusty driveway that led to the highway, Riley left the window open, enjoying the fresh spring breeze.

Zane glanced over. "Did you get a chance to see the town when you first got here?"

"Not really. I was so busy searching for Delia Cowling's place, I wasn't even aware of what the town looked like." She turned to him. "Maybe I'll look up Delia while I'm there. She made us feel really welcome."

"I'm glad. If you'd have met her earlier, you wouldn't have had much good to say about her."

"You said she's changed. What happened?"

He shrugged. "A long story. Her brother was involved in some fraud, and he died at the hands of our deputy, who was the mastermind of the scheme. When our family extended our sympathy, she opened up to us about the pain of having loved and lost our grandfather, and now she's like one of the family."

Riley's eyes widened. "Lost love. Bank fraud. I never expected to hear about something like that in a town as small as Gold Fever."

Zane gave a short laugh. "Don't kid yourself. Passion and crime don't happen only in big cities, Riley. You can find broken hearts and bad guys anywhere."

She fell silent, staring out the window at the pretty blanket of vegetation that had emerged from beneath the snow. The air was perfumed with the smell of fresh sagebrush. The countryside was carpeted with brilliantly colored wildflowers.

Zane itched to catch a handful of dark hair drifting on the breeze. He closed his hand into a fist. "You're awfully quiet."

"Just enjoying the view."

"Me, too."

At the change in his tone she glanced over to see him watching her. "Montana, at least what I've seen of it, is really beautiful."

"It doesn't hold a candle to what I'm seeing."

"Zane…"

"Okay. I get it. Keep it impersonal." He held up a hand. "Tell me about Philadelphia."

"A whole lot of city streets and a whole lot of traffic. Neither of which I miss at all."

He smiled. "Why Montana?"

She shrugged. "Why not? It was new and unique, and as far away as I could get."

"I'm betting the distance was the real motivator."

She looked away, not liking where this was headed. "Tell me about Gold Fever. What do you like about it?"

"Not much." He chuckled. "Only kidding. To an outsider, as towns go, if you blink, you miss it."

They shared a laugh.

"And to an insider like you and your cousins?"

He sobered. "It hasn't changed much since I was a kid. They've added a medical clinic, and a high school. There's a developer trying to buy up ranchland to build some houses. But most of the businesses have been here for years. And the folks are like folks anywhere. Some nice, others not so much."

She smiled. "That's interesting. So everybody knows everybody else?"

"Just about. That can be good or bad, depending on how much of your business you want them to know. But they're neighbors. If you can't pay your bills, they'll carry you. And if there's a sickness in your family, they'll do whatever they can to ease your burden until you're back on your feet. And if you're in trouble, they'll do what they can to help."

As they rolled into town, Riley studied it with a new awareness, trying to see it through Zane's eyes.

"It has to be comforting to know that so many good people are looking out for you."

"And discussing every little bit of your most personal life, whether you like it or not." He parked in front of a big brick building. "This is Orley Peterson's grain and feed store. I'll give Cal's list to Orley and leave the truck here. When we're ready to head home, he'll have the back filled with Cal's supplies."

"And nobody would be tempted to steal it before you drive home?"

Zane laughed. "I'd like to see somebody try. First, there's the brand on the door. Everybody knows this truck belongs to the Lost Nugget Ranch, and they know every wrangler who ought to be driving one of our vehicles. Then there's the fact that a potential thief would have to answer to Orley. He's no giant, but he's as wide as he is tall, and it's all muscle from lugging hundred-pound sacks of feed and grain for a lifetime. If he ever wanted to use one of his arms as a club, I'd feel sorry for his victim."

He was still laughing as he turned off the truck and walked around to open her door. He took her hand as she stepped down, and she had to fight the ripple of pleasure that surged through her veins at his touch.

Still holding her hand, he led her across the sidewalk and into the huge store.

"Hey, Orley."

The stooped figure of a man stocking cans on a shelf straightened and turned. His bald head glistened with sweat.

He was, as Zane had described him, as round as he was tall. He wore a stained leather apron that emphasized his large middle.

"Hey, Zane." His gaze shifted to the woman beside the cowboy.

"Riley, this is Orley Peterson. Orley, meet Riley Mason."

"The new accountant." A slow smile spread across the man's face, causing his jowels to jiggle.

"How did you know...?"

"Delia Cowling. She was really taken with you and your little girl. Summer, is it?"

"Yes, but..."

Zane squeezed her hand and she fell silent.

Zane handed Orley a list. "Cal said you have all this in stock."

"I'll check it out. If I don't have it, I'll order it." He glanced out the window. "Leave your truck right there and I'll have your order filled in an hour or two."

"Thanks, Orley. Take your time. We have some things to take care of here in town. We won't be heading back until late this afternoon."

Orley smiled at Riley. "Nice to meet you. I'll tell Delia you're as pretty as she said you were."

Riley dimpled. "Thank you, Orley. I'm hoping to get time to pay a call on Delia before I head back to the ranch."

"She'll be at the Fortune Saloon at noon. She's meeting her Blue Hair ladies for lunch."

"I think it's Red Hat ladies," Riley corrected.

Orley shook his head. "Not in this town. Delia founded the group, and said she didn't want it to be like any other. At first they were going to call themselves Blue Hats, but then they changed it to Blue Hair."

Riley was still laughing as Zane led her out of the store and along the sidewalk toward the Bits and Pieces Shop.

She paused outside the store. "What's this?"

"The only place in town where you can buy hiking boots and high heels, woolen long johns or fancy silk underwear." He looked her up and down. "I have you pegged for silk instead of wool."

She laughed. "You've got that right."

"I thought so. And I'd love to see you in it sometime." He opened the door and held it for her. "While you shop in here, I'll run the rest of my errands. I'll come by to pick you up in..." He glanced at his watch. "Will two hours be enough?"

She nodded.

"Okay. And then we'll have lunch at the Fortune Saloon."

She rolled her eyes. "Amy and Marilee have told me a few things about it. I can hardly wait."

Zane eyed the packages in Riley's arms. "Did you buy out the store?"

"Just about." When he reached out a hand, she offered him several bags and kept the others for herself.

"Come on. We'll stash these in the truck before going to lunch."

If Riley was surprised by the way he kept hold of her hand, she tried not to show it.

After depositing the bags, they headed for the Fortune. Just as Cal had predicted, the day had turned warm enough to be out in shirtsleeves. Montana weather, it seemed, went from calling for parkas to calling for swimsuits in the blink of an eye.

"This used to be the old grain and feed place before the Spence sisters bought it and turned it into a saloon. At first they figured they could make a living with the grain business while they built up the saloon traffic. In no time they had to sell the grain and feed business to Orley to concentrate on food and drinks."

Riley caught the sound of voices as they paused outside the door. "Business seems to be booming."

"It's the hottest spot in town. I should warn you, Daffy and Vi are…interesting characters." Zane opened the door and stood back as Riley preceded him inside.

Her first impression was the wave of sound. Not only voices, but the twang of country music blasting from speakers overhead. Her second impression was the haze of smoke that drifted like a pall in the air.

"Well, look who's here." A bony woman, wearing skintight jeans and a T-shirt that read "Spare a Horse— Ride a Cowboy," had Zane in a bear hug. As if her purple-spiked hair and eyebrows penciled like half-moons weren't enough, she'd outlined her lips with smoky pencil, giving her the look of a pouty vampire. "Where've you been hiding, my gorgeous cowboy?" After a lifetime of smoking, her whiskey voice sounded like the creaking of a rusty gate.

"Hey, Daffy. You know what it's like when the snows break."

"Yeah. Ranching's a bitc…" She shot a look in

Riley's direction. "Sorry. You look like one of those ladies that never heard a cussword. You must be the nerdy accountant."

Riley couldn't help laughing. "That's me." She stuck out her hand. "Riley Mason, nerdy accountant."

"Daffy Spence." She pointed with a menu. "Say hi to my twin, Vi, over at the grill."

As Riley turned, Daffy shouted, "Hey Vi, here's that accountant working at the Lost Nugget."

Riley cupped her hand to her mouth to shout above the din, "That's nerdy accountant." But at that very moment the entire place went silent, and her words could be heard all the way to the far side of the cavernous room.

Daffy slapped her on the back and turned to Zane, missing the look of shock mingled with embarrassment on Riley's face. "Now this one's got a sense of humor. I like her." She draped an arm around Zane's shoulders and snuggled her face close. "Ummm. You smell so good. You trying to impress the ladies?"

Zane chuckled. "Maybe one or two."

"I hope I'm one of them."

"You're always one of them, Daffy." He looked up as Delia Cowling came rushing over. The ridiculous blue wig, topped by a blue-feathered hat with a lacy black veil, looked completely out of place with her prim housedress and sensible shoes.

"Riley." She embraced the young woman before shooting a menacing look at Zane. "About time someone freed you from the ranch and brought you to town."

"I had a lot of work to catch up on."

Delia frowned. "You mean now that you're all caught up, you're planning on leaving us?"

"Not at all." She leaned close. "I've been offered a full-time job at the ranch."

"Oh, honey, that's such good news." Delia hugged her hard. "Now I want to hear all about…" Distracted, she turned toward the table where several older women were calling out to her that their lunch was ready. "I have to join them or they'll just keep nagging me. I'll come join you as soon as I'm through. You're not leaving without telling me everything."

As she hurried back to her table, Zane leaned close. "That little tidbit of personal information has now become topic number one over lunch with the Blue Hair ladies."

Riley looked perplexed. "Why would anybody care about what I do?"

"Spoken like a big-city girl." Daffy shot a look at Zane. "Doesn't she get that in this sleepy little burg she's just become the celebrity du jour?" She huffed out a breath. "Want a table up front, where you and the lady can be seen by all the curious? Or back in the corner, where you can whisper sweet nothings?"

He leaned close. "Corner. And if it's dark enough, I may even whisper sweet somethings."

That had her cackling as she led them through the crush of people to a booth in the corner of the room.

As they walked, they could hear the whispers and see the heads swivel to chart their progress.

"Told you. You're the talk of the lunch crowd," Daffy muttered as she dropped two menus on the table. "Should I bring two longnecks?"

Riley arched a brow. "A beer for lunch?"

Zane nodded, and in a pronounced drawl said, "Little

lady, when a cowboy rides in from the range, his first thought is a brew to wet his dry throat."

She was laughing. "And his second thought?"

He leaned close. "Let's just say, he won't be thinking about his throat." He turned to Daffy, who was laughing along with them. "Two longnecks, Daffy."

She walked away, returning minutes later to set the frosty bottles in front of them.

Zane didn't bother scanning the menu. "What's today's special?"

Daffy sat down across from them and slipped off her high heels to wiggle her toes. "Been on these dogs since sunup. Trying to look good for all the young studs sure can be painful." With a sigh of satisfaction she slid her feet back into her sexy shoes. "We're calling our special Pig-in-a-Poke. Actually that was Vi's idea. Pulled pork grilled with mushrooms and onions topped with her spicy homemade barbecue sauce and served in a pocket of sourdough bread. That comes with a side of Vi's pick-led onions and beets or, for the daring, deep-fried onion rings."

Zane nodded. "Sounds great. I'll have that with the onion rings."

"I figured you for the daring." She turned to Riley. "How about our nerdy accountant?"

"The same," Riley said.

Daffy arched a brow. "Honey, I had you figured for the pickled onions and beets. But hey, since you've man-aged to snag the most eligible bachelor around for a lunch date, it's a good thing you're willing to walk on the wild side."

"This isn't actually a date. We just…"

"Oh, yeah. That's what they all say." With a cackle at her own joke Daffy walked away, leaving Riley to stare after her in silence.

"Is that what they all say?" She turned back to Zane.

"You bet. And for your information, you may consider this just a trip into town, but I'm considering this a lunch date. And an all-afternoon date. And if I had my way, it would turn into an all-nighter, as well."

"I think you'd better settle for lunch and consider yourself lucky for that much, McCord."

He shrugged. "Can't blame a guy for trying. Especially since everybody in the place figures us as the latest twosome."

"So you say."

"Don't take my word for it. Just look around you."

Riley did just that, and she was surprised to find so many customers looking their way, their heads bent close in serious discussions.

"Small towns and gossip," Zane muttered.

Seeing the way Vi and Daffy were staring in their direction, Riley tried to suppress a giggle. But when she met Zane's eyes, she lost it.

The two of them threw back their heads and roared with laughter.

CHAPTER FOURTEEN

So." While Riley enjoyed what turned out to be an excellent sandwich, she fixed Zane with a look. "The town's most eligible bachelor, are you?"

He gave one of those self-deprecating smiles that she found so endearing. "It plays hell with my attempts to remain anonymous, but what can I say? All the women want me."

She glanced around. "I can see why. You're probably one of the few unmarried men that still have any teeth."

He gave her a toothy grin. "And they're all mine. Want to check?"

"I'll take your word for it. Is Daffy this crazy about all the men who come in here, or is it just you?"

He laughed. "I'd like to think it's my charm. But Daffy has been known to sweet-talk even old Mitch Cranston, who's at least ninety-four, into coming up to her place for a drink after hours."

"Well, she's certainly choosy. At least you're in great company with old Mitch."

Zane sat back, sipping his beer and enjoying the sound of her laughter. This was a side of Riley he hadn't seen before. Easy. Relaxed. With a great sense of humor.

He looked up as Delia crossed the room and swooped down on them.

Without waiting for an invitation she plunked herself down in the seat beside Riley. "Now fill me in on the details. Does this mean you'll be living at the Lost Nugget permanently?"

"It means that I have a full-time job handling payroll and paperwork so that Cal Randall can concentrate on other things."

"And you'll be living at the ranch?" Delia persisted.

Riley nodded.

Delia turned her attention to Zane. "My friends were all saying what an attractive couple you two make."

"Would you mind telling Riley that?" Zane turned his smile up to full wattage. "She's been too busy to give me the time of day."

"Well, she does have that beautiful little girl to think of." Delia turned to Riley. "Which brings me to my next question: Where is Summer? I'd have thought you would have brought her along so we could have a visit. You know, since I was the first in town to meet her, I consider myself her honorary grandmother."

"That's sweet, Delia. I think she considers you her honorary grandmother, too. I wanted her to come, but she's doing some secret project with Amy today, and she couldn't be persuaded to leave."

"Really?" Delia's brows shot up. "Summer and Amy?"

"Amy has become her teacher. The two have really bonded."

Delia nodded. "I'm not surprised. Amy loved teaching in Helena, but she had to give it up when she came back here to take care of her father during his illness. Then she and Jesse got married, and there was no going back to Helena." The older woman sighed. "I'm so glad those two found each other. But I have to say I'm a bit jealous. I was hoping to be Summer's nanny and teacher while you worked."

"Tell you what." Zane touched her hand. "Why don't you ride up to the ranch with us? You can stay for dinner, have a nice long visit with Summer, as well as Aunt Cora and the rest of our family, and I'll drive you home later."

"That's an awfully long drive, all in one day. You wouldn't mind?"

"I'm used to long drives. If you'd like to go with us, I'll pick you up at your place when we're ready to head back."

Delia took less than a second before coming to a decision. "I'd love that, Zane. Thank you. It's been awhile since I had the chance to visit with Cora and the family."

With a quick hug for Riley, she hurried to catch up with her friends who were waiting for her at the door of the saloon.

She was no sooner gone than three men shoved back their chairs and crossed the room to their table.

"Stafford." Zane nodded toward the taller of the two. "This is Riley Mason. Riley, Stafford Rowe is the mayor of Gold Fever."

The tall man with salt-and-pepper hair, dressed in

denims and a plaid shirt, shook her hand. "Miss Mason. It's nice to meet you."

"And you, Mayor Rowe."

"Call me Stafford. Everybody else does. The only reason I'm mayor of this town is because nobody else will have the job." He turned to include his friend. "This is Stan Novak, a local developer and building contractor."

Riley shook the hand of a tall, stocky man, dressed like the mayor in a plaid shirt and denims.

"And this is Gabriel Pasqual. Gabe, Miss Mason and Zane McCord. You've met his ranch foreman, Cal Randall."

They shook hands all around. Pasqual wore a dark suit and tie. Despite the warm spring day, he carried a sheepskin-lined jacket over one arm.

After a handshake, Pasqual continued holding Riley's hand while staring at her in a way that made her extremely uncomfortable, though she didn't know why. "You're not from around here, Miss Mason."

She firmly extricated her hand from his and tried not to give in to the shiver that tingled along her spine. "No. I'm not."

"I hear you've living on the Lost Nugget Ranch."

"Yes." To deflect any further questions about herself she turned the tables. "And you, Mr. Pasqual? Are you a local?"

He cleared his throat, as though equally unwilling to say more than necessary. "I've lived so many places, I don't call any single place home." He turned to Zane. "I'm hoping to change your foreman's mind. He doesn't want to hear about my plans for this town." He flicked a gaze over Zane's face. "But I'm told you and your cousins are actually the owners of the land. I'd like a chance to talk to the three of you."

"You've been told wrong. My cousins and I consider Cal Randall to be not only ranch foreman, but part of our family. We never second-guess his decisions."

Stung by the rebuke, Pasqual turned to the mayor for support.

Stafford pulled out a chair, prepared to join them. "I told Stan and Gabriel that I'd arrange another meeting between them and your family so they could present their plans for future development. Pasqual would like an opportunity to see your spread up close. Maybe we could set up a meeting."

"This is our busiest time of year, Stafford."

The mayor squirmed under Zane's steely look. "I know. Maybe Mr. Pasqual could present a few preliminary plans right now, and you could pass along his ideas to the others."

Zane's smile remained, though his eyes appeared, to Riley, to have turned flinty. "As we've said repeatedly, our family's in the ranching business, Stafford."

Pasqual's tone was challenging. "I've heard your family's in the fortune-hunting business."

Zane's words sharpened. "We've never tried to hide that fact. It's common knowledge that my cousins and I intend to continue our grandfather's search."

"I hear you've had some fancy high-tech stuff shipped to your place."

"Whatever does the job." Zane turned to the mayor. "As I said, we're not interested in selling or developing the land."

"But you haven't heard Gabriel's latest proposal."

Stan followed the mayor's lead and sat in a chair facing Zane. "This town could use a hospital, to replace that small clinic. And the high school needs a track and football field, maybe an indoor pool and theater. Then there are the retail stores that could bring jobs to the area. And…"

"Yeah. A shopping center," Zane deadpanned. "Of the millions pledged, how many real dollars have you brought to the table, Mr. Pasqual?"

There was an awkward silence as the mayor and the building contractor turned to the man whose face had gone from friendly to fierce in the blink of an eye. "I haven't produced any hard cash yet, but then your town hasn't produced any land, either. I've said that my backers are ready to pledge millions of…"

The three men looked up, annoyed, when Daffy bent down to Zane, blocking his view from the others.

"Phone call, Zane. Sounds important. You can take it at the bar, honey."

"Thanks, Daffy." Zane shoved back his chair and stuck out his hand. "Nice seeing you again, Stafford, Stan. Nice meeting you, Pasqual."

The men accepted his handshake.

When it looked as though they would remain and make small talk with Riley, Zane waited a beat before saying, "Thank you, gentlemen. Have a good day."

The three were left with no choice but to shove back their chairs and return to their own table.

With a wink at Riley, Zane said, "I'll be right back."

He crossed the room and accepted the phone from Daffy's hand. He said something, smiled, then handed the phone back to her before sauntering back to his table.

All the while Riley could see Gabriel Pasqual studying her from his position across the room. She felt like squirming under his dark gaze.

"Bad news?" Riley asked when Zane reached her side.

"Not at all." He picked up his longneck and drained it.

Before he could explain, a man in rumpled hospital scrubs and a woman in a nurse's uniform stopped by the table.

"Hey, Doc. Elly." Zane introduced the two. "This is Riley Mason. Riley, meet Dr. Frank Wheeler and his nurse-practitioner, Elly Carson, who run the medical clinic here in town."

The doctor, with tufts of white hair and rimless glasses that gave him an owlish appearance, chuckled. "So you're the new accountant who has already been practically canonized by Cal for cleaning up his paperwork."

While Riley blushed, Elly caught her hand. "If you think Doc's kidding, all I can say is, in the years I've known Cal, I've rarely heard him say more than a dozen words. But when he started talking about you, he couldn't say enough good things."

Riley shook her head. "It's nice to hear Cal is so pleased with my work."

"'Pleased' is an understatement." Dr. Wheeler patted her shoulder. "I have an idea that we'll be seeing you around Gold Fever for a long time to come."

"Oh, I hope so." As they made ready to walk away, Riley called, "I hope I'll see you again."

"But not in a professional manner," Doc said with a laugh. "Most folks in town prefer to see us at the saloon rather than at the clinic."

The two were still laughing as they made their way to the door.

Riley glanced over at Zane with a rather dazed look. "How sweet of Cal to praise me to strangers."

Zane nodded. "It's more than sweet. It's completely out of character. As Elly said, Cal is a man of few words. I'd say you've really impressed him."

For the next hour people stopped by their table, eager to exchange a few words with Zane and to get an up close view of the stranger now living and working at the Lost Nugget.

After meeting Judge Wilbur Manning, Reverend Martin, Sheriff Ernest Wycliff, and half a dozen other strangers, Riley's head was swimming with names and faces. How, she wondered, would she ever be able to remember all of them?

They looked up when Daffy approached with their bill.

Zane stood and handed her the money before leaning close to press a kiss to her cheek. "Thanks, Daffy."

"My pleasure, honey." She squeezed his arm. "All part of my job."

"And nobody does it better."

She turned to Riley. "I'd be careful with this one, honey. The way he looks at you, if you were one of Vi's specials of the day, you'd be devoured by now. And I have to say, there are a whole lot of females in this town who'd give a year's pay to have him look at them the way he's been looking at you for the past hour."

She saw the blush that reddened Riley's cheeks. "Well, now I don't even have to ask any more questions. Your eyes are a dead giveaway. They just told me everything I wanted to know." She gave a shake of her head and said to Zane in a loud stage whisper, "You'd better move fast, or you may be the one that gets devoured, honey."

When she walked away, he caught Riley's hand and the two of them made their way to the front door. Once again Riley could feel the stares of everyone in the room.

A quick glance at the mayor's table affirmed that he and Stan Novak and Gabriel Pasqual were all watching. The look in Pasqual's eyes had her shivering.

When they were outside, the warmth of the sunlight helped Riley shake off the gloomy feeling. "You're right. Daffy's quite the character. Why were you thanking her?"

"For getting rid of a pest."

She looked confused. "A pest?"

"Pasqual."

She shivered. "I didn't like that man."

"You're not the only one. He's only been in town a short time, and he's determined to be invited out to the ranch to talk about buying some of our land for development. There's something about him that doesn't add up. And, like Stafford Rowe, he refuses to take no for an answer."

"But the phone call . . . ?"

"Pure fiction on Daffy's part. She could see my frustration clear across the room, and did what she does best, which is to make sure that all her customers are comfortable."

"Did you know before you left the table?"

He merely grinned and patted his shirt pocket. "Anybody wants me, they call on my cell. Daffy has the slyest wink in the world. When she leaned in to tell me about that call, I could've kissed her."

Riley laughed. "I'm thinking that would have made her day. She has a thing for you."

Zane joined in the laughter. "Yeah. Our Daffy is about as subtle as a train wreck. She can't help herself. She just purely loves men. All men. Not that I'm complaining, of course. It's always nice to know somebody finds you irresistible."

Riley strolled along beside him and held her silence. But the truth was, she found him every bit as irresistible as Daffy Spence did.

Zane paused beside the ranch truck. "Still here. And all the supplies stored in back as promised."

"Not that you expected anything less."

He shot her one of those famous grins. "Now you're getting the hang of things. Not too much changes from year to year in Gold Fever." He held open the door and waited until she was seated inside before closing it and walking around to the driver's side.

He turned the key in the ignition. "Now to pick up Delia." He dialed his cell phone. "Dandy? I'm bringing along company for dinner. Tell Aunt Cora that Delia Cowling will be joining us."

As he returned the phone to his pocket, he said with a laugh, "Dandy is always happy to have guests. That means more compliments for the cook."

"He deserves them." Riley touched a hand to her stomach. "I haven't eaten this well in a lifetime. If I'm not careful, I'll start gaining weight."

Zane glanced over. "I bet you were cute when you were expecting Summer."

She seemed completely caught off-guard by his comment. "I don't know. I never really thought about it. But now that you mention it, I recall friends telling me that I was glowing."

"What did Summer's father say?"

When Riley turned to stare out the window, he regretted his impetuous remark. She was silent for so long, Zane thought she might refuse to answer.

Then, without warning, she said softly, "He never got a chance to see me."

Zane pulled up in front of Delia's house. "He never...?"

Before he could ask Riley what she meant by that, the older woman came hurrying down the walk and stood waiting for Zane to help her into the truck.

As they drove to the ranch, Delia kept up a running conversation with Riley, leaving Zane to ponder her words.

In the span of scant months Riley had faced birth and death. And faced them, apparently, alone. What sort of fears had she dealt with? What sort of strength did she possess?

So many questions. And any hope of getting answers would have to wait for another time.

As the truck ate up the miles, Riley kept her smile in place and allowed Delia to do what she did so well. Talk, talk, and then talk some more. This dear old woman never seemed to tire of conversing. Maybe, Riley thought, it was because she was so alone and hungry for company.

Though she tried to concentrate on Delia, Riley was distracted by the things Daffy had said.

Was she so transparent? If Daffy could see her reaction to Zane, could others see it, too?

She didn't want to want him. But she couldn't seem to help herself. The more time she spent with him, the more attracted she was.

Attracted. It was too tame a word.

Daffy was right. She could easily devour him in one quick bite. And that frightened her.

Delia opened a bag and removed a children's book. "I bought this for Summer."

"Oh, Delia." Riley read the title. "We haven't read that yet. Summer will love it."

"I'm looking forward to reading it to her before she goes to bed tonight." Delia patted her hand. "I hope you don't mind." She glanced across Riley to where Zane was driving in silence. "There's something very special about reading to a child. Have you ever done it?"

"No. At least not yet." Zane gave her a smile.

"I highly recommend it." Delia linked her fingers with Riley's. "I know it's silly, but since you spent that first night at my place, I've begun to feel connected in a special way to you and Summer."

"It isn't silly, Delia. Summer and I were both taken with you. We were strangers in a strange town, and you made us feel so welcome. I hope you'll always be a part of our lives."

The older woman gave a sigh of pleasure and fell silent.

As they started along the driveway leading to the ranch house, Riley chanced a quick glance at Zane's face. In profile he seemed almost stern. But then he turned and winked, and her heart actually tumbled in her chest. She touched a hand to her heart, wondering if he could hear it thundering.

Oh, the man was dangerous. And so damnably charming, she wanted to wrap herself around him and never let go.

She was falling. Hard. And wasn't that exactly what she'd vowed she would never do?

CHAPTER FIFTEEN

———◆———

As soon as the older woman stepped into the kitchen, Cora hurried across the room to greet her with warmth and affection. "Delia. How lovely to see you."

Cora turned to Summer, who was seated beside Amy. The two were whispering behind their hands. "Summer, look who's here."

"Auntie Delia." With a yelp of delight the little girl flew across the room into the open arms of Delia, who had dropped to her knees to embrace her.

"Oh, I've missed you so much." Delia buried her face in Summer's hair.

"I've missed you, too, Auntie Delia."

When Riley stepped into the kitchen, Summer raced to her side. "Miss Amy and I made you a surprise. But you can't see it until after dinner." She turned to include Delia. "And now that Auntie Delia is here, she can have some, too."

"Some what, dear?"

At Delia's question, Summer gave a shake of her little head. "It's a surprise. You can't know until later."

"Oh." Getting into the spirit of the moment, Delia put a finger to her lips. "Not another word, then. I'll just have to be patient and wait."

When Dandy announced that dinner was ready, Cora caught Delia's hand and led her to a place beside hers at the table. "I'm so glad you were able to ride out here with Zane and Riley."

"Me, too. Oh, I've missed all of you." Delia glanced around the table, noting the absence of Cal.

She turned to Cora. "Where's that good-looking ranch foreman?"

"Up in the high meadow with the wranglers. He'll be back in a day or two."

She glanced at Wyatt and Marilee, shoulders brushing, fingers twined under the table. "You two look happy. How are you dealing with this big, noisy family, Marilee?"

That had Marilee smiling. "It's more than I ever dreamed of having. I never have time to be lonely since marrying Wyatt."

"And you, Amy?" Delia turned to the fair-haired young woman seated beside her husband. "I can see how happy Jesse is. Tell me about your father. How is Otis doing?"

"Doc has declared him to be in complete remission. He's right back to where he was a year ago, doing all the ranch chores that would exhaust three men."

That brought a round of laughter from the others. They all knew Otis Parrish well enough to appreciate that his daughter wasn't exaggerating. He was known around Gold Fever as a hard-driving, hardheaded rancher.

"Do you spend much time with him?"

Amy shook her head. "Dad's a bit of a loner. He enjoys an occasional meal with me, or here with the McCords, but he prefers his own company. And I'm really busy, especially now that I have my new pupil." She smiled at Summer across the table.

"That has to be very satisfying for you. I know you were missing your job as teacher."

"I was. But this is so much better. Instead of a classroom full of noisy students, I get to work one-on-one with someone whose quick mind never fails to amaze me. Like today's lesson..."

"Shh." Summer put a finger to her lips. "You promised, Miss Amy."

"So I did. It will be your secret, honey. And after dinner, you'll get to reveal it."

Cora laid a hand over Delia's. "And how are things with you in town?"

Though it remained unspoken, everyone knew what she meant. After Delia's brother, Ledge, a respected bank president, had been caught up in a scandal that resulted in his murder by the sheriff's deputy, Harrison Atkins, the old woman had been convinced that she would have to leave town rather than face the cruel gossip of former friends. It was Cora who had persuaded her to give the townspeople a chance.

"I'm so glad I listened to you, Cora. Things are just grand. I've formed the Blue Hair Club. A group of old biddies like myself who meet to discuss books over lunch once a week at the Fortune Saloon."

"You're not an old biddie," Cora said firmly.

"And why not?"

"Because," she explained, "that would make me one, too."

"You?" Delia's brows shot up. "Believe me, Cora McCord, if I had a successful career like yours, or a handsome cowboy looking at me the way Cal Randall looks at you, I couldn't possibly consider myself old."

Cora turned several shades of red before coughing into her napkin while the others merely exchanged grins. She seemed genuinely surprised. "Whatever do you mean? Why..." Words failed her as she turned from Delia to the others and back again.

"Oh, for heaven's sake," Delia blurted. "Is everybody around here blind except me?"

At the sudden silence, she gave a shake of her head, a clear indication that she was about to launch into a long-winded monologue about lost romance and roads less taken.

It was Zane who took pity on his aunt and managed to quickly change the subject. "What's new in town, Delia?"

Her eyes danced, and Zane had the idea that the old woman knew exactly what he was up to. Mercifully, she went along with him.

"Same old things as always. Stan Novak's bending the mayor's ear about the need for a bigger school, hospital, city hall. This time he has some big money to back it up. Someone named Gabriel Pasqual. I think Stafford has been hearing it so long, he's begun to believe it himself. If you ask me, our mayor has become this stranger's biggest advocate. They say he spends more time with Pasqual than he does with all his old cronies."

"Are the townspeople buying into the idea of building the town into a big city?"

She shrugged. "The longer the mayor talks it up, the more some folks are going to start to think it could bring more people, which would bring more business, which would be good for everybody."

Zane and his cousins exchanged a meaningful look. They needed to prepare for yet another visit from Stafford Rowe and his new friend, armed with yet another high-pressure sales pitch.

"Then there's the gossip about all the high-tech gadgets being delivered up here. That has to mean you're once again taking your grandfather's treasure hunt seriously. Folks are speculating on which McCord will be next to fall victim to the curse."

"Curse." Zane spit the word with venom. And though he felt like issuing a few curses of his own, he held back in deference to little Summer and the women seated around the table.

Delia wasn't about to be sidetracked. "Well, you have to admit. Both Amy and Marilee were threatened as soon as they got too close to the McCord family."

Zane's frown deepened. "In both instances, those threats came from someone bent on derailing the search. How can anybody consider this part of a curse?"

"Maybe." Delia sat back in her chair, always pleased to engage in a heated debate. "But they were real threats nonetheless. And you can't deny that both Amy and Marilee were in real danger."

"But not from any curse. That rumor has been around for so long it's become part of the town's folklore. But any sensible person knows the difference between a curse and a criminal bent on destruction."

Sensing his anger, Delia decided to change course.

"So, what about those high-tech gadgets? This sounds serious. Does this mean you think enough gadgets will finally end the search and lead you to the lost treasure?"

"You bet." Zane managed a smile. "We've just returned from a couple of weeks in the wilderness, and we're still on an adrenaline rush. We plan on going full steam ahead."

"You know I wish you well, even though I always thought Coot was chasing a pipe dream. But it was his dream, and I'm sure he'd be happy to see his grandsons chasing after it."

"Auntie Delia, what's a pipe dream?" Summer asked.

Delia smiled at the little girl. "It's like you saying you intend to go out to the barn, saddle a horse, and win all the medals at the rodeo."

Summer thought about that for a moment. "Zane says when I'm ready, he's going to let me ride Vanilla. I bet once I do, I could ride in a rodeo. Can't I, Zane?"

"Honey, I'm convinced that you're smart enough to do anything you set your mind to do."

"Then I'm going to live with wild horses like you did."

Delia joined in the laughter of the others. "If you say you will, I've no doubt you'll do it, Summer. Just look at your mama. Now there's a strong woman." She glanced over at Riley and clapped a hand to her mouth. "Oh, for heaven's sake. I completely forgot. The day after you left my place I had a phone call from someone asking for you."

"A phone call?" Riley's laughter faded. "Who was it from?"

Delia shook her head. "He didn't identify himself, but

he seemed agitated when I said you weren't staying at my place as you'd planned. He refused to leave a message, but I think he was somewhat appeased when I told him where you were." Delia looked around at the others, clearly enjoying her importance. "I hope you don't mind, but I couldn't help bragging just a bit. I told him you were working at the Lost Nugget Ranch, the biggest, most successful ranch in all of Montana."

Seated beside Riley, Zane heard the little hiss of annoyance that escaped her lips. While the dinner table conversation swirled around her, he noticed Riley's sudden silence and the way she seemed to have drawn into herself.

Cora glanced around at the others. "Shall we take our coffee and dessert in the great room?"

"I'd like that." Delia followed Cora from the table.

Summer and Amy exchanged knowing smiles. While the others left, both teacher and student remained behind with Dandy.

A short time later, while the family gathered around the cozy fireplace, Dandy wheeled in a serving cart and began pouring coffee.

Delia looked puzzled. "I thought you said there was dessert."

Cora turned to the cook.

Before she could say a word he merely held out a hand. "It's all part of Summer's surprise. I'll leave it to her to explain."

Amy stepped from the kitchen carrying a silver tray on which rested a cake and candles.

"Is it somebody's birthday?" Delia asked.

"Yes. It's part of our 'prise." Summer trailed behind Amy. In her arms was a stack of colorful papers.

She set the stack down so the others could see that it was a collection of pages punched with three holes and tied together with pink, yellow, and blue ribbons to make a book. The top page, carefully hand-lettered, read "Mamas and Babies." Underneath the title was Summer's name. As she opened the cover, she revealed a drawing of a vanilla-colored horse and a brown foal.

"I wonder who that is," Zane deadpanned, much to the delight of the others.

"It's Vanilla and her baby, Star." Summer had assumed the role of teacher, and Amy sat back, looking as proud as Riley.

"And who do you think this is?" Summer turned the page to reveal a drawing of a brown and white cow and its tiny calf.

Though the drawings were primitive, they showed real talent.

"That looks like Bessie and her new calf."

"That's right. And tonight we're having a birthday party for all the new babies on the ranch."

At Summer's words, everyone smiled and made appropriate noises about the delightful drawings and the neatly printed words.

Amy was quick to point out, "I'll have you know that every drawing was Summer's idea, and every letter was made by her hand. I didn't help at all except to tell her how to spell the words. The printing is all hers."

"Our very own little prodigy," Delia said with pride.

Dandy held a lighter to the pink, yellow, and blue candles. "Summer, would you like to blow these out?"

The little girl nodded. "But first, we have to sing 'Happy Birthday.'"

Everyone joined in the song to the new foals and calves, and clapped hands when she successfully blew out the candles.

For the next hour, while they enjoyed cake and ice cream, they passed around the book, remarking on the clever little girl in their midst.

Through it all Summer glowed with pride. It was clear to all of them that this little girl was reveling in the opportunity to shine.

Zane studied Riley, smiling along with the others. He was relieved to note that she'd been able to put aside her earlier dismay at Delia's announcement and simply enjoy her daughter's accomplishment.

A short time later, seeing Summer yawning, Riley said softly, "I think, after so much excitement, the time is catching up with you. Want to go upstairs to bed?"

Delia picked up the new book she'd brought. "I hope you can stay awake long enough to let me read this to you."

"Oh, boy." Summer caught Delia's hand before turning to Cora. "Are you coming with us, Miss Cora?"

Cora was clearly delighted to be included. "I'd love to, honey."

Summer circled the room, calling good night to everybody before climbing the stairs.

As they climbed, Summer's voice drifted down to the others. "I can't wait for my new story, Auntie Delia."

Upstairs, Riley led the way into her suite of rooms.

Cora paused to look around. "I've always loved this suite. I hope you and Summer are comfortable here,

Riley." Out of deference to Delia, who'd loved Coot even before he married another, she carefully avoided mentioning the name given this suite of rooms by the family. It may have been a retreat for Annie, but it would be a painful reminder of loss to Delia.

Riley turned, seeing the look of pleasure in the older woman's eyes. "I can't imagine a more comfortable place than this. I love everything about it. The lovely fireplace, the pretty feminine furniture, the view from every window."

Delia was taking her time looking around. "I've never been in here before, but I couldn't agree more. It's lovely."

Riley opened the door to Summer's bedroom. "Come on in. I'll get Summer into her pajamas, and then you can read her the story." With a laugh she added, "Though I won't guarantee that she'll be able to stay awake until the end."

As she helped Summer out of her clothes and into her night things, the two women wandered the room, noting the place of honor where Floppy lay on the little girl's pillow.

Cora paused to study the drawing hanging over the bed. Leaning closer, she stared at it for long moments before turning to Riley.

"Where did you get this picture of Summer's stuffed dog?"

Riley glanced over her shoulder, then returned her attention to her daughter. "I made it."

"You did?" Cora touched a hand to the frame. "Would you mind if I took it down and held it closer to the light?"

Riley shrugged. "Not at all, Miss Cora."

Cora removed the framed art from the wall and carried it close to the child's lamp atop her dresser, studying it with the eye of a professional artist. "This is so very clever. How did you achieve this three-dimensional look?"

Riley chuckled. "Nothing very complicated. I drew the same picture over and over, and cut out each one with an X-Acto knife. I did this one over a dozen times on various shades of paper so that it appears to go from light to dark to light again."

"I love the fact that each part of the dog spells out a different letter of Summer's name. Could you see the letters in your mind while you were drawing the dog?"

Summer, clad in her pajamas, was busy climbing into bed and pulling Floppy into her arms.

Riley crossed the room to stand beside Cora. "I do see the letters while I'm working. I don't quite know how, but it all comes together in my mind by the time I've finished the initial sketch."

"Could you do this for anyone besides your daughter?"

At Cora's question, Riley paused to think, before nodding. "Zane would be easy. If I were sketching his name, it would probably be in the form of a mustang. Something rather wild and beautiful, with its mane and tail billowing in the wind. Just picturing it in my mind, I can see the letters of Zane's name forming the mane, the tail, the hooves. Of course, I could completely change it around and draw a video camera that spelled out his name. Both horses and video cameras are such an integral part of Zane, either one would personify him."

Cora was watching her carefully as she spoke. "Yes, you've easily captured Zane, though he's more complicated than most men."

"You think so?" Riley wasn't aware of the way her eyes grew dreamy at the mere thought of Zane.

"What about me?" Cora asked softly. "What would you draw to form my name?"

Riley smiled. "That's easy. An artist's easel. Bright, almost neon colors that would scream your name as vividly as every one of your beautiful canvases does."

"Yes. Yes." Cora's voice was little more than a whisper before she reached out to frame Riley's face with her hands. "Oh, my dear." She stared down into Riley's eyes. "Of course. How could I have so completely missed this?"

At Riley's look of confusion the older woman said simply, "My heart knew. And has from the moment we met. But I pushed it aside, because you're so good at keeping Cal's ledgers. I actually convinced myself that I was wrong, and that your real talent lay with numbers."

Riley was staring at her with a look of consternation. "I don't understand, Miss Cora."

Cora smiled down into her eyes. "Of course you do. Though you've probably nudged it aside as I did, and tried to deny it, you have to know in your heart of hearts. We're sisters. Soul mates. Like me, dear, you're an artist. And from what I've seen, a very gifted artist."

CHAPTER SIXTEEN

At Cora's words, spoken with such passion, Riley's eyes filled with unexpected tears. Though she was mortified at such a display, there was no hiding her emotions.

"Sorry." She struggled to blink back her tears.

"Don't be." Cora continued cupping the younger woman's face in her hands. "How long have you been in denial about your gift?"

Riley gave a strangled laugh. "You call it a gift. My aunt called it a curse."

"Your aunt?" Cora was instantly alert. In the time Riley had been at the ranch, it was her first mention of family.

"I was raised by an aunt and uncle. My parents died in a traffic accident when I was seven. I felt so lost. My uncle Frank was my father's oldest brother, and he was more like my grandfather than a father. He and Aunt Janey are"—at a loss for words, she spread her hands—"stern, prissy people. They like everything perfect, you know? And seven-year-olds are rarely perfect. At least I wasn't." She took in a breath. "They let me know that they expected certain things of me, and I…I did my best to make them proud. When I went off to college, they warned me not to take any frivolous courses."

"Frivolous meaning art classes?"

Riley nodded. "I've always had an interest in art. I couldn't get enough of it. They both hated it, and demanded my promise that I wouldn't waste their money or my time on such foolishness. I was there strictly for business."

"That would explain the math and accounting classes."

Riley sighed. "I showed an aptitude for them and graduated at the top of my class. Uncle Frank believes that the most important thing in this life is being able to earn your own keep. He delivered hundreds of such lectures to me over the years."

"So, if being a top scholar was the only goal they approved of, I'm sure they would have disapproved of"—Cora glanced across the room where Delia was reading to Summer—"anything that got in the way of such a goal."

Riley bit her lip before giving a slight nod. "When I told them I was expecting a baby, they cut off the rest of my college funds and let me know that I was no longer welcome in their home."

"Oh, my dear." Without another word Cora gathered Riley into her arms and held her. Just held her.

At first Riley stiffened. She wasn't quite sure how to react to such tenderness. Denied her mother at such an early age, she had no displays of affection during her growing-up years. And now, in the space of minutes, this dear woman had, without question, recognized her talent and accepted her with such warmth and grace, she was feeling completely overwhelmed by an array of overpowering emotions.

The longer Cora held her, the more rigid Riley grew, until she felt as though the slightest movement would cause her to shatter like glass.

Sensing her discomfort, Cora released her.

Riley swayed slightly, fighting for control. "Thank you, Miss Cora. For…everything. You'll never know what this means to me."

Cora laid a hand on her shoulder. "Never forget, dear. You're a beautiful, talented, and loving young woman. You deserve to be loved in return. And you deserve to pursue those things in life that make you happy."

"Happy." Riley gave a long, deep sigh. "Aunt Janey said the pursuit of happiness is the ruination of my generation."

"Happiness is not something we strive for, dear. But it is surely something we deserve." Cora looked her in the eye. "I see that you're not convinced."

"I'm…"

Before she could reply, Delia called softly, "You were right, Riley. I only managed half the book before our girl was asleep. I hope you'll let me come back another time to read to her again." The older woman smoothed the covers before setting aside the book. "I'll leave this here for her to enjoy another night."

Riley looked over at the bed where her daughter lay sleeping. "As Summer's honorary grandmother, you're welcome here anytime, Delia. I know Summer would love to have you read to her again."

"Well," Cora said softly, "I hope we can resume this conversation at another time. For now…" She returned the framed artwork to the wall above Summer's bed before turning to her friend. "Zane will be waiting to take you back to town. We'd better get you downstairs." She gave Delia a hug.

Delia looked puzzled. "Why are you saying good-bye here? Aren't you coming down with me?"

Cora shook her head. "If you don't mind, I'll say my good night here." She turned to Riley. "I'd like to sit by the fire awhile, and just watch your beautiful daughter sleep. Why don't you run along and accompany Zane to town with Delia?"

"We could be hours, Miss Cora."

"I have nothing else to do, dear. Go."

Though Riley was surprised by the offer, she didn't know how to refuse such kindness. "If you're sure you want to stay."

"I'm very sure, dear."

"Thank you again, Miss Cora." She gave the older woman an awkward hug before following Delia from the suite of rooms and down the stairs.

When they were gone, Cora sank down into a soft rocking chair in front of the fire, deep in thought.

She'd been privileged to grow up in a family that not only loved her but respected her independence and encouraged her talent. That had freed her to travel the world, learning from the best and brightest artists of the day. Oh, she'd made mistakes along the way. Given her heart to some who weren't worthy. Had her heart broken a few times. But she'd never had to endure the censure of those who loved her. They had always accepted her, warts and all.

She sighed. Delia had been right about little Summer. She was fortunate to have a mother who displayed such strengths.

But at what cost? Cora wondered. What price had Riley Mason paid to remain strong through so many trials in her young life? And what price did she continue to pay in order to maintain such rigid control in the face of so much adversity?

As always, Delia dominated the conversation all the way back to town. She talked about the books she and the members of her Blue Hair Club had read and discussed. She talked in great detail about the latest town council meeting chaired by Mayor Stafford Rowe, in which developer Stan Novak and Ben Rider, owner of the Grizzly Inn Diner, had joined forces to push for new roads. Then she turned the conversation to the gossip swirling around Paula Henning, her late brother's bank assistant, and the new bank owner, Jeremy Peterson, a distant cousin of Orley Peterson.

"Everybody knows that Paula and her husband are having some problems," Delia said matter-of-factly. "Every marriage has a few now and then. Not that I speak from experience, you understand. But if you ask me, Jeremy Peterson is nothing more than a womanizer taking advantage of the situation. I know for a fact that he's asked her to stay after hours to help with the bank audit. As you can imagine, Paula's poor husband is in a tizzy over it. I have half a mind to tell Paula what I think, but I just can't bring myself to walk into that bank since Ledge's death."

Zane glanced over. "How do you handle your banking?"

"By phone and by mail. I know it sounds crazy, with the bank just a block from my house, but I simply can't face seeing somebody else in Ledge's office." She sighed. "Sooner or later, though, I know I'll have to bite the bullet."

Zane patted her hand. "Whenever you decide to do that, give me a call. I'd be happy to go with you the first time. Maybe that would make it a little easier."

"Oh, you sweet thing." Delia turned to Riley. "See why I love this young man? Ever since I reconnected with the McCord family, Coot's grandsons have been like my own."

When they reached her house, Zane pulled up to the curb and climbed out before walking around to the passenger side of the truck. He and Riley walked with Delia to her front door.

"Thank you for today, Zane. That was such a thoughtful, generous thing to do."

"My pleasure, ma'am." He brushed a kiss to her cheek.

She turned and gave Riley a warm hug. "I hope I see you and that sweet little girl soon."

"Very soon. Promise." As was her custom, Riley returned the hug awkwardly.

Zane unlocked Delia's door and walked in ahead of her, switching on the lights so that she wouldn't have to step into a darkened room.

"Thank you, Zane."

"You're welcome. We'll wait until you lock the door."

When they heard the click of the lock, Riley and Zane made their way back to the truck.

Zane turned the key in the ignition. As they started along the street, he looked over and winked. "Listen."

Riley frowned. "To what? I don't hear a thing."

"Exactly. Listen to the silence. After a hundred miles of nonstop Delia, this is great."

She couldn't help laughing. "She does get tedious. But I think the poor thing is just starved for company."

"Or it could be she just loves the sound of her own voice."

They shared a chuckle.

Once they hit the highway leading away from town, the darkness enveloped them, making the stars seem even brighter.

Riley lowered the passenger-side window, then, to keep her hair from billowing about, reached into her pocket and, with a few deft twists, tied her hair back in a knot atop her head.

Zane looked up at the night sky. "I love this time of night. And I love the way the countryside looks." He pointed. "There's Treasure Chest. You can just make out the peaks by the light of the full moon."

"It's really breathtaking."

Riley turned away to stare out over the moon-washed countryside. As their truck ate up the miles, she fell silent.

Zane studied her profile. "Was it my imagination earlier this evening, or did Delia's mention of a phone call upset you?"

She glanced toward him, then away. "I...may have been a bit surprised."

"I wouldn't call it surprise. You appeared pretty shaken by the news. Want to tell me why?"

When she offered no explanation, he tried again. "I'll tell you how I see it. Somebody found out that you were supposed to be living with Delia Cowling. But when they called her and asked for you, they learned that you're no longer living there. That would have been just fine with you, except that Delia unknowingly gave this party much more information. I'm thinking she gave out details you were hoping to keep secret." He looked over. "Am I right?"

She gave a long, deep sigh. "Yes."

"So now somebody knows exactly where you live and work, and how to find you." He waited a beat before adding, "And where you are, Summer is bound to be."

When she turned to stare out the side window, he said softly, "And your job, to keep her safe, is now in jeopardy."

He saw a single tear course down her cheek, the only sign that he'd hit his mark.

Without a word he veered off the highway and continued for some miles along a stretch of flat grassland until they came to a swollen creek. He turned off the ignition.

"When I was a kid, I called this my thinking place." He stepped out of the truck and opened her door, catching her hand.

In the darkness they made their way to the banks of the creek. The rushing water was illuminated by the light of millions of stars. Out in the deepest part of the creek, a ribbon of golden moonlight rippled across the water.

Zane's voice was hushed. "I had a lot of problems when I was a kid. My parents were involved in an unhappy marriage. My mother hated the ranch. Hated Montana. Hated life in general. And I was caught in the middle. I loved my life here, and couldn't imagine living anywhere else. But kids have to do what grown-ups demand. So, whenever things got to be too much for me, I'd come here and sit by the creek's banks and do some heavy-duty thinking. But no matter how miserable my life got, I always had Jimmy Eagle. Jimmy was my friend, my mentor, and even in those years when I was living in California, the voice of my conscience. There were times when the only place I could turn to for help was my longtime image of Jimmy."

He glanced at Riley, who hadn't said a word. Out of deference to her somber mood, he fell silent.

Her voice, when she finally spoke, trembled with nerves. "I wish I'd had a Jimmy Eagle. I thought I'd made a clean break. But now..." She clenched her hands together, twisting and untwisting her fingers.

He waited, knowing that she needed to do this in her own way, her own time.

"When I came here..." Her voice was soft, breathy, as though she'd been running for miles. "All I wanted was a chance to earn my keep in a place where nobody knew me. When Cal offered me not only the job, but a chance to live on your ranch, I couldn't believe my good fortune. Not only was the pay more than I'd hoped for, but the ranch was so isolated, I knew nobody could find us."

"And that was important."

She nodded. "But I never expected to find such good people here. I thought...hoped that I could just earn my pay and keep my distance from all of you."

"Why was that so important?"

"Because"—she stared down at the water, as though weighing her words—"I've never met a family like yours.

All of you have been so kind, so loving to Summer and me. From Cal, who treated me like a valued part of the team from the first time he met me, to your sister-in-law Amy, who took Summer under her wing and has patiently taught her so many new things. And then there's the way you introduced her to your beloved horses. She loves being with you. She repeats everything you say. Remembers every little compliment. You're becoming the…man she hungers for in her life. She's a different child since coming here. I see her blooming like a lovely flower. And tonight your aunt told me…" Just thinking about that scene with Cora had tears stinging the backs of Riley's eyes.

"She told you what?" For a moment his heart stopped.

"That I'm an artist. Her sister. Her soul mate. Do you know what that means, coming from Cora McCord, an artist whose paintings I've admired for all of my life?"

Zane felt his heart start to beat again and smiled down into her eyes. "I'm not surprised. But why is any of this a problem?"

"Because…" She bit her lip and tossed her head, choosing to stare out at the glistening water rather than face him. "Oh, Zane. I've made such a mess of things. I never wanted to care this much about any of you. And now, hearing what Delia said, I realize that I've brought trouble to your doorstep. And I can't bear to think that all of you could be hurt because of me. Don't you see? I can't stay here any longer. I have to run. I have to take Summer far away to keep her safe, and I have to do it now, before they get a chance to hurt all of you, as well."

"They?"

She shook her head. "It's too complicated. But I have to leave right away. First thing in the morning. Now that I know I've been found out—"

"Hold on." As she turned, he caught her by the wrist, holding her fast. "Riley, this involves more than just you and Summer now." Though his words were spoken softly, there was a hint of something beneath.

Fury? She wondered. Was he angry because she'd admitted to bringing trouble to their doorstep?

"I know. I'm sorry to put you and your family in such..." She turned to him, and her words were instantly forgotten. One look at his eyes revealed the depth of passion there.

Not anger. Something much, much deeper.

His voice was little more than a raspy whisper. "Sorry, Riley. I can't let you leave. Not without telling you how I feel."

"Zane..."

"Don't. Don't cut me off again. And don't deny what we both know in our hearts. You're not the only one caught by surprise by all of this. I didn't want this to happen. I worked damned hard to keep it from happening. But the truth is I've fallen. Hard. Not only for you, but for your daughter. Believe me, this wasn't at all what I expected to admit to you. And certainly not like this. In the dark, by the river, after a tedious day with Delia."

He almost smiled, and her lips curved slightly at his words.

"If I could choose the time and place for this soul-baring declaration, we'd be alone somewhere in a soft bed, miles away from the ranch, the family, the town. Far away from work and worries. And after a long, lazy night of making passionate love, I'd confess my true feelings. But sometimes we don't get to choose the time and place."

She opened her mouth, but he stopped her. "This isn't some fantasy about romantic love. I've been there, done that in my misspent youth. This is real and deep and crazy, and at the worst possible time in both our lives. I don't know how it happened. Frankly, I don't care. But I know this: I love you, Riley Mason. And I think, though you've been burned, and probably fighting as hard as I've been to deny it, you love me, too."

She was too stunned to do more than stare at him. Her mouth opened, then closed. She swallowed hard and tried again.

Her heart was pounding; her palms sweating. She could actually feel her head spinning in dizzying circles, as though she'd just stepped off an out-of-control merry-go-round.

And then, because she was afraid her poor heart might just stop beating altogether, she threw her arms around his neck and did the most unexpected thing of all.

She burst into a torrent of tears.

CHAPTER SEVENTEEN

Zane held her, his lips pressed to a tangle of hair at her temple, while her scalding tears soaked the front of his shirt. He felt such a welling of tenderness for this woman. For so long now she'd put up this strong, brave front, but he'd seen through the facade to her fear and, more, to her emotional fragility.

When at last her tears had run their course, she sniffed and accepted his handkerchief.

"Feel better?"

She hiccuped a laugh. "I feel like an absolute idiot. I think I've shed more tears today than I've shed in a lifetime."

"My beautiful, wonderful Riley." He lifted her face and brushed a kiss over her lips.

As he lingered over the kiss, she wrapped her arms around his neck and returned his kisses with a sudden sense of urgency that caught them both by surprise.

He lifted his head to stare down into her eyes. Though

the hunger was still there, he softened it with a smile. "I believe you just gave me your answer. I'd say you're feeling much better."

"Oh, Zane." She leaned into him before continuing, "I didn't want this. I fought so hard against it. God knows I tried every way I could not to care about you. But I just can't help myself. You've found a way past all the barriers I'd been so clever to set up."

"Thank God," he breathed before taking her offered lips.

The kiss spun on and on, by turns filling them, draining them, until they were both struggling for breath.

He held her a little away and pressed his forehead to hers. "You have to know how much I want you, Riley. But unless we stop right now, we're about to cross a line. I want this to be your decision."

His words, spoken so tenderly, touched her more deeply than anything he could have said. Most men would take what they wanted, without regard for the consequences. But then, she'd already learned that Zane McCord wasn't like most other men.

These things she was feeling weren't just passion or a spur-of-the-moment hunger, though she'd tried to convince herself they were when she'd first been drawn to him. Now she knew beyond a doubt. She could feel her heart swelling with love for him.

She touched a finger to his cheek. "Delia was right about you. You hide behind this tough cowboy image. But inside, you're kind and caring. Another reason why you've become so special to me, Zane. And why, whether you like it or not, I want you, too. Now." She lifted her face to his. "Please. Before I die of wanting."

"I'll thank God later. For now..." He caught her in a

bear hug and lifted her off her feet while he devoured her with kisses until they were both trembling.

Locked in an embrace, he backed her up until she was pressed to the gnarled trunk of a tree.

For a moment she was startled by the roughness of his kiss. His arms were almost bruising, his kisses by turn demanding, then coaxing, as he seemed to be fighting a war within himself.

Then with a sigh she leaned into him, losing herself completely in the pure pleasure of the moment.

Touched by her total surrender, his kiss gentled. His lips moved over hers, tasting, nuzzling, drawing out all the sweet, sweet flavors that were uniquely hers.

She sighed and her lips parted for him. His tongue tangled with hers and he took the kiss deeper until they were both sighing.

When he lifted his head, she felt bereft. But when his lips whispered over her face, pressing light kisses to her eyelids, her cheeks, the corner of her jaw, the sweetness of it had her heart stuttering. All she could do was stand very still absorbing each new pleasure.

"Riley, do you have any idea how special you are?"

His words, whispered against her ear, made her shiver with delight. No one had ever made her feel like this. As though she were the center of his universe. His sun and moon and stars.

To a woman starved for affection, his were the sweetest words in the world.

"Show me, Zane."

She'd expected him to take her quickly. Instead, his movements were slow and deliberate, as though now, in this place, they had all the time in the world.

With his tongue he traced the curve of her ear, nibbling, tugging, then darting inside until she gave a
strangled laugh and pushed a little away. He dragged her
close and burned a trail of kisses down her neck. When
he buried his lips in the sensitive hollow of her throat, she
shivered and clung to him, afraid that at any moment her
legs would fail her.

As though reading her mind, he released her to remove
his denim jacket and toss it to the ground. Then, lowering
her to the spot, he kissed her until she was breathless.

"Last chance to change your mind," he whispered
against her ear.

She twined her arms around his neck. "I couldn't if I
wanted to. I want you too much. I've waited so long for
you. For this. Please don't stop now."

In reply he kissed her with a hunger that rocked them
both. And she responded by pouring herself into the kiss,
hoping to show him in every way she could just how
much he meant to her.

When she reached for the buttons of her shirt, his
hands stopped her. "I want to do this." His eyes stayed
steady on hers as he unbuttoned first one, then another,
until he slid the shirt from her shoulders, baring a sheer
lace bra that revealed more than it covered.

He undressed her with a kind of reverence that had
her fully aroused. The brush of his big hands down her
body, the whisper of his lips on her bare flesh, had her
trembling with need.

The look in his eyes made her feel beautiful. The sigh
that escaped his lips made her feel cherished.

She reached for his shirt, slipping it aside to reveal a
body beautifully sculpted, corded with muscles. With all

the ranch chores, this cowboy had no need for a personal trainer.

She brought her lips to his hair-roughened chest and thrilled to the little moan that escaped his lips.

It was exciting to know that he was as fully engaged as she, and that it was her touch that could make him respond like this.

When her fingers fumbled with the fasteners at his waist, he helped her until his clothes lay discarded beside hers.

He reached up and removed the clip from her neat knot, causing her hair to tumble wildly around her face and shoulders. He watched it with a look that reminded her of a wild creature. Without a word he plunged his hands into the tangles and pulled her head back, with a low moan of pleasure, before covering her mouth with his.

His kiss was no longer gentle, but demanding. It spoke of a hunger so deep, so abiding, it longed to be filled. Of a need so long suppressed, it could no longer be contained. A need to touch and be touched.

And he did, over and over until she felt her body trembling for him.

Riley wrapped her arms around his waist and clung to his strength. At that simple contact she felt his muscles contract violently, as though pulled by invisible strings. His hands moved over her, followed by his mouth. Enticing, arousing, taking her high, then higher still, until her body hummed with need.

He'd spoken to her of a big bed, far away from the world. Right now, with his lips and tongue and fingertips arousing her, she had no need of fantasy. This was real. This was now. This rough cowboy possessed her, body and soul. And this place, with the starlight above and the sweet smell of earth beneath, was all she wanted or needed.

She thought she knew the sweet, gentle man with the delightful grin and the quick joke. But this darker, passionate side of Zane McCord excited her beyond all her wildest dreams.

The more aroused he became, the bolder she became. It was exciting to know that it was her touch, her kiss that he craved. And she gave all she could, pressing soft kisses down his throat, across his chest, and lower, along his stomach, until he moaned and clutched her fiercely.

Like two people starved, they feasted. Crazed with need, they gave and took, coming together with a blaze of passion that had them slipping beyond reason.

With great care Zane levered himself above her, his mouth teasing her breasts until she writhed beneath him. Without warning she reached the first crest, stunned and reeling. Her mind went numb as her body reacted in a purely physical way, sending shock waves through her system.

He gave her no time to recover as he continued kissing her, touching her, leading her even higher, until her entire body was a mass of nerve endings.

Her breath came harder now, faster, as she clutched the jacket beneath her and struggled for air.

The night breeze was fresh, but nothing could cool the heat that rose up between them, clogging their throats, pearling their flesh, blinding their vision.

She trembled as he moved over her, heated flesh to heated flesh. And still he kept the final relief just out of reach, as he continued to kiss, to touch, to tease until she thought she would go mad from wanting him.

Their world had narrowed to this place, this moment in time.

A night bird cried, and its mate answered. The rushing waters of the creek seemed to keep time to the erratic pounding of two hearts. Their chests rose and fell with each measured breath.

Riley's eyes, glazed with passion, remained steady on Zane's. She hadn't thought it possible to want more, but she did. As he entered her, she enfolded him in her arms, moving with him, matching his strength. Oh, it felt so heavenly to have him inside her, deepening her arousal until she was half-mad with desire.

She filled herself with the dark taste of him. Heard his voice, low, urgent, as he whispered words never heard before, and took her to places she'd never gone before.

And then they were moving to a rhythm as old as time itself. Climbing, soaring.

She felt her body shudder and heard her name torn from his lips as together they seemed to reach the very center of the bright, full moon high overhead.

For a space of a heartbeat they hovered, suspended somewhere between heaven and earth. And then they were shattering into millions of glittering, golden pieces before drifting like gold dust to the ground.

It was a most incredible journey.

It was Zane who finally broke the silence.

Still joined, he lifted a hand to her cheek. "You all right?"

Her eyes were closed, but she could still see stars. "Better than."

"Better than what?"

Her lids flickered, then opened. "Much better than all right. That was..."

"...fantastic," he finished for her.

"I was just about to say that."

"Good. Two minds." He gave a long, deep sigh. "Am I too heavy?" Without waiting for her response he shifted, rolling to one side before drawing her into his arms. "Better?"

"Much." She snuggled closer, until her head was resting on his shoulder. "You make a great pillow."

"Happy to oblige, ma'am."

She gave a dreamy smile.

They lay that way for long minutes, until their world gradually settled, and their heart rates returned to normal.

It was Riley who finally spoke. "There are things you need to know."

When he didn't respond, she sighed. "You know what I love about you?"

Though he wondered if she realized she'd used the L word, he waited, unwilling to shatter the mood.

"You don't push. You give me time. But now that we've..." She chose her words carefully. "Now that we've shared this, I need to tell you what I couldn't tell you before."

Again he merely waited, knowing that she would tell him in her own time, in her own way.

"I told you that Summer's father was in Special Forces, and was killed on a mission in the Middle East."

He nodded.

"What I didn't tell you was that Nick's background was pretty...unsavory." She took a breath. "He was a street-tough kid who'd been in foster care until he ran away. I learned later that he'd been on his own since he was twelve. When I met him, I was working in a coffee shop off-campus while going to college. He was always quiet, always alone, always seated in a corner, where he could watch the door. I thought it was amusing. Like a gunslinger from the Old West who had to watch the door of the saloon for the approach of the bad guys. I had no idea that's what he was actually doing. Then one day he came in wearing his uniform, and told me he was celebrating the fact that he had broken with the past and was leaving in the morning for special training before shipping overseas. I jokingly told him I thought having a latte wasn't much of a celebration."

She fell silent for long moments, and Zane waited, eager to hear more, but giving her time to collect her thoughts.

"He stayed until my shift ended. And then he offered to walk me home. I don't know why I agreed. I didn't really know him. But he was so alone. And it touched something in me. Maybe because I was always alone. I've been alone my whole life."

She glanced over. "I guess, since I told your aunt about my family, I owe you the same." Very quickly, without emotion, she told him about the loss of her parents, and the way she'd been raised by her very cold, very distant aunt and uncle.

Zane listened in silence, giving her time to tell him as much as she felt comfortable admitting. As he listened, his heart ached for her.

When she paused, he said quietly, "So two loners connected."

"Exactly." She fell silent before adding, "When we got to my place, it seemed the most natural thing to invite him in. Though I'd never before been with a stranger, it didn't seem wrong. Oh, I knew my aunt and uncle would have strongly disapproved. And I rarely veered from their rules. But there was so much sadness in him. And we were both so lonely." She sighed. "He was my first." She gave a dry laugh. "Pretty pathetic, isn't it?" She didn't wait for a response. "He stayed the night and left in the morning. But through the night he opened up about his life. He told me about his troubled childhood, and about the fact that he'd been coerced into becoming part of a gang. I was thinking he meant a street gang, but he said these weren't kids. These were men involved in every kind of criminal behavior. Very well-connected. Some of them, he said, had infiltrated the ranks of law enforcement, politicians. A lot of very important people. When he left them to join the military, they accused him of being disloyal. He knew too much. They vowed to make him pay for his disloyalty. He told me that they wouldn't dare hurt him, because he had something they wanted. And as long as it was in his possession, he was safe."

"Did you ask what he had?"

She shook her head. "I didn't ask and he didn't volunteer anything more. But I figured that was why he'd signed on for such a dangerous military mission. After the life he'd led, he had nothing to lose." In a low voice she added, "When he was leaving the next morning, he promised to keep in touch, and he gave me a contact number, but we both knew we wouldn't see one another again."

"How did you know?"

She shrugged. "I don't know how to explain it. There was no connection. No real feeling between us."

She looked up, watching the path of a shooting star. "By the time I learned of my condition, he'd already shipped out. I wrote him via the contact number to let him know that I was expecting his baby. It seemed the right thing to do, even though I assured him that I didn't want or need anything from him."

"And then he died."

She nodded and sat up, too agitated to continue lying in Zane's arms. "Afterward, I received his letter, written before his death, saying that he wanted to do right by his child. To that end, he was sending me something that was worth a great deal to certain people. When I received it, I was to take it to the state's attorney general, and I would be given a reward, generous enough to guarantee my future and that of my child."

"What did he send you?"

"A list of names, dates, amounts of money paid. And photos and videos. Dozens of them, of prominent people in the act of accepting money."

Zane whistled. "Did you follow Nick's instructions?"

"I tried to. I contacted the attorney general's office. Of course, I never got to actually speak with him. I was given an associate, who promised to relay my information that I had something of value. The next thing I knew, I was visited by a man who claimed to be from the attorney general's office, saying I was to give him the 'Green File.'"

"End of story?"

She shook her head. "It would have been. But I hadn't said exactly what I had. When he mentioned the Green File, I knew that this man wasn't from the attorney general's office. I'd never mentioned Seth Green by name."

"What did you do?"

"I told him I'd mailed the folder to his office. That it would arrive before the close of business the next day."

"A lie?"

"Yes. I was playing for time. And scared to death. But he left, promising that I'd be in very big trouble if that file wasn't in his hands by the following day."

Zane had a flash of memory, and he sat up beside her. "You once mentioned being set up by someone who wanted to discredit you and cause you to lose custody of Summer. Do you suspect the attorney general of doing that?"

She held up a hand. "Not really, though I can't prove or disprove it. The law professor who was kind enough to lend me some legal advice suggested that a band of criminals that well connected could have a paid operative in the attorney general's office and in several other locations as well. Their job would be to pass along any information that they deemed important. Whoever it was, they seemed determined to discredit me so that anything I might say later would be tainted. What better way to discredit a woman than to prove her unfit to raise her own child?"

At Zane's sudden frown she added, "That same law professor suggested that I was up against money and political influence that could eventually cost me much more than my daughter. He said such criminals wouldn't flinch at taking a life. With no one to protect me, I accepted a job as far away from Philadelphia as possible, hoping I could just hide out and this would all go away."

"And now, thanks to Delia, they know where you are."

She nodded. "And now they know how to find Summer." She held herself stiffly, hands twisted in her lap, gaze fixed on the sky.

"Did you keep the file with you?"

"I was afraid to. I hid it."

"In a bank vault, I hope?"

"I was afraid to go there. I was convinced that I was being followed." She gave a shaky laugh. "Of course, by then I'd become convinced that my phone was bugged, my child threatened, and my life on the line."

"What did you do with the file, Riley?"

"I put it in a post office box and...hid the key."

He gave a sigh of relief. "Smart move. Now, you need a plan. Let me help."

She shook her head. "Don't you see? Now that I know about that phone call to Delia, I have to get away. What if that wrangler, Cooper Easley, was one of them?"

That had Zane's brows knitting together. "I thought he was just looking for something to steal. But he could have been sent here to spy on you."

"You see? I can't bear to think I've brought trouble to you and your family, Zane. These people are ruthless."

"The McCords are pretty tough, too. We have a few connections of our own. And my cousin Wyatt knows a private detective who might be able to do some digging. He's helped us in the past."

She was already shaking her head. "I can't..."

"Sorry. I'm about to overrule you, Riley Mason. You're not alone anymore. We're going to figure this out together." He dragged her into his arms and kissed her until she stopped fighting and returned his kisses.

When her arms encircled his neck, he smiled down into her eyes. "Now that wasn't so hard to do, was it?"

"You're not playing fair."

"You know what they say. All's fair. And, my beautiful Riley, this isn't war. Which only leaves..." Instead of saying more he covered her mouth with his and kissed her, long and slow and deep.

Love? She'd never believed it possible. Oh, she knew that what she was feeling for Zane was special. But after Nick, she'd convinced herself that she wasn't worthy of a good man's love. Especially a man like this.

It was difficult to deny what her heart was whispering. But love? Men often lied to get what they wanted. Would Zane?

Oh, why had this happened now, when her whole world was coming apart at the seams?

And then, as the kiss spun on and on, all thought fled. She could actually feel her heart tumble in her chest. And as he took the kiss deeper, she could feel the ground tremble beneath her as he laid her down and took her on a slow, sensuous ride to paradise.

CHAPTER EIGHTEEN

Zane and Riley climbed the stairs hand in hand, both of them careful to avoid the squeaky step halfway up.

When they reached Riley's suite, she expected Zane to say good night, but instead he opened the door and stood aside to allow her to precede him.

Cora was curled up in the rocker, an afghan tucked around her shoulders. The fire had long ago burned to embers.

Zane set a log on the grate and closed the fire screen. The movement had Cora lifting her head.

"Oh. You're back."

Riley knelt beside her chair. "Miss Cora, I'm sorry we were gone so long. That was really thoughtless of me."

"Of us," Zane corrected.

Suddenly alert, Cora looked from her great-nephew to the young woman kneeling beside her.

A slow smile crept over her lips, illuminating all her features. "There's no need to apologize, dear." She patted

Riley's hand. "I was young once myself. You haven't had a single night away from Summer since you arrived at the ranch."

"I don't need to be away from her."

Cora touched a hand to Riley's cheek and stared directly into her eyes. "Of course you do. That's why I insisted on staying here."

Riley's eyes widened with sudden recognition. "You . . . wanted us to be alone?"

Cora saw the look exchanged between Riley and Zane, who was standing beside the mantel, and her smile deepened. There was no denying the look of intimacy between them.

She set aside the afghan and got to her feet. "I'll say good night now."

"Good night, Miss Cora. I can't thank you enough."

Zane took his great-aunt's hand and lifted it to his lips. "'Night, Aunt Cora. I'll walk you to your suite."

She winked at him. "No thanks, dear. You stay here and say a proper good night to Riley. I believe I'll go to the kitchen and make myself some hot chocolate before I go to bed." Her steps were brisk as she crossed to the door. "After that lovely nap, I'm not feeling at all tired just now."

With a smile at both of them, she let herself out.

Zane chuckled and gave a shake of his head in admiration.

"What's so funny?"

"Us." He twined his fingers with Riley's and drew her close. "That sly old woman orchestrated this whole thing. And she knew, the minute she saw us, that we'd played right into her hand."

"Oh. I knew it. I knew, by the look in her eyes when

she stared into mine. She wanted us to be alone. She was pushing us together, whether we were ready or not."

"Who knew that my sweet Aunt Cora is a hopeless romantic?" He brushed a kiss over Riley's lips. "Well, I for one, am grateful as hell."

"You're not the only one."

They were still laughing together as they walked to the door and shared a lingering kiss good night.

"Remember," Zane said against her mouth. "You're not running. Whatever happens, you're not alone anymore. We're in this together."

She pulled back. "I can't help thinking you're wrong. I have a very bad feeling about this. I couldn't bear it if I brought trouble here."

"With your permission I'd like to let the family know in the morning, so they can be advised of the situation and be prepared. It will mean revealing things about you and Nick and his background. I'd like to do this before Summer is awake, so she doesn't overhear any of it. Is that going to be all right with you?"

She took in a deep breath, considering the implications. The McCord family was about to learn intimate details of her life. Details she'd never shared with anyone except Zane. And though she would like to be the one to tell them, she knew it was better this way. With Summer unaware that anything was amiss.

Reluctantly she nodded.

Zane tipped up her chin, staring into her eyes. "Are you willing to abide by their decision?"

She shrugged. "I'll consider it. But as I said…"

He kissed her again. "Just promise me that you'll take their suggestions into consideration."

She sighed. "Why do I get the feeling that you're going to have your way?"

"Because you know I'm right. Besides, we would never agree to anything that doesn't first have your stamp of approval."

When she pursed her lips to say something more, he kissed her lightly before turning away.

Riley stood in the doorway until Zane disappeared down the hallway. Then, with a thoughtful look, she closed the door and dropped down into the chair vacated by Cora.

The McCords were an extraordinary family. Accepting, forgiving. So openly loving. The kind of family she'd yearned for in her lonely, troubled childhood. But just how loving and forgiving would they prove to be when they learned that their very safety was at stake because of her?

Too wired to think about sleep, she leaned her head back. She had a great many things to mull, and she couldn't think of a better place to do that than right here in front of a blazing fire.

Zane was downstairs early, drinking his first cup of coffee when Wyatt and Marilee entered the kitchen.

As always, his first thought was how completely happy and contented they both were. Though their courtship had been stormy, their marriage seemed, from his vantage point, to be thriving.

"'Morning, cuz." Wyatt slapped his arm in passing.

"You're the very person I've been waiting for." Zane topped off his cup and settled himself at the table beside his cousin. "I have need of your old friend Archie."

Wyatt shot him a look. "Are you in some kind of trouble?"

Zane was shaking his head just as Jesse and Amy walked in.

"Who's in trouble?" Jesse demanded.

"Trouble?" Cora opened the door. "Did I hear somebody say trouble?"

Before Zane could answer, Cal came in from the trail, shaking rain from his hat and scraping mud from his boots before carefully washing his hands at the big sink. He stepped into the kitchen and picked up a mug of coffee, listening in silence as Zane turned to include all of them.

"Riley's concerned about that phone call that Delia fielded at her place. Delia let it be known to the caller that Riley lives and works here. And that could spell trouble, since she left some... unfinished business back in Philadelphia."

"What kind of unfinished business?" Wyatt's attention sharpened.

As briefly as possible Zane explained the situation, while the others listened with matching looks of concern.

When he'd finished, Cal set down his mug. "The first thing we do is call Sheriff Wycliff right away."

Jesse nodded. "I agree. Ernie can keep an eye out for anybody who looks out of place, or asks for directions to our ranch."

Zane glanced around the table. "Gold Fever may be a small town, but it's grown big enough that strangers, even those asking for directions, won't always be spotted by the law. I think we need to have Wyatt's pal Archie investigate these gang members, and let us know who and what we're dealing with. But in the meantime, while he's doing his search, we need to have a plan to keep Riley and her daughter safe."

Jesse looked at the others. "How about posting a couple of wranglers here at the house to keep an eye out for trespassers?"

Cal shook his head. "What are they supposed to do all day? Walk the perimeter of the place with rifles like some old Western movie?"

"Then I guess you won't agree to setting up guards around our property?" Jesse added with a half-smile.

Cal frowned. "I can't think of too many bad guys who will just drive up and announce themselves. Wouldn't you expect them to arrive under cover of darkness? Besides, I can't pull valuable wranglers from the herds to drive around a couple hundred thousand acres of land from morning until dark looking for out-of-state license plates. I just don't have any wranglers to spare. It was bad enough that I had to fire Cooper."

At the mention of the wrangler, Zane's head came up sharply. "Riley is wondering if he might have been sent here to spy on her." One look at his cousins, and he realized that they were on the same wavelength.

"You think Cooper could have been on the payroll of this gang?" Wyatt asked.

Jesse nodded slowly. "Stranger things have happened."

"Especially to us." Wyatt squeezed Marilee's hand.

Zane turned to Cal. "Okay. Cooper may have been here to do harm. But he's gone. Since you want to strike the idea of guards, do you have any suggestions?"

While the older man mulled, Wyatt spoke up. "The important thing is that we're all on alert. I'll contact Archie as soon as Riley gives me names and other information that he can go on."

"There's one thing we could do now." At Cal's words they all turned to him.

He glanced at Cora. "You've been itching to go up into the hills and paint. Why not invite Riley and Summer to go along? It'll get them out of the house for a week or two, and once you settle in and let me know your location, I'll arrange for a couple of wranglers up in the hills with the herds to drop by every day to see how you're doing."

Cora seemed delighted at the prospect. "That's brilliant, Cal. Not only will I get my fill of painting, but I'll be able to share it with a fellow artist."

At the puzzled looks of the others she went on to explain, "Just yesterday evening I realized Riley's talent. I think it would do her a world of good to be exposed to something other than those ledgers she's been working on."

"Just a minute." Cal turned to Cora with a look of surprise. "Are you suggesting that, now I've discovered the best darned accountant I've ever had, I'm about to lose her?"

"Not at all." Cora laid a hand over his. "Riley is as committed to your paperwork as I am to my art. And she's the most conscientious worker I've ever known."

Cal nodded. "She is that."

"And now you've thought of something we can do for Riley. I love your idea of a wilderness trek, Cal." Cora's eyes twinkled. "Think what fun it will be. A girls' retreat. Fresh air. Sunshine. Hours of painting whatever and whenever we please. And plenty of mother-daughter time for Riley and Summer. And when we come back, I'm sure Riley will return to her ledgers with renewed energy."

The ranch foreman shook his head from side to side while giving her a warm smile. "You're a sly one, Cora."

The others around the table merely smiled. The deep well of affection between these two was always such fun to watch, especially since neither seemed aware of it.

Cora smiled with delight. "Oh, Cal. This will be so good for Riley. Not to mention the fact that I'll have someone along who loves art as much as I do."

"And a four-year-old child who may prove a bit of a distraction," Amy said drily.

Jesse shot a glance at his wife beside him. "Why are you raining on Aunt Cora's parade? Are you angling for an invitation to go along on this?"

Amy flushed, and he realized she'd been doing exactly that.

"I think"—she weighed her words carefully—"that it might be an advantage for Aunt Cora and Riley to have some backup around, when Summer needs a nap, or a diversion, so they can continue painting without interruption."

Marilee surprised them by chiming in. "Mind if I come along, too?"

Wyatt shot her a look of surprise. "What's in it for you?"

"A chance to camp out in the wilderness. To climb rocks. Besides, if the rest of the girls are going, why should I stay behind and miss all the fun?"

"What fun?" The door opened to reveal Riley and Summer.

The minute Riley stepped into the kitchen, Zane was beside her, taking her hand in his.

While Summer took her place at the table, Riley and Zane stood very still, hands joined. The look that passed between them wasn't lost on the others. While the women smiled in sudden understanding, Jesse and Wyatt turned to each other with arched looks. Everyone knew it was just a matter of time before they would be teasing their cousin mercilessly.

"What fun?" Riley asked again.

"I'm planning my latest trek to the wilderness for some marathon painting." Cora looked quite pleased with herself. "I was hoping, since Amy and Marilee asked to go along, that you and Summer might join us."

Riley settled herself at the table beside her daughter. "This might not be a good time for me to think about leaving the ranch. There are things you don't know."

Zane put a hand on her shoulder. "I've already told them."

Before she could protest, Cora interrupted. "We think this would be the perfect time for you and Summer to take a break. I hope you'll give it some thought, dear. We'll paint to our hearts' content. And when we're not painting, we can explore some of the foothills of Treasure Chest Mountain. And at night, if you don't care for the tent, we can sleep under the stars or in the back of my vehicle."

Summer picked up on one thing. "We can sleep in a tent?"

"If you'd like."

She turned to her mother. "Oh, boy, Mama. Can we?"

Riley looked up at Zane. "You think we'd be safe out there?"

"Maybe safer than here"—he glanced at Summer, to see how much the little girl was following their conversation— "for now, at least. Nobody but those of us gathered around this table would know where you're headed when you leave." He squeezed her hand. "It doesn't get much safer than that."

"I don't know..." Riley chewed her lip.

"Please, Mama?" Summer tugged on Riley's arm. "I've never slept in a tent. Can we please?"

Zane was matter-of-fact. "It's wilderness. It's isolated. And it's on our land. We'll have wranglers posted nearby, just as a precaution."

"And you think we should go?"

He nodded. "And while you're gone, we intend to work on your...situation."

She glanced around the table and saw heads nodding. She fell silent for long moments, swallowing the lump in her throat.

When she found her voice she said softly, "You're all amazing, to be so accepting of this. I guess it's decided, then." Riley turned to her daughter. "Looks like we're going camping with Miss Cora, honey."

"And we'll get to see bears and coyotes and lions." Summer was carrying on a long conversation with Floppy, lying on the floor beside her little suitcase in the kitchen.

The thought of it had Riley shivering.

She turned to Cora. "I have to warn you. I'm not much

of an outdoor person. In fact, I've never been camping in my life."

"Not even when you were little?"

She shook her head. "Not once."

"What about Girl Scout camp?"

"My aunt wouldn't allow it. She called it permissive foolishness."

Though Cora's lips pursed in a tight little frown, she refrained from making a comment.

Zane picked up their bags and hauled them out to the truck, parked behind the Jeep that Cora always took on her wilderness jaunts. They had arranged for Cora to drive Riley and Summer, with Marilee driving the ranch truck, and Amy along as her passenger. That way they had room for all their supplies in the back of the two vehicles.

After securing Summer in her car seat, Riley turned to Zane. "I still can't believe I'm running away and leaving you behind to deal with my troubles."

"You're not running away." He touched a finger to her lips and felt the quick rush of heat. "I'm sending you away. There's a difference."

"But…"

"And I'm going to miss you like hell every day that you're gone."

He glanced around. Wyatt was busy hugging Marilee. Jesse had Amy in a passionate embrace.

He didn't care if the whole world saw him. He wasn't letting her go without a final kiss.

"Enjoy your girls' retreat."

He bent and kissed her, much to the delight of Summer, who clapped her hands and shouted, "Look, everybody. Zane and Mama are kissing."

That had heads turning.

Zane grinned and kissed her again for good measure.

Cal had made half a dozen trips from the house to the Jeep and truck parked outside, until every available space that wouldn't be used by a passenger was filled to capacity with supplies. When all was in readiness, he took Cora aside.

In low tones he asked, "You have your rifle and handgun?"

"Of course."

"You've packed extra ammunition?"

She nodded.

"Remember to keep the safety on. For Summer's sake."

"I've already checked." Cora touched a hand to his cheek. "You look worried. Is there something you haven't told me?"

He hissed in a breath. "I always worry when you go away. Why should this time be any different?"

"You tell me."

His eyes looked bleak. "Maybe I'm just getting too old for this."

"Too old for what?" She lifted her other hand until she was framing his face. "Tell me what's troubling you, Cal."

He merely shook his head and pulled away.

As they made their way to the Jeep, he kept his hands tucked into his pockets, to keep from reaching out to keep her from going.

Once in the driver's seat she lowered the window. "We shouldn't be any longer than a week. Maybe two."

"If you are, I'll send out the troops." Cal watched as Jesse, Wyatt, and even Zane indulged in a final kiss before stepping back from the vehicles. It only tightened the band around Cal's heart.

He'd spent a lifetime watching Cora leave at will. In earlier times he'd told himself that it was her right to live her life as she pleased. She answered to no one, and he admired that in her. But now, suddenly, he was feeling overwhelmed, and he couldn't understand why. She'd left hundreds of times before, always returning with a renewed zest for life.

Why should this time be any different?

He had no answers. Only the terrible, urgent feeling that it was his suggestion that had brought this about. He should have kept his mouth shut. He should have done more to persuade her to stay.

Should have, could have...

He had very bad feelings about this. There was a real and terrible threat to their safety, and he wanted, needed, to be beside Cora, just in case.

With a wave and a shout, their little convoy took off in a cloud of dust.

The men stood to one side, watching until they were out of sight, before going their separate ways to resume their chores.

CHAPTER NINETEEN

With their women gone, the four men did their best to stay busy, and were mucking stalls when Wyatt's cell phone rang.

Archie's cockney voice came over the line.

Wyatt set his phone on speaker and motioned for Zane, Jesse, and Cal to gather around and listen.

"Okay, Archie, give us all you've got."

"Quite a lot so far, and none of it good. This fellow you asked me to check on, Nick Porter, did indeed die in the Middle East in a roadside bombing. Before he joined the military and left the country, he'd been running with some bad apples. This is a well-organized band of bad actors. At first glance they seem to be simply buying up foreclosed land and buildings in the heart of Philadelphia for renovation. That makes a lot of citizens happy. But upon digging deeper, it seems they're getting much bigger discounts on those properties than their competitors.

After sniffing around, I believe I know why. They're very well connected. Some city commissioners, the top honcho in the city's legal department, even the head of the tax tribunal, have made considerable deposits in their accounts since this group was allowed to play on their turf."

Zane's hands fisted at his sides. "Riley had good reason to be afraid."

Archie's voice faded a bit before growing louder. "There's talk of a big shake-up at city hall. The city's newspaper has their top investigative reporter sniffing around. He's been asking a lot of questions about this group and some land they sold back to the school board for several million more than it was actually worth. The word on the street is that the district attorney's office has refused to cooperate, saying there isn't enough evidence."

Zane's mouth compressed to a thin, tight line.

Wyatt asked the question that was on all their minds. "So, if that particular office should be corrupted, they'll continue their free ride?"

"Makes sense."

Wyatt frowned. "Thanks, Archie. You'll keep digging?"

"How could I stop? I'm already up to my knees in muck here. And I see no end to it."

"One more question." Cal caught Wyatt's hand and spoke into the phone before he could disconnect. "How far do you believe this gang's power is capable of reaching?"

"Are you asking me if I believe they can do harm there in Montana?"

"I am."

"My best guess is they'll go as far as they have to in order to hold on to their power base. Their greatest fear is that if one of them should topple, the rest would fall like dominoes."

Archie's reply had the four men staring at one another with somber expressions.

The somber mood remained throughout the dinner hour. While Dandy served a hearty beef stew, the men were more interested in discussing how to help Riley get Nick's information to the proper authorities, without having it intercepted by someone who was corrupt.

Jesse pushed aside his dinner. "She's already phoned the Philadelphia district attorney's office, and right after that, she was paid a visit by someone who threatened her."

Wyatt asked, "How about the chief of police?"

Cal nodded. "Good point."

Zane shook his head. "Do you think the chief of a big-city department takes all the calls made to him? That's why they have assistants and secretaries."

Cal gave a sigh of disgust. "Then how do we guarantee that Riley's file will reach somebody who can be trusted to follow up?"

Zane slapped a hand on the table as the thought struck. "The newspaper reporter."

The others looked up.

"Archie said the city's newspaper had their top investigative reporter sniffing around. His name is bound to be listed on the articles he's written so far for the paper. If we can contact him, we've got the perfect destination for Riley's file."

"Would she just contact him and trust that he'll follow up?"

Zane shrugged. "I'm not sure. We need to give this some thought. But it certainly seems wiser than sending word to a district attorney who may or may not even get the message if it's intercepted by the wrong party. I'm betting an investigative reporter reads his own mail and answers his own phone. After hearing from Riley, don't you think he'd want to pursue an important lead on an investigation into the corruption in his city? I'd think his paper would fly him out here to interview her and get a firsthand read on how much he's willing to trust her."

Around the table heads nodded.

Wyatt spoke his thoughts aloud: "And once the information is in his hands, there would be no reason for anybody to threaten Riley's life. The information would be out of her hands."

"All right then." Zane sat back, wondering why he didn't feel any sense of relief. Probably, he thought, because of the enormity of the corruption. This was so much bigger than he'd first expected. "We'll pass this information along to Riley. It's her decision."

He pushed away from the table and followed Cal's lead into the great room. There the four men stretched out their long legs toward the heat of the fireplace.

"I've been meaning to ask, cuz." Jesse settled into a big, overstuffed chair. "Riley Mason strikes me as pretty secretive. In the time she's been here, I don't think she's ever said two words about herself. How did she happen to trust you with such personal and volatile information?"

Zane tried for humor. "Haven't you noticed? Women have always trusted me. It's part of my charm."

The others shared a look before shaking their heads.

"Why you, cuz?" Wyatt pressed. "Why didn't she bare her soul to Cal? Or Aunt Cora?"

Zane saw Cal turn to him with a piercing look.

He shrugged, determined to keep things light. "She needed a friend. She sensed that she could trust me with her secret. And I'm glad she did, because that was way too heavy to carry alone."

That had the others nodding in agreement.

It was Cal who finally spoke. "Just so you remember, Riley's not only an employee, but she's a valued part of our family now."

Zane held up a hand. "I haven't forgotten, Cal."

The older man pinned him with a steady look, as though weighing his words. "Since coming back home, you've cut a pretty wide swath through the females in Gold Fever. Riley doesn't strike me as someone to be sweet-talked and then set aside. That sweet young woman has been hurt enough."

Zane's chin came up, but he refused to look away. "I would never hurt her." His tone had grown dangerously soft. "You're not the only one who thinks she's too special to ever do her wrong."

At that, Cal's eyes narrowed in thought before understanding dawned. "It's like that, then?"

Zane felt a sense of wonder as he acknowledged the truth to Cal, to his cousins. "Yeah. It's like that."

Dandy entered, wheeling a tray of desserts and coffee.

"Where're you going?" he called to Cal's back.

"To the barn." The ranch foreman's voice was gruff with emotion. "I've got some work to see to."

When he was gone, Zane ignored the tray of coffee and desserts and headed for the stairs.

"You going up to bed?" Jesse called.

"Yeah."

As he climbed the stairs, his two cousins picked up their coffee and drew close, talking in low tones.

Alone, Zane made his way to his room. Odd, he thought, that he and Cal both knew, though neither of them had spoken the word.

Love may be the hardest word in the world to say aloud.

Riley tucked Summer into her bunk in the tent before dropping down beside her to hear her daughter's prayers.

"Bless my mama and Miss Amy and Miss Cora and Miss Marilee. And bless Floppy and"—her smile was quick and bright—"bless Zane and Vanilla and..." She rubbed her eyes as she struggled to stay awake after a very long day of travel and excitement. "Bless everybody in the whole world."

"That was a very nice prayer." Riley leaned close to press kisses to Summer's face and neck.

She breathed her in, as always loving the smell of her daughter's skin. "Did you enjoy today?"

"It was fun."

"What did you like best?"

"Riding in Miss Cora's Jeep. Walking with Miss Amy along the stream and finding those pretty stones. Helping carry sticks for the fire. Eating outdoors. And this." She looked up. "Look, Mama. I'm sleeping in a tent."

"Yes, you are. Imagine that."

"I always wanted to."

"I know. I hope you get to do all the things you've always wanted."

Despite her excitement, Summer's eyes closed. Her breathing grew soft and easy. She was asleep before Riley walked from the tent.

She joined the women around the campfire.

Marilee held up a paper cup. "Wine?"

"Why not?" Riley accepted the cup from Marilee and settled herself on the opposite side of the fire, with her back pressed against a rock warmed by the flames.

She leaned her head back to stare at the night sky, ablaze with millions of stars that looked close enough to touch. "I can see why you love this, Miss Cora."

"It's grand, isn't it?" The older woman stretched out her legs to the warmth of the fire. "This is my favorite spot in the whole world. I can't imagine not being able to come here. The mountain, the buttes, the slow pace, all restore my soul."

Marilee gave a shake of her head. "It's the sheer size of everything out here. The vastness makes me feel very insignificant."

Riley turned to Amy. "You grew up here. Do you feel it, too, or is it all very ordinary to you?"

"There's nothing ordinary about this part of Montana. I may have grown up nearby, but our ranchland was tame compared to this." Amy took a sip of wine. "You could ride out here for days and never see another human."

Riley sighed. "That suits me just fine."

The others exchanged looks.

With an impish grin Amy said, "Would that happen to include Zane?"

Riley flushed and stared at the cup in her hand, avoiding their eyes. "He's...very sweet."

"Not to mention tall, dark, handsome, and extremely sexy," Marilee said with a laugh.

The others, including Cora, joined in.

"Really?" Riley didn't know if it was this place, or the company she was keeping, but whatever the reason, she was able to let down her guard and simply enjoy the moment. "I hadn't noticed."

That had the others laughing harder.

Amy arched a brow. "A woman would have to be blind not to notice Zane McCord. That man drips sex appeal. And," she added with a laugh, "if you repeat what I just said to my husband, I'll have to kill you."

That brought another round of giggles.

Marilee circled the fire, topping off their paper cups with more wine.

Cora removed her hiking boots and wiggled her toes. "Coot was so proud of his grandsons."

"He had a right to be, Aunt Cora." Marilee settled herself closer to the warmth of the fire. "Were you ever married?"

The older woman shook her head. "I came close a time or two. But it never seemed right."

"Are you sorry?" Riley asked.

Another shake of her head. "I can't miss what I never had. But I think I always knew that my career would come first in my life. The passion is so great, it doesn't leave room for any other."

Marilee thought about that before saying cautiously, "I don't know. Maybe if you were commuting to some big-city office building, where you were an officer of the company, climbing the corporate ladder, it would make marriage difficult to maintain. But being an artist doesn't strike me as being so all-consuming that you couldn't make room for a man. If you really loved him, of course."

Cora nodded. "That's the key. I guess I've never loved a man as much as I love my chosen career."

"Not even Cal?" The question was out of Amy's mouth before she could think.

Cora smiled in the growing darkness. "Cal is very dear to me. But he doesn't love me, Amy. Coot used to say that the ranch was Cal's very demanding mistress, and any woman foolish enough to lose her heart to a cowboy like that would always have to take second place."

"And you believed him?"

Cora's tone was as patient as if she were lecturing a child. "Why wouldn't I? My brother was one of the wisest men I've ever known. Not to mention the fact that he was Cal's closest friend for a lifetime." She turned to Riley. "What about you, dear? Did you come close to marrying?"

Riley gave a firm shake of her head. "My only goal was to graduate at the top of my class. After Summer was born, I had to shift gears radically. I never knew I could love anyone or anything as much as I loved that baby. She changed me. I decided that I had to improve my own life in order to improve hers. But then, when I realized that we were in danger, I became obsessed with keeping her safe. It's still my only thought."

"And Zane?" Amy asked. "Does he have a place in your thoughts?"

Riley drew her knees up and wrapped her arms around

them. Staring into the flames she said softly, "He's a really good man. And a persistent one. But though I trusted him with my secrets, I can't expect him to take on my responsibilities. That wouldn't be fair to him."

"Has he said as much?"

Riley shrugged. "Of course not. He's too much of a gentleman for that. But every man has a right to want a wife that comes into marriage without baggage."

Marilee gave her a gentle smile before stifling a yawn. "Maybe some other time I'll tell you about the baggage I brought to my marriage. But not tonight."

She poured the last of her wine into the grass before tossing the paper cup into the fire. The flames hissed and leaped before devouring it.

She got to her feet. "'Night. See you in the morning."

"I believe I'll join you." Cora slowly rose to her feet.

Amy glanced at Riley. "I'm with them. After all this fresh air, I can't keep my eyes open another minute."

As the others made their way to the tent, Riley remained by the fire, letting the silence of the night wash over her.

Their questions about Zane were understandable. It was obvious that he held a very special place in their hearts. They were looking out for one of their own. But the questions, and her answers, weighed heavily on her mind. What she and Zane had shared had been very special. And she had trusted him with a secret that had become too heavy to carry alone.

But sharing a secret wasn't the same as love. Not that she knew much about such things. The only person she'd ever loved completely was Summer. She was absolutely determined that no one, especially not a man, would ever be more important to her than her daughter.

So where did that leave Zane McCord?

It didn't matter, she told herself. She'd meant what she'd said earlier. A man like Zane, living a charmed life, had the right to find a woman who could concentrate all her love and energy on him, without the distraction of a child or other baggage.

For all the passion that pulsed between them, it was only that. Passion. Lust. Desire. Need. She had to face that hard truth if she was going to move ahead with her life. She couldn't allow herself to confuse lust with love. Want with need.

What she needed right now was a sense of safety, and she'd found that with the McCords. She was so grateful that they were willing to circle around her and Summer until this nightmare was somehow ended.

Would she ever feel completely safe?

She shivered. In truth, most of her life had been spent in fear. The loss of her parents had left her terrified. The threats by her aunt and uncle of what would happen if she didn't measure up to their standards had been harsh enough to make her work harder than any of her classmates. Facing debt and danger after the birth of Summer had uncovered hidden strengths within her. And now, after a taste of normal life, it was all being threatened once more.

She squared her shoulders. She wanted to run. Wanted, more than anything, to spare these good people even a threat of danger. But Zane seemed so certain that he and his family could bring her through this. And she wanted to believe him.

A part of her was desperate to take Summer and run. Now. Before they could be found.

Another part of her yearned for this threat to be gone, once and for all, so that she could get on with her life.

What if it was never over? What if they ran, and hid, and were found again and again?

Was that why she'd agreed to stay?

Or was Zane the real reason? The tantalizing chance, no matter how slim, that he wasn't just using a tired old line to get what he wanted, but instead...

She refused to go there in her mind. More than most women, she'd learned the painful lesson about the use of the *love* word. Men tossed it around, knowing how women needed to hear it. Family members said it, until the rules were broken. Friends said it, until their own needs were more important. And all of them disappeared, never to be seen again.

In her life, love had been real only once. Summer. That child was perfect love.

Riley hugged the thought to herself. She loved and was loved. That would have to be enough.

It was hours before, with the campfire burned to embers, she finally gave in to the need to crawl into her bunk.

She was asleep instantly.

CHAPTER TWENTY

———◆———

Summer took another bite of Marilee's flapjacks smothered with syrup. "These are good."

"You think they're as good as Dandy's?" Marilee asked with a straight face.

The little girl chewed, swallowed, all the while mulling. "Mama says it's wrong to lie. But they're really good, Miss Marilee."

"What a good girl. Even under stress, she can't tell a lie." Marilee winked at Amy. "I'd call that a halfhearted compliment."

That had all of them laughing.

When Riley's cell phone rang, she noted the caller and stepped away from the others. "Good morning, Zane. How're things at the ranch?"

"Lonely as hell."

That made her smile.

"How have you city girls taken to camping out?"

"With Marilee cooking over a fire, and Summer sleeping soundly in the tent last night, I'd say day one was a complete success."

"I'm glad you're enjoying yourselves. Are you feeling safe way out there?"

"Amazingly safe. Isn't that strange? We're miles from civilization, and feeling unafraid for the first time in years."

"I'm glad. We may be joining you in a couple of days."

"What does that mean?"

"We've heard more from Archie, and after talking it over, we're in agreement that you should contact a man named Jack Manning, a reporter with the *Gazette*."

"The *Gazette*? That's Philadelphia's biggest newspaper. Do you think that's wise?"

"I do, and I'll tell you why." As quickly as possible he explained their concerns about going to any public officials whose office staff may have been corrupted.

"The last thing you want is a repeat of that incident with the district attorney's office."

"How do we know we can trust this reporter?"

"Who better than the one digging up all the dirt? If he's serious about this, and I believe he is, he'll want to fly out immediately to interview you."

"Should I return to the ranch?"

"We think you should agree to meet him out there. Once he arrives at the ranch, we'll drive him to your campsite."

"I won't have to be alone with him?"

"We'll all be there with you, if you'd like."

"Yes." She gave a deep sigh. "I'd feel better if you and your family could be with me while I talk to a stranger."

"Count on it." He gave her the reporter's number, which Archie had provided. "You'll call him now?"

"As soon as I hang up."

"Riley."

At the sudden change in his tone she was instantly alert. "Yes?"

He thought about all the things he wanted to tell her, but said simply, "It's going to be fine."

"Yes. I know." Seeing Cora drawing close, she said, "Thank you for this information. I'll call now."

After disconnecting, she took a deep breath and dialed the number he'd given her.

Later, while Amy and Summer were busy collecting pretty stones along the banks of the creek, she filled in Cora and Marilee on what she had done.

Zane spoke with Sheriff Ernie Wycliff, asking about any strangers in town who had shown an uncommon interest in Riley Mason or the ranch.

"Hell, the whole town's talking about Miss Mason, Zane. Especially after you brought her to town and had lunch at the saloon."

"But that's typical of Gold Fever, Ernie. What about strangers?"

"The only stranger in town the past few days was Gabriel Pasqual."

"Was?"

"He left town without a word. You ought to see Mayor Rowe and Stan Novak. All those big dreams about Pasqual pouring millions of dollars into development, and all they have to show for it now is a pile of paperwork, and all without his signature." He chuckled.

"I know it isn't funny. It would have been nice to have a deep-pocket investor. But right now, they're left to shovel manure, if you know what I mean."

Zane was in no mood to laugh. As quickly as possible he told the sheriff about the threat to Riley's safety, and asked him to keep an eye out for strangers who might be heading toward the ranch.

"You want me to bring the state police in on this?" the sheriff asked.

"Not yet. But I have a private detective on it. If he sees any clear danger, I'll let you know, and then I'd appreciate you contacting them."

"Will do."

When he rang off, Zane sat staring at the phone. He'd promised Riley that he'd keep her and her daughter safe. Now he had to pray he'd done all the right things.

Zane pocketed his cell phone and turned to his cousins. "The *Gazette* reporter, Jack Manning, is flying in tomorrow. Since he can't get a direct flight, he'll fly to Helena, then catch a commuter plane to Gold Fever. We're to pick him up at the airstrip and drive him out to Aunt Cora's campsite."

Wyatt finished administering the antibiotic to a young calf before stepping from a stall in the cattle barn. "That was quick. I guess that proves he's eager to get his hands on that file."

"I'll say." Zane frowned. "I figured he'd be sharp enough to recognize what he's being offered. But this is moving even faster than I expected."

"It's all good." Cal stepped out of the stall behind Wyatt. "This can't be over soon enough to suit me."

The others nodded in agreement.

"One more night without my bride," Wyatt said with a grin. "And then we'll be together again."

Cal shook his head before striding from the barn. "She's only been gone for a couple of nights. What'll you do if you have to be separated for months?"

"Let's hope he never has to find out," Jesse muttered. "Now let's see what Dandy whipped up for tonight's he-man menu."

"I don't care what it is," Cal said over his shoulder, "as long as it has something to do with steak. Rare."

"Dandy, this is just what I was craving." Cal looked around with satisfaction at the platter of steak and an array of baked potatoes and salad served with thick slices of home-baked garlic bread.

The four men dug in, savoring every bite.

Dandy nodded his approval. "I figure, after a day of chores, nothing satisfies like red meat."

They were too busy eating to respond.

An hour later, relaxing around the fire with coffee and longnecks, they looked up at a visit from the mayor.

"Stafford." Cal got to his feet to shake the man's hand. "We just finished dinner, but I'm sure Dandy could bring you some."

"No thanks." The mayor patted his stomach. "I ate at the Fortune Saloon before leaving town."

"Will you have coffee or a beer?"

"Coffee, thanks." He accepted a cup and settled himself in one of the big chairs.

Zane polished off one of Dandy's chocolate chip cookies. "Kind of late to be driving out here just for a visit, isn't it?"

"More business than pleasure." Stafford took a moment to sip his coffee. "I figured all of you would be interested in hearing that the deal Stan Novak had with Gabriel Pasqual has fallen through."

Cal arched a brow. "We already heard from Ernie Wycliff. But he didn't know why. Did they have a falling-out?"

"Stan swears he didn't do anything to ruin this deal. One day Pasqual is talking about pumping millions of dollars of his investors' money into our town, and the next thing we know he's checked out and left without a word."

"No explanation?"

"None. We didn't even know he was gone until we went over to the house he was renting. Mrs. Soames said he still had two weeks to go on his rent, and he told her he wouldn't be back. He left no forwarding address, and calls to his cell phone go unanswered."

Cal scratched his head. "That's a puzzle."

The mayor nodded. "All those meetings, and all those parcels of land that Stan and I fought to buy, and now it's all for nothing." He shot them a sheepish look. "I guess you're relieved to know that you won't be bothered with any more requests for your land."

"A glimmer of light in all that mess," Wyatt said with a grin.

"Sorry. I knew you were getting annoyed with all those requests for meetings, but I really thought we'd be doing something good for the town."

The mayor finished his coffee and shook hands with each of them before taking his leave, looking more like a whipped dog than the proud mayor of Gold Fever.

When they were alone, Cal glanced at the three cousins. "I wonder what that was all about?"

Zane's mind was working overtime. "I know it's a stretch, but I can't help wondering if it has anything to do with Riley."

Jesse slapped his arm. "More than likely Pasquale's investors just left him high and dry, without a dime, and he was all hot air. Not everything in the world revolves around Riley, cuz."

Zane nodded. "Yeah. I guess you're right. Still, it's weird."

"So is life." Stifling a yawn, Wyatt drained his beer and set it on the trolley. "I'm heading up to bed. It'll be a long day tomorrow, picking up the reporter at the airport and driving all the way to Treasure Chest."

"Yeah," Zane added with a smile, "but think about who'll be waiting for us at the end of the drive."

"There's that." Wyatt was chuckling as he strolled away.

Riley awoke to a countryside lush with spring wildflowers after an overnight rain. She stood outside their tent and watched a herd of deer drinking at the stream. Such a deceptively tranquil sight. But even that wasn't enough to quell her nerves.

She hadn't been completely honest with Zane when she'd told him she felt safe here. Though it was a far cry from the perils of the city she'd fled, the truth was, until she was assured that Nick's file was in the proper hands, and the guilty ones exposed, she would never feel completely safe anywhere.

"Mama. Look." Summer had crept from her cot and was standing just behind Riley, pointing to the deer.

"I see. Aren't they pretty?" She picked up her pajama-clad daughter and brushed a kiss to her cheek.

"Um-hmmm. Do you think I could feed them?"

"I think they'd run away, honey." She continued holding her little girl, to give her a better view of the herd.

"Why?"

"Because they're wild creatures, and they're afraid of people."

"If we lived way out here and they saw us every day, would they let me feed them?"

"I don't know. Would you like living way out here?"

"Yes."

"Wouldn't you get lonely?"

"Not if I had some deer to play with."

Riley laughed as she and Summer watched the deer drift away and gradually blend into the surrounding woods, until they were completely invisible.

She set her daughter on her feet. "Let's get dressed. We have a big day ahead of us."

"Miss Cora said she was going to let me help her paint a canvas."

Riley stood still as her daughter danced into the tent. The thought of being allowed to paint beside a gifted artist like Cora McCord sent a thrill through her already charged system.

It was promising to be a memorable day. She and Summer would paint with Cora, and then she would meet with a reporter who could possibly change her life forever.

All of this ought to be enough to calm her frazzled nerves, but in truth, she was feeling very uneasy just thinking about the coming interrogation. Once again she would be opening herself to a past experience that continued to bring her a sense of shame.

Still, she reminded herself, if it hadn't been for her unfortunate introduction to Nick, she wouldn't have Summer in her life. And for that she would be eternally grateful.

"Time to go." Zane tucked a video camera into his shirt pocket.

The four men piled into the ranch truck and headed toward town to pick up the reporter.

When Zane flipped open his cell phone, Wyatt glanced over. "Who're you calling?"

"Craig Matson."

They all knew Craig, the longtime mechanic who worked at the tiny airstrip in Gold Fever, servicing the small fleet of private planes, and doing double duty by also manning the tower.

"Hey, Craig. Zane McCord. Is the flight from Helena running on time?"

Zane listened, then gave the others a thumbs-up. "Great. Thanks, Craig. We're picking up one of the passengers. We'll be there within the hour."

When he disconnected, Wyatt burst into laughter. "We're picking up one of the passengers? What do you want to bet our reporter is the only passenger?"

That had the others joining in the laughter. They all knew that their little town was too insignificant to attract visitors, except at rodeo time, when the town swelled to nearly three times its size. The rest of the year it was a virtual ghost town.

An hour later they arrived at the airstrip. The commuter plane from Helena was already on the tarmac. They waved at Craig, who was driving the fuel truck toward the plane. The pilot stood watching, ready to oversee the refueling.

As they pulled up beside the small building, Zane glanced around. "I expected our reporter to be standing outside watching for us."

"Probably helping himself to something from the vending machine." Wyatt opened the door and stepped out, with the others following.

Inside the small terminal they looked around the empty interior.

Jesse pointed to the restroom. "I figure he'll be along any minute now."

Cal dropped a bill in the vending machine and twisted the top off a bottle of water.

Zane arched a brow. "Why bother buying water when we've got a case of it in the back of the truck?"

"I saw how carefully Dandy packed all that stuff. I wouldn't want to mess anything up. This is easier." He took a long pull and, like the others, stared expectantly at the door of the restroom.

Minutes later the outer back door of the building opened and a powerfully built man hurried inside, carrying a backpack and looking slightly out-of-breath. When he saw the four men staring, his expression changed. He managed a smile before striding forward, hand outstretched.

"Hey. Jack Manning."

"Zane McCord." Zane's hand was engulfed in a surprisingly strong grip. The man facing him looked more like a prizefighter or professional wrestler than a reporter. "My cousins Jesse and Wyatt, and our ranch foreman, Cal Randall."

They shook hands all around.

"Is that all your luggage?" Jesse pointed to the backpack looped over Jack's arm.

The man shrugged. "I'm traveling light. I figure a day here and back, I don't need a thing."

Zane couldn't hide his surprise. "We expected to put you up at the camp before you fly back."

"I got lucky and booked a return flight leaving late tonight."

"I hope it's really late. We've got a long drive ahead of us." Zane turned away and the others followed.

Cal remarked casually, "I didn't think they ever flew more than one plane in here in a week."

The reporter shrugged. "My publisher pulled a few strings."

Zane shot him a look. "Must be nice to have that kind of clout."

Jack Manning gave a dry laugh. "I guess I live a charmed life."

Outside, they climbed into the truck and Zane honked at Craig, standing beside the plane, busy refueling. The old man waved and returned his attention to the job at hand as they took off in a cloud of dust.

CHAPTER TWENTY-ONE

———◆———

This is Gold Fever," Zane announced as they drove through town.

"Or what there is of it." Jesse grinned. "I guess, in Philadelphia, this would take up less than a city block."

While the others laughed, their visitor merely stared through the truck window, his head swiveling this way and that, as though searching for landmarks.

"Your first visit to Montana?" Zane asked.

"I was here once before. Did some elk hunting."

"Really? Maybe you should sign up to write the *Gazette*'s nature column instead of investigative reporting."

Jack joined in their laughter, though he seemed distracted.

"How does somebody become an investigative reporter?" Cal was determined to engage the man in conversation, since he seemed so reticent to talk about himself.

"Hard to explain. A curious mind helps."

"And a degree in journalism," quipped Wyatt.

"That, too."

As he drove, Zane studied their visitor in the rearview mirror. "I expected you to be in a rumpled trench coat, notebook in hand, snapping pictures of everything along the way."

Jack looked up, meeting his eyes in the mirror. Zane thought, for just a moment, he saw temper. But just as quickly the man smiled. "Sorry to disappoint you. But I am making notes and snapping pictures in my mind."

"And you're able to remember it all without writing a thing?"

"Total recall. I'm blessed with a laser memory."

Wyatt chuckled. "That would come in handy when I forget my wife's birthday."

His little joke had the others laughing.

Zane watched as the reporter turned away to scan the horizon.

"You worried about the weather? Don't worry, the predicted storms have moved to the north of us."

Jack's gaze swung again to the mirror. This time Zane was certain of the flare of temper.

Maybe in order to be good at his job he felt he needed to intimidate. But Zane had the feeling there was something more here. He struggled to dismiss the nagging thought that Jack Manning wasn't at all happy to be here. Shouldn't he be excited at the prospect of getting some key facts for his investigation?

It could be, Zane reasoned, because he was engaged in such a sordid scandal. Maybe the enormity of the city's fraud was dragging him down. Maybe he felt that he was helping to take down a city he loved, and wished it could be otherwise. Or, Zane thought, maybe he was jaded by all the corruption, and running on empty.

Whatever the reason, Jack Manning couldn't hide his impatience with the company he was forced to keep. To tune them out, he plugged his cell phone button into his ear and leaned his head back, closing his eyes as he listened to his messages. Zane couldn't tell if Manning was asleep or just a very good actor. At any rate, their visitor spent the rest of the journey locked in his own thoughts without any interaction with his hosts.

It was just as well, Zane thought. They couldn't discuss the investigation with this reporter without revealing what Riley had already told them. He wasn't here to make small talk with them. It was better if Jack Manning got all his facts from the one person who had been unwittingly caught up in this whole sordid matter.

As they drew near the foothills of Treasure Chest Mountain, Zane used the vehicle's hands-free speaker phone to keep in constant contact with Cora, who talked them through the twisted trail they would need to take to their well-hidden campsite.

At the first sound of her voice Jack Manning's eyes snapped open and he took his cell phone from his pocket, silently touching buttons and scrolling through various messages, his words spoken too softly to be overheard by the others.

After nearly an hour of twisting and turning, jostling over hills and crossing a swollen stream, they rolled into the campsite, completely obliterated from the outside world until they drove past a stand of trees and dipped below a foothill abloom with wildflowers.

"Zane." Riley and Summer were dashing up to the truck as soon as it came to a halt.

Mother and daughter stood back until he exited the vehicle and strode up to them, gathering them both into a quick, hard hug.

"Are you having fun?" Though Zane directed his question to Summer, he kept a hand on Riley's arm.

"Uh-huh." She held up her stuffed dog. "Floppy and I were painting pictures today with Miss Cora."

"I can't wait to see them."

Beside her daughter, Riley absorbed the warmth of Zane's touch and shivered.

As the others climbed from the truck, Zane turned and focused his video camera. "Riley, this is Jack Manning. Jack, Riley Mason."

"Riley." He gave her a long, steady look, nearly crushing her hand in his while keeping his head averted from Zane's camera.

"And her daughter, Summer."

His head nodded in Summer's direction before turning toward Zane with his hand in front of the camera. "What's with the video?"

"I'm filming a documentary of my family."

"Turn it off." His words were stiff, his voice harsh. "This is my show."

"Sorry. I didn't know you objected."

"I do. In case you've forgotten, I'm an investigative reporter. I need to remain anonymous in order to do my job."

"Anonymous?" Zane was caught by surprise. "Your byline is listed on every one of your newspaper articles. I'd hardly call that anonymous."

"They know my name, but they don't ever see me." He glared until Zane switched off his camera. "I'd like it to stay that way."

Keeping a hand on Riley's arm, Zane led them toward the other side of the truck, where Jesse was busy embracing Amy, and Wyatt was holding firmly to Marilee. Cal had a hand on Cora's shoulder, and the two were talking quietly.

They all looked up as Zane handled the introductions of Jack Manning to the women.

Except for a curt nod of his head, he barely acknowledged them, as if to signal that he was here on business.

"I expect you're hungry and tired after that long flight and the drive out here, Mr. Manning." Cora pointed to the fire, where burgers, onions, and sliced potatoes were grilling, giving off the most heavenly fragrance. "Why don't you sit and catch your breath before we eat."

He remained standing. "I thought Riley and I might go off somewhere alone where I could conduct an interview."

Riley shot a pleading look at Zane, who said smoothly, "Sorry. I promised Riley that we'd all be with her while she told you what she knows."

Jack allowed his gaze to trail over the others, as though assessing their feelings on this matter. "I see. Then you've all been made aware of the facts in this case?"

"What we're aware of," Zane said firmly, "is that Riley was caught up in this reluctantly and just wants to turn over the information she has, so that she can get on with her life."

"Of course." Jack looked around the campsite, then up at the sky, as though assessing how much daylight was left. "If you don't mind, I'd like to forgo eating and get right to the file, so I can catch a flight home."

"Tonight?" Cora looked dismayed. "We thought perhaps we'd have the night with our men before they had to leave us."

"We thought so, too." Wyatt squeezed his wife's hand, looking as unhappy as his aunt. "Jack changed the game plan by booking a late flight back."

"I see." Cora flipped the burgers, noting that their food was already cooked to perfection. "Then why don't we all refresh ourselves by the fire, and you can ask Riley anything you'd like over a meal. That way our men will have a little time with us before they have to drive you back to town."

As the others gathered around the fire, Jack stood back, waiting until they had all settled before choosing a spot between Riley and Summer, keeping his backpack alongside him in the grass.

Riley took the time to cut her daughter's burger and potatoes into bite sizes, before reaching across the reporter to hand over the little girl's plate.

While Summer ate, and pretended to feed Floppy, Riley sipped water, feeling too nervous to consider eating a thing.

Seeing her nerves, the others were more determined than ever to carry on a steady stream of conversation, in the hope of putting her at ease.

Wyatt brushed a kiss over Marilee's cheek. "You really lucked out on this weather."

Cora took a bite of hamburger. "I heard rain through the night, but by morning there wasn't a drop in sight."

Amy nodded. "We thought we'd need sleeping bags at

night, but it turned mild enough to sleep with only a light blanket on our cots."

Cal glanced at Cora's bright smile. "Looks like you've been enjoying your girls' retreat."

"Oh, Cal, I'm loving every minute. It's funny." Cora leaned back against the big rock. "All my life I've been surrounded by men. Coot's sons and their sons. Dozens of wranglers. Maybe that's why this has been such a rare pleasure. I have company while I paint. And at night, around the campfire, we talk about the most fascinating subjects."

"Like men?" Jesse asked.

They all laughed.

"All right," Cora said. "I'll confess. We have spent some time talking about men, but only because it's such a fascinating subject."

More laughter ensued.

"But we've also talked politics, religion, relationships, life in general. And it's been so satisfying to share all this with other women."

"I'm glad, Cora." Cal closed a hand over hers and gave her a warm smile. "Nobody deserves a retreat more than you."

Jack Manning glanced at his watch. "Sorry to interrupt this fascinating conversation, but I have a plane to catch. Riley, if you don't mind, I'd like to take your statement now, and get this show on the road."

Riley set aside her water bottle and took a deep breath. "Where would you like me to begin?"

"This file you claim to have. Have you read it?"

"I've looked through it. But I certainly haven't memorized names and dates."

"But you've seen it. I—"

Zane interrupted. "I thought you'd at least be taping this conversation." He pointed to Jack's backpack. "Don't you have a tape recorder with you?"

Manning shot him a look of disgust. "I told you I have total recall."

"Then humor me." Zane's tone had turned deceptively soft, a sure sign that his temper was heating. "I want you to have a tape of this conversation with Riley."

Manning reached into the backpack and pulled out a tape recorder. It took him several long minutes to check the buttons before he pressed one.

Ignoring Zane, he turned back to Riley. "You were saying that you've seen the file. I assume it contains the names of political figures who have been... compromised."

"Yes."

"Photos?"

"Yes."

"Videos?"

She nodded, then, remembering the recorder, said softly, "Yes."

He arched a brow. "Amounts of money involved?"

"Yes."

"And you'll be willing to testify in court to the contents of the file and how you happened to obtain it?"

"I..." She looked at Zane when his cell phone rang. "Yes. If I have to."

Not wanting to disturb Jack's interrogation again, Zane stood and walked a short distance from the fire. Seeing the identity of the caller, he said to the sheriff, "Hey, Ernie. What's up?"

"Where are you right now, Zane?"

"At Aunt Cora's campsite."

"Who's there with you?"

"Cal. Jesse. Wyatt. And a reporter from the Philadelphia *Gazette*, Jack Manning. He's talking to Riley right now about the evidence she has against the thugs who've bribed those eastern politicians."

"Listen to me, Zane. I'm at the clinic. I got a call from Craig Matson over at the airstrip. He found a man in the trunk of his car, more dead than alive."

"What does...?"

"Just listen. The man had no identification on him. But Doc was able to patch him up enough to learn that he's Jack Manning, from Philadelphia. When he walked into the terminal, he was strong-armed by a big guy who hauled him out the back door, shot him, and stuffed him in the trunk of Craig's car. If Craig hadn't needed a couple of his tools, this guy would have died before being found. And I'm sure that's what our bad guy planned. He expected to be long gone before the body was discovered."

Zane turned away, keeping his voice low. "Call out the state police, Ernie. And get them up here as fast as you can. The campsite is well-hidden, just over a ridge on the southern tip of the foothills of Treasure Chest. Once they're in this area, they'll see the smoke of our campfire and our vehicles, which are parked in plain sight."

"I'm on it."

Fearing that the police might be too late, Zane set his video camera on a stump facing their campsite. At least, he reasoned, there would be a record of what happened here if they didn't survive.

If they didn't survive.

He clamped his jaw. They'd been through so much. His family had escaped death threats. Riley and Summer had fled across the country, seeking a safe haven. And now, all of their lives were being threatened yet again.

There was no time for a plan, but he would do everything in his power to keep those he loved safe.

He returned to the campfire in time to hear the man say to Riley, "Now, I need to know where the file is. I assume you've hidden it?"

She nodded. "It's in a post office box in Philadelphia."

"Name and number."

As she answered him, he gave a smug smile, the first show of emotion other than anger since the interrogation had begun.

"I assume you have the key?"

"Yes. I—"

"Riley." Zane's voice, low and urgent, had her looking away from Manning.

"What?" She looked up at this unexpected interruption.

He carefully stepped in front of her, so that he was between her and the stranger. "I've decided this isn't a good idea."

"What . . . what are you saying?" Her eyes went wide.

The others were staring at him as though he'd suddenly lost his mind.

The reporter's eyes narrowed. "What's this about?" He was suddenly alert. "Who were you talking to?"

"The sheriff." Zane shot a meaningful glance at his cousins. "It seems Craig Matson found a half-dead man in the trunk of his car who claims to be Jack Manning. If he's telling the truth, it means that this guy is an impostor."

Everyone was on their feet, and all of them staring in stunned surprise as the impersonator pulled a handgun from his backpack.

Zane's voice grew dangerously low. "What're you going to do? Kill all of us?"

"If I have to." The gunman was actually smiling now.

"You don't have time." Zane's words were clipped with anger. "You might take one or two of us, but the rest will get to you before you can squeeze off another shot."

"All I'll need is one." In the blink of an eye the man scooped up little Summer and aimed the gun at her head. "I've been told this kid is all the insurance I need to get out of here alive."

Chapter Twenty-two

M ama! Mama!" The startled little girl began kicking and screaming.

To silence her, the gunman clamped a hand over her mouth.

"You're suffocating her! Oh, sweet heaven, Summer." With her heart in her throat, Riley cried out Summer's name and started toward them. She couldn't bear the sight of her terrified daughter in this madman's arms.

"Don't take another step or I'll waste her." For emphasis he removed his hand from Summer's mouth and pressed the muzzle of the gun to her temple with such force it caused her to cry even louder.

Everyone, including Riley, froze.

"That's better." He looked around, his eyes now as feral as a vicious animal's. "And if you think I'm bluffing, just try me. I've killed enough people that I don't care about adding one more. In fact, I'd like a good reason to silence her whining once and for all."

"Don't cry, Summer. Be quiet for me, honey," Riley crooned as tears streamed down her own cheeks.

The little girl struggled to do as her mother asked, though her tiny body continued to shudder in silent anguish.

In the distance came the sound of a low drone. As it drew nearer, they all looked up in stunned surprise at the sight of a helicopter coming over the ridge of Treasure Chest Mountain.

The gunman gave a cruel laugh. "Here's my chartered flight now."

He spoke into his earphone and the copter began to circle, searching through the dense trees to spot their exact location.

"That's what you were up to earlier," Zane said through gritted teeth. "Giving directions to the pilot." To the others he said, "He's been directing this operation all along."

"You think you're smart, don't you?" the gunman snarled. "But not smart enough to figure it out in time to stop me." He turned to Riley. "I want the key."

"I . . . hid it."

His eyes narrowed. "Don't play for time, woman." With the gun he menaced the little girl in his arms. "Get it. Now."

Instead of turning away Riley walked closer to the fire and bent down to pick up Summer's stuffed dog.

With tears streaming down her face she held it out. "The key is in here."

"Do you take me for a fool?"

"It's in here." Her voice rose on a note of near hysteria. "I sewed it in there myself."

"Prove it. Dig it out."

She gave a fierce shake of her head. "First, release my baby."

"Damn you, woman." His hand swung out in an arc, the pistol catching Riley on the temple with such force her head snapped to one side, and she dropped to her knees, dripping blood.

That sent Summer into a screaming frenzy. She twisted and kicked and bit the hand of the man who had dared to hurt her mother, causing him to swear and nearly drop her.

While Zane rushed to Riley's aid, Cal used that moment of distraction to charge the stranger. He managed to get one hand on little Summer's arm, pulling her free of the man's grasp and tossing her to safety.

Zane caught the little girl in a bear hug and curled himself over her and Riley, to protect them from possible bullets.

"You old fool," the gunman shouted, taking aim.

A gunshot rang out, sending Cal backward with such force he fell to the ground. He pressed both hands to his upper chest as blood spurted from the wound, spilling through his fingers to form a mottled pool around his body.

With a scream Cora dropped to her knees beside him, then suddenly stood and raced toward the tent.

A rope ladder was lowered from the belly of the helicopter and descended toward the stranger.

He crouched down and grabbed hold of the stuffed dog, tearing it from Riley's hands.

With a shout Zane reached out, catching one of the floppy ears.

Jesse and Wyatt surged forward, determined to tackle the gunman, but he managed to loop one arm through the rungs of the rope ladder, kicking out his legs frantically to hold them at bay until he was lifted just out of reach.

As the gunman became airborne, they heard the sound of his cruel laughter.

While the helicopter lifted, Zane was lifted off his feet. It took all of his strength to keep his hold on the stuffed dog. Stretched to capacity, it suddenly burst open, spilling its cotton stuffing like snow on the ground. A small shiny key fluttered to the ground as well.

Zane got to his feet and experienced a moment of desperation. "He's getting away. Even without the key, he knows the location of the box. We have to stop him."

"Zane."

At his aunt's cry, Zane looked up just as Cora tossed him her rifle.

There was no time to think. Barely time to take aim as he lifted it to his shoulder and reflexively pulled the trigger.

An explosion of sound echoed and reechoed over the hills.

As everyone watched in horror, the helicopter, with its dangling passenger, burst into flames, crashing into the side of Treasure Chest Mountain. The ground shuddered with the force of an erupting volcano, sending flaming debris and a wall of rock showering down the mountainside.

For the longest time they were too stunned to speak, to move, even to breathe. Then, as realization dawned, everyone turned to see Zane standing as rigid as a statue, the rifle still at his shoulder.

It was Cora who finally broke the silence.

"I'm sorry for the loss of their lives," she cried. "But I told Coot that I couldn't let them hurt the people I love. Coot knew I was shaking too hard to fire, so he told me to trust you to take care of us all, Zane." Through her tears she added, "And you did it. You did just fine."

With a cry of anguish she dropped to the ground beside Cal, who lay as still as death in an ever-widening pool of blood, while the others gathered around.

"Oh, Cal." Cora snatched up a blanket that had been spread on the ground beside the campfire and began mopping at the river of blood that flowed from the gunshot wound.

"Let me do that, Aunt Cora." Marilee raced from the tent with her ever-present first-aid kit. All her years of training as a medic kicked in as she tore open Cal's shirt and located the wound.

"It isn't his chest." She breathed a sigh of relief. "It's his shoulder."

"Oh, thank heaven." Cora wiped tears from her eyes, though her poor heart was still pounding.

"A clean wound. The bullet appears to have gone clear through." Marilee sponged the blood and applied disinfectant and a heavy dressing to stem the flow while Cora knelt beside her, holding tightly to Cal's hand, unwilling to break the connection for even a moment.

"I'm going to give you something for the pain," Marilee said. "It'll make you pretty groggy."

Cal hissed in a breath. "I'll take whatever you've got right now."

"Good." Marilee waved the men over to carry him to the tent. There he was tucked into a sleeping bag, with Cora curled up beside him, in case he needed anything until help arrived.

It was plain to all of them that Cora had no intention of leaving his side.

Marilee turned her attention to Riley, being comforted by Zane and little Summer. "Let me take a look at you."

Riley hissed out a breath as Marilee touched a gauze pad to her bloody temple.

"That's a nasty wound. I'd feel better if you had a few stitches."

"I'm fine." Riley cuddled her daughter in her arms, afraid to let her go for even a moment. "Now that my baby's safe, nothing else matters."

Summer's tears had dried, but she clung desperately to her mother.

Riley remained still while Marilee applied ointment and a dressing to the wound, including butterfly bandages to bond the skin together.

Marilee touched a hand to the corner of Riley's eye. "I'm betting you'll have a lovely shiner by tomorrow." She held out a pill. "Take this for pain."

Riley looked at it with a frown. "Will it make me sleepy?"

"A little. But I guarantee you'll feel a lot better after you take it. Maybe you and Summer could join Cal and Cora in the tent. It would do you all some good to rest for an hour or so."

Riley took a mouthful of water and swallowed down the pill.

When Marilee was finished with them, Zane gathered

Riley and Summer close. "Let's go to the tent now. I'll feel a lot better knowing you're resting."

"What about you?"

He shook his head. "Jesse, Wyatt, and I have decided to climb the mountain. Though it's hard to believe anyone could have survived that crash, we have to make certain."

When she started to protest, he pressed his lips to her temple. Against her ear he whispered, "Do this for me. I won't be able to relax until I know that you and Summer are able to relax."

She shivered. "What if we aren't safe here? What if that horrible man escaped? Or has friends in the area? What if we're never safe again, Zane? What if ... ?"

"Listen to me." He held her a little away. "I know after all that's happened, it's hard to believe that it's really over. But trust me. The state police are on their way. Amy and Marilee have agreed to stand guard outside the tent. They have Aunt Cora's rifle and handgun. If they see anything at all suspicious, they'll fire off a shot to alert us. And they know how to use those weapons."

With great tenderness he picked up little Summer and, with his arm around Riley's shoulders, led them across the campsite to the tent.

Summer buried her face in his shoulder, refusing to let go. Even after her mother was settled comfortably on a cot, the little girl clung to his neck and begged him to stay with them.

"I won't be far away. And Miss Amy and Miss Marilee will be keeping watch while I'm gone. By the time you wake up from your nap, I'll be back."

"Promise?" Her eyes, big and round with fear, fastened on his.

"Promise." He laid her gently on the cot beside her mother and tucked them into the blankets, knowing the shock and fear had left them chilled, despite the heat of the afternoon.

Summer lifted her head. With tears still shiny on her lashes, she framed his face with her chubby hands and said, "Mama told me my daddy never came back."

Zane stared into those big eyes, so round and fearful, and felt his heart nearly break in two.

"I give you my word, Summer. I'll be back by the time you wake up."

He stood and walked from the tent. When he looked back, she was still watching him.

He lifted his hand in a salute, blew her a kiss, and turned away to join his cousins.

But his heart remained with Riley and Summer. They were two of the bravest little females he'd ever known. The sudden knowledge hit him with all the force of a thunderbolt. He was hopelessly in love with both of them.

CHAPTER TWENTY-THREE

R emember." Jesse gathered his wife close. "One shot means you've spotted a stranger. Two shots will mean immediate danger. Either way, we'll come running."

"You've been watching too many movies." With false bravado, Amy patted his cheek. The truth was, her own nerves were none too steady, but she knew she had to be brave for all of their sakes. "You said yourself the police are on their way. We'll be fine."

"I know. But humor me, baby."

Amy kissed him full on the mouth.

Marilee was busy assuring Wyatt in that same calm, measured voice. "We'll be fine here. We have guns and ammunition. And in case you've forgotten, it was your sweet old aunt's quick thinking, fetching her rifle from the tent the minute Cal was shot, that had Zane bringing down that helicopter."

"Yeah." Wyatt couldn't help beaming his pleasure. "Isn't she something?"

"She's amazing."

"So is my little cuz. I may even tell him some day." He turned away, slinging a duffel over his arm that contained a few meager medical supplies Marilee could spare. Just in case there was a need for them. "We shouldn't be gone more than an hour. We'll check out the crash site and then get back here while it's still light enough to see the trail."

"Good." Marilee blew him a kiss.

Zane retrieved his video camera from a tree stump. At the questioning look from the others he explained, "When I took that call from the sheriff, I decided to record everything, just in case."

"Quick thinking, cuz." Wyatt punched his arm. "Were you thinking we might not make it out alive?"

Zane shrugged, uncomfortable with the question. It was too close to the truth. On the slim chance that none of them survived, he'd wanted to leave credible testimony about what had gone down here.

The three cousins started up the mountain, pausing occasionally to turn and wave until they were too far away to be seen.

While the women kept watch at the campsite, Jesse, Wyatt, and Zane followed a circuitous route up the steep trail, using the path of debris as their compass.

Throughout the climb, Zane recorded everything with his camera, adding narrative from time to time.

Even before they reached the crash site, they recognized the first body as that of the gunman.

Zane studied the grisly scene and shook his head. "We don't even know his name."

"I'm sure the authorities are already on it." Wyatt walked up behind him.

"At least there's enough here to identify." Jesse stared at the trail ahead. "From the pile of twisted metal up there, I'm not sure we'll be able to say the same for the pilot."

They continued climbing until they reached the site of impact. It looked like a war zone. The helicopter had crashed into the side of the mountain, shearing off a wall of rock to reveal a cave the size of a small shed.

Acrid smoke plumed from what had probably been the engine, though now it was nothing more than a pile of red-hot metal. From the shattered glass to the burning seats, there was nothing left to identify the vehicle. They could make out an arm and a boot, all that was left of the pilot, buried beneath the twisted metal.

They walked around the smoking wreckage, hoping to locate anything that could be used to identify either the helicopter or its passengers.

Zane looked over at his cousins. "I think we're going to have to give it up and let the state police figure it out. They'll probably send a team of investigators to comb through the wreckage."

"Yeah." Jesse kicked at a smoking piece of rubble. "Hell of a way to die."

Wyatt had grown so quiet, both men glanced over.

He dropped down to sit on a rock, staring at the carnage. "This could have been Marilee and me, when her plane was sabotaged."

"Hey." Zane walked over to lay a hand on his shoulder. "Don't go there, cuz. You both survived."

"You should have seen her." He gave a slow shake

of his head, remembering. "When the engine quit, she was so calm. If she was shaking inside, it didn't show." He looked up at Zane. "Sort of the way you handled all this. A guy with a gun terrorizes us, is about to get clean away, and you calmly fire off a single shot that changes everything."

Zane swallowed. "I did what I had to. You and Jesse did the same when the ones you love were in danger. But I agree with Aunt Cora. The one directing all of this was really Coot. He saved us today, and he was there during your crash with Marilee, keeping the two of you safe."

"Yeah. I can't argue with that. There's no other explanation for the fact that we survived all that we've been through." Wyatt ran a hand through his hair and got restlessly to his feet. "This place has me spooked. Let's get out of here."

"I'm with you. In fact, I can practically feel Coot tapping me on the shoulder." As Zane turned, he caught sight of the gaping wound in the mountain. Aiming his camera, he called, "Look at this."

The others remained where they were while he ducked his head and stepped under the shelf of rock and into the cave. "This place is huge." His voice sounded hollow as it bounced around the rock walls.

"Hey," he called suddenly. "Bring the flashlight."

Jesse dug it out of the duffel and turned it on before stepping in behind Zane.

"Shine it over there." Zane pointed to something in a corner.

"Bones." Jesse's voice was hushed.

The two walked closer and knelt down.

"Human. There's the skull." Zane filmed it before

turning to look over at his cousin. "Looks like it's been here for a long time."

"Yeah." Jesse shouted, "Wyatt. Look at this."

At his call Wyatt entered the cave and crossed to their side. At the sight of the bones he gave a mock shudder. "Creepy."

"I wonder who it was." Out of respect for the dead, Zane's voice dropped to a whisper. "And how long he's been hidden."

"Probably some poor, cold miner who took shelter from a blizzard and never made it home," Jesse mused.

"Or a claim-jumper hiding out from a posse." Zane got to his feet and caught a glint of something in the far corner. "Shine the light over there, Jess."

As the light played over the rock wall, the three men went perfectly still.

Zane was the first to find his voice. "Is that what I think it is?"

They were across the cave in an instant, staring at the pile of what appeared to be, at first glance, stones.

Zane picked up one in his hand and tested its weight before shining the light over it to reveal dull glints of metal beneath the layers of dirt. Without a word he passed it to Wyatt, who studied it carefully before handing it to Jesse.

The three men had gone perfectly still, as though afraid to say aloud what they were thinking.

Zane knelt. With the camera in one hand he reached out with the other, moving the pile of nuggets aside. Beneath were a few fibers of rough cloth that had nearly completely decomposed with age.

Now his voice trembled. "In his journal Nathanial

claimed that his gold was in a potato sack when it was stolen from the saloon."

He looked up at his cousins, and their faces reflected the range of emotions they were all experiencing.

Automatically he lifted his camera, panning their faces.

He held up one of the biggest nuggets. It was the size of his fist. The others, much smaller, were the size of his thumb.

"Could it be?" Jesse whispered.

"It has to be." Wyatt knelt beside Zane and picked up a handful of nuggets, weighing, testing.

As they passed the nuggets from hand to hand, they grew even more silent and thoughtful, struggling to absorb the enormity of their discovery.

So many lives spent in the search for the illusive gold. So many ancestors who had fervently believed. So many more who had scorned them for that very belief.

Suddenly, the three burst into spontaneous laughter. Throwing back their heads, they gave a roar of excitement before getting to their feet and hugging one another, pumping their fists, slapping each other's backs, before dropping once more to the ground to weigh the nuggets in their palms, as though unable to believe their good fortune.

They were all talking at once.

"We did it, Coot." Jesse's face was beaming.

"I always knew we would." Wyatt kept shaking his head from side to side, trying to take it all in. "That's why I stayed. I wanted to be a part of this."

"Best of all, we found it together, just the way Coot wanted." Zane continued filming them as he spoke.

They remained together in the cave for the longest time, unable to tear themselves away from the spot that had been hidden from sight since gold had been discovered at Grasshopper Creek in 1862.

"I just thought of something." Zane looked around. "If this is what we think it is, it proves something important. All those years ago, it wasn't our ancestor who killed Grizzly Markham. It was some stranger who probably was at the saloon that night and saw Grizzly leave with the sack of gold after slitting Jasper's throat. He could have easily followed Grizzly, waited until he made camp, and then did to Grizzly what Grizzly had done to Jasper. Maybe he got caught in a storm, or maybe he figured he'd hide out here until Nathanial gave up the search, and he'd be rich."

"Instead," Wyatt said in hushed tones, "he died in here like a cornered animal. And the gold has been waiting all these years to be found."

"Waiting for the McCords," Jesse said with a grin as the enormity of their discovery continued to sink in.

"You really think it's our lost treasure?" Zane couldn't stop palming the nuggets, as though afraid they would disappear before his very eyes.

"I do." Jesse did the same, holding first one nugget, then another. "But whether our ancestor found real gold or pyrite, only an assayer can say."

"Fool's gold." Wyatt spoke the words that had been whispered about his family for generations.

"I have the strongest feeling that it's real," Zane said.

"Why?" The other two stared at him.

"Because Aunt Cora felt Coot's presence when she tossed me her rifle. Because it was that shot that brought the copter into the mountain, uncovering a spot that had been hidden for all these years. For all our sophisticated equipment, we'd have never penetrated all those layers of rock. Remember, I actually felt a touch on my shoulder before I decided to step into this cave, as though Coot himself was directing me. And there's one more thing." He looked from Jesse to Wyatt. "Remember those boulders we found when we resumed the search?" Without waiting for their reply he added, "This is the direction those boulders were pointing to."

Jesse nodded. "Treasure Chest Mountain."

"And this is where Coot was searching when Vernon McVicker pushed and killed him." Zane's voice lowered with feeling. "He was here. At this site. He'd finally come within reach of finding his treasure, when it was snatched from his grasp by a jealous claim-jumper, the same way it had been taken from old Jasper McCord."

The other two nodded in wonder.

"I think," Zane said carefully, "that we ought to make a pact."

"I know what you're thinking," Wyatt said.

Jesse nodded, reading their minds.

"We're in agreement, then? We don't say a word about what we found here until we've had a chance to determine whether it's real or fool's gold." Zane spit in his palm before holding out his hand. The other two did the same, before joining their hands with his, just as they'd done all those years ago when they were kids.

"Jasper revealed his secret too soon, and it cost him his life. And cursed the succeeding generations to search for the lost treasure for all these years. This time," Jesse said, "we need to be sure before we say a word to anyone."

"How do we hide this?" Wyatt asked.

Zane reached for the duffel and began filling it with the nuggets.

When the bag was filled, he tested the weight. "Heavier than I'd expected. But we can manage it."

"It's going to be hard to keep this from our wives." Jesse sighed. "Amy will kill me when we do reveal the truth, one way or the other."

"It's only for a couple more days," Wyatt said. "Still, I expect that Marilee won't be too happy with me, either, for holding out on her."

"Not to mention Aunt Cora and Cal. It's as much theirs as ours." Zane considered his words carefully. "But we really need to take this one step at a time, so we don't get everybody's hopes up, only to have them dashed."

The three couldn't hold back their smiles as they made ready to leave.

Zane turned away from the cave, carefully documenting every step with his camera.

As they started back down the trail, they heard the sound of a helicopter, and looked up to see the emblem of the state police as it flew overhead.

When it passed, Jesse pointed to a rainbow in the sky. "Look. It's got to be a sign from Coot."

The three paused to stare.

Jesse removed the rainbow keychain their grandfather had always carried. The same keychain he'd given Amy on their wedding day. It had become their good-luck charm, and one he'd carried this day in his grandfather's honor. "Coot always said one day he'd find his pot of gold at the end of the rainbow."

As they continued toward the campsite, their hearts

were light at the knowledge that Coot was still with them, and still showing them the way.

It was, to all three of them, a sign that they had finally found the family's lost treasure. Whether true gold or pyrite, they wouldn't know for some time. It would be up to the experts who tested the nuggets to determine that. But at least now the search had ended. For now, regardless of the outcome of the tests, it was enough to know that they'd come through yet another bout with danger, and had survived for another day, their family intact, the nuggets stolen from their ancestor at last revealed.

CHAPTER TWENTY-FOUR

———— ◆◆◆ ————

Zane, Wyatt, and Jesse walked into organized chaos at the campsite. Besides the helicopter, there was a convoy of trucks bearing a squad of state police officers as well as Sheriff Ernie Wycliff.

A team of officers was already headed up the mountain toward the crash site. The three cousins had paused to inform them of the bones in the cave. Another team was preparing Cal and Riley to be flown to town for treatment at the clinic.

Both Cal and Riley were adamantly refusing.

Cora rushed toward her nephews, imploring their help.

"Please, make Cal understand how important it is that he gets medical assistance."

The three men hurried toward the tent.

Jesse knelt beside the ranch foreman. "Aunt Cora's worried about you, Cal. Why won't you let the officers fly you out of here?"

"I'm not leaving Cora."

Jesse turned to Sheriff Wycliff. "Is there room for my aunt on the copter?"

"I'll make room." The sheriff walked away and returned minutes later to affirm that she could ride along.

Placated, Cal agreed to go. With his arm around Cora's shoulders, he made his way slowly toward the waiting helicopter.

Riley sat on a cot, holding Summer, who reached out to Zane the minute he entered the tent.

"You came back." Wrapping her arms around his neck, she buried her face against his shoulder and began to cry.

"Hey, now. What's this?" He tipped up her face. "I told you I'd be back."

"I know." She held on tighter. "But I was afraid."

"It's okay to be afraid." He caught Riley's hand in his. "Sheriff Wycliff just told me that he wants you to go with Cal and Aunt Cora in the copter."

"I'm not leaving Summer."

"I'll see that she goes along."

Riley gave a firm shake of her head. "I'd rather stay here and ride back with you."

"I'd rather be with you, too, but we're facing a long, dusty drive back, and I'd feel a lot better if you could have Doc look at this wound. Marilee thinks you need stitches."

"What about Summer? She's terrified."

He tipped up the little girl's face, forcing her to look at him. "You're afraid of riding on a whirlybird?"

"What's a whirlybird?"

Zane looked into those big, trusting eyes and felt his heart melt. "That big noisy machine out there."

She shook her head. "The other one caught fire. I'm afraid. I don't want to ride in it."

"But it'll get your mama to town faster so the doctor can take away her pain."

She glanced over at her mother and touched a hand to her cheek. "He can take away her boo-boo?"

"That's what doctors do."

"Just like Mama does?"

"Uh-huh. Just like your mama."

She thought about that a moment. "Will you come, too?"

"If there's room. But if there isn't, I'll follow in the truck, and I'll get there in time to take you back to the ranch. Okay?"

Another long pause before she looked up at him with such trust, he found his world settling despite all the crazy commotion going on around them.

"Okay. But I want you to go with us."

"I'll do my best." He stood, still holding her in his arms, and went in search of the sheriff.

Within minutes he was back to assure Riley that both he and Summer would be riding with her.

While the others dismantled the campsite and loaded everything aboard the convoy of trucks, Zane, Riley, and Summer joined Cal and Cora in the helicopter, along with the state police pilot.

Before they left, Jesse ran up and tossed the duffel into Zane's hands. "Since we're driving back in a convoy, I figure you ought to keep this with you."

The two exchanged foolish grins before the door was

slammed, and the blades began sending up a cloud of dust.

Holding tightly to Summer, Zane set the duffel on the floor of the helicopter and watched as the campsite seemed to fall away from his line of vision.

The next hours passed in a blur of excitement, with no time to think about all that had transpired. While they flew over wilderness, Zane took the time to explain to Riley and Summer where they were in relation to the ranch house.

When they set down at the airstrip on the edge of town, another state police car was waiting to take them to the clinic.

Once there, Dr. Frank Wheeler and his nurse-practitioner, Elly Carson, whisked them into examining rooms and began treating their wounds.

With that finished, Zane led Riley into the room where the reporter, Jack Manning, was recovering from his ordeal. After the introductions, Zane sat off to the side quietly holding Summer, while Riley sat by the man's bedside.

Manning looked rumpled and bleary-eyed, struggling to focus through a haze of prescription painkillers that had left him groggy. But his look sharpened when Riley began to tell him about the file that Nick had entrusted to her care.

"When I'm stronger," he said, "I'll want to talk to you myself. But for now, because I can't seem to hold more than one thought at a time, I'd like you to meet with a trusted lawyer who can take your deposition. Are you agreeable to that?"

Riley nodded. "Whatever it takes. What about the file?"

"For now, because I don't trust too many officials in my own city, I'd prefer to leave it where it is. I figure if it survived without detection this long, it'll be there when I'm ready to read it."

"Here's the key." She set it on the bedside table.

When Riley turned away, he stopped her. "Miss Mason, I want to thank you. There are some who will say that what you did was very foolhardy. I'm here to tell you, it was a very brave thing you did. Without you and that file, I might have never been able to dig through the lies to find the core of truth. Without you, desperate criminals would have walked away, to spread their slime in yet another city."

"Will I need to return to Philadelphia?"

He shrugged, then winced at the sudden pain. "Probably. But that's not my call. I intend to write the truth. It will be up to others to decide whether or not to prosecute. If I were a betting man, I'd say they're all going down, thanks to you."

"No," she said emphatically. "I was just the keeper of the file. My daughter's father was the one with the courage to not only walk away from a life of crime, but to turn his life around and give it up for his country. I want you to see that he gets the credit for your story when it's written."

"I'll do that." As she started to leave, he called to Summer, "You should be very proud of your mama. She's a brave woman."

The little girl beamed at the unexpected praise.

Through the glass doors of the clinic they could see a

ranch truck idling at the curb, with Cal and Cora already in the front seat beside Jimmy Eagle at the wheel.

When he spotted Zane, Jimmy hurried around to open the back door and help Riley up.

Minutes later they were headed to the ranch. Noting their exhaustion, Jimmy held his silence, allowing them to take a breath and collect their thoughts.

When they arrived at the ranch, Dandy looked up from the phone. "I heard from Wyatt and Jesse, who figured you'd want hot soup." Seeing Cal's heavily bandaged shoulder, and the dressing at Riley's forehead, he said, "You folks rest. I'll bring the food to you when you're ready for it."

"Thanks, Dandy." When Cal turned as though to head to the bunkhouse, Cora steered him toward the stairs.

"Where are you taking me?" he demanded.

"To Coot's rooms. Your rooms now," Cora said softly.

He offered no protest as Cora, watching like a mother hen, helped him maneuver the stairs.

Behind them Zane carried Summer, who was rubbing her eyes and fighting to stay awake.

Riley climbed to her suite, her back stiff, her head high. But when they stepped into the rooms and the door was closed, she slumped into the chair by the fireplace and gave in to the exhaustion that had left her drained.

"Come on, sweetheart," Zane whispered to Summer. "We'll let your mama rest there while I read you a story."

A short time later, when he covered a sleeping Summer with her blanket, he stepped into the parlor to find Riley asleep in the chair.

He picked up the ever-present duffel and headed to his own suite.

Cora turned back the covers and helped Cal lie down on the big bed. Though he frowned, he was helpless to stop her when she began pulling off his boots. After smoothing a cover over him, she retrieved several pillows from the closet and leaned across him to position them under his wounded arm.

"How does that feel?"

"Perfect. Thanks, Cora." He looked up and was caught completely by surprise when he spied tears in her eyes. "Hey, now. What's this?"

When she tried to turn away, he caught her by the shoulder, forcing her down on the edge of the bed facing him.

"It's nothing. I'm just a foolish old woman."

"There's nothing old or foolish about you, Cora." His eyes narrowed on her. "Now tell me what's wrong."

"I was so afraid you were going to die."

He gave a wry laugh. "So was I."

Instead of smiling, her lower lip trembled. "I couldn't bear to lose you, Cal. You're so very dear to me."

With his good arm he drew her close. "You're never going to lose me, Cora. I'm too ornery to die."

Though she didn't say a word, he could feel the dampness of her tears on the front of his shirt, the tremors as her body shook with silent tears.

Alarmed, he pressed his mouth to her temple. "Here I am letting you treat me like some helpless infant, when you have to be overwhelmed by all that's happened. You were a hero out there, Cora."

"I was no hero." Her words, spoken against his chest, had him shivering. "I couldn't let that awful gunman get away with hurting the people I love."

The people I love. Her words were a soothing balm to his frayed nerves.

She lay against his chest for so long, he thought she was sleeping. But then she sat up, brushing hair from her eyes.

"You need your rest."

"No." He caught her hand in his. Instead of looking at her, he stared at their linked hands. "You mentioned the people you love." He cleared his throat. "I'm sure you wondered why I hired Riley so quickly, without even bothering to check her references."

Cora shrugged. "I've always trusted your instincts, Cal. I'm sure you had your reasons."

"I did." He looked up, meeting her eyes. "I'd like you to hear them."

There was something in his tone that alerted her to the seriousness of what he was about to say. Instead of speaking, she merely nodded her head in encouragement.

"When I met Riley, it was like looking at my own mother."

"Your...mother?"

"She was seventeen when I was born. I never knew my father. It was tough to be a single mother in those days. A lot of people thought of her as less than human. I watched her take on two and three jobs, cleaning houses, and in order to survive, doing ranch chores that would stagger a man twice her size. By the time I was seven or eight, I was doing the work of a man. Mucking stalls, hauling feed to the high country, doing whatever I could to help her make ends meet. We never had a real home. Just drifted from ranch to ranch. A few of the ranchers' wives were kind to my mother. Some were suspicious, waiting to see if she'd make a move on their man. She carried the double burden of trying to raise a son alone and trying to forever live down the mistaken image of her as a loose woman. She died too young, still bearing the stigma of having had a child out of wedlock."

"I never knew. Did Coot know this?"

Cal nodded. "He did. Your brother never cared about such things. He trusted me the way few men ever had. He was a true friend. That's why…" He paused, choosing his words carefully. "I knew I could never betray that friendship."

"And you never did."

"But I was tempted."

She arched a brow.

"When I first met Coot's little sister, I thought I was looking at an angel. I looked at you, Cora, and you took my breath away."

"Cal." She looked down, knowing he could see the blush on her cheeks.

"It's the truth. When you came home from Europe, so wounded, so distant, I was so taken with you, I'd get all tongue-tied whenever you walked by. I couldn't eat. Couldn't sleep. All I could think about was how beautiful you were and what a fool I was to ever think I could be anything except your friend. If I was truly Coot's friend, then I knew I could never allow myself to be anything more to you than a friend, as well. But I have to tell you, I've been mighty tempted through the years."

"Oh, Cal." She felt those damnable tears spring to her

eyes again and blinked furiously. "Couldn't you see that I wanted to be more than your friend?"

He hissed in a breath, and for a moment she thought he was in pain. Then she looked more closely and could see him staring at her with his heart in his eyes.

"Didn't you wonder why I didn't want to move into Coot's old rooms?" he asked softly.

She shook her head.

"I would have been just a room away from you. And that wasn't safe. Even now, after all these years, I'd have been too tempted. So I stayed out in the bunkhouse, where I belonged."

"Belonged." She spit the hateful word. "Oh, Cal. I can't bear to think about all the pain you suffered through the years. But to think that you're continuing to believe that you're somehow less worthy just breaks my heart."

"Cora..."

"Shhh." She leaned close and brushed her mouth over his.

When she started to pull away, he drew her back to him and kissed her with more urgency.

With a sigh she wrapped her arms around his waist and rested her head beside his on the pillow.

"You'll stay?" he whispered. "Through the night?"

"Don't you even think about asking me to leave," she said fiercely. "Not now. Not ever. I love you, Cal Randall."

"And I love you, Cora. Always have. Always will." He sighed, long and deep, and kept his good arm around her.

All the sadness, all the unease of the past hours, slipped away as she lay beside her dearest friend, absorbing the warmth of his touch. Hadn't she always known he was the great love of her life? But she'd waited, never knowing, yet needing to know. And now she did. After a lifetime of wondering. But they hadn't wasted a lifetime. They'd merely needed to grow into the people they were now.

Old friends.

New lovers.

She smiled. It would make a great title for the portrait she could see in her mind's eye. Of a handsome, white-haired cowboy and his woman.

Oh, it was so dear, so special, that she hugged the tumultuous knowledge to her heart.

His woman.

Her man.

It was her last thought before she drifted into the most peaceful, bliss-filled sleep she'd known in years.

Chapter Twenty-five

The ranch house was as quiet as a tomb as Zane, Jesse, and Wyatt drove away in the ranch truck. Two hours later, when they returned, everyone was still sleeping. The house was permeated with the wonderful fragrance of Dandy's soup, simmering on the stove, and freshly baked bread.

Nothing had changed. And yet, everything had changed. In the blink of an eye, in the assayer's laboratory, they had learned the difference between gold and pyrite. Real gold and fool's gold. But the three had sworn an oath to keep their secret, even if it killed them, until the time came to reveal it.

Hearing that the sheriff was waiting downstairs with an initial report, the family began drifting down to the great room to gather around the fireplace.

Wyatt and Marilee sat beside Jesse and Amy on the

hearth cushions alongside a roaring fire. Cora and Cal chose the sofa. Riley and Zane sat in chairs on either side of little Summer, who had brought along her crayons and sketch pad and was lying on the hardwood floor, busily drawing pictures of her adventure.

The drawings had been Amy's suggestion. The teacher in her saw this as a learning experience for Summer, as a way to address her fears and exorcise them. The little girl had leaped at the opportunity to express herself.

"State police have identified the pilot and the passenger of the copter that crashed." Ernie Wycliff held up a printout of the report. "Both had extensive criminal records." He looked around the silent, watchful group. "There's more. Cooper Easley is the name of a dead man, buried in a cemetery in Wyoming. This mob of criminals has a long list of names and identifications they use as aliases. Anyway, Cooper Easley, whose real name is Vincent Fisher, signed on as a wrangler, hoping to gain access to the ranch house. The plan was to kidnap Summer to force Riley's hand. When he was fired, they had to come up with a backup plan. That's when they sent Gabriel Pasqual, another alias, real name Joseph Blair, to Gold Fever, posing as a moneyman interested in developing land. His job was to get himself invited out to the ranch, where he would do what Cooper couldn't. But when someone intercepted a call to Jack Manning, these guys knew they had to act quickly."

Zane looked startled. "They actually wiretapped the reporter's phone?"

The sheriff nodded. "It was no secret that he was investigating corruption for the *Gazette*, and they were desperate to learn how much he knew. Manning's not very happy about that. Now, he says, he'll have to have his line swept regularly." Ernie shrugged. "The price of being an investigative reporter in the electronic age."

Zane's voice was filled with self-loathing. "And I led us all into the trap."

"It wasn't your fault, cuz." Wyatt was quick to defend him. "We all agreed with you."

He shook his head, heavy with guilt. "I nearly had my whole family killed."

"No." Riley put her hand on his. "This was my fault. I'm the one who brought all this on your family."

Cal spoke for all of them. "I think we've heard enough mea culpas. We're all amateurs in the deadly game they were playing. But we had some angels on our side."

He shared a smile with Cora. "We may not be able to see Coot, but I'm convinced that he's still looking out for all of us."

The sheriff got heavily to his feet. "I've got to get back to town." He turned. "One more thing. Miss Mason, I'll be bringing a lawyer out to get your deposition next week. Will you be here?"

She looked toward Cal.

The ranch foreman nodded. "She will."

Her voice, when she finally spoke, seemed tentative. "I'm not sure what my future will be, Sheriff."

"You can call me when you figure it out."

When the sheriff was gone, the family grew quiet. One by one they drifted back upstairs, still shaken by all that had happened, and still trying to digest it.

Zane let himself into Riley's suite of rooms. Once again she had fallen asleep in the chair, in front of the fire. From the silence, he knew that Summer was sleeping as well.

The day had been so crazy, there had been little time to eat, so he'd retrieved a tray of soup and sandwiches from the kitchen. Setting it on the coffee table, he went to check on Summer. The little girl lay in the middle of her bed, covered with her favorite blanket.

He watched the slow, easy rise and fall of her chest and thought about the shocking blow he'd taken to his heart when that gunman had snatched her up and held the gun to her head.

In that moment, he'd known that if anything happened to this very special little girl, his life would never be the same.

How had this happened? When had this one little creature managed to wrap herself around his heart so tightly that when she hurt, he bled?

And her mother. What amazing strength she'd displayed. His chest grew tight just thinking about all she'd endured.

He walked to the other room and stood watching as Riley slept, curled up in the rocker. When he realized that she was beginning to wake, he walked closer, to kneel beside the chair.

"Zane." Her eyes focused on him and her smile was quick. "Look at you. All freshly shaved and showered and dressed."

"I didn't want to look like a trail bum. That's happened too many times."

"I wouldn't mind."

"Good. I hope that means that if I asked you to spend years with a scraggly trail bum, you wouldn't be scarred for life."

"My life was pretty scarred before I ever caught sight

of a trail bum." She sat up, shoving hair from her eyes. "How many years are you talking about?"

"What would you say to a lifetime?"

Her hand paused halfway to her lap. Her mouth rounded in surprise, but she didn't speak a word.

"I'm going to take that for a yes."

"No. Wait a minute." She got unsteadily to her feet to face him. "You're being serious now."

"In case you haven't noticed, I'm always serious. That is, when I'm not teasing you."

"But you're..." She tried again. "Are you teasing? Or are you proposing?"

A little voice from the doorway of the bedroom called, "What's pro...posing?"

They both turned in time to see a sleepy-eyed Summer looking from one to the other.

Zane got down on one knee and opened his arms. "Come over here and I'll tell you."

Summer barreled into his arms.

He gathered her close and whispered against her ear, "I'm asking your mama to marry me."

Summer's eyes grew round.

Turning to Riley, she said, "Mama? Can we marry Zane? Please?"

Riley had to bite back the laughter that bubbled up. Crossing her arms over her chest, she said, "Two against one? You're not playing fair."

Zane gave her a heart-stopping smile. "All's fair in love, Riley. You know that. Now answer your daughter. Will the two of you marry me? Please?"

Getting into the spirit of the moment, Riley knelt down and beckoned Summer over.

After a whispered conference, they both looked at him with matching smiles.

Riley turned to her daughter. "Go ahead. You can answer for both of us."

Summer's eyes danced with delight. "Mama said we each get a vote. I voted yes. And Mama voted..." She turned to her mother. "What does...firmative mean?"

Riley covered her mouth with her hands and leaned close to whisper. "It means yes."

Summer pumped her little arms up and down in a victory salute. "Zane, it means yes. Yea," she shouted. "We're getting married."

For the longest time Riley and Zane stared at each other across the space that separated them. Then, with a laugh of pure delight, Riley barreled into his arms just the way her daughter had.

Zane lifted her off her feet and kissed her until they were both breathless. And then, for good measure, kissed her again and again, while little Summer danced around the room on a wave of delicious happiness.

The family drifted down the stairs, talking quietly, helping themselves to glasses of freshly squeezed orange juice, foaming milk, and cups of steaming coffee. Dandy was busy at the griddle flipping flapjacks and turning crisp bacon. A platter of toast and biscuits and a little jar of strawberry preserves stood on the counter.

Cora and Cal sat close together on one side of the table, watching with matching smiles as first Jesse and Amy, and then Wyatt and Marilee joined them.

A short time later Zane walked in behind Riley and Summer. The little girl was practically bouncing off the walls with excitement as she bounded across the floor and climbed into her seat at the table.

Cora glanced at Riley. "Summer seems none the worse for her ordeal, dear."

"Aren't children resilient?" Amy wrapped both arms around Jesse, and the two shared a secret smile.

"How're the new house plans coming, cuz?" Wyatt asked.

"I thought I'd have Stan Novak out here next week to walk the site with me and see what he thinks."

"This is getting serious." Marilee shared a look with Amy.

"How about you, Wyatt?" Jesse grinned at his cousin. "Amy says you and Marilee are thinking about building your own place, too."

"What's this?" Cora looked across the table at her great-nephew.

He nodded. "We think it's time."

Cora turned to Marilee. "You never said a word about this while we were camping out."

Marilee smiled at her husband. "We'd been thinking about it, but nothing was firm until last night. Now we've decided the time is right."

Cora was shaking her head. "But the house will be so empty."

"Maybe not." Zane handed Summer a glass of milk. "How would you like another addition to the family, Aunt Cora?"

A guilty flush crept up Cora's cheeks. She turned to Cal. "You told them?"

He shook his head.

"Told us what?" Zane snagged coffee for himself and Riley before taking a seat at the table.

"Cal and I are…" Cora paused and Cal placed a big hand over hers on the tabletop.

"Cora and I have decided…"

Marilee sighed. "Oh my gosh, this is just wonderful."

"What is?" Wyatt, Jesse, and Zane looked puzzled, while the young women were suddenly surrounding the happy couple and kissing their cheeks.

"Holy…" When they caught on, the men were on their feet, pumping Cal's hand, kissing their aunt.

Cal and Cora accepted their congratulations and continued staring at each other with matching smiles as though they couldn't quite believe their good fortune.

When the noise faded and they settled down to eat, Zane cleared his throat. "When I asked if you'd like an addition to the family, I didn't know about you two. I was talking about Riley and Summer."

"I'm glad to know you aren't leaving us now that the bad guys are behind bars," Cal said with a chuckle. "I was afraid, after what you told the sheriff, that you had decided to return to Philadelphia. It would make sense, now that the bad guys can't hurt you."

"Too late for her to leave," Zane deadpanned.

"What's that supposed to mean?" Jesse looked up.

"I believe I'll let Summer tell you." Zane turned to the little girl.

Her eyes grew big. "Can I tell our secret now?"

At Zane's nod she said, "Mama and I are marrying Zane."

After a round of laughter there were more congratulations as the women hugged and kissed, and the men slapped backs and insisted they weren't surprised.

Over the longest breakfast of their lives, which

stretched into the noon hour, they talked and laughed, discussed the possibility of a double wedding, and began to make plans for a huge family celebration.

The family gathered in the great room. Cora and Cal sat side by side on the sofa. Amy and Jesse were snuggled together on a love seat. Wyatt and Marilee had chosen floor cushions, where they could lean their backs against a hassock and hold hands. Riley and Zane sat in one of the big overstuffed chairs, with Summer on Zane's lap.

A fire blazed on the hearth. The enormous television, usually hidden behind the closed doors of an armoire, was tuned to the public channel. Dandy wheeled in a cart with bowls of popcorn and soft drinks, as well as frosty longnecks.

When Steven Michaelson's documentary on the annual migration of wild horses began, everyone fell silent.

At the sight of a magnificent black stallion standing on a snow-covered Montana mountaintop, Zane's voice could be heard describing the leader of a herd of wild mustangs that he'd trailed for years while documenting their adventures in the wilderness.

Summer's eyes went wide. "I hear you. Where are you?"

"Behind the camera."

"But why can't I see you?"

"Because this is all about the mustangs."

"Oh." She watched and listened with the others until, caught up in the adventure, she began wriggling. "Why is that horse trying to hurt our horse?"

"They're fighting over a lady horse."

"That's not nice."

That had everyone chuckling.

When the stallion ran off the intruder, Summer settled back. "Good for our horse, Zane."

"Yeah. The good guys always win, don't they?"

She smiled dreamily. "Uh-huh."

A short time later, as they watched a newborn foal taking its first halting steps in a meadow of wildflowers, she said, "That's like Star, Vanilla's baby, isn't it, Zane?"

"Yes, it is. And in no time, that foal will be running alongside its mama and making the same journey across the wilderness that its family has made for generations."

At his words, Cora squeezed Cal's hand. The two shared a secret smile.

Later, when the documentary concluded, the family watched and listened as Zane's cell phone began ringing with phone calls from friends around the country, including a call from famed documentary filmmaker Steven Michaelson himself.

"Thanks." Zane was smiling. "I appreciate that. Yeah, we do work well together. It was the fulfillment of a lifetime dream, and I thank you." He paused. "Sorry, Steven. I won't consider it. I'm editing my own documentary at the moment. And I have something even more important that's going to keep me right here in Montana for the rest of my life." Another pause before he added, "I'm positive. But of course I'll stay in touch."

When he disconnected, he saw his family watching in silence and waiting for an explanation.

He shot them one of those devilish grins. "He offered me the chance to spend a couple of years in the Outback of Australia filming his next documentary. He promises that it will be a huge blockbuster that could earn us both a fortune."

"And you told him no?" Riley's voice was hushed.

Zane winked at Jesse and Wyatt before lifting Riley's hand to his mouth for a quick kiss. "How could I ever turn away from what I've found here?"

CHAPTER TWENTY-SIX

It was a perfect spring day in Montana. Rain had turned the hillsides into lush green meadows, dotted with an array of wildflowers. In the distance cattle lowed. The horses had been turned out of the barns and into pastures, where the foals raced alongside their mothers. It was a sight that ranchers never tired of stopping to watch as they went about their daily chores.

The air of excitement at the Lost Nugget Ranch had reached a fever pitch.

In the kitchen Dandy was preparing a feast. Beef tenderloin with mushroom caps. Potatoes grilled with onion and green peppers. He'd baked two very distinctive wedding cakes. One chocolate with buttercream frosting, requested by Cal and Cora. On top Dandy had created a silver-haired bride and groom. The other, suggested by little Summer, was a white cake with strawberry-cream filling and fresh strawberries from the ranch garden dotting the rich frosting. This cake bore three figures. A bride, a groom, and a little flower girl. Dandy couldn't wait to see Summer's reaction when she saw what he'd done.

Though he thought he hid his secret well, everyone in the family was aware that he had fallen hopelessly under the little girl's spell. As had the entire family.

"Zane." Riley was laughing as he and Summer took her by the hand and led her out of the suite. "I should be getting ready."

"You will. But first, there's something we have to show you."

Intrigued, she allowed herself to be led down the stairs and out to the barnyard.

"What more could you possibly show me? Wasn't last night's viewing of your documentary on mustangs enough to last a lifetime?"

That had him smiling. "Old news." He led her to a corral. "Stay right here."

He and Summer raced off to the barn.

A short time later Zane stepped out leading Vanilla. Seated in the saddle on her back was Summer, looking so proud and happy.

"Oh." Speechless, Riley put a hand to her throat as the little girl waved.

Zane led the mare inside the enclosure and they made a slow, easy circle around the corral before coming to a stop in front of Riley.

"Look at me, Mama."

"I see. Oh, honey, you're so brave."

"Want to go again?" Zane asked.

Delighted, Summer nodded and they made another turn around the corral.

Jimmy Eagle walked up to stand beside Riley. "She reminds me of another kid I once knew."

"Amy? I heard she grew up nearby."

He shook his head. "I'm talking about Zane. Tough little cookie. Did he ever tell you how he got that scar on his chin?"

She turned to the old wrangler. "No. He didn't."

"He took a nasty fall from a horse's back. I wanted to take him to town and have Doc stitch it up, but he wouldn't hear of it. It would've wasted the whole day, he said. So I just patched him up as best I could and he was back in that saddle in no time. Zane just purely loved horses. Couldn't get enough of them." He pointed to Summer. "She's going to be just like him, I figure. Those two have a lot in common."

Riley's heart did a strange dance inside her chest just as Zane brought the mare to a halt in front of them.

"Mama, Zane said I'm a..." Summer looked at him for the word.

"A natural. You were born for this. Don't you agree, Jimmy?"

There was such fierce pride in Zane's voice, Riley glanced over at the look on his face. When Jimmy agreed with him, he looked like a proud papa, she realized. Somehow, without knowing how or when, Summer had already become his. His child. His own. His pride.

She had to fight back tears as Zane helped Summer dismount before handing over the reins to Jimmy Eagle.

"That was my wedding gift to Zane, Mama."

As her daughter skipped along beside her, Zane

dropped an arm easily around Riley's waist and winked, sending her heart into a spiral. Would he always have this effect on her?

"I can't think of a better gift, honey. Wasn't that your gift to your mama, too?"

"Uh-uh." She smiled, that secret little smile. "Aunt Amy's helping me with that."

When they reached the house, the little girl dashed off to find her aunt Amy, while Riley hurried upstairs to dress for the big event.

At a knock on her door Cora called, "It's open."

Marilee peered in.

Cora was wearing a robe and holding a pair of scissors to her hair.

"Aunt Cora." Marilee crossed the room. "What in the world...?"

"Just giving myself a little trim." Cora laughed. "You should see the look of horror on your face, dear. Don't be alarmed. I do this all the time."

"But today is your wedding day." Marilee was shaking her head.

"Yes, it is." Cora snipped another strand and watched as the end curled neatly.

She set down the scissors. "Tell me what you think of this." She led Marilee to her closet to reveal a lovely white skirt and jacket with a beaded shawl collar.

"Oh, Aunt Cora." Marilee touched a hand to the material. "This is just gorgeous. Where did you find it?"

"I phoned an artist friend of mine who lives in Milan. She described it to me and when I approved, she overnighted it."

"Have you tried it on?"

Cora nodded. "Earlier today, after Cal went downstairs. If fits perfectly. Do you think he'll be surprised?"

"Surprised?" Marilee wore a stunned expression. "If Cal fell in love with the artist who wears her brother's cast-offs, this little bit of finery is going to give him heart palpitations."

Cora touched a hand to her own heart. "Don't even think such a thing. I wouldn't want to be a bride and a widow on the same day."

The two women shared a laugh.

"Now," Marilee said, "let me see those hands."

Cora dutifully held out her hands and the younger woman shook her head. "I'm going to give you a manicure."

Cora withdrew her hands and tucked them behind her. "I'll wear an elegant suit, but I draw the line at having my nails painted. It would be a complete waste, since I'll just have my hands back in paint and thinner tomorrow."

"I won't polish them. But I'm going to file and shape them, and massage oil into the cuticles."

Before Cora could refuse, Marilee was leading her toward a table and chairs set up in the corner of the room. After filling a bowl with warm water, she began setting out little bottles of oil. In no time the two women were laughing together as Cora submitted to Marilee's ministrations.

Riley indulged in a long, leisurely bath before wrapping herself in a towel and starting on her hair.

Amy and Summer had left earlier, whispering and

laughing about their secret mission. Amy had promised to return Summer in time to be ready for the ceremony.

The ceremony. Riley paused to study herself in the mirror.

This had all happened so quickly. And yet, oddly, she hadn't a single doubt. She'd never before felt about any man the way she felt about Zane. He was everything she would ever want in a husband and lifelong companion. Smart and funny and caring. And watching him with her daughter, she knew he would always be the father Summer had longed for.

Riley hadn't been one of those girls who grew up dreaming about her own wedding. She'd never seen herself in a long white gown, walking down the aisle of a church filled with people. She would be forever grateful that she could share this day with Cora, so that she wouldn't have to be the center of attention. She would leave that for Summer, who couldn't wait to slip into the ruffled little white dress Amy had made her for the occasion. With every fitting, Summer had preened and danced about, eager to have it finished so she could model it.

She would let this day be Summer's and Cora's. As long, she thought, as the night belonged to Zane. They'd decided to wait until after the ceremony to merge their two suites together. For now, Zane was still sleeping in his room, while she and Summer remained in here, even though workmen had been knocking out walls and hammering and painting for days.

But tonight...

With a smile she returned her attention to her hair. She wanted to look beautiful for her husband.

Husband. What a strange and wonderful word.

• • •

"Good." Jesse and Wyatt shared knowing grins when Cal and Zane finally joined them in the small wrought-iron enclosure some distance from the house. The tombstones bearing the names of Coot and his wife, Annie, and their ancestors were testimony to the generations that had cleared and maintained this land before them. "We figured you two lovebirds might forget all about this little tradition."

"Forget?" Cal laughed. "Hell, I've been doing this longer than any of you."

He passed around cigars and held a match to the tip of each, while Zane filled four tumblers with good Irish whiskey and handed them out.

Jesse lifted his tumbler. "Here's to Zane and his beautiful Riley, and their ready-made family. May you be happy all the days of your lives."

The others lifted their tumblers and drank.

Wyatt lifted his tumbler for the second toast. "Here's to you, Cal, and to our great-aunt Cora. I don't know what took you so long, when the rest of us knew all along that you were perfect for one another. We wish you a long and happy life together."

With a rumble of laughter the others lifted their glasses and drank.

Cal couldn't stop smiling. "I waited a lifetime for this day, boys, and I intend to enjoy every minute of it." He lifted his glass. "Here's to Coot, my best friend. May he continue watching out for us as we follow the path he charted."

The three cousins shared a quick glance before drinking.

Zane took a last pull on his cigar before setting it

aside, along with the empty glass. "We'd better get up to the house. The women will have our hides if we hold up the ceremony."

The others drained their glasses and turned to follow him.

Only Cal remained beside the graves. As he watched the younger men walk away, he lifted his glass one more time. "I don't know what kind of magic you have, my friend, but you did the impossible. Not only are your three grandsons best friends again, but they've all managed to find remarkable wives." He started to drink, then paused. "Of course, not as remarkable as the woman I'm about to marry." He shook his head, as though unable to believe his good fortune. "Marry. I never dreamed I'd be saying Cora's name in the same breath as marriage. That's a miracle in itself. But then, Coot, you were always able to surprise me." He drained his glass. "Thanks, my friend."

Without a backward glance he strode toward the ranch house, and toward the woman who had owned his heart for all of his adult life.

Reverend Martin was standing in front of the fireplace, holding the family Bible and chatting with Jesse and Amy and Wyatt and Marilee, who would be the official witnesses. The men wore Western-style suits with string ties and hand-tooled leather boots. Their wives were pretty in ankle-length dresses with handkerchief hems. Amy's was peach, giving her the look of a pale angel, while Marilee's was buttercup yellow, to complement her fiery curls.

The only invited guests were Delia Cowling, Jimmy Eagle, and Dandy, who had settled themselves on the sofa to await the ceremony.

Cora and Cal descended the stairs together.

"Oh, just look at you," Delia said with a sigh. "I don't believe I've ever seen a prettier bride."

"That's just what I told her." Cal paused to lift Cora's hand to his lips. "I can't take my eyes off her. I can't believe this beautiful woman would consent to marry me."

"Oh, Cal." Cora actually blushed. "I ask you, Delia. Have you ever seen a better-looking groom?"

"You've snagged yourself one handsome cowboy," the old woman said with a laugh as they continued toward the preacher.

At the sound of footsteps on the stairs they turned to watch Zane and Riley walking toward them. Riley, in a slim column of white silk, wore her hair long and loose, just the way Zane loved it. Zane, like the other men, was wearing a Western suit and boots.

Walking between them was Summer, in the lovely, floor-length dress Amy had made her, her hair softly curled, her hands holding a satin pillow on which rested four gold rings. Because she took her job seriously, she stared straight ahead, measuring each step until they reached the preacher.

Cal and Cora spoke their vows first, and when they kissed, the room erupted into cheers while hugs and kisses were exchanged.

Then it was Zane and Riley's turn to speak their vows. Breaking with tradition, Zane lifted Summer off her feet, holding her in his arms while he promised to love, honor, cherish. That was all it took to bring the tears to the eyes of the others, and especially to Riley, who fumbled for her handkerchief.

When he lowered Summer to her feet and took Riley

in his arms, the crowd went silent as they all seemed to sigh in unison.

After another round of hugs and kisses, they were toasted with glasses of champagne before heading into the dining room for a formal supper.

As they were seated, Amy got Summer aside before the little girl announced her gift to her mama.

"Actually, it's two gifts," Amy explained. "The first is from Jesse and me. And we wanted Summer to be the one to make the announcement."

"Announcement?" Zane's question had everyone around the table turning to look at Summer.

The little girl solemnly said, "Miss Amy said I'm going to be a cousin, just like Uncle Jesse and Uncle Wyatt are cousins to my daddy."

It took a moment before her words began to sink in.

On a breath of excitement she blurted, "Miss Amy and Uncle Jesse are getting a baby."

While the others jumped up to thump Jesse on the back and hug Amy, Cora began weeping until Summer asked her, "When are they getting it?"

"Whenever heaven says it's ready, dear."

"Oh." Summer turned to her mother. "Can heaven send it today?"

"I think they may need a little more time," Riley said with a laugh.

When the family finally settled down, Amy caught Summer's hand. "Summer has another wedding present."

With Amy's help Summer produced a copy of Jack Manning's column in the *Gazette*, naming Nick Porter a hero for turning his back on a life of crime to serve his country, and stating that, to the city of Philadelphia, he would always be a hero.

"See, Mama." Summer handed her mother the newspaper column. "I asked my daddy in heaven to give me a brand-new daddy, and he did."

Cora sniffed back more tears. "I see that Coot isn't the only one still looking out for us."

"Speaking of Coot." Zane got to his feet, followed by Jesse and Wyatt. "We have an announcement of our own."

As quickly as possible Zane explained about the cave that had been exposed by the helicopter crash, the bones they'd discovered, and the nuggets.

An expectant silence fell over everyone in the room.

"We took the nuggets to a lab." Zane caught Riley's hand. "Would you love me even if we were paupers?"

She smiled. "You know I would."

"That's good to know."

He paused and glanced at his cousins before saying, "The gold is real. Not pyrite, as some thought. And, according to the experts who've weighed it and had a chance to run their tests, it's the richest gold strike ever recorded."

For a moment longer silence reigned. Then, as one, they leaped up and began laughing and talking, firing questions, shouting comments.

Throughout all the commotion, Zane sat beside Riley and held her hand in his.

She studied their joined hands. "Why did you wait to tell everybody about the gold?"

"Because it wasn't as important as this." He leaned close and brushed his mouth over hers. "I've already found my treasure. You and Summer mean more to me than any gold."

Above the din Amy asked the question the others were thinking. "What will we do with the gold?"

Zane shared a look with his cousins. "It will be up to a family vote. The treasure belongs to all of us. And all will get to vote. Wyatt, Jesse, and I are leaning toward loaning it to the state, to be put on display in the Capitol Building. I'm sure there will be other great suggestions. We're open to any and all."

Cora, holding tightly to Cal's hand, was openly weeping.

"Happy tears, Aunt Cora?" Zane asked.

She nodded. "Very happy. Not just because Coot's search has ended, but because I believe he arranged for all three of you to find it together."

"With your help," Jesse added. "It was your quick thinking that had Zane bringing down that helicopter, which tore apart the very cave where the nuggets have been hidden all these years."

She shook her head. "It was all Coot's doing."

Zane stood, holding aloft a glass of champagne. "Do you remember Coot's toast every year after roundup?"

Solemnly, Jesse and Wyatt picked up their glasses and stood.

"Life's all about the road ahead, boys," Jesse began.

"What's past is past," Wyatt added.

"Here's to what's round the bend," Zane finished for them.

Across the table, Cora held Cal's hand, and the two of them felt the soft brush of cool air, as though someone had touched them.

Seated beside her mother, little Summer felt the same quick brush of air, as though she'd been kissed on the cheek. That had her thinking about the prayers she said each night to the father she'd never known. Though she was too young to understand the words her new daddy and his cousins had just spoken, she felt their meaning deep in her heart.

She couldn't wait to see what was around the bend. Just being part of this big happy family, she knew whatever it turned out to be, it would be a grand and wonderful adventure.

Amy Parrish was the
only woman Jesse McCord
ever loved.
Now she's back in town—
but an unseen enemy is
fast closing in…

———◆———

Please turn this page
for an excerpt from

Montana Legacy

The first book in the trilogy, and
discover how it all began.

Available now.

In the kitchen Jesse loosened his tie and poured himself a tumbler of Irish whiskey. Like his grandfather, he wasn't much of a drinker. But every New Year, and at the annual roundup barbecue, Coot would pour a round of whiskeys for himself and the crew, and offer a toast to the future.

"Life's all about the road ahead. What's past is past. Here's to what's around the bend, boys."

Jesse could hear his grandfather's voice as clearly as if he'd been standing right there. There had been a boyish curiosity about the old man that was so endearing. He'd truly believed he would live to find his ancestor's fortune. The anticipation, the thrill of it, had influenced his entire life. And it was contagious. Jesse had been caught up in it as well. It's what had kept him here, chasing Coot's rainbow, instead of going off in search of his own.

Not that he had any regrets. He couldn't imagine himself anywhere but here.

He crossed the mudroom and stepped out onto the back porch, hoping to get as far away from the crowd as possible.

Just as he lifted the drink to his lips, a voice stopped him.

"I thought I might find you out here."

He didn't have to see her to recognize that voice. Hadn't it whispered to him in dreams a hundred times or more?

His tone hardened as he studied Amy Parrish standing at

the bottom of the steps. "What's the matter, Amy? Make a wrong turn? Lunch is being served in the front yard."

"I noticed." She waited until he walked closer. "I just wanted to tell you why I came back."

"To gloat, no doubt."

"Don't, Jess." She pressed her lips together, then gave a sigh of defeat. "I'm sorry about your grandfather. I know you loved him."

"Yeah." Her eyes were even greener than he remembered. With little gold flecks in them that you could see only in the sunlight. It hurt to look at them. At her. Almost as much as it hurt to think about Coot. "So, why did you come back?"

"To offer some support to my dad while he had some medical tests done."

His head came up sharply. "He's sick?"

She nodded. "The doctor in Billings sent him to a specialist at the university. The test results should be back in a couple of days, and then I'll be going back to my job, teaching in Helena."

"I'm sorry about your dad. I hope the test results come back okay." He paused, staring at the glass in his hands because he didn't want to be caught staring at her. "So, I guess you just came here to say good-bye before you leave. Again."

"I just..." She shrugged and stared down at her hands, fighting nerves. "I just wanted to offer my condolences."

"Thanks. I appreciate it."

The breeze caught a strand of pale hair, softly laying it across her cheek. Without thinking he reached up and gently brushed it away from her face.

The heat that sizzled through his veins was like an electrical charge, causing him to jerk back. But not before he caught the look of surprise in her eyes. Surprise and something more. If he didn't know better, he'd swear he saw a quick flash of heat. But that was probably just his pride tricking him into believing in something that wasn't there, and hadn't been for years.

He lowered his hand and clenched it into a fist at his side.

She took a sideways step, as though to avoid being touched again. "I'd better get back to my dad."

"Yeah. Thanks again for coming."

She walked away quickly, without looking back.

That was how she'd left in the first place, he thought. Without a backward glance.

Now he could allow himself to study her. Hair the color of wheat, billowing on the breeze. That lean, willowy body; those long legs; the soft flare of her hips.

Just watching her, he felt all the old memories rushing over him, filling his mind, battering his soul. Memories he'd kept locked up for years in a small, secret corner of his mind. The way her hair smelled in the rain. The way her eyes sparkled whenever she smiled. The sound of her laughter, low in her throat. The way she felt in his arms when they kissed. When they made love...

He'd be damned if he'd put himself through that hell again.

He lifted the tumbler to his lips and drained it in one long swallow, feeling the heat snake through his veins.

"What's past is past," he muttered thickly. "Here's to what's around the bend."

Marilee Trainor
likes her freedom
and lives for trouble.
But she's met her match
in sexy cowboy
Wyatt McCord...

———◆———

Please turn this page
for an excerpt from

Montana Destiny

Available now.

Wyatt." Amy McCord turned to watch as her husband's cousin paused at one of the food booths set up at the rodeo grounds. "You've already had two corn dogs. Don't tell me you're buying another one."

"All right. I won't tell you." Despite his faded denims and scuffed boots, with his hair blowing in the wind, Wyatt McCord looked more like an eternal surfer than a cowboy. "But I can't get enough of these." He took a big bite, closed his eyes on a sigh, and polished off the corn dog in three bites.

Wiping his hands down his jeans he caught up with his cousins, Jesse and Zane, and Jesse's bride, Amy.

Their grandfather's funeral had brought the cousins together after years of separation. Now the three had begun to resolve years of old differences and were quickly becoming the same inseparable friends they'd been in their childhood.

Wyatt glanced around. "Where did all these people come from? It looks like half of Montana is here."

Jesse grinned. "Gold Fever might be a small town, but when it's rodeo time, every cowboy worth his spurs makes it here. In the past couple of years it's become one of the best in the West."

The four paused at the main corral, where a cowboy was roping a calf. While they hung on the rail and marveled at his skill, Zane whipped out his ever-present video camera to film the action. During his years in California he'd worked with famed director Steven Michaelson filming an award-winning documentary on wild mustangs. Now he'd become obsessed with making a documentary of life in Montana, featuring their ongoing search for a treasure stolen from their ancestors over a hundred years ago.

The search had consumed their grandfather's entire adult life, causing the people who knew him to give him the nickname Crazy Old Coot. He'd embraced the name, and in his will, he'd managed to entice his three grandsons to take up his search, no matter where it might lead them.

Jesse looked over at a holding pen, where riders were drawing numbers for the bull-riding contest. "There's one you ought to try, cuz." He laughed at Wyatt's arched brow. "It doesn't take just skill, but a really hard head to survive."

"Not to mention balls of steel," Zane remarked while keeping his focus on the action in the ring.

Wyatt merely grinned. "Piece of cake."

Jesse couldn't resist. He reached into his pocket and withdrew a roll of bills. "Twenty says you can't stick in the saddle for more than ten seconds."

"Make it a hundred and I'll take that bet."

Jesse threw back his head and roared. "Cuz, you couldn't stay on a bull's back for a thousand."

"Is it a bet?" Wyatt sent him a steely look.

"Damned straight. My hundred calls your bluff."

Wyatt turned to Zane. "You're my witness. And you might want to film this. I doubt I'll offer to do a repeat."

Without waiting for a reply he sauntered away and approached the cluster of cowboys eyeing the bulls.

Half an hour later, wearing a number on his back and having parted with the fifty-dollar entry fee, he stood with the others and waited his turn to ride a bull.

While he watched the action in the ring he noticed the ambulance parked just outside the ring. In case any fool wasn't already aware of the danger, that brought home the point. But it wasn't the emergency vehicle that caught his attention; it was the woman standing beside it. There was no way he could mistake those long, long legs encased in lean denims, or that mass of fiery hair spilling over her shoulders and framing the prettiest face he'd ever seen. Marilee Trainor had been the first woman to catch Wyatt's eye the moment he got back in town scant months ago. He'd seen her dozens of times since, but she'd always managed to slip away before he'd had time to engage her in conversation.

Not this time, he thought with a wicked grin.

"McCord." A voice behind him had him turning.

"You're up. You drew number nine."

A chorus of nervous laughter greeted that announcement, followed by a round of relieved voices.

"Rather you than me, cowboy."

"Man, I'm sure glad I ducked that bullet."

"I hope your life insurance is paid up."

Wyatt studied the bull snorting and kicking its hind legs against the confining pen, sending a shudder through the entire ring of spectators. If he didn't know better, Wyatt would have sworn he'd seen fire coming out of the bull's eyes.

"What's his name?" He climbed the wood slats and prepared to drop into the saddle atop the enraged animal's back.

"Devil. And believe me, sonny, he lives up to it." The grizzled old cowboy handed Wyatt the lead rope and watched while he twisted it around and around his hand before dropping into the saddle.

In the same instant the gate was opened, and bull and rider stormed into the center ring to a chorus of shouts and cries and whistles from the crowd.

Devil jerked, twisted, kicked, and even crashed headlong into the boards in an attempt to dislodge its hated rider. For his part, Wyatt had no control over his body as it left the saddle, suspended in midair, before snapping forward and back like a rag doll, all the while remaining connected by the tenuous rope coiled around his hand.

Though it lasted only sixty seconds, it was the longest ride of his life.

When the bullhorn signaled that he'd met the qualifying time, he struggled to gather his wits, waiting until Devil was right alongside the gate before he freed his hand, cutting himself loose. He flew through the air and over the corral fence, landing in the dirt at Marilee Trainor's feet.

"My God! Don't move." She was beside him in the blink of an eye, kneeling in the dirt, probing for broken bones.

Wyatt lay perfectly still, enjoying the feel of those clever, practiced hands moving over him. When she moved from his legs to his torso and arms, he opened his eyes to narrow slits and watched her from beneath lowered lids.

She was the perfect combination of beauty and brains. He could see the wheels turning as she did a thorough exam. Even her brow, furrowed in concentration, couldn't mar that flawless complexion. Her eyes, the color of the palest milk chocolate, were narrowed in thought. Strands of red hair dipped over one cheek, giving her a sultry look.

Satisfied that nothing was broken, she sat back on her heels, feeling a moment of giddy relief. That was when she realized that he was staring.

She waved a hand before his eyes. "How many fingers can you see?"

"Four fingers and a thumb. Or should I say four beautiful, long, slender fingers and one perfect thumb, connected to one perfect arm of one perfectly gorgeous female? And,

I'm happy to add, there's no ring on the third finger of that hand."

She caught the smug little grin on his lips. Her tone hardened. "I get it. A showboat. I should have known. I don't have time to waste on some silver-tongued actor."

"Why, thank you. I had no idea you'd examined my tongue. Mind if I examine yours?"

She started to stand but his hand shot out, catching her by the wrist. "Sorry. That was really cheesy, but I couldn't resist teasing you."

His tone altered, deepened, just enough to have her glancing over to see if he was still teasing.

He met her look. "Are you always this serious?"

Despite his apology, she wasn't about to let him off the hook, or change her mind about him. "In case you haven't noticed, rodeos are a serious business. Careless cowboys tend to break bones, or even their skulls, as hard as that may be to believe."

She stared down at the hand holding her wrist. Despite his smile, she could feel the strength in his grip. If he wanted to, he could no doubt break her bones with a single snap. But she wasn't concerned with his strength, only with the heat his touch was generating. She felt the tingle of warmth all the way up her arm. It alarmed her more than she cared to admit.

"My job is to minimize damage to anyone who is actually hurt."

"I'm grateful." He sat up so his laughing blue eyes were even with hers. If possible, his were even bluer than the perfect Montana sky above them. "What do you think? Any damage from that fall?"

Her instinct was to move back, but his fingers were still around her wrist, holding her close. "I'm beginning to wonder if you were actually tossed from that bull or deliberately fell."

"I'd have to be a little bit crazy to deliberately jump from the back of a raging bull just to get your attention, wouldn't I?"

"Yeah." She felt the pull of that magnetic smile that had so many of the local females lusting after Wyatt McCord. Now she knew why he'd gained such a reputation in such a short time. "I'm beginning to think maybe you are. In fact, more than a little. A whole lot crazy."

"I figured it was the best possible way to get you to actually talk to me. You couldn't ignore me as long as there was even the slightest chance that I might be hurt."

There was enough romance in her nature to feel flattered that he'd go to so much trouble just to arrange to meet her. At least, she thought, it was original. And just dangerous enough to appeal to a certain wild-and-free spirit that dominated her own life.

Then her practical side kicked in, and she felt an irrational sense of annoyance that he'd wasted so much of her time and energy on his weird idea of a joke.

"Oh, brother." She scrambled to her feet and dusted off her backside.

"Want me to do that for you?"

She paused and shot him a look guaranteed to freeze most men.

He merely kept that charming smile in place. "Mind if we start over?" He held out his hand. "Wyatt McCord."

"I know who you are."

"Okay. I'll handle both introductions. Nice to meet you, Marilee Trainor. Now that we have that out of the way, when do you get off work?"

"Not until the last bull rider has finished."

"Want to grab a bite to eat? When the last rider is done, of course."

"Sorry. I'll be heading home."

"Why, thanks for the invitation. I'd be happy to join you. We could take along some pizza from one of the vendors."

She looked him up and down. "I go home alone."

"Sorry to hear it." There was that grin again, doing strange things to her heart. "You're missing out on a really fun evening."

"You have a high opinion of yourself, McCord."

He chuckled. Without warning he touched a finger to her lips. "Trust me. I'd do my best to turn that pretty little frown into an even prettier smile."

Marilee couldn't believe the feelings that collided along her spine. Splinters of fire and ice had her fighting to keep from shivering despite the broiling sun.

Because she didn't trust her voice, she merely turned on her heel and walked away from him.

It was harder to do than she'd expected. And though she kept her spine rigid and her head high, she swore she could feel the heat of that gaze burning right through her flesh.

It sent one more furnace blast rushing through her system. A system already overheated by her encounter with the bold, brash, irritatingly charming Wyatt McCord.

THE DISH

Where authors give you the inside scoop!

From the desk of Roxanne St. Claire

Dear Reader,

I'm the youngest of five, a position of little power but great benefits. Yes, it meant I got the car floor on road trips (seriously, the floor!) but that position also allowed me to reap the rewards of parental guilt for sometimes treating #5 as an afterthought. On my tenth birthday, that meant the ultimate gift for a budding writer: a typewriter. I think I've had my fingers on a keyboard ever since.

So when I decided to launch a new romantic suspense series, I knew I wanted to anchor the stories around a big family. I hoped to translate the always-fascinating sibling dynamics into complex relationships and unforgettable characters. Since I married into an Italian family, I'd been given a window into one of the most colorful of all cultures, and choosing that background for my characters was a natural move. But this couldn't be an ordinary Italian family, since I like extraordinary characters. To work in my stories, they'd have to be fearless, protective, risk-taking, rule-breaking, wave-making heroes and heroines, willing to take chances to save lives. Oh, and the guys must be blistering hot, and the ladies? Well, we like them a little on the feisty side.

Thus, the Guardian Angelinos were born. They are the five siblings of the Boston-based Rossi family and their two Italian-born cousins, Vivi and Zach Angelino. The security and investigation firm these two blended families form is created in the first book, EDGE OF SIGHT. When soon-to-be law student Samantha Fairchild witnesses a murder in the wine cellar of the restaurant where she works and the professional hit man has her face on tape, she seeks help from her friend, investigative reporter Vivi Angelino. Sam gets the protection she needs, only it comes in the form of big, bad, sexy army ranger Zach Angelino...who stole her heart during a lusty interlude three years earlier, then went off to war and never contacted her again.

I had fun with Zach and Sam, and just as much fun with the extended family of renegade crime-fighters. One of my favorite characters is eighty-year-old Uncle Nino, who is grandfather to the Rossi kids and great-uncle to the Angelinos. He joins the Guardian Angelinos with typical Italian passion and gusto, carrying a spatula instead of a Glock, and keeping them all in ziti and good spirits. Oh, and Uncle Nino is a mean puzzle solver, a trait that comes in handy on some special investigations. But what he does best is Sunday Gravy, a delicious, hearty meat dinner in mouthwatering red sauce that the family gathers to enjoy at the end of a hard week of saving lives and solving crimes. He's agreed to share his secret recipe, just for my readers . . .

Uncle Nino's Sunday Gravy

Ingredients

- 1–2 pound piece of lean beef (eye of round)
- 1–2 pounds of lean pork (spare ribs)
- 2 pounds of hot or sweet Italian sausages
- 4 tbs olive oil
- 4–5 garlic cloves, sliced
- 1–2 Spanish onions, chopped
- Pinch of dried chili flakes (optional)

- Pinch of sugar
- 1 can tomato paste
- 2 26 oz. cans whole, peeled San Marzano tomatoes
- 2 cups dry red wine
- 1 tsp dried thyme
- 1 tsp dried oregano
- ½ cup torn fresh basil leaves
- Salt and pepper to taste

Instructions

1. Cut and trim the meats into smaller pieces; halve the sausages, cut eye of round in four sections
2. Heat olive oil in large pan or Dutch oven (deep, heavy casserole) over medium heat
3. Sear meats in hot olive oil until golden brown; may be done in batches and removed from pan, set aside
4. Sauté onions in the same pan until translucent
5. Add garlic and continue to sauté until garlic turns golden (spicy Italians—and these guys are—add the chili flakes here)
6. Add tomato paste and constantly stir until paste reaches rich, rusty color
7. Add thyme and oregano and stir
8. Deglaze the pan with red wine, using spatula to scrape all bits of charred meat (Uncle Nino says this is the key to success) until reduced by half
9. Crush whole, peeled tomatoes (by hand!), then add to sauce
10. Season sauce with salt and pepper and—this one from Grandma Rossi in the old country—a pinch or two of sugar to balance the acidity of the tomatoes
11. Add seared meat into the sauce and simmer for two hours, stirring occasionally

12. Serve over pasta (Uncle Nino recommends rigatoni)
13. Sprinkle fresh basil on top just before serving

(Note: with one pound of pasta, this recipe serves six. Hungry heroes may want more to keep up their stamina, so feel free to add homemade meatballs. Sorry, but Nino's recipe for meatballs remains a family secret. Stay tuned for future books to unlock that and many more mysteries.)

Mangia!

Roxanne St. Claire

www.roxannestclaire.com

♥ ♥ ♥ ♥ ♥ ♥ ♥ ♥ ♥ ♥ ♥ ♥ ♥ ♥ ♥ ♥

From the desk of Caridad Pineiro

Dear Friends,

I want to thank you for the marvelous reception you gave to SINS OF THE FLESH! Your many letters and reviews were truly appreciated and I hope you will enjoy this next book in the Sins series—STRONGER THAN SIN—even more.

From the moment that Mick's sister, Dr. Liliana Carrera, walked onto the scene in the first book, I knew she had to get her own story. I fell in love with her caring nature, her loyalty to her brother and her inner strength. There was no doubt in my mind that any story where she was the heroine would be emotionally compelling and filled with passion.

Of course, such an intense and determined heroine demanded not only a sexy hero, but a strong one. A man capable of great love, but who needs to rediscover the hero within himself.

Jesse Bradford immediately came to mind. Inspired by the many sexy surfer types I encounter on my walks along the beach, Jesse was born and bred on the Jersey Shore. A former football player who had to leave the game he loves due to a crippling bone disease, he is a man who has lost his way, but is honorable, caring and loyal. Jesse just needs to meet the right woman to guide him back to the right path in his life.

Together Jesse and Liliana will face great danger from a group of scientists who have genetically engineered Jesse, as well as the FBI Agents entrusted with his care. The action is fast-paced and will keep you turning the pages as you root for these two to find a way to be together!

If you want to find out more about the real life Jersey Shore locations in STRONGER THAN SIN, please visit my website at www.caridad.com where you can check out my photo gallery or my Facebook page at www.facebook.com/caridad.pineiro.author@Caridad Pineiro!

Wishing you all the best!

Caridad Pineiro

♥ ♥ ♥ ♥ ♥ ♥ ♥ ♥ ♥ ♥ ♥ ♥ ♥ ♥ ♥ ♥

From the desk of R.C. Ryan

Dear Reader,

My family and friends know that I'm obsessively neat and organized. I work best when my desk is clean, my office tidied, my mind clear of all the distracting bits and pieces that go into being part of a large and busy family.

And so it is with my manuscripts. When I created the McCord family and started them on their hunt for their ancestors' lost fortune, I had to find a satisfying ending to each cousin's story, while still keeping a few tantalizing threads aside, to tempt my readers to persevere through this series until the very end.

My editor remarked that, until reading MONTANA GLORY, she hadn't even been aware that the family needed the balance of another generation. Cal and Cora provided the narration for much of the family's history, and a steady anchor for these three very different cousins. Jesse, Wyatt, and Zane provided enough rugged male charm to stir the hearts of even the most unflappable female. The women they love brought excitement and fresh flavor into the family dynamic. But it was four-year-old Summer who changed each member of this fascinating household in some way. It is the ultimate gift of a child. They touch our lives, and we are forever changed.

In MONTANA GLORY, I was free to delve even deeper into the McCord family's history to reveal long-held secrets. I made a point to reveal a bit more about Cal, Cora, and the things that shaped them and the other members of this family. And, I hope, we learn things about ourselves in the process.

I hope you fell in love with this diverse, fascinating family as much as I did while writing their stories. And I hope you're as satisfied with the ending as I am. Like I said, tidy, organized, with all the loose ends neatly tied up. I'm a sucker for a happy ending.

Happy Reading!

R. C. Ryan

www.ryanlangan.com